KILLIAN MILSON

Executive Bounty

GEORGE I. DUHART JR.

ISBN 978-1-959182-24-5 (paperback)
ISBN 978-1-959182-25-2 (digital)

Duhart Ink
817-891-7655

Printed in the United States of America

This book is dedicated to the memory of Ivy
G. Senior and Mable A. Duhart.
Thank you, Mom and Dad.
Love.

PROLOGUE

Thursday, November 5, 2009. The day had started off like any other day at Fort Hood Army Installation in Killeen, Texas. I and a couple of my battle buddies had taken a temporary break from PT (Physical Training Exercises) this morning because several of us in my unit were going to have to report to the Soldier Readiness Center, in building 42000 on Seventy-Fifth Street and Battalion Avenue, for deployment orders. We were scheduled to report for SRP (soldier readiness processing) because of our upcoming deployment to Iraq. Every soldier had to go through SRP when it came time for overseas deployments and assignment to foreign duty stations. Each soldier from each unit had to receive a medical evaluation, financial education, and combat readiness awareness training (this last being for both the soldiers and their families) to prepare themselves for an extensive tour of duty in a foreign land. I and one of my barrack buddies, Private First-Class Brandon Pike, were assigned to the Sixty-Fourth MP Company, under the Seven Hundred Twentieth Military Police Battalion attached to the Eighty-Ninth Military Police Brigade. We had been ordered by our platoon sergeant to head over there this afternoon to get things squared away for deployment next month, either before or after the Christmas holiday.

Pike and I were brand new to the company. Both of us were nineteen and straight out of high school. We had just come out of basic training at Fort Leonard Wood, Missouri, nicknamed "Fort Lost in the Woods," where soldiers are trained to become MPs and engineers. We first arrived at the post in the beginning of the summer, June, right after Leonard Wood. We met up with several other soldiers we knew from basic training who were already there, and they showed us the ropes—how things were done in a line platoon and an MP company. My platoon sergeant was Sergeant First Class (E-7) James Hunter, who previously had done three tours in Iraq and one in Afghanistan. One could tell that he was a tough SOB, a no-nonsense NCO who didn't put up with any BS. But he was fair, equitable, and honest. He was a former member of an SRT (special response team) in the army's Military Police Corps, which is identical to a SWAT team and similar to other special reaction units in the law enforcement community responsible for first response tactics related to counterintelligence, terrorism, and reconnaissance, such as hostage rescue, riot control, and urban assaults. He had told us we were scheduled to arrive there after lunch to undergo the second phase of our processing.

Pike and I had arrived ten minutes early, at about ten minutes to one o'clock, to get ahead of everyone else who was coming for the same thing. We met up with several guys from our unit, but there were a lot of other soldiers from different units too. Many of them were from engineering companies, and a few were from medical detachment units, but most were National Guard and reserves. It seemed that of the whole bunch, we were the only MPs there—five to ten of us.

The briefing started at 13:00 hours. The guys and I were seated on the far-right side of the room, next to one of the two exit doors. As we were sitting there taking in the information the instructor was telling us, Pike told me he had forgotten one of his SRP folders, having left it out in the hallway. He got up from his seat to retrieve it. Later I noticed it was taking him a long time to get back. Around 13:20, while the instructor was still engaged in his discourse about our deployment, I suddenly had to go to the latrine, having drunk a large amount of water at lunch. Afterward, our platoon sergeant told us, we were going to have PT formation at 17:00 hours and a four-mile run at the end. He wanted us to be fully hydrated for that event, not wanting his soldiers to pass out from heat exhaustion. I had known that the army was tough when it came to physical exercise, but I had no idea that it would be this ridiculous.

Well, I had to go bad, and I couldn't hold it any longer, so I excused myself and headed right for the latrine. I was in there for only a couple of minutes, no more than usual. As I exited the restroom, I walked down the corridor and headed back to the classroom. When I was halfway to the classroom entrance, I heard it: several gunshots that sounded as if they'd come from a fully automatic weapon, with screams and shouting sounding out between each discharge. Everyone was confused about what was going on, including me. I ducked down to stay safe. As I tried to figure out what was going on, I saw several individuals rushing out of the classroom to which I had been returning. The shooting continued with some strange screaming and shouting from a distinctive-sounding voice: "Allah u Akbar! Allah u Akbar!"

It was coming from inside the classroom. Sounds of screaming and distress were coming from the classroom too, along with other sounds, such as of chairs and objects being thrown against walls. I saw Pike in the distance as he ran out of the classroom. I hollered at him to try to get his attention, but he just ran the other way to get out of the shooter's line of fire, whoever it was.

As I was positioned on the other side, trying to escape myself, I finally saw who the shooter was. To my surprise and disbelief, it was another soldier—an officer. He had two semiautomatic pistols, one in each hand, and was firing both of them into the crowd. It seemed that he was shooting only at soldiers and no one else. Once I was in position to get a good look at him, he saw me as well. He pointed one of his guns at me. For a moment, I was scared out of my mind, but then I reacted, running away before he could get off a shot at me. I ran to one of the other rooms in the building, to which several other military personnel had escaped with the same intention of getting out of the shooter's crosshairs. The shooter kept discharging both his weapons while shouting "Allah u Akbar!"

The entire ordeal seemed as if it took forever, but really it was only minutes—ten to be exact.

As I was huddled in a corner with several other individuals, I heard a faint voice in the background saying, "Drop your weapon now!"

The gunshots continued after the warning from this individual, possibly a police officer who had finally made his or her appearance. The shooter chose not to heed the warning and continued his deadly assault. Soon, several shots rang out from the side of the building opposite the shooter. We who were huddled up weren't sure if the danger had passed or not as we stayed hidden.

We heard a voice. It belonged to a person who evidently had witnessed the whole thing. The person said loudly, so that everyone in the building could hear, "They shot him! They shot him! He's down! He's down!"

Everybody slowly got up and checked themselves to see if they were wounded or injured. Then we all checked on each other to see if everyone else was okay, but unfortunately, not everyone was.

Thirty individuals had been severely wounded and had to be rushed to the hospital. Later, as the count continued, it was discovered that thirteen had been killed instantly, one of whom was, unfortunately, a pregnant soldier. This whole event was a horrific thing to witness. I had never seen so much carnage in my life. It was something that I truly had not been ready for, even when I was prepared to go overseas.

I tried to help out, giving aid to the injured and giving the authorities my statement about the whole ordeal.

While I was talking to the police about what had happened, Pike and three others ran up to me to see if I was okay. "Mil, Are you all, right?! Are you okay?!" shouted Pike as if he were yelling in a noise-filled room.

"Yeah, I'm all right. Are you guys, okay?" I replied, expressing the same concern.

"Yeah, we're good. We're all here."

"What the fuck just happened?! I was on my way back from the can, and suddenly I heard gunshots!" Pike said.

"Dude! I was sitting in the front corner near the exit when suddenly this guy rose up from the back and started yelling, 'Allah u Akbar,' then he pulled out two pistols and pointed them at everyone! He was shooting up the whole damn place! I ducked and got the hell out of there!" Pike was angry. "Who the hell was he, and how in the hell did he get on post with two guns in the first place?!" I asked myself out loud.

One of the other guys in our platoon, Specialist David Cash, answered my question for me: "The DOD cop says that he's an officer—a major! And he probably had clearance to have those weapons on post!"

"What?! Are you fucking serious, Cash?! One of ours did this shit? You've got to be fucking kidding me!" I was so angry that both Pike and Cash had to calm me down. All three of us sat down on a curb, trying to gather ourselves physically and mentally.

Sergeant Hunter, surprising all of us, came up and asked if we were all right. We told him what had happened and informed him that we had given our rendition of the event to the DOD police officers. He wanted us to go to Carl R. Darnall Army Medical Hospital, where some of the victims had been transported, so we could get checked out, but we told him that we were fine. Being our platoon sergeant and responsible for our well-being, he insisted that we go anyway. We decided to do as he had asked.

Just as I was about to leave for the hospital, Sergeant Hunter grabbed me by the shoulders and said with concern, "Specialist Milson, are you sure you're all, right?"

I responded, "Roger that, Sergeant. I'm good. Just a little shaken, but I'm fine."

"All of you go get checked out, then come back to the company immediately so we can go over what happened in more detail. I'll inform the first sergeant and the company commander [i.e., the captain] about what happened here. Our sergeant major and battalion commander [i.e., the lieutenant colonel] are going to want to hear your side of the story. Go ahead and get yourself looked at, Milson. Call me on your cell if anything goes wrong or if you need something."

"Roger that, Sergeant." He patted me on the back as if I were one of his kids, then told me to go ahead. I ran to catch up with the other guys. As I did so, I watched in horror as some of the victims were being hauled off in ambulances and medevacked to other medical facilities in the area. I didn't know what to make of all this. It seemed like something right out of an action flick, but this was not make-believe or fantasy. It was real—real enough for me to realize that there are dangerous people out there who don't care whom they hurt or how many lives they have to take to get their point across, whether it's a political, social, or religious point of view. I'd had to find this out the hard way. I had seen death for the very first time in my military career, and I knew that this time was not going to be the last. I was mad as hell because of it and wanted others to know of my pain and rage.

I extended my enlistment in the army for a few more years and became a warrant officer, until I left to become a company man.

My name is Killian Antonio Milson. I am the product of an African American father who served in the US Army in the Gulf War of Operation Desert Storm, and a Latin American mother who was a professor of a prestigious university for fifteen years. I'm a veteran of both the Iraq and the Afghanistan Wars; a former CID (Criminal Investigation Division) official, US Army Military Police Corps of the Office of the Provost Marshal; and former army intelligence. I was also a CIA (Central Intelligence Agency) officer for five years, until I resigned from the agency. I now work as a bounty hunter (bail enforcement officer) in Baltimore, Maryland. And this is just *one* of many stories to come.

CHAPTER 1

DECEPTION FROM WITHIN

Monday, October 1st, 2029. A distinguished-looking man in his early to mid-thirties woke up at six o'clock in the morning without the sound of an alarm clock alerting him. He rubbed his eyes a few times and stretched his arms to revive his body after a restful seven-hour sleep. He leaned over the side of his bed and pulled out a small rug from underneath it. The rug appeared to be elaborate, very well woven and colorful. From the design, it looked to be Middle Eastern—Persian. He rolled it out flat on the carpet and knelt on it to pray, committing to what is called salah or salat, a prayer ritual practiced by all faithful Muslims. He did this for a couple of minutes, saying, "'Ashada 'al-la ilaha illa-llahu wa 'ashadu 'anna munammadan rasulu-llah" (I testify that there is none worthy of worship except God, and I testify that Muhammad is the messenger of God), a creed recognized as the Shahada or Sehadet that all Muslims recite when saying their prayers.

After finishing his religious obligations, he retreated to his bathroom and turned on the shower. After taking three to five minutes to wash, he shaved his face and brushed his teeth. He left his bedroom and automatically turned on his fifty-five-inch flat-screen television. After it flickered for a second, he went into the kitchen and prepared some coffee. The sound of the TV started off loud, so the gentleman rushed to the remote to turn down the volume. As he prepared his breakfast of wheat toast, scrambled eggs, fresh fruit, black coffee, and orange juice, he caught a glimpse of a show on one of his favorite channels, a popular news station that he watched every morning. His attention was piqued by what the anchorman was saying:

> Well, America, it has finally happened, and now it's official. After a ten-year process of talks and negotiations, an international agreement has finally been reached on the treaty. The remaining countries of the Arabian Peninsula, namely, Iraq, Afghanistan, and Pakistan, as well as Palestine, have finally come to an agreement. A peace accord has been signed, and a brand-new alliance has been established with the United Earth Administration—UEA—which was founded by the United Nations and the European Union Alliance almost twelve years ago. Benefiting from this partnership and this new global administration is the United States, Russia, England, Canada, Mexico, the rest of Europe, and all of Asia. All member countries have pledged their allegiance to the alliance, which has been touted as a beacon of prosperity, fortitude, and peaceful coexistence for the past twelve years. This indeed marks an outstanding moment in human history, and it will remain so for generations to come, with the possibility of prosperity, peace, and unity extending into the future.
>
> The only countries that have not signed the treaty are Syria, Yemen, Libya, Lebanon, Iran, and the communist country of North Korea. They have all pronounced that they wish to stay neutral and will not join the UEA unless matters of humanitarianism, economic awareness, and independence are acknowledged by the influential Western governments—the United States,

Great Britain, Canada, and Mexico. These countries have even demanded that China and Russia acknowledge them as independent states, to be treated equally by the global community. It has been stated that these remaining countries are still skeptical about the alliance of the world's governments. They reportedly feel doubtful and cautious about certain Western ideologies that have infiltrated certain foreign cultures and societies. They believe the UEA is a manipulative scheme to promote self-centered agendas, false beliefs, and principles contrary to their own all across the world. Ever since the People's Republic of China set up the naval blockade three and a half years ago in the South Pacific, allegations of espionage have been made against the United States, which has also been accused of secretly shipping weapons to force rebelling against the policies of China. This arose in the wake of trade negotiations and other agreements made between the United States and Japan and other countries in the South Pacific. This has, in fact, made both Iran and North Korea very suspicious of the United States and has led them to remain independent from the West. But since China has had a change of heart and dismantled the blockade it set up four years ago, which led to several naval skirmishes in the South Pacific, this has engendered a new cooperative outlook that has led to the signing of the treaty and the peace accord between the two superpowers.

With the signing of the UEA treaty, old, prejudicial concepts and pointless political philosophies, once the foundation of the member countries, have been eradicated. But since Iran and North Korea refuse to budge, the UEA and the UN have made several proposals to impose sanctions on these nations that wish to stay outside the treaty, claiming their independence as self-owned, self-reliant governments. Both countries have separated themselves from the rest of the world to independently pursue engineering developments in nuclear power and self-defense, which entails a buildup of their military forces. These views have arisen from their mistrust of the United States and its allies. This has caused more suspicion within the UN and the UEA that both countries exited the peaceful negotiations in order to arm themselves with weapons of mass destruction and other forms of military might. The possibility has raised many eyebrows all over Europe and Asia, as well as the rest of the world. This has led to even more distrust of the unified governments of the world, who, the declining countries allege, are seeking to put forth their own set of rules and regulations to benefit themselves alone and advance their political agendas. These countries have falsely identified themselves as being less powerful and are claiming they have been victimized and ostracized by Eastern and Western powers alike along with their philosophies, adding that they do not wish to conform to what they think of as a false ideology of unity.

Meanwhile, in other news, there has been speculation that US government secrets have been made public by unknown sources who hacked into the secure system of the Department of Defense, the DOD. The allegation is that the United States and its allies have fabricated a scheme to throw off foreign governments not aligned with the United States. At the same time, the United States believes that classified intelligence has been stolen from several secure servers. This information is protected by the Privacy Intelligence Act—PIA—of 2015 to keep government records from falling into foreign hands. It has been speculated that breaches such as this one has been carried out under the direction of the DOD, though the DOD has denied this. Officials from the National Security Council and the DOD issued a statement saying that such rumors are mere fabrications, a ploy to divert suspicion away from radical groups that wish to create disruption and controversy. But the intelligence community, along with the US State Department, has concluded that these are nothing but false rumors made up by conspiracy theorists and antipeace demonstrators who want to create a distraction whereby to defeat the UEA's goal of having peaceful negotiations across the world. The State Department has denied such allegations, saying it will conduct an internal and an external investigation into these matters as soon as possible.

On a lighter note, a new military organization has been formed that will concentrate on space itself as well as its boundaries. It's called the United Space Force Exploration Agency, or more commonly USFEA, and it operates under the aegis of the US Air Force—a military spin-off. It was created by the president, the secretary of the air force, the Pentagon, and the governing body of the UEA. This organization will differ from its predecessor, NASA. It is described as a new branch of the military for the earth's defense and for space exploration and scientific research. Its main purpose is to explore our solar system and go beyond the boundaries of space, in addition to exploring the uncharted portions of the Milky Way galaxy. Now for the weather ...

After listening to the news, the slender gentleman lowered the volume on his TV and went back to eating his breakfast. After finishing, he headed back to his bedroom to dress for work. He produced several items of clothing from his closet; they appeared to be components of a uniform. He laid them out neatly on his bed and put the items on one by one. It was his US Navy uniform, traditional service dress blues (SDB), the class-A uniform worn by all navy personnel. It looked very much like a black civilian-style suit with a white dress shirt and a simple black tie. His rank of lieutenant commander was made plain by the insignias at both ends of his sleeves. His nameplate, on the upper right of his suit jacket beside his lapel, read, "Ad-dam Omar Assad."

The man was of Lebanese and Iraqi descent. His father was a military scientist for the Republic of Lebanon, who later emigrated to Iraq, and his mother was a college professor and activist for women's rights in Baghdad, Iraq. He and his family had lived in Iraq for the last few years of Saddam Hussein's regime, before US and coalition forces invaded Iraq in March of 2003. His parents left right after the invasion began, when he was a little boy, and became US citizens right after the fall of Saddam's government.

Assad gathered some documents together and placed them in his briefcase. He cleaned up after himself, setting aside the rest of his personal items, then started to head out the front door to go to work. His apartment, located to the north of Baltimore City in Towson, had two bedrooms and one bath. It was plenty large for him since he was single and living alone.

Assad lived on the third floor, not too far from his personal carport, which was beneath the complex. A couple of his neighbors, who were also on their way to work, waved and greeted him as he passed by them. Being polite and courteous, Assad reciprocated with a tip of his white combination cap and a word of hello. One of his neighbors, the one who greeted him first, was a young woman who lived in the unit just under his. She was very attracted to Assad and made her intentions known. Assad was a very handsome man. Slender and tall with an average muscular build, he impressed a lot of people, including his neighbors, because of his dress, his choice of career, and the way he carried himself. He was confident, sophisticated, and urbane. He was very popular with the opposite sex but did not flaunt his looks or advertise his achievements. He was more modest and humbler, never conceited or vain.

Assad did not look at all Arabic judging from his facial features and complexion. On the contrary, having been in the United States for so long, he had taken on the attributes of an American more than one would expect given his Middle Eastern heritage. He was very fair-skinned, which caused people to assume he was Caucasian rather than being of Iraqi and Lebanese heritage. But he recognized his true identity as an Islamic Arab. Another feature that made him irresistible to women was his eyes. Commonly, Arabs had dark eyes, but Assad's genetics had given him the unique gift of light blue eyes instead. This along with his handsome good looks made it easy for him to blend in with Caucasian Americans.

Assad stepped into his silver BMW and turned the key in the ignition. When he was about to put the car into reverse to exit the carport, he suddenly remembered something. He took his cell phone from his coat pocket and removed the back. Then he turned to his briefcase, which was on the passenger side, to open it. He took out a very small metallic object that appeared to be a computer chip or perhaps a SIM card for a cell phone. Taking the original out of his phone, he replaced it with the one from his briefcase, then slid the back cover into place. With that done, he dialed a number.

Preoccupied with the phone, Assad managed to drive out of the carport and begin along the route to his usual destination. While holding the phone to his ear, he began programming the automated guidance control system (AGCS) on his dashboard to put the car in autonomous drive mode. The GPS system allowed for automatic operation of the vehicle so the driver could attend to other things as the vehicle piloted itself, navigating its way to the preprogrammed destination.

Still occupied with the phone and waiting for someone to answer his call, Assad heard a click on the other end as if someone had finally answered. When he suspected the individual, he was hoping to reach was on the line, he immediately began to speak.

"Hello, it's me. … Yes, I have the scrambler installed. No one can trace this call or access the data from the memory chip. I'm heading to work now. Once I'm in my office, I'll send you the rest of the info. Do you have my papers and documents ready? … Good. What about the money we agreed on? Has it been wired to my private account? … Perfect. Once I check the amount that's been deposited and read the agreement, I will send you the rest of the data you requested, along with a flash drive that has copies of all the files. I will bring the original drive and an extra one as well. … I know that this isn't part of the arrangement, but I must have some insurance to prevent against any double-cross or trickery on your part or the part of your organization. … It's just a precaution, that's all. … If you don't receive the info I send you, the thumb drive will serve as both the backup and a safeguard. … I know what I'm doing this for and why. You don't have to question me or remind me of where I should put my loyalties or whom I should obey. You just make sure to tell your superiors that I'm taking a big risk by doing this, so I expect to be reimbursed very generously for it. … You just make sure that they're prepared on their end. I don't want any surprises. … Yes, I know. Once the info is sent to you, I must delete all evidence of these transactions and the materials themselves from the mainframe's database. I'll also erase all memory and backup files from the library so that nothing will be traced back to me or you. … Yes, I've got that covered as well. I'm bringing them with me. Don't worry about that; I'll take care of it myself. You just make sure that the information on my ticket matches that on my new passport and ID. … Yes, I saw the news this morning, and I heard what they said, but it doesn't matter. The State Department doesn't have a clue about what's going on or who's leaking the information. Not even the CIA, the NSA, the NIA, the DCS, or the DIA knows what is going on, apart from where the information is coming from. I've covered every base here. They are clueless and have no way of finding out what is really going on. … Have you forgotten who I work for? … Yes, yes, I know. When the Americans find out about this, it will be too late. It will take them decades to recover from it. … Yes, of course, it will be their downfall. Listen, I must go. Once this call ends, the transmission will automatically delete itself and the resulting data will be erased. … Yes, yes, of course I know. Just have everything ready for me today. … Yes. Wa alaikum as-salaam [Peace be upon you too]. Bye."

Assad abruptly put down the phone as he saw that he was almost at his destination. His car was driving up to the entrance gate of a highly secure naval facility called the National Maritime Intelligence Center, located in Suitland, Silver Hill, Maryland, in Prince Georges County.

Assad disengaged the automatic drive and resumed steering manually. Decreasing his speed, he drove up to the gate, where two armed marine guards were posted. One of the marines came up on the driver's side and saluted Assad, asking for his ID. Assad gladly brought out his billfold, showing his military ID and his security pass. The guard took only a second to glance at it, knowing full well who Assad was. He waved him through and gave him another salute as he drove past.

Assad turned several corners and passed a number of landmarks before he came upon the area he was looking for. The building he worked in was one of the navy's oldest and most highly classified secure facilities in the world apart from CIA headquarters in Langley, Virginia. The building itself was called ONI (Office of Naval Intelligence), its creation dating back to 1882, when the ONI's primary objective was to gather information on foreign navies and discern their purposes. But as times changed at the turn of the century, the goals of this establishment changed as well.

The ONI is part of the United States intelligence community. It works side by side with the CIA (Central Intelligence Agency), the NSA (National Security Agency), the NIA (National Intelligence Agency), the DCS (Defense Clandestine Service), the DIA (Defense Intelligence Agency), DHS (Department of Homeland Security), and the FBI (Federal Bureau of Investigation). It is also partnered with other military entities, such as the intelligence agencies of the army, air force, and marine corps. Assad held the position of senior assistant analyst for foreign military relations and counterintelligence. His primary job was to gather information and intel from allied foreign countries and their militaries for the use in counterespionage. Another part of his job was to decipher codes and encrypted software slated for use against the United States and its allies. But Assad did not come into this job by chance. He had been recruited long ago when in his early twenties, right out of college. At the tender age of seventeen, he'd been accepted to go to Yale University right out of high school because of his high scores on the SAT (Scholastic Aptitude Test) exams. His test scores were impressive at fifteen hundred. When he graduated second in his class from Yale, he made the decision to enlist in the navy and applied to the United States Naval Academy in Annapolis. He studied at the academy for two years, graduating early as a lieutenant JG (junior grade) instead of an ensign like everyone else because of his academic skills and high IQ. He impressed many of his professors and senior officers, who took a liking to him. They encouraged him to use his intelligence and skills in the mainstream of the navy to advance his career. He had worked as an assistant cryptanalyst for the NSA and as an assistant internet operator for USCYBERCOM (United States Cyber Command), a highly sophisticated intelligence organization created by the United States Strategic Command Center, the Central Security Service, and the NSA. Its purpose is to monitor and surveil radio communications and transmissions from computer networks worldwide for cyberspace threats within and outside military jurisdiction. Another purpose of the agency is to deter and combat cyberterrorism and prevent hacking by either hostile foreign countries or hostile domestic organizations, such as privately owned businesses and corporations, along with rogue nations and foreign military networks.

In his third year of being in the navy, after having graduated from the academy, Assad took advantage of the combat and tactical side of the branch. He trained with several special elite forces such as Navy SEALs, Army Green Berets and Delta Force, and even Marine Recon Expeditionary Forces, known as MARSOC (US Marine Corps Forces Special Operations Command). Once again, he impressed his superiors so much that they encouraged him to apply for a position at

ONI. His recommendations got his application so far up the ladder that it reached a full-bird captain and two rear admirals, the latter being the position to which they appointed him. Assad was highly decorated from every phase of his astonishing career, from his time since the academy to his job at ONI. The brass was so impressed by this young man's combat skills and intellectual prowess that they forced him to take the position at ONI, even if he might have preferred to decline. He made full-grade lieutenant in three years and lieutenant commander in two. He had performed in an exemplary fashion in terms of his obligations and duties for the navy in his years of service—*until now.*

He drove into his personal parking space with his name and rank printed on a sign in the ground beyond the curb. He got out, secured his car with his remote, and walked to the entrance doors to his left. As he entered the facility, he was greeted by several fellow officers and high-ranking enlisted men who were obviously marine NCOs and naval chiefs. Continuing to walk down the corridor at a comfortable pace, he managed to catch an elevator that was going in his direction. He quickly jumped on board with one person holding the door for him. As he entered, he was stunned to realize that his boss was also a passenger on the elevator.

"Just made it on time, Ad-dam?" The gentleman who had made this remark was a full-grade commander by the name of Sean Jacob Dixon, Assad's supervisor and his closest friend.

"Ah, yes, sir. Just in the nick. Morning, sir," replied Assad, who was surprised to see Dixon. "Morning, Ad-dam. Have you finished those reports I asked for last week?"

At first, Assad did not know what Dixon was talking about, but then Dixon gave a gesture that triggered Assad's memory. "Yes, sir, I've got them here in my briefcase. I spent all weekend working on them and getting them in order."

"Good, Ad-dam. The colonel and our new director want to see the latest intelligence reports we have on the Iranians and North

Koreans, not to mention our new friends the Chinese. But since the Chinese have signed the UEA charter, there's no longer any need to look at them, what with that nasty blockade they set up years ago having disbanded."

Assad gently nodded his head.

"True, sir. But don't we still have operatives down there watching over the Chinese?"

Dixon nonchalantly put a finger to his lips to indicate that Assad should keep quiet about that. Even though the elevator was occupied by only two individuals, namely, Assad and Dixon, any important information uttered there was still deemed top secret, no matter if any individuals who might have overheard worked for the facility and had security clearance. Precautionary measures were still implemented, and anything discussed as part of casual conversation was to be kept secret unless intervention was required from a superior—an admiral, a general, or a high-ranking political official.

Assad, realizing his mistake, respectfully acknowledged Dixon's request. Noticing from the digital display that the elevator had made it to its destination, the two commanders got off in haste. As they were walking to their respective offices, Assad took the opportunity to offer an apology. "Sean, I'm sorry. I didn't realize that we were still keeping that hush-hush."

Dixon gave a wave with his right hand to assure Assad he needn't be apologetic, tapping on his chest at the same time.

"Nah, don't worry about it. You didn't know. The CIA, NSA, and DOD still want to keep tabs on the Chinese. They want to make sure that they don't try to build any secret bases in the South Pacific, such as in the Solomon Islands or Indonesia, that our satellites won't be able to detect. Ever since the blockade, we've been suspicious that they might have set up covert facilities around those areas, especially since there were patrol routes leading into and out of there."

"Well, we know that that will never happen," Assad replied. "The Australian government, along with the governments of New Zealand, New Guinea, Japan, and the Philippines, will never allow the Chinese to build up any military base on the Australian coast without express permission and consent. To do otherwise would be to violate the treaty of the Federated States of Micronesia, stipulating neutrality and nonaggression for independent countries like ours with big navies. Not to mention the UEA treaty accords." The Federated States of Micronesia is a sovereign nation made up of four island states: Yap, Chuuk, Pohnpei, and Kosrae. When the Chinese ended their naval blockade four years ago, a treaty was signed by the governments of the United States and China at a neutral location in Micronesia stating that no military installations would be established in the South Pacific on islands near to larger occupied areas for the purpose of secret surveillance. The treaty allowed for both countries to set up installations for humanitarian purposes only. "In turn, if the Micronesian government ever were to find out that the Chinese were setting up bases in those areas, heavy stipulations, fines, and sanctions would level against them, and a declaration of war would be made," Assad concluded.

"Correct, Ad dam. That's why Washington wants to make sure they are still upholding their end of the bargain. Even though we and the Chinese are allies on paper, we must not underestimate our neighbors from the East. China is considered a world power just as Russia, Great Britain, and the United States. That's why we still have people down there looking at every move the Chinese make and working side by side with the local governments and military agencies down there."

As they continued to walk and discuss current events and world affairs, Assad noticed that he was about to pass by his office.

"Here's my stop, Sean. I'll see you later at lunch."

Dixon was about to head off to his own office, but he stopped suddenly.

"Oh yeah, that reminds me. Don't forget that we have a briefing to get to at eleven hundred hours. The director wants to see the entire staff about our workloads and go over about what's been happening in the news."

"The news? What news?" Assad asked disingenuously, knowing very well what Dixon was referring to.

"Rumors have been circulating that highly classified information has been leaked beyond the confines of Washington and the Pentagon. They think that sensitive materials, based on certain intel, may have been compromised or taken. The FBI and the NSA think that someone is giving such info to either the Iranians or the Koreans, possibly even to Pakistan. The admiral and the colonel want to debrief everyone, including junior staff, on this, so don't forget—and don't be late."

Assad gave a nod to his supervisor, ensuring him that he would be there promptly. As he entered his office, he was greeted by one of his aides, a marine staff sergeant who served as his personal secretary by the name of Beverly Crawford. Beverly had an endearing appearance that made Assad smile when he looked at her.

"Morning, sir. How are you doing today?" The young NCO smiled as she stood up and gave him the proper greeting.

"I'm fine, Sergeant. How are you?"

"Never better, sir. … I put those documents on your desk that you requested Friday."

"Thank you, Beverly. Oh, by the way, I don't want to be disturbed for the next two hours, unless it's Commander Dixon or Colonel Remington. There's a meeting I must attend at eleven hundred hours. Remind me around ten thirty, will you, Bev?"

Once again, the sergeant smiled at the charismatic officer who had a charm about him that appeal to women. "No problem, sir. I most certainly will."

"Thank you, Sergeant Crawford." Returning her smile, Assad opened his office door and entered, closing the door behind him. Afterward, he started to wonder about what Dixon had said earlier about the news and the mandatory meeting. At first, he felt a little uneasy, but the anxiety, initially overwhelming, lasted for only a couple of seconds, because suddenly he remembered his confidence, his knowledge, and the true circumstances. After he had worked out his diabolical project in his mind, the anxiety subsided quickly. He was again felt at ease with himself. He knew exactly what was going on as he had planned the entire scenario precisely. He went over every contingency and, in his mind, executed his scheme without a single mistake. If his devious plan were to give rise to any backlash and he ended up being implicated, he knew that serious consequences would befall him. Assad was too smart to allow for that. He knew enough to create decoys that would point the authorities in some other direction if something were to go wrong. He already knew that he himself would not take the fall. He would find a patsy, someone to take the blame for what he'd done, a person who might look innocent and appear to be beyond reproach—unless he wanted to cast suspicion on this person so as no one would look at him as the true culprit.

After going over everything again in his mind, Assad dashed to his desk and turned on his personal touch screen laptop. While waiting for his computer to boot up, he moved the forms that Sergeant Crawford had laid out on his desk to the side and replaced them with his briefcase, which he put on top, next to the computer. Fumbling with the combination lock, he opened the briefcase and pulled out some top-secret documents. Glancing at the forms for only a moment, not putting too much emphasis on them, he placed them to the side, right next to the others. He then took out a flash drive that he had hidden beneath his desk, along with another flash drive that served as the backup. Both drives were very small in size, but they suited his purposes because they each held thousands of megabytes worth of data. The capacity of the flash drive was 2.75 gigabytes.

When Assad's computer finally powered up, he plugged the thumb drive into the USB port to begin downloading information. Meanwhile, he opened several personal files from his favorites and enlarged them to match the size of the screen. He had several files there containing information from different intelligence agencies. A few discussed new top-secret weapons being developed by the DOD and DIA. He scrolled through a few file names until he found the six important ones he was looking for. The first of these was titled "US and British Naval Development of Counter weapons and Their Deployment." The second was "Department of Defense Schematics for Upgrades to Specialized Weapons: US Air Force General Atomic MQ-1, -2, -3, and -4 Unmanned Aerial Drone Vehicles—Predators—SAM (Surface-to-Air Missiles), and AMRAAM (Advanced Medium-Range Air-to-Air Missiles) Long-, Medium-, and Short-Range Penetrating Detonation Missiles." The title of document number three was "The Defense Intelligence Agency's Strategy on Counterintelligence and Covert Operations in Foreign Countries." These three topics were his main area of interest. Another of the files he had pulled up was titled "Names of All US and Allied Intelligence Operatives, Military Intelligence Agency Groups, and Federal Law Enforcement Agencies Working Overseas Doing Covert Operations with Interpol and Other Foreign Military and Law Enforcement Agencies and Services." The fifth document was titled "New Military Aerial Combat Vehicles/Fighters and New Ship Designs under Development by the Department of Navy and DOD for US Armed Forces and British Royal Armed Forces." The sixth and final one was titled "DARPA (Defense Advanced Research Projects Agency), an organization responsible for the development of technological advancement for the use of military and for scientific research." These files contained information vital to the security of the United States and its allies. Assad looked over them carefully. Then he typed in a pass code that he alone knew. "Password approved" flashed on his screen. He began to download the information he wanted to the thumb drive. Later, he accessed the mainframes of the NIA, the NSA, the DOD, the DIA, the DCS, and the CIA to get more files with, hopefully, some useful information on top secret military hardware.

After having hacked into the US intelligence network, he moved on to USCYBERCOM, his previous employer, where he had worked years prior as a junior officer just starting out, and dismantled several USCYBERCOM security protocols and firewalls, which were making it impossible for him to retrieve the data. He was able to do this because he had an insider's knowledge of USCYBERCOM's security protocols and how often they changed the pass codes to access their network. Assad had hacked in and stolen classified information from the very heart of the most important US database. He managed to outwit USCYBERCOM's IT protocols and sneak in past the same electronic barricades he had helped design when he was employed there.

After taking a hurried look at all the data and realizing that he was satisfied, he took an hour and a half to copy the files to his drive. After removing the device from the USB port, he replaced it with one designed specifically to erase the memory, including workloads and outputs, linked to individual PCs and government networks. He also typed in a sequence of codes whose purpose was to distribute a computer virus that he had designed himself in case anyone tried to hack into the system to retrieve information. In addition to this, he prevented against any unauthorized pass codes granting access to the hard drive by initiating a program to destroy both the software and the hard drive. These viruses would soon cause an immediate shutdown of the system and would destruction of the mainframe by instantly frying its circuits. After doing this, Assad created a protocol that would send the virus not only from his laptop but also from his cell phone, in which he had installed a chip he had designed to distribute the virus to all relevant email addresses and websites in the event his computer was incapable of doing so. He reminded himself to dispose of the chip once the virus had been distributed across the world.

Assad was clever, too clever for his own good. He had masterminded this entire scheme down to the last precise detail and knew what to do and how to do it while keeping himself clean, a facade he would have to uphold until he arranged for safe passage and left the country for good.

Perhaps an outsider would see Assad's motives as arbitrary and reprehensible, but that was not Assad's point of view. His issues were political and emotional in nature, almost to the point that he thought that what he was doing was justifiable and fair, with the financial support to prove it. He knew that by doing this, if he were to get caught, he could be brought up on serious federal charges as well as military charges under the UCMJ (Uniform Code of Military Justice). The charges he was looking at were espionage, conspiracy, aiding the enemy, and treason, seeing as he was giving classified information and materials to foreign countries that were hostile to the United States and its allies. Assad realized he could spend fifty years to life in a military or federal prison without the possibility of parole, and probably even get the death penalty if any innocent lives ended up being lost. But Assad knew what was at stake, and he knew he could get away with what he was doing hands down. His reasons for doing this were very deep and personal. Judging from his facial expression, he was feeling rather calm about it, to the point of being unemotional.

Two hours had passed. Sergeant Crawford knocked gently on the door to Assad's office, saying, "Sir, the time is ten thirty. You wanted me to remind you of your staff meeting."

Assad had almost forgotten about it. He managed to gather all his things, including the flash drives with the downloaded information, and put them back in his briefcase. Then he deleted the memory, erasing all the information from his taskbar and favorites. While closing his briefcase and turning off his computer, he told Crawford that he would be right out. Looking up at the clock positioned above his doorway, he put his laptop in the sliding drawer under his desk, and put his briefcase into a combination safe located on the left side of his office. After dusting himself off, he walked around his desk and toward the doorway. As he turned to leave his office, he was surprised to be greeted by Dixon, who was standing in the middle of his doorway with his arms crossed. Assad looked over to Crawford and asked her why she did not inform him of Dixon's presence. Just as she was about to answer him, the commander interrupted, beating her to the punch and saving her hide.

"Ad-dam, I just arrived a second ago and told her not to call me out. I'm here to pick you up for the meeting. Are you ready?"

Assad looked at his watch and gazed at his supervisor.

"Yes, sir, I am. Do we need to bring anything with us, like a pen and a pad to take notes?" Dixon replied.

"No, this is not a study session with take-home work. It's a casual, albeit impromptu, setting. The director and deputy director just want to debrief us on what's going on and tell us what to look out for. Come on, Commander, let's go."

Bent on leaving in a hurry, they both exited the doorway quickly, with Assad giving Crawford a friendly hand gesture to indicate she should oversee things while he was gone. The tentative staff sergeant smiled while filing some documents in her file cabinet, watching her commanding officer and his supervisor leave the office.

As they were walking through the hallway and down the stairs, Dixon and Assad met up with several senior and junior officers who were heading in the same direction as they were. Most of these were navy and marine personnel, with some army and air force mixed in. As Dixon and Assad continued their stride, talking together, with the familiar crowd surrounding them as they moved casually through the corridors, they finally arrived at their destination. It was a conference room of average size that could hold maybe fifty to seventy-five people, a hundred max. It was well-lighted and very spacious, but there weren't enough chairs or tables to accommodate everyone. Most of the high-ranking officials in attendance were majors / lieutenant commanders and lieutenant colonels / commanders, who were sitting in most of the seats, while the junior officials—captains / full grade lieutenants and their subordinates, that is, first and second lieutenants / lieutenants JG and ensigns—were standing around the conference room. There were a few NCOs there as mandated, all of which were grade E-6 and above.

Assad and Dixon sat down in the front close to the door, looking over at the crowd in the room with a digital clock hanging overhead that read 10:59 on the dot, which meant that either the admiral or the colonel was about to arrive, but this did not change the mood of the audience, who were all questioning why they had to be there in the first place. Some of them knew, but most of them did not. Everyone was in a jumble, talking and laughing amongst themselves. While the crowd was getting comfortable, a tall, husky sergeant major entered the room and shouted at full volume, his voice echoing throughout the entire room as if he were a drill instructor, "Attention on deck!" Everyone stood up at full attention as they kicked their chairs from up under them with the junior officers already standing stiffly behind their chairs.

As the audience continued moving, a full-bird colonel dressed in a class-A marine brown uniform walked through the door first. It was Colonel John (Jack) Remington of the US Marine Corps, executive officer and deputy director of ONI. Remington was a statue of a man who was in his mid-fifties with a tuft of gray hair on each side of his head that was cut close in the standard marine "high and tight" hairstyle. To his staff and subordinates, Remington was a tough SOB. A standard marine officer with the attitude and toughness of a marine boot camp drill instructor/sergeant. He was mean and surly, to the point of being outrageously nasty and brutish at times. He walked in as if he owned the place, seemingly on a mission, with determination and grit. He strode through the room and came to stand on the opposite side, waiting for his commanding officer to make his entrance. Remington stood straight and stiff, staring hard and fast, awaiting the arrival of his CO, who was coming right behind him. Everyone remained motionless in anticipation of the senior supervisor who would make his presence known.

In just a few seconds, he finally arrived. A middle-aged man between the ages of forty-five and forty-nine; fifty to be exact. The individual happened to be an African American with a statuesque build and a robust demeanor. He walked through the door without breaking a stride. Dapper and mild-mannered, the one-star flag officer stepped up to the front table close to the podium in the center and looked around the room at his potential underclass audience. This was Rear Admiral Wayne James Cooper, chief director and senior commanding officer of naval intelligence.

Cooper's physique and facial features made him appear to be younger than he was. He looked distinguished and commanding. He resembled a young Thurgood Marshall (former Supreme Court justice who served during the mid-to late twentieth century). He had a dapper ink-line thin mustache that made him appear more mature and sophisticated. But no matter his age and vitality, according to the younger officers and his battle-hardened deputy director, he still had the look of a younger man trying to appear older than he really was with the facial hair pasted under his nose. Everyone took notice of the two combat badges Cooper wore on the left breast of his uniform, just to the side of his lapel, of his formal navy SDB class-A black uniform.

Assad, who was impressed by the admiral's decorations, was familiar with the first insignia thanks to his previous duties as serving as a liaisons officer for Naval Special Forces. This was the Special Warfare insignia, famously known as the *SEAL Trident*, an honorable pin worn only by SEAL team members who had earned the right to wear it by going through the rigorous training course known as "BUDS" (Basic Underwater Demolition SEAL Training). That alone established them as honorary SEALs, and entitled them as US special forces members who have served under USSOCOM (United States Special Operations Command) performing covert operations. Cooper wore this prestigious badge with pride and honor, and he made it stand out by wearing it close to his lapel so the entire audience would know that their director and senior commanding officer had been and still is a member of the elite unit, as well as being damn proud of it also. Assad of his own accord had the privilege of owning the Trident badge himself, but out of respect for the unit and his division, he chose not to wear it because he was not an official SEAL. Yes, he had been trained by the unit and had gone on several missions with them because of his background and linguistic expertise, but Assad has never been a member officially and has never gone through the BUDS training like the admiral and other brave men who pledged their lives to a career as an honorary Navy SEAL.

Cooper's second pin was the Submarine Warfare Officer insignia. This spoke to his previous service as either a submariner or submarine commander. Cooper had landed that job after his successful tours of duty as a SEAL in Iraq and Afghanistan. He previously had served as a submariner when he was a young enlisted sailor. After he received his commission as an officer and finalized his career as a SEAL, he was recruited to the submarine fleet service under COMSUBPAC (Commander, Submarine Force, US Pacific Fleet). He served as a commander for the submarine fleet for several years, until he was promoted to captain and received his first supervisory role as a solo submarine captain. He was one of five submarine commanders who had engaged the Chinese navy during the blockade three and a half years ago. He managed to sink a Chinese Han-class nuclear submarine that had drawn first blood by attacking the US Surface and Submarine Naval Fleet. After having exercised his exceptional combat tactics at sea and commanded one of the newest Columbia-class ballistic missile nuclear submarines, a.k.a. "boomers," Cooper landed his current job on the basis of his reputation and his experience as a submarine captain and special ops coordinator. His previous command tour was aboard the USS *Leviathan* (SSBN-830), serving as supervisor for more than three years. He was promoted to rear admiral after that, which gave him the opportunity to direct the most secret intelligence organization in the US navy. At the time, he did not want the job, but ultimately, he was persuaded to take it by one of his mentors, Three-Star Vice Admiral Patrick Taylor, who was nicknamed Torpedo Taylor on account of his reputation for being a hard-driving, hard-nosed submarine commander. Admiral Taylor, the VCNO (Vice Chief of US Naval Operations), had, under congressional authority, given Cooper his promotion to command ONI one year ago, right after his tour had ended in the Pacific. Since then, Cooper had been the top dog of the agency and had run it efficiently. Little did he know of the dastardly deed committed by one of his officers who would, by doing as he had, change the outlook of the organization's operations and intentions for years to come.

Quickly glancing at everyone present in the room, Cooper looked over to Colonel Remington, who had held the rank of colonel for the past twenty-five years, to command everyone to take their seats.

"At ease!" Colonel Remington said. He followed this with,

"Take your seats!" in a harsh and pounding tone as he stood on the opposite side, facing the crowd. After all the officers and NCOs had sat down, Cooper opened the proceedings in a calm and casual way.

"Afternoon, ladies and gentlemen." Everyone responded to the admiral with the same courtesy. "I know that all of you were ordered by your supervisors and COs to attend this briefing recommended by me and Colonel Remington, but I assure you that this will not be a waste of your time, or of ours, since we have a lot of work to do afterward. So please bear with me, and I promise you that I'll make it quick and painless.

"You all know what's been reported in the news today. The remaining Arabian and Islamic countries have agreed to sign the treaty and join the United Earth Administration, pledging peaceful coexistence with their neighbors in an effort to end the long-lasting hostilities with the West. They're still trying to hammer out some of the minor details and deal with the points on which they disagree, especially as concerns Israel and its policies, but many of the new signatories, such as the Palestinians, are willing to listen open-mindedly to suggestions on how to improve negotiations under the UEA charter. We still have some concerns about Syria, Iran, Libya, Yemen, Somalia, Pakistan, and North Korea, and we are confused about what are their primary roles will be, because they are refusing to join the global unification effort that the rest of the world has embraced. But it seems that they have not bothered to interfere in the proceedings between their neighboring countries and the rest of the world, so that may be a good thing. But they still regard us as untrustworthy, and they wish to stay neutral and to build themselves up as separate independent nations. On our end, we will still regard them as a threat to the security of the United States and the world.

"There is some speculation about weapons development despite the nuclear sanctions, weapons that these countries have produced under the noses of the United Nations and NATO. But the UEA, along with us, Great Britain, Russia, and China, has begun an investigation to find out if Iran and North Korea are building WMDs for their own use. True, both countries have nuclear power and capabilities, but we do not want to underestimate these or take them for granted.

"Speaking of the Chinese, the People's Liberation Army has embraced us with open arms and wants to work toward accomplishing the UEA's goal of world peace by providing humanitarian services, ensuring cooperation between governments worldwide, and contributing to global security. But Washington still feels uneasy about China in terms of territorial matters, particularly China's desire to govern the South Pacific and Central Pacific. This was one of the many issues we had when they set up the blockade four years ago. I know because I was right there in the heart of things when it happened. We do have operatives down there in the Solomon Islands and Indonesia surveying China's every move, with cooperative local governments having given us permission to be down there in the first place. But under international law, and according to the treaty and charter, we are not to retaliate against them unless what they are doing violates the treaty or the law. We must remember that they are still partners and allies of the United States and of all the other unified countries that follow the UEA's guidelines and policies. So, for that, we're required by law to stay neutral and out of the way until we hear otherwise.

"But unfortunately, we have something more serious and disturbing to talk about today. It seems that we have a serious breach of national security on our hands. In other words, we may have a conspirator or a mole within our midst." Even though the room had remained quiet throughout Cooper's presentation, his last statement made everyone fall utterly silent as they looked at each other in puzzlement and confusion. The remark had made Assad feel a little inadequate, but this bit of news in no way shocked him because he'd been aware of it ahead of time. He knew the truth and the specifics behind the breach, and because of that, he made himself comfortable within his surroundings.

Cooper continued to state the facts and suspicions that had led to this meeting being called in the first place. "Several months ago, the State Department reported that large amounts of classified data from its internal archives had come up missing. At first, they thought it was just a glitch in their software or, perhaps, a simple matter of misplaced files. But when they went to retrieve some of the data that they thought might have been placed in other secure files, it became obvious to them that someone had been stealing classified military intel and economic information from their database. They immediately notified the FBI, the NSA, and the Department of Homeland Security, telling them of the missing info, but these agencies have found only a few leads. Their investigations have also turned up several instances of hacking into the mainframes of the Department of Defense and the Defense Intelligence Agency. These leads have brought them to the conclusion that someone may be involved, but they don't know who, or where. This individual or individuals, they believe, have successfully hidden their tracks, masking their location to prevent the possibility of being discovered. It seems that they have knowledge of our security protocols and are probably well experienced in dealing with high-profile computer databases, including microprogramming and encryption processing and sequencing. Whoever they are, they're smart as hell and cunning as foxes. Some of the investigators think the source may be from an external sphere of influence, but others think it may be an inside job."

Dixon raised his hand.

"Excuse me, sir, but do you think we may have a spy or a group of spies within our government?"

"Most likely, Commander. The idea is not that far-fetched," Cooper answered.

"We've seen situations like this before. When I was a young lieutenant many years ago, twenty years to be exact," said Cooper, not about to tell his subordinates his true age,

"We had a string of Russian spies in the United States that we didn't know about until a couple of months after the fact. The FBI and the CIA did an investigation into several unexplained emails and communications that had gone back and forth between the United States and Russia. Later, they figured out that these individuals were not registered via the proper international channels and that certain paperwork of theirs had already expired, most importantly, their passports and travel visas. Also, there was a case many years ago involving an FBI agent by the name of Robert Hanssen, who was charged with espionage and treason against the United States for giving classified documents to the Russian government for almost twenty years while he was employed with the Federal Bureau of Investigation. He is still serving a life sentence today. And I think some of you either are too young to remember or had not even been born yet when two gentlemen, Julian Paul Assange and PFC Bradley Manning, the latter of army intelligence, were tried for espionage and treason after having posted military information to a publicly accessible website. Assange, who is the creator and founder of the website called WikiLeaks, was distributing highly sensitive materials containing secrets of both the US government and certain foreign governments. These were materials considered highly classified by the IIC [international intelligence community] and by the SHIELD [Securing Human Intelligence and Enforcing Lawful Dissemination] Act. This information, which was mostly about battle plans and intelligence gathering, was used at the discretion of the United States during both the Iraq War and the War in Afghanistan. PFC Manning was caught red-handed when sending emails and text messages to Assange that included things for Assange to post on his website, which offered this information free of charge to anyone on the internet, meaning that terrorists and extremists could access it for use against the United States and our allies to disrupt military operations and diplomatic efforts in war-torn areas.

"The idea of doing something like this is not impossible to believe. In 2013, a former CIA and NSA contractor named Edward Snowden leaked top secret surveillance information from both the United States and the United Kingdom to the worldwide press. His actions left our surveillance procedures and classified materials at risk of being accessed illegally by foreign countries and governments that at the time were our adversaries. Snowden fled the United States, seeking asylum in other countries, namely, Russia, but was later brought to justice. Right now, all federal law enforcement agencies and military intelligence groups (army, air force, marine corps, and DIA) like ours are going to combine their efforts and do a full security sweep of all emails coming into and going out of every DOD mainframe. They are also prepared to install software detection nets for all algorithmic processors, with storage of both input data and output data. USCYBERCOM is getting involved in this effort as well, making it a joint investigation among all federal intelligence agencies. So, I want you to show professionalism as you assist these groups. Give them your undivided attention and be courteous as you help with this investigation. I want every computer system in this building, including all personal PCs, to be swept thoroughly by the end of this week or sooner.

"Ladies and gentlemen, we have a serious breach of national security on our hands, and I want to know who or what is responsible for this. The secretaries of defense and state are aware of this, as are the chairman of the Joint Chiefs and the national security adviser. They don't want to inform the president of this matter until we have evidence to prove that there is a foreign agent taking our secrets and selling them to a foreign adversary at the highest bid. They don't want to alarm him, and will only inform him if the story spins out of control before the media or some other form of social public internet communication. The press already has an inkling of this situation, but they don't know the severity of it. That's why the State Department is just feeding them what they need to know, not what they should know."

A young army captain raised his hand.

"Admiral, sir? Excuse me for interrupting, but you spoke of missing classified military information. Can you be more specific, sir?"

Cooper decided to oblige the young officer by answering his question.

"The missing information includes schematics and plans for new military weapons, including Predator drones; newly developed counter weapons that we and the Brits have been working on; new aircraft for the air force and navy, as well as designs for other new ships; and last but certainly not least, and an extremely important addition, the names and background info of all undercover operatives (both federal and military) working for both the Justice Department and DOD who are serving either overseas or right here in the States."

The expression on everyone's faces turned suddenly from one of confusion to one of concern and horror in a matter of seconds, although Assad maintained his relaxed look. This truly was a fragile situation that Cooper had laid out for them.

"This is why it is very important that we find out who is behind this. If any of this information gets out, the media and the public will go into a frenzy. This is not even counting the more immediate threat: that knowledge of this may fall into the hands of our potential adversaries, the Iranians and North Koreans, or into the hands of other rogue nations that don't share our views on democracy and freedom or don't accept the newly established government that the UEA is trying to expand across the world. This could seriously cripple us and our allies for years to come. We must find these individuals at once and stop them immediately before any real damage can be done. At all costs, by any means necessary, they must be stopped *permanently* and *expeditiously*." Everyone knew exactly what Cooper meant, even Assad, who had kept his cool throughout the session.

"All right, the colonel is going to dismiss you and go over the game plan with your COs and supervisors. Keep in mind, people, we're not accusing anyone here, and this is not a witch-hunt, so all of you can stop sweating and start breathing again. We're not suspecting anyone here or in any of the other aforementioned branches or agencies. But the secretary of defense and the chairman of the Joint Chiefs want everyone to be accountable and to come forward with any knowledge you might have. In any event, I want all of you to be observant of your surroundings and report anything out of the ordinary. Is that clear?"

Everyone responded with a loud and clear of,

"Yes, sir!" including Assad, who remained calm and collected.

Cooper looked over at Remington and gave him the sign to dismiss the group.

"On your feet!" the marine colonel shouted out assertively. Everyone got up and stood straight as Cooper left the room, with the sergeant major following directly behind him and other staff members of his entourage. As soon as the admiral left, Remington told everyone to be at ease. They all relaxed for a moment and talked amongst themselves for only a few seconds, before the abrasive colonel barked some more orders of his own along with making a few other remarks under his vocabulary.

"Okay, people, listen up! You heard the admiral! Go to your assigned areas and stations and start sweeping your equipment. Look for any unauthorized breaches or algorithms of any kind, including any network outages that have occurred or anything that has been integrated into your systems within the past few months. Clean your systems and files thoroughly, and go through every nook and cranny of your processors. Looking for any suspicious emails, messages, or texts that may have appeared on your web servers. Senior supervisors and assistant supervisors, go through and inspect your staff's personal materials and work-related materials! Check the mainframes to see if they might have been affected by hacking, viruses, or spyware. It is imperative that we detect anything that might be considered a cyberattack, internet hacking, or the common espionage. Dismissed, people!"

Everyone followed their usual routine after a meeting, discussing this remarkable news with each other. It certainly was an unprecedented event that had taken place.

In the back of his mind, Assad knew what procedures the brass was going to follow and how they were going to implement them. He knew he had everything covered, but there was no guarantee that he could stop the system from backing up the files for his own use, which was something he had started doing months ago. He had deleted all current files and downloadable materials from his recent transactions from his laptop and personal computer, but he had not taken into account that the network files embedded in certain mainframes that he had downloaded would leave memory signatures behind. If looked up later, even though the information had been deleted or erased, it could still be located and accessed if the person searching for it were to enter certain dates and time spans as part of the mainframe's log-in parameters. Assad was good, but he knew his limitations. He was confident that no one from outside, not even the smartest computer hacker in the world, could crack his codes or decipher his encryptions, but someone from inside the building? That was another story. All a person would have to do would be to go back several weeks or months to find, amid the transactions, the inquiries someone made recently while working on a computer logged into the system, the email messages the person had sent, and which websites he or she visited. Assad's expression changed from cool, calm, and collected to nervous, tense, and jittery within the space of a second. He knew he had to leave immediately, before he was discovered. His plans were to be safely out of the country before they could find out it was him who had stolen the data. He would make a trip to a foreign country with no extradition laws and with no international laws banning the providing of aid to individuals seeking sanctuary or asylum within their borders. His plan was to go to California first, then travel to Japan, China, or Australia, and then hide out in Pakistan, Saudi Arabia, Dubai, or Iran until everything blew over, which would take several months to a year. Then he would make his new residence in a secluded spot in one of seven places: Italy, Greece, Holland, Turkey, Ukraine, South America, or an island in the South Pacific where no one would be able to find him. The amount of money he was being paid for this treacherous act was three million US dollars. He was promised clean, untraceable currency, which was to be wired to an account of his choosing, preferably in Europe so he would have unlimited access to it.

As everyone was leaving the conference area to go back to their assigned duties, Assad made a sudden decision in haste that promised him a departure without suspicion. He turned toward Dixon.

"Sean, I know that this is an unexpected situation we're dealing with here, but I need to ask a favor of you."

"What is it, Ad-dam?"

Assad cleared his throat, sounding reluctant, and began to whisper so that only Dixon could hear: "I have some vacation time saved up, and I would like to use it now, before it expires."

"Ad-dam, I don't know about that. You heard what the admiral and the colonel said. We need to get on this hacker situation ASAP before the real shit hits the fan. I don't know if you can take time off right now."

"I know that this is short notice, and I've never asked for time off before. But I didn't want to tell you this until later. I got a call from my mother today. She informed me that one of my grandparents from the old country, Lebanon, has fallen ill. It seems that my grandfather is sick with tuberculosis. And they're not sure how much time he has remaining. I know that this is sudden, and I wouldn't ask you unless it was absolutely necessary and an emergency, but my family is leaving to go see him within the next couple of days, and they really want me to be there with them."

"Why didn't you bring this up with me earlier?" asked Dixon, concern in his voice.

"Well, for one, I just got the call from my grandmother this morning. I was going to tell you later today, after we got off work. I didn't know that today, of all days, was going to fall under a crisis. If it were any other circumstance, I would not ask you for leave time. And you know that. But unfortunately, this has to do with family, and it's something that I have no control over."

Dixon looked at Assad with concern. He realized that Assad had never requested leave throughout the whole time he had known him. The man had been loyal to ONI and was an asset to the organization. Never once had he complained about the workload or the stress that came with the job. Dixon rubbed his chin while looking at Assad, after having thought for a few seconds. Afterward, he gave Assad the answer he wanted to hear.

"All right, Ad-dam, you can have your time off. I'll go and talk to Colonel Remington about it, but you know that he has the final word. If he decides to deny your request, then that's it. But I'll try to bat for you… He is going to want to hear about this from you directly. And I know for sure that he's not going to be happy about it. He's going to want all your personal information plus contact information of your family ahead of time just in case we have to get in contact with you or your relatives so you can get you back here ASAP."

"Thanks, Sean. I appreciate it," Assad said.

"Don't thank me just yet. The final approval must come from the old man upstairs," he said, referring to Admiral Cooper, "and he must authorize it for you to get your leave. How many days are you asking for?"

"Two to three and a half weeks, possibly four, tops. That's how much leave time I've accumulated since I've been working here."

"A month?" asked Dixon, surprised. "Okay. I'll tell Remington about the total amount of time you have saved up. They might grant you this since it is a family emergency, but under any other circumstances, it wouldn't be possible, especially now that we may have a spy running around here giving away our secrets like candy on Halloween night. I'll go right now and talk to the colonel. You get your stuff together, and get squared away in terms of getting everything you need. I'll pull up some requisition leave papers from the ops center and give them to the colonel and admiral."

With a sly smile spreading across his face, Assad was pleased he had gotten his way. As devious and smart as he was, he had known he could get away with stealing top-secret information and never get caught. He was about to turn and walk away, when Dixon literally stopped him in his tracks. "Ad-dam, before you start planning your vacation, do me a favor. Leave all your work materials here at the office. While you're gone, we may have to go in to your computer and look at all your files and documents to try to track down these hackers and find out where they are located. And since you're one of the top analysts in cyber encryption and data recovery, we may need to look over the findings on your computer. Also, leave your laptop here so we can get into it later if we need to find something substantial to go on."

Not wanting Dixon to see the unexpected look that had come over his face when he heard Dixon's request, Assad turned around with a smirk-like smile, a substitute for the expression that otherwise would show how he actually felt, and said, "No problem. I'll even give the password to Sergeant Crawford. She'll be able to get you access."

"Good. I'll go and talk to Remington right now about your leave. Wish me luck. Let's hope it gets approved."

Assad's confidence turned to panic once again. He had been planning to take his laptop with him during his getaway. But he knew he had planted booby traps within the mainframe in case they did think to consider the files he had downloaded. Still, he had no intention of leaving his computer behind. He had had an inclination that this would eventually happen, so he had made a backup plan.

Assad ran back to his office, hoping to beat his colleagues to the punch and prevent them from discovering the truth of his treachery. Rushing in without acknowledging Crawford, he opened his office door. In haste, he took his computer from the desk drawer and started hooking up all the cords to gain him access to the internet. He quickly turned the laptop on and waited while it powered up. Then he dashed over to his safe to retrieve his briefcase. As he was fumbling with the combination lock, his laptop went online instantly. Immediately he received an email. Not aware of it, he was still preoccupied with getting something from his briefcase. Once he had accomplished that task, he turned his attention to the computer and saw the alert about the email. Pressed for time, he logged on with his password and opened the email. Surprisingly, it was a message from his mysterious contact to whom he was talking on his phone earlier this morning. While Assad was at the meeting, the individual had emailed him a message about meeting up with him at his apartment to retrieve his new identification papers and passport, along with some other materials Assad had requested. Knowing that this message could be traced easily, Assad downloaded the email into his personal mailbox then set up several electronic firewalls so the other analysts in the building would not be able to breach his mainframe or discover his subroutines. While trying to cover his tracks, Assad rushed to reply to the email, his fingers flying across the keyboard. He pressed the enter button quickly to send what he had written. Then he keyed in several encrypted protocols and codes to block anyone from seeing the message or finding the email address from which it had been sent.

Next, Assad went to his toolbar, clicked on the History tab, and scrolled down to see months' worth of material that he had looked up and downloaded from the DOD and DIA archives, with the intention of deleting it from his computer. He did not realize that his computer had stored so much information in its memory. It was going to take hours, perhaps even days, to delete this data, but it was imperative to do so if his colleagues were going to do what the admiral suggested. Going back through months of data stored in the mainframe was definitely time-consuming. The electronic signatures left behind by emails served as shadow trails on certain systems, making the information vulnerable to viewing by the public. Intel such as this had to be deleted. It was taking Assad a long time to accomplish this task, much more than he had anticipated. He had worked all the way through lunch and even into midday to get it done.

While Assad was still preoccupied with covering his tracks, going over every document that he had stolen within the past couple of months, the intercom on his desk buzzed.

Crawford's voice came through.

"Sir, sorry to disturb you, but Commander Dixon just called. He wants to see you in Colonel Remington's office right away."

Assad became nervous again. Realizing the short amount of time, he had to finish getting rid of the remaining evidence, he downloaded the files that hadn't yet been backed up to his pocket-sized thumb drive. Not having the patience to allow the data to finish transferring to the drive, he pulled the drive out quickly and answered Crawford in haste.

"Thank you, Beverly. Tell Commander Dixon that I'll be up there ASAP."

"Aye, aye, sir."

Anxious to get everything straightened up, Assad put his thumb drive into his pants pocket and closed his briefcase again, placing it to the side of his desk. He didn't bother to turn off his computer, thinking he had gotten rid of all the evidence that could lead back to him. He just closed his screen and disconnected his laptop from the internet. After straightening himself up by dusting off his jacket and pulling on his tie, he exited his office and informed Crawford that he would be out for a while.

"Beverly, if I get any calls, just tell the caller that I'll be gone for a while. Take a message if need be."

"Yes, sir," replied the young sergeant.

As Assad made his exit out the main door, he was unaware that he had just received another email message from his coconspirator. It was on the computer he had left unsecured. The cursor on his computer screen was blinking obviously, with a call sign address in the Arabic language, transliterated to read "at-Thalf Mn al-Lh," meaning "the Alliance of Allah," and with the initials "M. K." at the end of the email, which was displayed at the upper left of his screen.

Colonel Remington's Office

Assad got off the elevator, in a hurry to get to Remington's office. He came to the door that had the colonel's name plastered across it and continued through to the staging office, which was quite roomy and occupied by several enlistees from both the navy and the marines, with a few junior officers stationed around. Usually the atmosphere here was serene, but today it was busy and hectic because of the current situation.

Assad walked up to an E-7 female chief petty officer, one of the colonel's aides, and announced his presence. The NCO acknowledged him and pressed the button on the intercom.

"Colonel, sir. Commander Assad is here to see you."

"Send him in, Chief!" said Remington in a crass tone, the coarseness of his voice coming through the speaker.

Assad opened the door and saw Colonel Remington seated at his desk with a dark woven cigar protruding from the corner of his mouth. Assad also took notice of Dixon, stationed on the other side, standing tall and straight next to the intimidating full-bird colonel. As Assad was standing at attention, waiting for the colonel to acknowledge his presence, he happened to take a glance at the wall where Remington's diplomas and certificates were hung, boasting of some of the colonel's achievements and accolades. Amid several decorative plaques and awards honoring the colonel's distinguished career and his valor was one that stood out from the rest, a bronze plaque with both the Department of Defense seal and the marine corps seal. This was an honorary award commending a joint task force made up of soldiers from all military branches for the capture and killing of the notorious al-Qaeda leader Osama bin Laden. Remington had served as a first lieutenant marine recon infantry soldier during his tours in Afghanistan some eighteen years ago. Back then, he was working as an intelligence gatherer attached to a Navy SEAL unit known as SEAL Team Six, which was responsible for tracking down and killing bin Laden, who had eluded United States law enforcement for nearly ten years since the attacks on the World Trade Center in New York City and the Pentagon building in Arlington County, Virginia, along with the failed attack connected with United Airlines Flight 93, which crashed in Shanksville, Pennsylvania, all of which happened on the historic date of September 11, 2001, early on that Tuesday morning. Those events prompted two long-lasting wars, one with Iraq and the other a continuation of the War in Afghanistan.

At the time, SEAL Team Six thought the intelligence they had indicating that bin Laden was hiding somewhere in the mountainous region of Tora Bora on the border between Afghanistan and Pakistan was correct. But later, a different intelligence report told them that the al-Qaeda leader was located somewhere inside Pakistan. It took the task force, using the resources of the CIA, months to smoke him and his followers out of a secluded compound within the small remote town of Bilal, Abbottabad, near the capital city of Islamabad. The operation was called Operation Geronimo, a nod to the intricacy and importance of history. With an intense ground battle that lasted a few minutes at the most, Remington and the SEALs were able to identify bin Laden and execute the mission to terminate his life. Remington, along with several commando leaders of the SEAL team, received medals for distinguished service and honorary awards from the president at the time, Barack Obama, along with the nation's gratitude for neutralizing the most wanted, most dangerous man since Adolf Hitler, Saddam Hussein, and Muammar Gaddafi. Remington was promoted to captain after that. A few years later, he was promoted to major. It was in this capacity that he led marine troops in several skirmishes in South America and Mexico to fight the war on drugs, and also engaged several times with the Mexican cartels. He was also involved in the naval blockade, with Chinese forces landing on nearby islands for supremacy and control. In short, Remington was a highly decorated officer who later landed a position at ONI. When Cooper took over as the new director, Remington was instantly promoted to be the executive officer and deputy director of the facility.

Assad's eyes were glazed over as he started at the award hung in the center of the wall behind the colonel. He knew that Remington was a warrior at heart, but he had not realized that he was responsible for taking down a man who was, in Assad's mind, one of the greatest Islamic leaders of the twenty-first century. Assad felt disgusted and angry but kept his feelings to himself in the presence of his supervisor and senior commanding officer.

Looking over some papers, Remington failed to realize how long Assad had been standing at attention, until Dixon cleared his throat to remind the abrasive colonel that Assad was present in his office.

Remington looked up and said,

"At ease, Commander, at ease. I forgot you were standing there, son." Assad relaxed with a gentle sigh of relief and assumed the position of parade rest.

"I understand you have a family emergency, that Commander Dixon just relayed to me."

"Yes, sir!" answered Assad in a strong and firm tone.

"My mother, who is in California, called me this morning. She informed me of my grandfather's illness. He, along with my grandmother, resides in Lebanon. He has been diagnosed with tuberculosis and has only days to live. I know that this is short notice, especially in light of what's going on, sir, but the presence of my family and of me is needed there immediately for the days he has remaining."

Going over the leave papers that Dixon had given to him, Remington stood up from his desk, still smoking his cigar, and approached Assad on his right side.

"Son, relax. Despite my reputation of being a mean son of a bitch and a hard-ass, I'm not going to rip your head off and take a dump down your neck. Take it easy. I know that we're in a compromising situation right now, and to tell you the truth, I need every swinging dick here to help work through this shitstorm we're involved in. But family emergencies are just as important as the security of our nation. Commander Dixon informs me that you want about four to five weeks off. Is that right?"

"Yes, sir. It takes time to travel from here to California, then from the States to overseas, what with commuting from one area of a country to another, not counting the number of stops and layovers in between," replied Assad, presenting the itinerary that would make his escape possible, of course under false pretenses, namely that his grandfather was gravely ill.

Again, Remington looked over the papers, flicking each one, while circling the young lieutenant commander, who was still standing erect and motionless even though he'd been given permission to relax. Looking out of the corner of his eye, Assad followed Remington's movements. He also gave a quick glance at Dixon, who was positioned in the same manner but in the opposite direction. Assad was thinking to himself that this might not work after all.

Remington was, as already mentioned, a hard-ass. He had a reputation within ONI and the military community for being a stickler for the rules and for being a hard, no-nonsense commanding officer. He was strict in his attitude and beliefs—the stereotypical jarhead marine. The reasons for this were that his time within the marine corps and his adherence to their standards had overcome his sense of proportion. The man was identified as a hard-core indestructible fighting machine who was cold, calculating, and thought-provoking, your standard marine who relied on instinct instead of logic and reasoning. This was one of the many attributes that had led to his having been chosen to serve as deputy director of naval intelligence. Not only because of his combat service, experience, and history, but also because of his talent for perceiving a situation as perfectly doable that others might see as impossible or impractical. He would take over a situation without thinking twice about it and without regretting the outcome, even if the course of action he pursued turned out not to have been the best one.

Assad was getting edgy thinking of the idea, and Remington's circling him made things no easier. It was as if Remington were a vulture about to swing down and take his injured prey with one quick swoop.

What seemed hours to Assad was only minutes in real time. After going through the documents sheet by sheet and pausing for what seemed an eternity, not to mention the fact that the stench from his cigar was permeating the room, Remington looked over at Dixon, puffing proudly on the aromatic cigar, and said,

"Commander, go ahead and sign off on Assad's request." Assad was relieved. His plan was working. His supervisor and commanding officer were ignorant of his true intentions.

"I'll put my Hancock here and send it up to the admiral. Commander Assad, before you leave today, get with Commander Dixon and surrender all your work materials to him. We're going to need the pass codes to get into your computer files."

"I've already advised him of that, sir. He knows that we're going to need access to his e-files and documents for the next couple of weeks," Dixon said.

"Good, Commander. Thumbs up for staying well ahead of me. Well, Mr. Assad, it looks as if you have your leave." Turning to Dixon, he said, "Go and finish up today's workload and your other daily tasks, Commander." Turning back to Assad, he added,

"After seventeen hundred hours, you are officially on leave."

"Thank you, sir," Assad said, giving the colonel a full salute, a feeling of betrayal swelling within his soul for having fooled his naive friend and superior officer.

Assad's Apartment, 23:00 Hours

It was 23:00 hours (11:00 p.m. EST), late in the evening, and Assad had just arrived at the carport in front of his apartment. He had been away all evening, from the time he left ONI at 17:00 hours (5:00 p.m. EST) until the time he arrived at his soon-to-be-previous residence. During the time of his absence, he had been gathering materials in preparation for his departure. As he stepped out of his BMW, the carport security lights, which worked on a motion sensor, illuminated the small confined area. He went around to the back of his car to open the trunk with his key remote, then pulled out several items. One of these was a huge black duffel bag, bulky, that looked as if it weighed fifty or sixty pounds. It had something inside it. He also removed two black suitcases that were a little larger than average. The items that Assad retrieved from his trunk seemed to have been bought from a military depot. It was Special Forces–type equipment. He put the strap of the duffel bag on his left shoulder, tucked his briefcase in his left armpit, and used his two hands to carry the two cases. It took him five minutes to walk from the carport to the entrance of the complex. He traveled upstairs with ease despite the bulky items he was carrying, managing to make it to his floor. As he came to his door, he pulled out his keys, shuffling through them to find the one that will open the door. Unlocking the door, he pushed it open wide, struggling with the luggage. He managed to enter his apartment without any help while simultaneously trying to close the door behind him. Just when he managed to accomplish this, he was startled by a monotonous voice, someone with a Middle Eastern accent, which broke the silence within Assad's dark apartment.

Speaking only in Arabic, this mysterious person said, "Msa' al-Khyr, 'Assad. Han al-wqt lknt j'it mn wtnhm," which in English translates as, "Good evening, Assad. It's about time you made it home."

Knowing exactly who it was, Assad dropped his bags and immediately turned on the lights to get a better view of his uninvited guest. Now that he could see him, Assad realized who it was. He answered the intruder in the same Arabic dialect.

"Muhammad, what are you doing here? And how in the hell did you get into my apartment?"

The mysterious stranger was Assad's original contact, Muhammad Kareem, the individual who had sent him the email messages with the subject line reading "The Alliance of Allah," with his own initials, M. K., marked at the end. Kareem worked for the Iranian security force, but recently he had been taken on a number of freelance contracts for different government agencies—secret services and intelligence departments within Arabia. His dress was casual: regular blue jeans, a tan sports jacket, an eggshell-colored polo shirt, and black suede shoes with old-fashioned string laces. He stood at least five foot nine and weighed approximately one hundred sixty-five pounds, almost identical in build to Assad, but not as athletically endowed as he was. Kareem gave a slight snicker to Assad's question, answering,

"Oh, come now, Ad-dam. Remember our conversation earlier? I told you that I was going to meet you here later tonight to finish discussing the arrangements. I told you in the email I sent to you, and I told you when I broke into your apartment. Well, let's just say that you know of my skill and talent for getting into secured places that may seem impenetrable to others."

Angered by those audacious remarks, Assad replied with agitation,

"I'm aware of your so-called skills, but that doesn't give you the right in breaking and entering! This is my home, and there are laws here."

Once again Kareem snickered at Assad.

"Laws? Your home? Don't be ridiculous, Ad-dam. This place is not your home. Are you forgetting about the transaction we're about to make here tonight and the reasons why you are doing this? After tonight, you will no longer have a home here or anywhere else in the United States. And you will not be subject to the inferior laws and propaganda-based idealism that this country has used to establish itself as hypocritical—a nation of infidels. You are now a brother, as well as a member of our organization and a son of our Islamic agency. Once the Americans find out what you've done, they will consider you a traitor, an outcast. You will be branded as a terrorist and a treacherous spy, just like the late honorable Osama bin Laden. But among our people within the Arab and Islamic world, you will be called a hero and a savior."

"Do not patronize me, Muhammad. I know what I'm doing, and it's not for the glory of the Arabian or Islamic world as you put it. I'm doing this for my own personal reasons, purposes of self-proclamation. My issues are my own. And I expect to be well compensated for my knowledge and skills."

Kareem sneered at Assad's response, ignoring his comments as he pulled a couple of papers from his blazer pocket to hand over to him. "Here are the passports that you asked for, and your new identification cards to go along with them," he said. "I also have here statements of your pay, with the money to go into your private account. I did receive the emails that you sent me regarding the initial blueprints and plans for the secret weapons the Americans are developing, along with the names of all the spies they employ. I've told the organization of what you've accomplished, and they were very pleased to have heard that information. I've informed them that what I had shown them were just copies of the original, adding that you'd be bringing the real thing to them very soon. I presume that you have here some of the items that you plan on showing them?"

Kareem's attention was drawn to the bags that Assad had at his side. He had an idea of what was in them, but his anticipation and curiosity were overwhelming him. Assad noticed that Kareem was gawking at the bags, obviously intrigued Kareem. He was reacting in almost the same way as a child would react if he or she were stuck in a room filled with an abundance of toys and candy. Assad waved his hand, giving Kareem permission to look inside the bags, while continuing to look over the documents his Iranian contact had given him. Even though Assad's attention was drawn to the papers he was reading, he managed to answer Kareem's question without taking his eyes off the papers.

"Yes, I managed to 'borrow' some of the new weapons the DOD has been developing for quite a while. The Pentagon has ordered that these weapons be issued to all ground and elite forces within the US military."

"May I look, Ad-dam?" Kareem asked.

Still preoccupied with the papers to see if they were correct, Assad gave Kareem permission to look inside the bags. Kareem unzipped one of them and took out a state-of-the-art fully automatic assault rifle. It was small and compact but looked very durable.

"Is this the new FN-F2000 assault rifle that I've been hearing about?" Kareem asked.

"Yes, it is, but it's the 2020 series, with state-of-the-art telescopic magnification sights—one-point-six times magnification—that is equipped with both infrared and night vision. The firearm has a shooting range of six hundred to seven hundred yards without misfiring or jamming. It's durable and lightweight to carry around. DOD has a contract with the Belgium government to make fifty thousand to seventy thousand of these to distribute to army, marines, and air force infantry ground enforcement, not to mention all Special Forces units," Assad explained.

"This is impressive," said Kareem.

"The organization will definitely be pleased to get their hands on this type of hardware. What else do you have?" Assad pointed to the other bag while still looking at the documents in his hands. Kareem opened the other one, which had several other handheld weapons inside it. "These are truly remarkable, although I'm not familiar with their origins."

Assad looked up for only a split second, then returned to the papers that consumed his attention. "I'm surprised at you, Muhammad, since you hold yourself to be one of the top arms dealers in Europe and Arabia, a fact you frequently advertise. You should know these weapons like the back of your hand. The first one has been used by the Saudis and Pakistanis for years. It's the Steyr AUG assault rifle. There are four to five variations of this rifle in existence. The one you're holding is the A3 LSW [light support weapon]. It's a nine-millimeter with a barrel measuring three hundred twenty-five millimeters, or twelve-point-eight inches, in length, installed with a Picatinny rail system for smooth and accurate discharge. We also have a contact in the Austrian government who can hook us up to get several of these manufactured, all to go to special ops and covert agencies such as the CIA, NIA, and NSA. The rifles will also be distributed to local and state law enforcement agencies, and federal law enforcement agencies that fall under the jurisdiction of the Justice Department."

"And this one, what is it?" Assad looked up again at Kareem to give another presentation. "That is the military's pride and joy. It's the XM25 airburst grenade launcher. It shoots twenty-five-millimeter grenades at high velocity up to a distance of five hundred fifty yards within an area a thousand meters in range. The United States constructed these around 2010, but they weren't distributed to the military until 2015 and 2016. They are a superb usage against long-range weapons on the battlefield, especially when we were in Afghanistan twenty years ago."

Kareem nodded his head in agreement, holding the sophisticated weapon in his hand. He was very pleased by the three items that he saw, but the huge duffel bag that Assad had around his shoulder piqued his curiosity even more.

"Ad-dam, may I ask what that is?"

Assad turned his head and said,

"Oh, this. This is my prized possession." He took the harness from around his neck and placed the bag on the floor. He unlatched the security clips from around the bag and opened it up slowly.

"This is the Beretta ARX-160 rapid-fire assault rifle with an M203 grenade launcher attachment. This is a very sophisticated weapon, difficult to handle. I know because I operated a similar version when I used to train with the Navy SEALs and Army Delta Force units. The Italians made only a few of these and were not easily persuaded to part with them. But given the trade agreements between the United States and Europe, the United States was willing to give Italy financial support for its frail economy in exchange for several of these babies. The ARX does a rapid-fire seven hundred rotations per minute with an effectiveness range greater than the FN-F2020, and her range is six hundred to seven hundred meters longer and wider too. She holds only thirty rounds, but with a larger magazine capacity, she can discharge forty to fifty rounds every one and a half seconds. She could probably dish out more with a larger magazine drum, but in my expert opinion, anything bigger than a thirty- or forty-round mag is overkill. She's a formidable close-quarters combat weapon with a single shot—a forty-millimeter NATO low-velocity grenade launcher, which is the GLX-160. She can discharge up to three hundred yards or better, depending on how far the target is. She can also do some serious damage at long range, as I mentioned before. She has a polymer frame, which makes the weapon lightweight and easy to handle and shoot. DOD plans to replace all its M-16's and M-4 carbines with this beauty right here within the next month or so," Assad said.

"Can it be duplicated?" asked Kareem.

"Yes. With her polymer design, this weapon can be easily replicated using the schematics I personally have in my possession."

"Good. I'm impressed, Ad-dam—really impressed. And so will my superiors be when they have these in their possession. You have provided a good service for the organization and its cause. By the way, how were you planning to get these guns past US customs and their inspection detail? You're aware that they have detection scanners and X-ray monitors," Kareem said.

"You see these bags? Each has a lightweight fiber optic imagery casing between the interior fabric coatings. The purpose of this casing is to cause false image projections and false readings when the luggage with the weapons goes through the X-ray scanners at airport terminals. I programed all of them to emit a false image of clothing and other personal items, which is what the people monitoring the scanner will think is inside the bags. The computer's magnification and sensors will not be able to penetrate the luggage to see what's inside or be able to tell the bag is holding weapons once the scan does its probing. And even if the TSA agents do force me to open the luggage, I will have clothing in there as cover. The CIA, along with MI6, has been working on camouflage, illusion, and imagery technology for a while, and they came up with this material by chance. And since I work for ONI, I have security clearance and access to all such toys," said Assad.

"Extraordinary, Ad-dam. Truly extraordinary. Now I know that the organization will be impressed with you and what you have to offer them," Kareem said with pride and confidence.

"Well, they won't be so impressed with this shipment or anything else until I receive the rest of my money, Muhammad! What is the meaning of this?"

While Kareem was inspecting the condition of the rifles, at the same time being fascinated by them, Assad was going over every paragraph of the papers that Kareem had handed him. Assad kept his cool and maintained his usual composure until he came upon one document that showed the amount of money, he was supposed to receive from the mysterious organization that Kareem kept referring to.

"Why is there only one hundred fifty million deposited into my account instead of the entire three hundred?!"

Kareem took the papers from him and looked over them for himself. He gave a believable performance, acting surprised and shocked by what he was seeing. But he'd known about the ploy all along, and tried to make an expression of confusion appear on his face to fool Assad. He continued to look over the papers as if very concerned, with Assad standing over him in a state of rage and frustration.

"Oh, I see. It looks like they only deposited half the money to your account. I'm sorry; I forgot to mention this to you earlier. They won't put the rest up until you personally deliver all the information to them. For instance, the thumb drive you told me about over the phone. When you bring that and the rest of the info and place it into their hands, you will receive the final portion of your money," Kareem explained in a demented sort of way.

"That was not part of the agreement! I told them and you that I would not go along with this unless I had all the money up front! I sent you all the information I could download from the files! I made a copy for myself only because if what I had sent to you were to get lost or be misdirected in the system, you could use it to make another duplicate or to burn the info to a CD! I only made this backup in case something like this should happen or in the event that your people couldn't download what I sent them. But I see now how you and the organization do business! No part of our arrangement indicated that I would get half the money now and the other half later, namely, when I get to Saudi! I told you and your leaders that I expected to be well paid for my services! I want all the money, not some! All!"

Furious at what had transpired, Assad snatched the papers from Kareem's hand in such an aggressive manner that he almost tore them in half. He then started grabbing all the weapons that were out on display and began placing them back into the bags. Noticing the frustration and anger that had overcome Assad, and with his back turned toward him, Kareem slowly moved his right hand and slipped it inside his jacket near his chest. Unaware of what Kareem was doing behind his back, Assad kept ranting and raving about the dishonesty and mistrust between him and the organization that Kareem represented. While Assad was preoccupied with dismantling the hardware and growing angrier by the minute, Kareem produced a weapon of his own.

He pulled out a medium-caliber semiautomatic pistol from his jacket, a Walther P99 with a suppressor attached to the end of the barrel. He carefully pointed it at Assad's back. In a devilish tone to his voice, he said, "Well, we don't have to worry about your services anymore, Ad-dam. And you don't have to worry about traveling too Saudi either." Hearing the cold monotone of Kareem's voice, Assad had a pretty good inclination of what was going on behind him. He stood up slowly from his bent position and turned around carefully, coming to bear witness to the barrel of a gun, down which he was currently staring, that his cohort was pointing at him.

"So, this was their plan all along. They sent you here as an assassin to kill me to get the rest of the data and the merchandise. They never planned on giving me all the money up front, did they?" asked Assad as he slowly put his hands in the air.

"Oh no, Ad-dam, you are wrong. The organization was straight with you. They planned on paying you all along. They need your expertise and the knowledge you have about the Americans and their secrets. It's just me who wants to take you out of the equation. I am here personally to cut out the middleman, which is *you*. You see, I will tell them that some sort of backward moral sensibility overcame you, causing you to have a change of heart and back out of the deal. I'll say that we had an argument about your loyalties and your commitment to us. Later, a struggle took place. I overpowered you, and you gave me no choice: I had to kill you in the process, leaving me free to take the data and weapons you had in your possession."

Assad gave a lighthearted, carefree laugh while shaking his head in disbelief. "So, you set this whole thing up, Kareem: insisting that we meet at my place where there are no witnesses, staging this entire event by giving me the documents personally to frame me for the whole thing, then devising a story that I coordinated the espionage and embezzlement all by myself. And now you're going to kill me in my own apartment with the intent of leaving my body as evidence, with documents found on my person to give the authorities and my coworkers the idea that I am the spy they have been looking for all along. Not to mention that I was planning to leave the country with falsified documents and a fake identification in my possession—as well as having a secret bank account filled with money that they know nothing about. Clever, Muhammad, very clever."

Kareem snickered for a bit, showing his conceited self-confidence.

"Yes, Ad-dam. I thought that if I took the info from you and gave it to the organization myself, they would reward me instead of you. Of course, they will want to know about you and why you decided to change your mind so suddenly. I will have to tell them that trusting in a man who has denounced his birthright and culture for so long; who has acted as a traitor by deciding to side with the very infidels who have raped and pillaged our Islamic countries, meaning Iraq and Afghanistan, for more than twenty years; and who had intentions of extorting money for his own purposes is not the type of man they should want to do business with. I'll tell them that it was better that you died with the little bit of honor and dignity you had left. Now, place all three of the bags right by the door, and hand over both flash drives to me very, very slowly."

Assad did just as Kareem had ordered, picking up all three bags and placing them right beside each other next to the front door.

"Okay, slowly turn around to face me, and walk toward me with your hands in the air." Again, Assad did what he had been told to do, walking slowly up to Kareem without breaking his stride. He stopped at least two feet away from him with both his hands in the air.

"Now, take out the flash drives and give them to me carefully. I don't want to kill you just yet." Assad took his right hand and placed it inside his coat, moving it toward the upper left. He took out both items slowly, giving them to Kareem, who took each of them with his left hand, while his right hand kept a firm and stable grip on the gun, with the index finger positioned on the trigger, of course pointing the weapon at Assad. After taking the items, he told Assad to turn around and face away from him. Assad nonchalantly obliged and turned toward the door.

Just as Kareem was going to discharge his weapon, which was aimed directly at Assad's head, Assad spoke, saying,

"Muhammad, may I suggest something? If you plan on shooting me in the back of the head, you might want to pick another spot. The bullet's direction of travel will undoubtedly cause it to go through my cranium, exit through the doorway of my apartment, and go into another apartment, given that you're using a caliber of nine millimeters. Even though you have a silencer attached to the barrel to muffle the sound of the discharge, it will not allow you to carry out your original plan of making my murder look like a suicide attempt. Neither the police nor their forensic detectives will be fooled. I should know. I knew someone who used to work for NCIS [Naval Criminal Investigation Service]. Looking at the way you're pointing the gun, I can see that this is going to be considered a murder case instead of a suicide. I suggest you move me over to the right side, between the kitchen and my bedroom. That will give a more promising outlook for the authorities."

"Do you take me for a fool, Ad-dam? You're just stalling for time so I won't kill you quickly," said Kareem.

"Well, yes, that is one notion. But I am serious about your line of sight. It is not feasible. Move me in the other direction." Assad was too smart for his own good. He wanted Kareem to move him to the right because to the left of Assad's bedroom doorway was a large vanity mirror that, when the overhead light in the dining room was on, emitted a blinding glare that would literally blind anyone who looked directly into the mirror from far enough away.

Agitated by Assad's suggestion but willing to conform to it, Kareem did just what Assad wanted him to do. They both moved toward the center of the apartment, where the kitchen was, and toward the bedroom doorway. When Kareem moved a bit to the right to get himself in a good position to shoot Assad, the glare from the light shining onto the mirror temporarily blinded him. That split second gave Assad plenty of time to turn around and move against Kareem, which he did, thrusting a dagger into his midsection. As if they were both football players on the gridiron field, Assad tackled Kareem onto the floor and let a single shot fly from his gun, the bullet hitting the side of the mirror, distracting Assad. The two men flew across the room, breaking some furniture in the process. Assad, being in a mounted position on top, automatically went for the gun, with his right forearm against Kareem's' throat. Struggling to get back in control, Kareem grabbed ahold of Assad's face and pushed it backward, hoping he would lose both his leverage and his balance.

Assad managed to disarm Kareem by forcefully pounding his hand against the hardwood floor that they were wrestling on. In an incredible offensive move, Kareem threw Assad off him by tossing his body over and above his own. Caught off guard because of this maneuver, Assad was not aware that Kareem had composed himself so quickly and was now starting to move towards the gun that Assad had kicked to a far corner. When Kareem got to his feet and headed after the weapon, Assad catapulted from the floor and jumped on his back, grabbing his head and interlocking his arms around his neck as if trying to get him into a headlock or choke hold. Struggling to get him off his back, Kareem grabbed the back of Assad's neck and tried to flip him over to land in front. But given Assad's skill at hand-to-hand combat, he managed to hold on with a tight grip as if he were a pit bull clamping down on a piece of raw meat. Still struggling in the middle of the living room, Assad managed to drag Kareem, who was still on his back and struggling with the fierce choke hold. Locked in combat with Assad, Kareem struck Assad's midsection with his elbow, which of course caused Assad enormous and excruciating pain. But being in a compromising position, Assad would not let up or let go. He knew that if he were to give up, Kareem would kill him, so he persevered.

The Iranian agent, on the other hand, could not shake off the highly trained naval officer because of his grappling technique. Assad had the upper hand in this fight. Literally choking the life out of Kareem in a rear naked choke hold maneuver that he had learned in his time with the SEAL's. He tightened his grip even more, trying to inflict enough pressure to either incapacitate Kareem or break his neck. Kareem, who was desperately fighting for his life, managed to summon enough strength to pick himself up off the floor with Assad still clinging on his back. He slammed Assad against the bar table several times stunning him for the moment. Feeling the blows, Assad wanted to give up but knew that was going to be a bad idea. Causing him more pain to his already battered mid-section, but with adrenaline coursing through his body, Assad still would not let go. Gasping and fighting for air, Kareem's eyes were turning blood red due to the lack of oxygen and strain upon his neck. Assad could not see it, but Kareem's eyes were also rolling up into the back of his head. Though Assad was in agonizing pain himself from the number of blows he had sustained from Kareem's elbows and fists, he knew he had Kareem right where he wanted him and was not about to let him go. But at that moment, without realizing the amount of force he had applied to Kareem's neck, he heard several of the Iranian's vertebrae snap, which concluded the fight. Assad had broken Kareem's neck. He heard his final breath escape from his mouth, just prior to the struggling moans. Kareem's body finally went limp without one twitch or convulsion. Assad knew instinctively that he was gone. The entire fight had lasted between two and three minutes, with the victor exhausted and gasping for air himself.

Assad rolled Kareem's limp body away from him and got up slowly. Tired from the ordeal, he looked around to see the damage he and his opponent had caused during their struggle. Feeling the physical effects from the brawl, Assad gathered himself and headed toward his bedroom. Then he went to the bathroom, turning on the faucet and began to splash water on his face to revive himself physically and emotionally. Looking into the mirror, he noticed several cuts and bruises on his face, neck, and arms. He knew right away that he had to do something quickly in order to make his escape. He knew he had to clean everything up in the time he had left so he would not fall into an investigation that would delay his plans to leave Maryland and the country for good. He was thinking that he must dispose of the body immediately and remove any physical evidence that might show that a struggle or confrontation had taken place.

Assad quickly cleaned himself up and started to gather all the belongings he wanted to take with him. He straightened the items in his apartment, sweeping up all the debris and scattered remains of damaged furniture and glass left from the confrontation. It took him several minutes to get everything arranged and sorted, but with the time he had left, he knew everything had to be picture-perfect and properly set up. He managed to complete the task successfully and without interruption. After looking over everything to ensure all was in order, he glared down at the wrecked body of Kareem, who had blood trickling from the corners of his mouth and a broken appendage, his lifeless eyes staring off into the far corner of the room. Assad bent down to grab ahold of Kareem and sit him up against one of the chairs.

As Assad stared at the lifeless corpse, he said,

"Well, Muhammad, you were half right. We did have a struggle, but the overpowering that you mentioned earlier was you being overpowered, not me. I'll make sure to tell your superiors what really happened here." Afterward, he began to search Kareem's body for the items he had initially given him. He found both thumb drives in Kareem's coat pocket. Retrieving them, he slipped them into the duffel bag holding the four rifles. Then he went back to his bedroom and took several articles of clothing from his closet. He then rushed to the bathroom again and looked at himself in the mirror. After staring at his face for several seconds, he pulled out some things from his toiletries bag: some hair dye, barber-style hair clippers, colored contact lenses, and a prosthetic mustache and beard. Assad was planning to change his physical appearance to get out of the country, so he would not be recognized or identified by any local, state, federal, or military law enforcement agencies. This had been his plan from the start.

Assad went over and looked at the passport and ID that Kareem had given him. The pictures on both identifications looked to be of a middle-aged man, very conservative and in his thirties. Identical to Assad in stature, height, and weight, but having blond hair, dark blue eyes, and a goatee, the man was Caucasian. Assad studied the picture and tried to match his likeness to it. Remember, Assad appeared more Caucasian than Arabian, so it was easier for him to alter his appearance to match the photo on the false ID.

After an hour had passed, Assad now looked like the man in the pictures on his IDs, a dead ringer. Once again, he cleaned himself up by taking a shower. He trimmed his fake goatee and mustache to match the pictures, giving himself a distinguish haircut and changing the color. He then put on his civilian clothes. Taking only one suitcase, which had all his essentials, and leaving his military clothing and everything else behind, he looked one more time around his apartment, then checked his watch. The time was a quarter to four in the morning. He still had plenty of time to make his getaway, but he knew he had to get rid of Kareem's body in a hurry.

Assad gathered up all his things, including the guns, along with Kareem's Walther P99 and the remaining magazine clips. He carried them all downstairs to his car and placed them in the trunk. Later, after everything was packed, he ran back upstairs to retrieve Kareem's body. He wrapped him up in a large black trash bag and took the corpse to an unlighted area in the corner of the parking lot where there was a huge boxlike trash receptacle. Assad dumped Kareem's body into the trash receptacle, leaving the pair of latex gloves he'd worn so as not to leave any fingerprints behind. After disposing of the evidence, he closed the lid and headed back to his apartment for the last time. He looked over it one more time and saw that everything was in its original place with noting out of the ordinary. He turned off the lights and shut the door behind him. Thinking that he had gone over every nook and cranny inside the place, he had completely forgotten about the bullet encased in the wall right beside the mirror near his bedroom door. That piece of evidence would show that something had indeed gone on here. But in Assad's haste, he failed to think about the bullet. He got into his car with all his essential items and drove off into the darkness. Little did he know what had happened before his departure.

One of his neighbors had been awakened by the loud disturbance made by Assad and Kareem. At first, she was concerned about what was going on upstairs, but then she returned to her bed and fell back to sleep. Later, though, she was awakened again by loud banging and slamming noises. She got up and looked out her bedroom window, and saw Assad putting what looked to be something very large into the trash bin. At first, she dismissed it because it was very late, but later she thought, *what is that person doing out there at this time of the night?* Again, she did not think too much of it and fell back to asleep again. Little did she know that as she slept, a murder had taken place right above her apartment, with the evidence inside a public garbage bin, and with the perpetrator soon to be identified as a potential spy and traitor to the United States government.

CHAPTER 2

TRUTH REVEALED

ONI Headquarters, Suitland, Silver Hill, Maryland, 09:00–15:00 Hours

It was Wednesday morning, and the scene inside the Office of Naval Intelligence was one best described as hectic, busy, and frantic. The place was busier than the usual because there had been a serious information breach that was now consider a significant threaten to national security. During the past forty-eight hours since Cooper had made his intuitive speech about espionage, which took place on Monday afternoon, everyone had been on pins and needles, searching everyone's computer files, personnel records, and software and hardware. Emails and text messages were being searched at every computer station in every cubicle in the building because espionage was suspected. This high-tech stress had been going on around the clock for several days. The FBI, along with the NSA, Homeland Security, and USCYBERCOM, had enlisted several of their top computer analysts to help with the ongoing investigation and aid all ONI personnel. Even Dixon's staff, who occupied the third floor, foreign intelligence, which was considered highly classified and off-limits to personnel other than their own, was being heavily surveilled by their federal counterparts. Each ONI staff member had one or two agents hovering over top them or helping them with the investigation. The commander himself was going over his own files with the assistance of an FBI agent who happened to be the senior deputy director for the FBI's Internet Cyberspace Division and a former naval officer. He and Dixon had met each other on several occasions and had been selected by chance to work together on this project. Both were busy discussing the circumstances within the confines of Dixon's office, at the same time observing everyone else through the office window. With a bird's-eye view, Dixon concluded that things were indeed hectic and frantic. Everyone within the area was going back and forth, relaying information to each other about their workload and assignments. It was like watching ants scattering on hot pavement, trying to find shade.

As the clock ticked from morning to afternoon, nothing was turning out to be successful. No one had yet discovered Assad's treachery. When the clock on the wall struck three o'clock, a young female ensign, with the aid of another junior agent, happened to come across some very interesting and strange encryptions. The ensign went back through several years of deleted emails and downloaded materials that had come through ONI's database. She went over the information several times, and cross-checked her findings with the agent who was helping her. After determining that in fact it was conclusive evidence, she downloaded the relevant documents into her own files and printed out a copy of her findings to show to her immediate supervisor.

Both the ensign and the agent presented their work to the former's CO, who was a full-grade lieutenant. He looked over it carefully as she explained her findings to him. After discussing it amongst themselves for several minutes, all three individuals walked up to Dixon's office and discreetly knocked on the door. Dixon answered by telling them to come in. They promptly entered.

The lieutenant began by saying, "Sir, Assistant Director, excuse me, but I think you need to see this. Ensign Elena Diaz and Agent Kelvin Jones have discovered something interesting."

Dixon waved them in further so he could listen to what they had to say.

"All right, Ensign, what's going on? What do you have for us?"

The young officer, being nervous and jittery, reached out to hand over what she had discovered in her cubicle.

"Sir, I was going over all the logs and e-files from previous months within our database, and I happened to come across a strange set of algorithms attached to certain emails that had been deleted. I tried to go in and check the history of this sequence, but unfortunately, the emails all had been erased prior to its distribution. So, instead of looking at only the last few months' worth of e-files and records, I went back several years—three to be exact—and found something peculiar. I decrypted the emails sent in August 2026, three years ago, and found that some data had been downloaded from the DOD's mainframe—classified materials. I couldn't access any of these because I don't have the security clearance to do so, but I did go into the unsecure files open to public viewing. It was all common, basic educational information regarding certain types of weapons that our armed forces and the militaries of some other countries use today. Only certain types of information for public use are deemed unclassified, but all these emails mention weapons currently under development, to be distributed to our military at some point in the future. I also took the time to look at other dates that came to mind, for example, June of 2026, two months earlier. An email I found from this time span includes basic information about covert operations, including how the military and law enforcement agencies throughout the United States and in certain other countries plan and organize them. Of course, the emails don't mention the names of the branches, but they do describe how and why the United States is involved with foreign militaries in terms of contingency efforts. Whoever did the hacking downloaded the specifics about June 2026 as well. And then there was another email, this one from all the way back in December 2025. This one is very strange to me. It's an email that had been deleted mere minutes after it was sent. The message is about how to encrypt data to transfer it from one highly secure location to another without electronic detection, and how to disable the DOD's security locks and firewalls without compromising their systems and thereby allowing unauthorized access—in other words, getting in without the alarm going off. The same type of info was also downloaded from the NSA's database and USCYBERCOM's database around that same time. Sir, I looked over this information twice—no, three times—myself, and had Agent Jones go over my work, and it all came out precisely the same each time. I went over my findings again before I passed the information on to Lieutenant Davis for further analysis. Sir, information like this is handled only by the military's senior analyst of counterintelligence, which is either you or Commander Assad, and these emails and downloads were either sent from or sent to Commander Assad's personal account."

Dixon took the printed page out of the young officer's hand and looked at it for himself. He glanced over it carefully but shook off the accusations.

"Ensign, this doesn't mean anything. Commander Assad has security clearance to look up and download any classified materials specific to his position. You know this."

"That is true, sir. You and Commander Assad are the only ones who have that type of clearance. But, sir, why are there several emails of foreign origin that make use of Arabic, such as this one?" She pointed to the address on the email she had printed out. It was allianceofallah.com, in Arabic.

"This is addressed to Commander Assad. I also found several requests from the person who owns this email address asking that Commander Assad relay highly sensitive materials such as the documents I uncovered dating back to when the commander began working here two and a half years ago. The syntax of the algorithms embedded within the emails I decrypted all came from previously extracted files that had been sent to Commander Assad's email address and that later were deleted in the same manner in which they'd been sent. These emails also left an echo trail of hash numbers in the computer's log to notate that someone had either read the information in the digital file or downloaded it from an external or internal source. And the source of the downloaded information was recorded by several types of memory devices, for instance, a flash drive. And in this case, sir, the info was downloaded using a flash drive with two and three-quarters gigabytes—a large storage capacity. Sir, I'm not accusing a superior officer of wrongdoing in any way, but these dates, the secure emails from a mysterious source, and the recorded data all point to the senior analyst of military foreign intelligence, which is Commander Assad. This can't be a coincidence, sir."

Astonished by what the young officer was saying to him, Dixon gazed at her with skepticism in his eyes and questioned her conclusions.

"These are some serious accusations you're making, Ensign. You're proposing that one of our top analysts, who holds the second-highest position in counterintelligence and knows all our top-secret information on military operations and foreign affairs, including weaponry and intelligence, is a spy and saboteur of espionage?"

The young ensign, standing her ground, said,

"Sir, I'm sorry. But as I said before, this cannot be coincidental. All the facts are here on paper. Each of these emails was either sent from or sent to Commander Assad's personal address and has the link to this mysterious website."

Again, Dixon looked at the paper and shared it with his FBI counterpart, who asked his own subordinate.

"Agent Jones, are you sure about this? Are these findings correct?"

Jones answered without haste.

"Sir, we went over these several times. I even logged onto another computer, one next to Ensign Diaz's, to find out for sure. We both came up with the same thing three times. It's conclusive, sir, right down to the fine print. Each set of emails, along with the dates they were sent and received, and the downloaded information, matches up precisely and leads directly to this Lieutenant Commander Ad-dam Omar Assad. Sir, Commander, I believe that this is our guy we've been looking for."

Admiral Cooper's Office, 15:34 Hours

Cooper was sitting behind his desk, looking over some forms his secretary had given to him earlier. These were daily surveillance files and reports on covert ops from every intelligence agency in the Pentagon. He was consumed, going over each document one by one, not letting simple distractions break his concentration. While still engrossed in reading the papers, subconsciously he was unaware of the intercom buzzer on his desk sounding off. At the last moment, realizing his annoyance, he nonchalantly answered the call, still preoccupied with his work.

"Yes, Chief, what is it?"

"Sir, I have Deputy Director Remington here to see you. And there are several other individuals in his party. He says it's urgent, sir."

"Send the colonel in, Chief."

"Aye, sir."

The door opened quickly. Remington was in the lead, with Dixon, Ensign Diaz, and two FBI agents following right behind him. Remington opened the discussion with a hint of agitation in his voice: "Admiral, sorry to disturb you, but I think you need to hear this. I think that we may have found the culprit behind our security breach. Commander!" Remington pointed in Dixon's direction, indicating that Dixon should finish the explanation.

"Sir, thirty minutes ago, one of my junior officers by the name of Ensign Elena Diaz informed me and Assistant Deputy Director

Daniel Moore that she uncovered some startling evidence relevant to our internal investigation. Several unauthorized emails were sent or received through our servers. The emails show evidence of foreign influence. They point to a website and an email account belonging to someone who may have in his or her possession top secret information about the United States military. The emails contain military intelligence from the DOD, the DIA, and other intelligence agencies. Our own naval archives have probably been probed into. Ensign Diaz discovered this by going back and looking into emails from three or four years ago. Diaz and Moore even compiled a list of the names of all undercover operatives working in intelligence or for the Justice Department. The surprising thing is that we might know who is responsible for stealing our secrets and leaking them to this unknown source."

"Well, Commander, who or what is it? An outside agency or a single individual who has ties to a terrorist organization?" asked Cooper with intense curiosity in his voice.

Commander Dixon cleared his throat, hesitant to give the admiral the answer.

"Well, sir, it is not an outside agency so far as we know. Unfortunately, it is an individual, one within our own ranks. We believe that Lieutenant Commander Assad may be responsible for the leak and the breaches, sir."

Cooper stood from his chair very slowly with an intense expression on his face. "Lieutenant Commander Assad! Are you serious, Commander?!" Cooper's voice rose an octave higher in shock and anger. "Are you sure of your analysis, Ensign?" He looked straight at Diaz, who stepped from behind Dixon to give her interpretation.

"Yes, Admiral. I went over them several times and checked them out thoroughly before I reported my findings to Commander Dixon. The information is solid and sound, sir. Several of these emails were sent to Commander Assad on different occasions. These emails contain information about our military, especially weapons, covert operations, foreign intelligence gathering, and secret weapons development. They are all included right here, sir, on the printout I made at my workstation."

Cooper was enraged as he snatched the paper from the ensign's hand to have a look for himself. "Didn't he just go on leave two days ago?!" yelled Cooper. Everyone in the room twitched at the decibel level of the admiral's voice.

"Uh, yes, sir, he did. But Director Moore has contacted his people to request a court-ordered affidavit for Assad's arrest. If it is approved, they will go to his place of residence in Towson to pick him up."

"It's probably already too late. He knew we would find out about this sooner or later. That's why he cooked up that bullshit story about some family emergency. He said he needed to go home because his grandfather was dying. Goddammit! That little sneaky-ass bastard! He planned the whole thing all along! Son of a bitch is going to try to sneak out of the country!" said Remington in the same tone Cooper had just used.

"All right, Jack, calm down. He pulled the wool over our eyes, and we didn't see it as it was happening. Remember, we signed off on his leave, so we're responsible for letting him go. Right now, we need to figure out where exactly he's going and what his true intentions are. It's not for me to say what his motives are." Cooper walked from behind his desk and went over to Moore and Jones.

"Director Moore, I highly suggest that you contact your bosses at the J. Edgar Hoover Building. Inform them of what we've found, and ask them how we should deal with this situation. Inform the rest of the NSA, and tell the Homeland Security agents downstairs, that we found our mole so they can inform their superiors. Also, you need to put out an APB on Commander Assad with all federal, state, and local law enforcement authorities. If what Colonel Remington says is true, Assad is going to try to leave the country as soon as possible. Distribute his likeness to every international airport in the country so he can be quickly identified and apprehended expeditiously."

"Right away, Admiral. I'll find out if my agents have made it to his place. I'll also contact the Baltimore County Police Department. I'll ask the state police to meet them there for backup." Moore and Jones exited Cooper's office, while the rest remained. "Commander, I want you to take Ensign Diaz down to Assad's office and see if you can get into his computer. I imagine he'll have some safeguards and booby traps set up inside it, but if you can, you need to bypass them and find out exactly who is involved, what is happening, when and where it's going to happen, and why and how Assad did this. I'm putting you in charge of this. You know the man personally and what he's capable of. Brief your staff on this, and make Ensign Diaz the primary analyst on this case. Since she is the one who cracked it, she should be the one in charge of finding out what else he has done. Have everyone on your staff report any other findings or substantial evidence related to Assad immediately."

"Aye, sir. I'll get right on it now. Come on, Diaz, we've got work to do." Dixon, with firm determination in his voice, motioned Diaz to his side and began to brief her as they were leaving Cooper's office.

The only one left was Remington, who was still upset about the whole ordeal. He closed the door so that he and his commanding officer could have some privacy. "Goddammit, Wayne! How in the fuck did we not see this?! One of our own giving out classified information to some unknown terrorist organization as if he were handing out candy on Halloween night! This is going to be a real shitstorm when Washington hears about this!"

"I know, I know, Jack," said Cooper. "This is something way beyond a breach of our own security protocols. This is a serious national security event that could cripple our defenses for years or even decades. We have got to find out why in the name of God Assad would do such a thing. I can't imagine what would cause someone who has been in the navy as long as he has and who has the knowledge and expertise that he has to commit an act of treason and engage in espionage. He must be considered very important to someone or something outside our control. Not to mention that he's a very dangerous individual, both to himself and to his contacts. Washington is going to make sure that the blame will fall at someone's feet—and that someone is going to be us. We're going to have to find out what his plans are and who his immediate contacts are."

"I'll tell you one thing, Wayne, when we catch that son of a bitch, I am personally going to bring him up on UCMJ charges and break his fucking neck! I want them to put him in a hole so deep in Leavenworth that he'll never see the light of day again!" shouted the full-bird colonel, who was irate beyond belief.

"You and me both, Jack." As Cooper, hunched over his desk. Angry and dismayed about the circumstances that had been belayed upon him due to this unfortunate situation, Cooper tried to comprehend the terrible scenario in his mind and the devastation it will have to America's national security and beyond. As he grappled with this terrible event, he seemed to have a moment of clarity that lasted for a couple of seconds. Looking at his computer monitor as well as a few papers lying in front of his desk, he looks over towards his deputy director for reassurance and presides with several suggestions that might help them with their situation.

"Jack, do me a favor: have someone look into Assad's background and find if there's anything we might have missed when he was first screened to take this job. There must be something about his past that we missed. Go all the way back to when he was a kid if you must, and find out the truth of who his parents are, where they are really from, and where they reside now. Use all your contacts, all channels, and all the resources you need if you think you're on to something that might be of some help to us."

"No problem," replied Remington.

"I know a guy in NCIS who can dig up all kinds of dirt on anybody. He will go all the way back to when Assad's grandparents first met each other, and he'll find out how many times they fucked when they met each other. I'll get in touch with him right now."

Just as Remington was about to turn around and walk out of Cooper's office, the admiral stopped him.

"Wait a minute, Jack. Before you do that, go ahead and give a call to all directors of the IAs [intelligence agencies]: CIA, DIA, NIA, DCS, and NSA. Even call MI [Military Intelligence Corps, US Army], AFISR [Air Force Intelligence Surveillance and Reconnaissance Agency], and MCIA [Marine Corps Intelligence Activity] about this. Give them a heads-up on what we discovered."

"You got it." As Remington turned to walk out, he paused for a second to say more to Cooper. "In the meantime, what are you going to do, Wayne? You know the brass will have to be notified about this."

Upon hearing Remington's statement, Cooper flopped down hard in his chair as if he collapsing in exhaustion and despair. Contemplating the situation that he now had to deal with, he rubbed his face profusely as if wiping sweat from it. He was troubled, his anguish written across his forehead. Sighing, he said,

"I know. I don't have much of a choice but to call the CJCS [Chairman of the Joint Chiefs of Staff], SECNAV [Secretary of the Navy], and Admiral Taylor [Vice Chief of Naval Operations] about this. I'll give them a sitrep of what's going on, but I know they're not going to be very happy about it. After they hear what I have to tell them, they're going to want to have a meeting with everybody, including yours truly, along with the secretary of defense, the national security adviser, and the president himself."

"Jesus! For once, I'm glad I'm not in your shoes, Wayne. Just being around those egocentric, egotistical, stuffed-shirt assholes who think that their shit doesn't stink makes my skin crawl. I can't stand to be around that much brass or that many bureaucratic bullshitters in one spot."

Listening to Remington's colorful repartee, Cooper shook his head in a manner to acknowledge the humor of what the hard-core, crass, outspoken colonel who always said what he really thought and felt had just said.

"Jack, my friend, you do have a way with words." Cooper laughed softly.

"Let me know later when you get ahold of everybody at the Pentagon and your guy at NCIS. I've got a feeling that we're going to be working past quitting time on this one."

Remington gave a nod to his commander in response and headed out the door. With that, the admiral picked up his landline phone and started dialing a number in the directory. When he held the receiver to his face, he heard a click just before his call was answered.

"Yes, this is Rear Admiral Cooper of ONI. I need to speak with Vice Admiral Taylor at once. It's urgent." Cooper waited on the phone for no more than five seconds before he heard another click.

"Afternoon, sir, this is Cooper. ... I'm fine, sir, but I must inform you of something that's very serious. Our internal investigation may have turned up the mole that we were looking for, but I must warn you, it is not good news, Admiral."

Assad's Apartment, 16:15 Hours (4:15 p.m.)

The FBI, along with several Baltimore County police officers, had arrived at Assad's apartment complex. Two agents with four uniformed officers were positioned at the entrance of what appeared to be the manager's office. They were conversing with someone who seemed to be either the apartment manager or the landlord. They explained to him what their purpose was and why they were there, then showed him a document issued by a federal judge—a search warrant and arrest warrant for Assad. The manager complied with their request for his assistance in locating Assad's apartment and locating the now fugitive naval officer. Looking confused but curious about what was going on, the manager asked the agents to follow him. He led all six men upstairs to the third-floor area. As they arrived, the manager started to pull out a large ring of room keys that he had in his pocket, which suggested that he had access to every apartment for maintenance purposes. While the manager was retrieving the keys, one of the agents halted his action and told him to wait a minute so they could announce themselves.

The first agent knocked forcefully on the door and said,

"Commander Assad? This is the FBI! We advise you to open the door immediately and surrender. We have a federal search warrant to enter the premises. If you do not comply, we will be forced to enter!" The agents stood patiently, waiting for a response, but silence was the only answer they heard after the announcement. On that note, the agents and officers remained cautious, waiting to be prompted to proceed.

Because there had been no response, the agent gave the manager permission to open the door with the key, instead of the agents having to using brute force to gain entry. The agents and the police all had their hands on their firearms, waiting to pull them from their holsters. The landlord, fumbling around with several of the keys on his ring, finally found the right one to open the door. He opened the door carefully, and the agents and the officers entered with extreme caution. As they stepped in, they continuously scanned the area as if expecting something to happen, but to their surprise, the scene was clean and in good condition.

The first agent took one of the officers and went into the bedroom, while the second one told the other two to go outside and scour the rest of the complex in search of anything suspicious or out of the ordinary. The agents swept the entire area and found nothing but an empty apartment with the furnishings still intact. After going through everything, the first agent went over to the manager to ask about Assad's personality and how good of a tenant he was.

"Mr. Kelly, have you seen Commander Assad recently, like, today or yesterday?"

"No, not really. I mean, the last time I saw him was when he came to the office to pay his rent. That was four days ago, after he'd given his final notice."

"His final notice? Do you mean he was moving out?" the agent asked with curiosity.

"Yes. It was kind of strange. He's been an outstanding tenant for the past couple of years, never late on his rent. But for some strange reason, he paid me an amount in excess of his monthly rent, which was not required in his case. His contract wasn't up until February of next year, and for moving out early, he would have had to pay a penalty, but he paid me all the way past the deadline, to March. And then he said that he might be leaving all his belongings here."

"Did he tell you where he was going?" asked the agent.

"No. All he said to me was that he might be leaving early and that all his personal stuff was going to remain in the apartment. I told him that we're not responsible for furniture or other personal belongings left by previous tenants, but he didn't seem to care. He just said that he'd be leaving soon and told me that whatever was left behind, I could either give it away or sell it."

"Did you happen to notice anything unusual going on in or around Mr. Assad's apartment, for example, strange people who stood out, people he probably hung around or associated with that didn't look right to you?" asked one of the agents.

"No, not really. I mean, the boy kept to himself most of the time. I never pay attention to any of my tenants' personal lives. Sometimes I might have seen a number of people come and go from his apartment, but I gave it no thought. Tell you the truth, I never have time to snoop around or spy on any of my tenants, unless they are deadbeats or late on the rent. But I didn't have to worry about that with Mr. Assad. He was always prompt with his payments and kept his apartment clean, as you see now."

While the lead agent continued interviewing the manager, the second agent, with the assistance of one of the police officers, happened to spot something. "Matt, come over here. Look at this." The agent politely excused himself from the landlord and went over to his partner to see what he has discovered. "One of the officers just pointed this out to me. Look at this. It's a bullet hole. The caliber looks as if it's nine-millimeter, and it seems the weapon was fired at close range. From the looks of it, it came from that direction." The agent turned around and scanned the area at which his partner was pointing. He walked over to the center of the room and instantly looked down at floor. There he spotted something peculiar.

"Mike, look at this." He bent down and pointed to what he'd found, being careful not to touch it. "What does that look like to you?"

It took the agent only a second to realize what he was seeing. "Well, I'll be damned. That's blood. And it looks like it's small specks, like a trail. And look at the scuff marks on the floor, as if a skirmish took place."

"Not just a skirmish, but a fight—a big fight from the looks of it. Look how deep the scratches are, Mike. If someone else was here with Commander Assad, they must have had one hell of a disagreement."

"We'd better call this in, Matt."

"Yeah, looks like our missing fugitive has turned into a possible murder suspect. Where there's blood, there must be a body somewhere. Call CSI [crime scene investigation] and forensics about this. Have them bring over some more locals to help with cordoning off this area. I'm going to call Director Moore and tell him what we found."

Assad's Apartment, 17:49 Hours (5:49 p.m.)

An hour had passed, and the apartment complex was now surrounded by more police and FBI personnel than previously. Agents Matthew Smith and Michael Lawyer, who were first on the scene, were debriefing Assistant Deputy Director Daniel Moore on what had been found within Assad's apartment. With extra manpower from the Baltimore County Police Department and Maryland State Police assisting, the agents were entitled by federal warrant to confiscate Assad's furniture and personal belongings because of his probable involvement in murder. But they could not seize it until the crime scene unit finished with the physical investigation of the domicile, and which was taking a while because the bullet stuck in the wall had given the forensics team plenty to work on. Attracted by the enormous number of the police swarming around the area, people who lived in the complex started to gather at the scene. The police had their hands full with trying to secure the area and fielding questions from the residents, which was becoming too overwhelming for the local officials to handle. Some agents helped out with crowd control, while others continued to gather information from Assad's neighbors.

One agent happened to take down some interesting information from a tenant who was the woman who'd seen Assad that night in the parking lot. He asked her to come with him, then escorted her to his immediate supervisors, Smith and Lawyer, to tell them of what she had witnessed that night.

"Excuse me, Assistant Director, Agent Smith, Agent Lawyer. I have someone here whom you should listen to. Her name is Ms. Elizabeth Derby. She resides on the second floor of the apartment building. She says that she may have seen Commander Assad Monday night." The young agent motioned her to the front. She was very attractive and young, in her early twenties, he thought, judging from her appearance and the clothing she had on. She was very nervous and a little hesitant to talk to the agents, but Smith adopting a coaxing tone to calm her down.

"Ma'am, my name is Special Agent Matthew Smith of the FBI's Criminal Task Force Division. This is my partner, Special Agent Michael Lawyer, and my supervisor, Assistant Deputy Director Daniel Moore. You seem a little nervous. Are you all, right?"

"Yes. I mean, I'm a little nervous. I've never seen so many cops around here before. Nothing like this has ever happened in these parts, not since I've been here."

"It's quite all right, Ms. Derby, I understand your concern. We're searching for a missing naval officer. Are you familiar with Lieutenant Commander Ad-dam Assad?"

"Yes, he lives right above me. Hell of a guy, and very cute."

Smith, Lawyer, and Moore all perceived Ms. Derby to be naive and immature for her age, but the other young agents and police officers, who were each taking a hard look at her, were not thinking the same thing. Instead, they were thinking about and looking at her exterior, all the while indifferent to her interior personality. She was very athletic-looking and well proportioned, with curves in all the right places and a body to die for.

Smith, trying to ignore Ms. Derby's anxiousness, continued to listen to her story even though it sounded like an adolescence talking.

"I've seen him a couple of times, including when he was in his uniform and going to work. God, he is so fine! He is so good-looking and so hot. He looks damn good in his navy apparel. I bet he works out a lot."

"Excuse me, Ms. Derby," Deputy Moore said, interrupting her in the hopes of preventing any further absurd statements about Assad's masculinity,

"But one of my agents said that you may have seen Mr. Assad last Monday night."

"Oh yeah. It was three forty-nine in the morning, close to four o'clock. I was awakened by a disturbance going on above my apartment. I didn't think too much of it at first. It sounded like some people were moving a lot of heavy stuff around up there, so I ignored it and went back to sleep. But later, I heard a huge crash outside my window, so I got up and looked outside. It was Ad-dam. He was carrying something big and bulky to the dumpster. I couldn't understand why he was taking out the garbage so late that night, especially when the trashmen wouldn't be picking up the garbage until Friday afternoon."

"Wait a minute," said Smith, "you saw him carrying something to the disposal bin?"

"Yes. He had to carry it with both hands because it was as large as he was."

Smith and Lawyer looked over at Moore simultaneously, and Moore was looking at them. They all had the same expression on their faces, and they were all thinking the same thing.

"Ms. Derby, can you show us where this disposal unit is?"

"Sure, I'll take you to it."

Smith told Jones to gather up some of the officers and have them follow them to the place where the young woman saw Assad carrying an object whose identity was obvious to everyone but her. Having walked the two meters around the building, they arrived at their destination. Ms. Derby pointed to the huge dumpster that was sitting close to the visitors' parking lot. Smith had one of the agents look after Derby while the rest of them, accompanied by three police officers, went over to inspect the dumpster. Two of the officers got on top of the huge can and opened the two lids simultaneously. To their surprise, they found what they had expected to see.

"Agent Smith, Agent Lawyer, you should have a look at this!" one of the officers said loudly.

Smith got up on top and saw a black plastic bag holding an oblong shape with a hand and foot sticking out from a tear. Smith took a pair of latex gloves from his pocket and put them on before going to identify who was in the bag. He tore the bag open from the top. Inside he saw the body of Muhammad Kareem, which was in the early stages of rigor mortis. He looked over at Deputy Moore and said,

"Sir! I think you'd better send CSI over here with a body bag! We definitely have a homicide! "Not only that, but we may have found one of the conspirators that is linked to our investigation." Moore turned to one of his agents and said,

"Call the director and Admiral Cooper at ONI. Tell them of what we found and that Commander Assad is on the run."

Los Angeles International Airport, 6:10 p.m. PST

Assad was walking casually along one of the airport's mainstream corridors, which was very crowded. His demeanor was quite relaxed as made his way to his gate, where he'd board a flight that was scheduled to leave from Los Angeles, bound for Hawaii, at 6:30 p.m. PST. He carried himself with a swagger, not in an arrogant or conceited way, but more in a way suggesting overconfidence and presumption. He had completely altered his persona to fit with his new identity, doing his best to act and sound like the individual whose passport and ID Assad was now using as his own. He had to look and sound the part so as not to give himself away, hence his determination to appear relaxed, amiable, and cordial. He knew that sooner or later the ONI was going to find out what he had done, and the FBI, along with other law enforcement agencies, were going to paste his likeness all over the TV and the internet. Thinking about this likely eventuality, he happened to catch a glimpse of the local news playing on a small flat-screen TV sitting in the window of a small electronics kiosk as he was making his way, walking nonchalantly, to his departure gate. He happened to see his own face displayed in the corner of the TV screen while the local anchorperson was reporting the news. He could not catch all of what was being said, only a portion of it.

"The FBI, along with other federal, state and local law enforcement authorities are looking for this man, who is wanted for questioning by the State Department for unlawfully distributing classified government information to outside sources. The information is considered to be extremely important and highly valuable to the Department of Defense and the State Department. The man's name is Ad-dam Omar Assad. He is a lieutenant commander in the United States Navy and a computer analyst for the navy's intelligence agency. He disappeared two days ago from a naval yard in northern Maryland and has not been heard or seen from since. He is also wanted for questioning in relation to two homicidal murders within the Tri-State Area of Maryland, Virginia, and Washington,

DC. The FBI considers the discovery of this man's whereabouts to be a top priority and is asking that the public cooperate with this investigation. The FBI is offering a substantial reward to anyone who provides information about Assad's whereabouts within the last few days." As this grabs Assad's attention, he quickly turns his head away from the TV set and slumbers his face into his cell phone that projects the same coverage on the outlet screen. But while doing that, the anchor man continues with his report.

"But if you should happen to locate this individual, do not try to apprehend him yourself. If you have seen this man, be sure to contact your local and state law enforcement authorities at once. It is vital to the navy and the FBI that Commander Assad be found and questioned immediately... And now on to sports. The four-and-three San Francisco Forty-Niners are scheduled to play the six-and-one Dallas Cowboys this coming Saturday afternoon. They will ..."

Assad turned away quickly so as not to arouse the suspicion of anyone near who was also watching the program. The disguise he had on was very convincing to an onlooker. But to the trained eye of a professional, Assad's disguise would easily be seen for what it was, a lie.

Assad began walking again toward his gate, looking at his ticket to remind himself of the number. Looking around, he spotted Gate 9, from which his flight would be boarding. His seat was in section 4 on Flight 308 from Los Angeles to Hawaii, which had a scheduled departure time of 6:35 p.m. and which, the monitor showed, was expected to arrive on time.

Assad looked down at his watch and saw that the time was 6:20 p.m. He noticed that most of the passengers were already boarding the plane. Each of them was handing over their boarding pass to the attendant and showing her their ID. Assad got in line with one of his carry-ons, this one carrying the four rifles he'd stolen from the armory. When it was his turn to surrender his boarding pass, he pulled out his passport to show the attendant. She gave Assad a complimentary greeting and looked at his passport. Having only glanced at it, she gave it back to Assad with a courteous and pleasant smile.

"Thank you, Mr. Brown. Enjoy your flight."

"Thank you, ma'am. I will."

Assad's photo ID and passport both showed that he was a conservative middle-aged man named Gary Brown who lived in Miami, Florida and whose occupation was as a chemical engineer. Kareem had confiscated the ID from Gary Brown himself. He'd met up with this Gary Brown in Miami a few days prior and killed him so as to allow Assad to assume his identity. Kareem had many people working under him, including some employed by the secret organization he'd kept mentioning to Assad. Assad had a clue of what this organization was and who belonged to it, but he hadn't speculated too much about it. He did think that the organization had ties to both al-Qaeda and the Taliban, and with other radical Islamic groups that were seeking to destroy the United States and its allies, but his intuition told him that this organization was large and well structured. It seemed to him that this was not your simple run-of-the-mill type of terrorist group with members hiding in caves and living up in the mountains or out in the desert. These people were very well funded, well established, and well organized—better than either the Taliban or al-Qaeda. Given the amount of money and intelligence they were willing to give Assad in exchange for the information he had, and given the sophisticated measures at their disposal, which had allowed them to recruit many new members into their fold, Assad knew that he was dealing with some serious players. He wanted to meet these individuals personally to find out who they were and how truly powerful and influential they might be.

Preoccupied with all these thoughts, Assad managed to board the plane successfully with no problems. Looking for his assigned seat in the front section of the plane, he caught a glimpse of an attractive woman with blonde hair seated right next to where he'd be sitting. He stowed the black duffel bag in the overhead compartment and politely squeezed past the beautiful woman to get to his seat. She smiled at him as he did so. He took his seat at the window, making himself comfortable.

"Good evening," he said to the woman next to him. "I hope that this flight doesn't take too long. I wouldn't want you to get tired of looking at my face."

She answered him with pleasantries of her own and a gleeful smile, not knowing that the man sitting next to her was very dangerous.

Friday, the White House, Washington, DC, 8:30 a.m.

An early morning meeting with the president had been called. Numerous officials had assembled in the Oval Office to discuss the matter of Assad's treason and espionage. These included several members of the president's cabinet, some of the Joint Chiefs, and the supervising directors of numerous federal law enforcement agencies and military intelligence groups. They were all standing and chatting about what had transpired within the forty-eight hours after their hearing the news about the former naval officer's actions. The others present were senior officials from the FBI, the CIA, the DIA, the NSA, and the Department of Homeland Security. There were also senior service members from all four branches of the military, along with their aides, who happened to be taking a special interest in this unique situation.

The two Joint Chiefs present were Four-Star General Charles Jacobson of the US Army, who was also senior chairman of the Joint Chiefs of Staff, and his second-in-command and vice chairman, Four-Star General Marcus Thomas, commandant and commander in chief of the US Marine Corps. The directors of intelligence agencies in attendance were Harold Richards, four-star general retired from the US Air Force and senior director of the CIA. Zachary Porter director of the FBI. Robert Tyler former US senator and four-star admiral retired from the US Navy, head of the NSA. Paul Goldsmith, three-star general retired from the US Army, head of the DIA. And Secretary John Kirby, four-star admiral retired from the US Coast Guard, director of Homeland Security.

The armed forces intelligence group was standing opposite the first group. Representing the Military Intelligence Corps, US Army Intelligence and Security Command/INSCOM, was Senior Director and Three-Star Lieutenant General Andrew Dreyfus. The Air Force Intelligence, Surveillance, and Reconnaissance Agency [AFISRA], Senior Director and Two-Star Major General Maxine Vaughn. And the Marine Corps Intelligence Activity Agency [MCIA], Senior Director and One-Star Brigadier General Samuel Carter. And of course, Admiral Cooper of ONI, along with his supervisor, the vice chief of naval operations, Vice Admiral Patrick Taylor, were present.

Everyone was packed into the spacious Oval Office, surrounded by portraits of the previous occupants of the prestigious office. Patiently awaiting the arrival of the president, the vice president, and the secretary of defense, each member of the executive cabinet stood observing those from the military with disdain and contempt, which they kept hidden. Cooper and Admiral Taylor both felt the tension in the room, which was obvious. One could almost see the finger-pointing that was going on inside people's minds. But because the guests were distinguished and had good reputations, no one dared exhibit their displeasure, as it would be unprofessional and indecorous to do so. As the minutes ticked past, the room filled with the sound of whispering as the members of the military and those of the cabinet spoke amongst themselves. Everyone was anxious, but the mood somehow seemed serene. They all knew that their commander in chief had an idea of what was going on but did not know the intricacies of the situation, nor the accusations against the suspected perpetrator. He had been briefed on the new developments, namely, the murders of Muhammad Kareem and Gary Brown, the latter of whom had been identified by local Florida authorities.

As everyone continued to wait patiently, the door, which was set in such a way as to appear to be a wall covering, suddenly opened, with a Secret Service agent making his way in first. As he held the door open, the president walked through, the vice president following behind him. But they were not alone. The secretary of defense, a retired four-star admiral, Todd Miller, was with them, as was a surprise visitor, the president's national security adviser, Shawn Atkinson.

The newcomers all stood still until the president had come around them to take up his position in front of the Resolute Desk.

"All right, gentlemen, as you were. We all know why we're here. Secretary Miller and Mr. Atkinson have already briefed me on some of the details related to our dilemma. But I need to hear this information personally from each of you. I want to know what's really going on and how we're going to resolve this problem quickly, before it escalates or gets spun out of control by the press. We don't want them getting ahold of it. I would like to hear your contingency plans to keep this from getting out of hand. Director Porter, Admiral Cooper," the president said, looking in their direction,

"Why don't you two start us off? Tell us what you know, gentlemen." The president waved his hand.

Porter, deciding to answer first, said,

"Yes, Mr. President. As you know, the FBI has been working with ONI and other intelligence agencies to apprehend Lieutenant Commander Ad-dam Omar Assad and arrest him for conspiracy, espionage, and treason according to the articles of the UCMJ. We are also trying to recover what's left of the classified data that he stole after hacking into the DOD archives, along with some USCYBERCOM files that he also illegally obtained. I have personally been in contact with both Director Tyler and Director Goldsmith, hoping to find out how much info was taken from the database. Unfortunately, sir, we have lost a considerable amount of high-profile intelligence related to our military and its network, including information about weapons and the operations of all our armed forces, including protection procedures as these apply to covert operations and intel. Also taken were personnel files and records, which include info about all undercover operatives and agents employed by the DOD, along with information about their missions."

"Wait a minute, Zach, are you telling me that this man has in his possession all our top-secret weapons, as well as a list of all our operatives—military, federal law enforcement, and federal intelligence—who are currently in the field?" The president was stunned.

"Yes, sir, I'm afraid so," replied Porter.

"How in the hell was this man able to retrieve these classified materials in the first place? How did he get past the firewalls and encryption protocols specifically designed to protect against such possibilities?"

Cooper turned toward the president in humility, clearing his throat and making a hand gesture. "Sir, he had top secret clearance, and indeed the usual security protocols were followed. His job title was assistant analyst for military foreign relations and counterintelligence. Only a very few individuals are privileged enough to hold such a position. Three of the ones who do are on my staff, not counting the accused Commander Assad. He had unlimited access to all military and federal government materials as per his MOS [military occupational specialty] as an analyst and intelligence officer. Plus, he is highly computer literate, sir. He knew the ins and outs of every mainframe and every bit of software we had."

"Well, aren't your people monitored daily, Admiral, to prevent against situations such as this? Just in case they decide to go rogue or get stupid? Not to mention losing their freaking minds and stealing highly classified government information that will land them in goddamn prison!" shouted the president.

"Sir, everyone working within the intelligence community—the CIA, the NSA, the DIA, and others—undergoes an intense screening process and submits to several interviews before they can even get a foot in the door. And they are subjected to constant surveillance, namely, the monitoring of all their computers, which create daily logs of their log-ons and log-offs," explained Cooper.

"Well, it looks like he found a way to get around that, didn't he, Admiral?" The president was so irate that he literally slapped the items on his desk to the floor, doing so with such ferociousness that everyone in the room flinched. Realizing what he had done, and noticing the reactions of his cabinet, the president quickly regained his composure and apologized for his outburst, singling out Cooper.

"Forgive me, Wayne, if I'm being belligerent toward you. I apologize. But none of this makes any sense. Why would a man who spent almost ten years in the navy, with a thriving career and the potential for even greater success, want to throw it all away by betraying his country, engaging in espionage, and inciting insurrection, not to mention masterminding a devastating breach of our security? I don't understand it! What would he gain by doing all this, knowing full well that the consequences he'd face once found out would be severe, including a ruined career?!"

Director Porter ventured,

"If I may, Mr. President. Our sources have concluded already that Assad might be working for either the Iranians or possibly the North Koreans. We know that each country has an investment in seeing the United States go down the proverbial toilet if it will benefit them militarily, politically, or financially—especially North Korea, since they tried to declare war on us and their neighbor South Korea eighteen years ago. Kim Jong Un and his generals would greatly benefit from having access to our secrets and military hardware. We even thought, Mr. President, that he might be working for the Chinese since they are still pissed about the blockade.""

"That is possible, Zach," said the president. "He may have been influenced by either of those countries, but something tells me that this is bigger than that. This Commander Assad jumped over a lot of hurdles just to hit us where it hurts. And besides, we have a treaty with the Chinese under the UEA charter. I doubt that Assad is working for them. We and China share info with each other and have a trade agreement. To me it seems like it's personal for Assad. I want to know the reason why he would do such a thing."

"I may have an answer to that question, Mr. President," Harold Richards, DCI of the CIA, said after having invoked his privilege to speak by raising his hand. "When I was contacted by Director Porter and by Admiral Cooper's deputy director, Colonel Remington, about this, I had several of my people go back and do an intensive search into Commander Assad's background. We obtained a huge amount of information from a reliable source in the navy's NCIS department thanks to the cooperation and efforts of Colonel Remington and his previous influence with the agency. In the past several years before his employment at ONI, Assad was stationed at two of our embassies, one in Iraq and one in Saudi Arabia, as a senior-grade lieutenant. He was assigned to a special type of SEAL unit that Admiral Cooper and Admiral Taylor are aware of. It's a naval special warfare development group that operates under the name of DEVGRU or SEAL Team Six. The identities of the SEALs are classified, known only to certain qualified individuals, but I can tell you, sir, that their missions are specifically related to counterterrorism and rescue. Commander Assad spent months with them downrange training and learning combat skills and operational tactics. He was assigned to the team as an observer and interpreter, helping to educate the Iraqi SIS and Special Forces units. But he also spent a lot of time with the locals in those regions as he spoke fluent Arabic, which is his ethnicity. He is of Lebanese and Iraqi descent. His father was a member of the Lebanese government, a chemical engineer who later immigrated to Iraq and then immigrated to the States, and his mother was a schoolteacher in Iraq who was an activist for Islamic women's rights. He had two brothers and two sisters. Two out of his four siblings live here in the States. All four of them have prosperous careers. Of the two who live here, one is a lawyer in New York, and the other is a doctor in California."

Upon hearing that last remark, Cooper said,

"Excuse me, General Richards. You said one of his relatives lives in California?" Richards shook his head as Cooper continued. "Assad requested a leave of absence to visit a family member in California—

his mother. Just before he left, he told us that his aging grandfather was ill and that his mother wanted him to join his siblings and the rest of his family so they could all travel together at the same time. His next destination is to Lebanon to visit his grandfather."

"That's probably half true, Admiral. Or it could have been a ruse to throw you, and all of us, off track. Either way, Assad's father and mother are with his sister, who is a doctor residing in Los Angeles, along with their grandchildren. The FBI sent agents over to their residence to talk to them. They all said they hadn't seen or spoken with Assad in more than three years. The agents also asked about the situation with Assad's grandfather in Lebanon. Assad's mother told our agents that Assad's grandfather and grandmother had both passed away years ago, in the early two thousand twenties. Assad's two other siblings still live in either Yemen or Iran."

"Oh, that's just perfect!" said the president, throwing up his hands. "Two out of the five children stay in two countries that have been complete thorns in our sides for almost four and a half decades and are still not willing to take part in the unification efforts that the UEA and UN have invited them to join! Now one of these siblings might be going over to Yemen or Iran to give them our military secrets and probably renounce their citizenship!"

Everyone fell silent at the president's outburst. Soon, Richards picked up the thread of conversation.

"That may be, Mr. President, but we do have undercover operatives in those areas to notify us if Commander Assad is spotted or identified or if he is apprehended."

"What good will that do us, General Richards?" asked an impetuous Lieutenant General Andrew Dreyfus of army intelligence. "He knows all our agents and operatives in every field; our measures and countermeasures for deep infiltration of foreign territories; and our specs for covert usage of said sites and their operation. It wouldn't do us a bit of good if one of our guys were to spot him and try to arrest him. He would know who the guy is before he could snatch him up, especially if he yells out 'Immunity!' or 'Sanctuary!' in a nation where they are likely to grant his request and provide him the possibility of citizenship or asylum. Not to mention the country he resides in likely has no extradition laws or policies."

"That would be highly unlikely, sir," replied Cooper.

"Such areas are liable to extradition treaties and immunity policies that oppose the granting of asylum, political or otherwise, especially when it involves the United States. Commander Assad will try to get to either Yemen, Iraq or any neighboring Islamic country that will grant him vacancy in order to give the intel he hijacked from us to one of his contacts, but he will not stay there indefinitely. I believe he will try to go someplace farther north, such as Turkey, Bulgaria, Romania, Greece, or the Ukraine—southern Europe or northern Asia—anywhere but Southeast Asia, West Asia, or the Middle East. That's what I would do if I were in his place."

"How do you know that for sure, Admiral? This officer was part of your staff for several years, and you had no idea that he was going to do something like this. It wouldn't surprise me if you discovered individuals in your department that are sleeper agents or part of radical Islamic terrorist cells. You have allowed someone to compromise our national security by giving away our nation's secrets, which could lead us into war with a terrorist faction, possibly a foreign country. This would be an immediate threat to our territories and military bases abroad! You fell asleep while on watch, Admiral! You dropped the ball!"

"Now wait one damn minute, General!" Admiral Taylor responded, rising to Cooper's defense. "Admiral Cooper is one of the best and finest officers under my command! His record and job performance are both exemplary, and he shows a superior keenness when it comes to leadership and supervision! I am not going to stand here and let you denigrate one of my men to satisfy your own conceited, pedantic-minded views of how protocol and policies should be handled! I handpicked Admiral Cooper to take over ONI, as I wrestled my conviction and decision to SECNAV and the chairman of the joint chiefs to have him appointed. As I see it, we are all at fault here except for the president!"

Dreyfus instantly looked over at the president with disbelief and confusion. His commander in chief acknowledged his expression by shrugging his shoulders, who was obviously in approval of Taylor's remarks.

"Now you can stand there and take pot shots of how things should be done in your own house all you want, but I will not let you stand there and insult a member of my staff or anyone else. The blame, without a shadow of a doubt, should be distributed equally to all of us. Everyone here in this room is accountable for our national security and the safety of our nation, including you and me. We are all responsible for this treacherous act! And we all must be held accountable for it. Do not shift the entire blame upon one man when you know damn well that we have the means and technology to foresee something like this from ever happening!"

Dreyfus's expression was one of agitation and embarrassment as the equally ranked admiral put him in his proverbial place. The president walked over to Taylor and put his hand on his shoulder, a gesture meant to calm the irate three-star flag officer down. Taylor responded with a nod to the president along with an apologetic expression.

"All right, gentlemen, we all need to relax. The tension in here is as thick as pea soup. I assure you that we're not going to get anywhere by pointing fingers, shouting at one another, or jumping down each other's throats. That won't solve the problem. But what Admiral Taylor said is correct. We need to look more closely at the way we do things and concentrate on dealing with this problem now, before it escalates into something bigger and we lose control of it. At the same time, we must find a way to capture this Commander Assad and retrieve the data he has stolen. Director Porter, I believe you have some more news to tell us."

"Yes, Mr. President. On the same day Admiral Cooper found out about Commander Assad, we sent several agents, along with a squad of local police officers to assist them, to Assad's residence to retrieve him. While investigating his apartment, our forensics team came upon several bullet holes in one of his walls. Ballistics determined the caliber to be nine millimeters, shot from a distinctive semiautomatic weapon, a German Walther P series."

Robert Tyler of the NSA interceded. "A Walther P99 to be exact, Mr. President, which of course is a firearm distributed around the world. But only a small handful are sold to the public."

"Why is that, Director Tyler?" asked the president.

"Because a weapon of that sort is only used by foreign operatives. The British, the Chinese, the Germans, the French, and even the Iranians use that type of gun, notably for the military and their security services. You can order a weapon like that online, but the process to obtain one is long and tedious. You have to either have a squeaky-clean record or be employed by a government agency, preferably federal law enforcement." The president, along with everyone else, was intrigued by what Tyler was saying.

Porter said,

"If I may continue, Mr. President? My men found scuff marks and bloodstains that left trails on the floor, which shows that a conflict took place, but there were no fingerprints found within or around the area. My men interviewed neighbors and other residents of the complex, but no one had seen Assad since that Monday morning when he left for work. But we were in luck. A neighbor living underneath Assad saw him late Monday, around three forty-nine in the morning, taking some trash to the nearby disposal bin. She even happened to hear a disruption earlier that evening. She showed my agents where Assad had taken his garbage, and surprisingly enough, they stumbled upon a body—a male, in his early to mid-thirties, who was in fact Middle Eastern. We ran his fingerprints through several databases and even sent them over to the NCIC [National Crime Information Center], but they came back clean. So, we sent the prints to Interpol to see if they could find a match. Fortunately, they did. And they came back to us with some interesting news."

Porter handed everyone several documents along with a photograph of the deceased. "His name is Muhammad Kareem. He works for the Iranian secret security force and is a top-ranking official in the Iranian government. But he also dabbles in independent contracting for other government agencies, and he deals in illegal arms, shipping them to foreign countries."

"So, he is an international arms dealer as well," said the president.

"Yes, Mr. President. He had ties not only with Iran but also with the entire Arabian region, plus North Korea. He did have several dealings with Russia, but when we contacted them, they denied knowing him altogether."

"Of course, they would. If the Russians were to mistakenly say that they knew him, they would be in hot water with the UN for affiliating with an illegal arms dealer with terrorist connections," said Todd Miller, secretary of defense. "But that's the least of our worries, gentlemen. If the Iranians find out that one of their own has been murdered on US soil, they will retaliate. And I'm sorry to say this, Mr. President, but we cannot afford to have any type of international conflict now, especially since we just patched up things with China and are still working out our situation with Afghanistan and Pakistan."

"You're right, Todd," said the president. "We can't expose this right now. But we also can't cover it up for too long either. If the Iranians do ask about their missing official and find out that he was over here, then the best thing to do would be to acknowledge it and come clean. At the same time, we can switch it around and question them why an associate of their government was involved in an arms deal and was trying to secure classified information about our military. They wouldn't be too quick to make an allegation against us, especially if we were to tell them that he was an arms trafficker. But apart from all that, do you think that this Muhammad Kareem was Assad's contact?" The president again looked over to Porter.

"Most likely, yes, sir, he was. During the internal investigation of Assad's facility conducted by Admiral Cooper and his staff, one of the admiral's junior analysts stumbled upon some unique emails that Assad had received. They included URLs linked to a possible terrorist organization that he was in direct contact with, as was the case with the deceased man found at Assad's apartment. The URLs led to sites operated by a group called the Alliance of Allah, and the initials of M. K. always appear at the end of the emails. We believe that these initials are Muhammad Kareem's, who we think might be linked to a new radical Islamic group. But unfortunately, sir, the analysis department at both the CIA and the NSA failed to find anyone who matches the description of Muhammad Kareem or anyone who is tied to or identifies with that name."

"So, in other words, Zach, we may have a new breed of terrorist on our hands, as well as a new faction of terrorists?" asked the president.

"Probably, Mr. President," replied Porter. "But this isn't the end of the matter. Another body was discovered in Florida by the Miami–Dade Police Department. The individual had some sort of connection with Muhammad Kareem, and his body was found in a city dumpster by some employees there. He has been identified as a local named Gary Brown, a chemical engineer for the Department of Biochemical Research and Development. Local authorities say that he was shot point-blank in the head by a round similar to the one found in Assad's apartment. And the two individuals had had similar interactions through email and by phone. We looked up his file just yesterday, sir. The connections were startling."

"So, what you're saying is that these two gentlemen had close dealings with Commander Assad somehow," proclaimed the president.

"Yes, sir. I believe so. Mr. Brown dealt with both biochemical materials and military hardware. We had contracted him to analyze the chemical and biological weapons we thought our enemies might possibly use against us. The discovery of that type of information probably piqued Mr. Kareem's interest in partnering up with such an individual. Assad's knowledge of and skills with military weapons and bioweapons could have been an important factor in their partnership, sir."

"My God, gentlemen! What I'm hearing is unbelievable! How could we have let something like this slip through our fingers? A naval intelligence officer who has turned rogue! Two bodies of people who might have been involved in a secret spy ring, to the point of establishing a terrorist cell and committing espionage! And then there's possibly a new, but as yet unidentified, terrorist organization! Why didn't we keep tabs on this guy from the get-go? And what about his finances? Have you found anything peculiar with his bank accounts, such as large sums of money being transferred or deposited?"

Cooper spoke up, saying,

"No, sir. In fact, NCIS and the FBI found that he withdrew all his money and closed out several accounts that he had with local banks and credit unions. He never took out a loan or has defaulted on any of his financial responsibilities. Assad was clean with his finances, sir."

Exasperated, the president fell back and came to rest against the edge of his desk, folding his arms across his chest in despair and disappointment. But that was not the end of the bad news he was about to hear next. Porter had left the best for last.

"Sir, that's not all. Homeland Security, along with some of my people, found out late Wednesday night that several weapons were reported missing from an army weapons depot at the Aberdeen Proving Grounds in Hartford County, Maryland. Four high-powered maximum-velocity rifles were supposedly taken out late Monday night by what some of the soldiers described as a"—he paused—"uniformed naval officer with top secret security clearance."

"What?!" shouted the president "You mean that this man got himself onto a secure military installation and took several of our weapons out with him when he left?!"

"Yes, sir. Commander Assad took the weapons that night: one experimental FN-F2020 series, one XM25 grenade launcher, one

Steyr AUG assault rifle, and one Beretta ARX-160 with a M203 grenade launcher attachment. Three of these weapons came to us by way of our partnership and arms exchange agreement with Italy and Germany. We developed the XM25 ourselves. All were experimental and ready to be deployed to our soldiers in the near future for combat use. We think that Assad may try to sell them to his contacts or find a fence to sell them on the black market. That's where I think Muhammad Kareem came into play. He was trying to buy the weapons from Assad, but they had some sort of disagreement and—"

"And now he's dead," replied Secretary Miller astutely. "Somehow, like you said, their transaction must have taken a wrong turn, and Assad killed Kareem because maybe he was blackmailing him."

"Or something else, Mr. Secretary," said Cooper.

"Explain, Admiral," said the president.

"Well, look at it this way, sir. Why would Assad go through all the trouble to amass so much top-secret information after having figured out how to get it if he knew the consequences and also knew that his chances for success would be slim to none—not to mention that he'd have to sacrifice his own well-being and likely get caught in the process? *Money*, gentlemen! Somehow, someway, he was going to be reimbursed for having stolen classified information and materials from us to give to some unknown agency so they could profit from it and use it against us. And it would have to be an incredible amount of money for him to turn against his country and do this. I'd say in the millions or billions."

"But what country has that type of money to give to an independent spy? Not Russia, China, Iran, or Korea. Not even Saudi Arabia, which happens to be the richest Islamic state, has that kind of loot in its treasury—and the Saudis are our allies, for Christ's sake. Certainly not Lebanon or Yemen. Who?!" asked General Dreyfus.

"From the looks of it, gentlemen, it seems to be some mysterious independent country or organization that has the means, including the financial backing to see our demise," said the president.

"The Taliban, al-Qaeda, ISIS [Islamic State of Iraq and Syria], or even the Haqqani network?" asked Secretary John Kirby of Homeland Security.

"No, Mr. Secretary. They're not funded with that type of cash, and really, all three of those terrorist groups lost their power years ago," replied Cooper, not mentioning anything about the Taliban.

"But it is possible that someone or something else has an incredible amount of pull and power over there in the Islamic world. I think it's the organization that owns that website we found linked to in Assad's emails."

"Sounds like you're describing some sort of criminal syndicate or powerful terrorist organization, Admiral—something out of a James Bond movie or Tom Clancy novel," the president said.

"I know it sounds far-fetched, Mr. President, but look at the number of terrorist organizations that have sprung up within the past thirty years since the attacks of 9/11 and the fall of both Saddam Hussein and Osama bin Laden—not to mention the anarchy that sprouted up in the Middle East nineteen years ago. Ever since the fall of the old regimes and the dictators who used to govern the Islamic countries years ago, several radical groups have come out of the woodwork, especially after the wars ended in Iraq and Afghanistan. This isn't even taking into consideration our distrust of the Pakistani government, which led to several skirmishes along the Pakistani border. We are still unable to figure out how these organizations came about so quickly or how they have endured, this in spite of the many peacekeeping tours we have sponsored over the years. And still, not even the UEA or the UN can find out who or what controls these groups. Iran, Lebanon, Libya, Yemen, Syria, Pakistan, and even North Korea might secretly support them, but we have no proof either way. But I feel that they're all too busy trying to solve their own problems to become thriving independent nations. They probably wouldn't have the time to look into such a small group of radicals who, although presenting an inconvenience, want only political glory and international recognition for themselves. It has to be something bigger than that for Assad to betray us so easily."

The president gave a hard and disturbing look at everyone who surrounded his desk. He appeared troubled and worried about this outcome. He stood up and walked around everyone, then came to the center of the huge presidential seal in the middle of the carpeted floor of the Oval Office. He looked up and addressed Chairman Jacobson, saying, "General, what will we be looking at if Assad does accomplish the handing over of our secrets to an enemy combatant such as the ones Admiral Cooper just described?"

Jacobson cleared his throat and placed his hands behind his back. "Sir, we would be looking at a national catastrophe with fallout on a worldwide scale, militarily, socially, economically, and financially. The stolen information is vital not only to our security but also to our stability as a unified nation. It is also important in that it will either enhance or decrease the confidence our people have in our government. Same goes for our allies' security. We would have to go back and change all our protocols, tactics, and procedures for handling terrorism and radical influences around the world. We would have to start from scratch and implement new security programs and protocols. This breach will do us more harm than good, especially if we have to replace the names of our personnel and equipment with new ones because of the sensitivity of the names that Assad has in his possession, not to mention his knowledge of our countermeasures and technology. That would make things very dangerous for the men and women who serve in the armed forces, also making it more difficult for them to maintain our security and uphold our freedoms. This is not even to mention their families, who might find themselves in harm's way whether or not they serve in the military. We would be set back decades. It would be catastrophic, Mr. President."

The president looked around at everyone and said, "Do all of you agree with this assessment?" Every official, including Cooper and Taylor, nodded their heads in agreement. "Then we have no other choice, gentlemen. We must find Commander Assad immediately and bring him back here to stand trial for treason, espionage, and possibly murder, and then retrieve what he stole from us, or eliminate him in the process *expeditiously.* Gentlemen, I want options on the table, and I want them now. I want to hear each of you give me your opinions and offer your solutions for how to get this man."

The president looked around for answers, but all he was receiving were looks of uncertainty.

"We could send more operatives to find out his last-known location within the past seventy-two hours," suggested Richards.

"No, that wouldn't be feasible or practical right now," answered the vice chairman, General Thomas, who was previous employed at MCIA before he became vice chairman of the Joint Chiefs. "He already knows the identities of most of our agents, and as you said earlier, Director Porter, he has the list of all covert operations and undercover operatives and teams from those classified files. Sending people whom he can easily recognize will be a waste of resources and American lives. We need to deploy someone he is not familiar with, someone he doesn't know personally or professionally, an individual he is not aware of, someone off the radar."

"I agree with General Thomas, Mr. President," said Admiral Taylor. "SECNAV and the director of NCIS wanted to be involved in this case because of Commander Assad's being a naval officer and intelligence analyst. They also wanted to implement a contingency plan for the situation, but I advised them that it would be a bad idea to begin such a campaign because Assad has that list of all our agents in his possession."

"Well, Admiral, we have to do something! We can't just sit around here with our thumbs up our asses waiting for this Assad person to hand over our secrets to an unknown terrorist organization that wants to obliterate us! We have to send somebody over there to get this guy!" said the president in anger and frustration.

The panel stood around contemplating what Thomas and Taylor had just said. It seemed a rather sensible and logical plan to everyone who thought it would be ridiculous to send someone with whom Assad was already familiar. So, as they continued to stand around motionlessly with the president pacing back and forth near his desk, thinking about what they needed to do, Cooper suddenly had an idea. "Mr. President, I may have a solution. Let's go with what General Thomas said earlier. We already know that we cannot send anyone out there whom Assad is already familiar with, so why don't we send someone he doesn't know?" Everyone looked at Cooper peculiarly, including the president.

"I'm sorry, sir, let me explain in more detail. Why don't we hire someone who used to work for us? We should find someone who has worked in intelligence and has been trained in covert military ops. Such a person would not be on the list since he's no longer in the military nor in the intelligence community. His name wouldn't appear in the files of the DOD or DIA."

"I'm intrigued, Admiral Cooper. Are you suggesting that we hire an independent contractor for a top-secret government operation? Would it be wise for us to assign a mission of such magnitude and importance to a freelancer we are not familiar with?" asked Secretary Miller, with an inquiring tone in his voice.

"Yes, Mr. Secretary, that is exactly what I'm suggesting. Instead of sending a group of sharks to hunt down the shark we want, why don't we send a killer whale instead." They all stared at each other in confusion, but Cooper had piqued their interest. The president especially was curios.

"Interesting how you put that, Admiral. I want to hear more about this 'killer whale' idea you're proposing," said the president as he invited Cooper to continue.

"Well, sir, we know of an individual who has prior experience with military criminal investigation—I'm speaking of the Army CID—and was a CIA operative for more than five and a half years. General Richards, you're probably familiar with this individual. He was one of your officers who was considered by the company to be the CIA's top 'dog catcher,' in apprehending and eliminating high valued targets."

As soon as Richards heard the phrase *dog catcher*, he knew exactly who the admiral was talking about.

"No! Absolutely not, Admiral. Out of the question. I know exactly who you're talking about. The idea is not feasible. He has been inactive for almost five years, and we've changed our policies and procedures since his time here. I personally don't think he's qualified for this assignment. And besides, Wayne, he was given a burn notice for leaving the CIA prematurely. I would not recommend him for this assignment." Richards said, using the official term adopted by the intelligence community to inform other intelligence agencies and federal, state, and local law enforcement groups that an individual or a group of individuals has been called out as an unreliable source of information and intel. A *"burn notice"* is an official statement issued by an intelligence agency to other agencies. It states that an asset or intelligence source is unreliable for one or several reasons, often fabrication, and must be officially disavowed. This is essentially a directive for the recipient to disregard or "burn" all information derived from that individual or group. It also means in simple layman's term that he or she perceives to be either a threat or of unimportance, and to seek new employment for him or herself because of the discrepancy that has been put on their record; henceforth the terminology.

"Maybe, General. But you have to agree that he was the best you had in the company before he quit," Cooper replied.

"Fired is more like it. He was insubordinate, irresponsible, and disrespectful to his superiors—a downright pain in the ass if you ask me. I don't know how he managed to make it through the army, let alone stay in the company for so long."

"Still, General, he was the best you had in covert intelligence gathering and apprehending international criminals. He was even responsible for finding bin Laden when still in the MP Corps as a staff sergeant working for CID and ISA [Intelligence Support

Activity] under the aegis of the Army Military Intelligence Corps. Do you remember that, sir?"

Richards's facial expression made it obvious that he was both cross and against Cooper's proposal, which reminded him of an individual he had no interest in, one whom he did not want to be considered for this task. Richards was extremely pessimistic and cynical about sending someone who, in his mind, refused to do things by the book. He was reminded of the deeds this person had performed in the past, but these gave him no satisfaction.

The president, on the other hand, showed more of an interest in knowing who this person was as he warmed up to the idea. "All right, Admiral, you've sold me. I want you to get together with Director Richards and Director Tyler on this. See if you can get ahold of this"—he paused to think of how to put it— "unique person whom you are infatuated with and see if he wants to work for us again. You will oversee hiring this man of yours. By the way, Wayne, what is his name?" Cooper looked over at Richards for only a split second to see the reaction in his face. Then he turned toward the president. "His name is Killian Antonio Milson. He's a bail enforcement officer for the Municipal County District of Maryland—a professional bounty hunter, Mr. President."

CHAPTER 3

THE CONTRACT

Monday, Downtown Baltimore, Maryland, 9:30 a.m.

A 2020 black Chevrolet Camaro ZL1 two-door was parked at the corner of North Avenue and Belair Road in downtown Baltimore about midmorning. Inside the vehicle was a darkly dressed occupant who had been surveilling a building across from where he was sitting for almost twelve hours; from ten o'clock at night to nine that morning, looking for something or someone. He appeared to be a little anxious and restless, but really, he was exhausted from having sat inside the vehicle for such a long period of time.

He took out a notepad from his jacket and flipped it open to look for something written inside it. Then he took out his cell phone from the side pocket of his jacket and dialed a number. He waited patiently as the phone rang on the other end. Someone answered.

"Hey, it's me … Yeah, I'm here. Are you sure that I'm at the right place? … You're sure now? … Yeah, I've been sitting here since last night around ten … No, I haven't seen him yet. … Now you're positive that he skipped bail? Because if he didn't, I've wasted a lot of time sitting around here for nothing… You're sure? … Okay, I'll bring him in. I read his sheet and know what's going on. You know he's going to go rabbit once he sees me ... Yeah, I know. I'll try my best to be gentle this time. If he cooperates, we won't have a problem, but if he doesn't, well, don't hold it against me if you see marks and bruises ... Yeah, I've got everything ... Don't worry about me. I'll be all right. Worry about him ... Yes, I'll follow procedures. I'll be as professional as I possibly can ... Yes, I understand ... Yeah, I'll see you later."

He placed the phone back into his jacket and continued to sit patiently, waiting for the arrival of the person he was looking for. After some minutes had passed, he slumped further down into the driver's seat, staring once again at the old building decorated with graffiti and gang signs. Just when he thought that this entire ordeal was a waste of his time and energy, he suddenly spotted the very individual he'd been looking for. The guy was walking casually from the other end of the street. Smoking a cigarette, he was dressed in baggy jeans, tennis shoes, and a black wool overcoat that made him appear to have served in the navy or the merchant marines. He walked up to the front entrance of the building and entered through the main door.

As the man on stakeout stood there watching the other guy go in, he reached into his glove compartment and pulled out several handheld weapons. One was a Glock 22, a forty-caliber pistol, which he loaded with a single magazine, then placed in his right ankle holster for backup purposes. The other was a SIG Sauer SP-2340, another forty-caliber handgun, which was his primary choice. He got out of the car and went around to the back, where he opened the trunk and took off his black jacket, replacing it with a lightweight black bulletproof vest, then fastened a pair of handcuffs to his belt. He put on the vest and covered it up quickly by putting the jacket back on. He went back to the driver's side of his car to retrieve his gun. After placing a fully packed fifteen-round clip in the gun, he put the weapon inside his coat pocket to secure it in his shoulder holster. Trying to be inconspicuous, he looked around cautiously to see if anybody was looking or had noticed him. When he thought it was safe enough to proceed, he started walking up toward the building, then entering through the same door his quarry had used minutes ago.

When stepping inside the premises, he realized that this was a high-rise apartment building. He noticed down the hall that the individual was getting into an elevator. His quarry was forty to fifty yards away from him, but he happened to catch a glimpse on the upper panel of the elevator of what floor he was traveling to. The number on the digital display was a five. He got into the elevator next door and pressed the same button, 5. There happened to be fifteen floors in this high-rise building, so he counted himself lucky that the guy lived on the fifth floor.

The elevator began to move upward as the man stood in the center of it, waiting for his floor to arrive. Once the elevator stopped and the door slid open slowly, he peeked outside to see where his guy might have gone to. He spotted the guy walking to the other end of the hallway and stopping at a corner door. The guy took a pair of keys from his pants pocket and unlocked the door. He opened the door and entered the apartment with no difficulty.

As soon as the unidentified person was inside, the other individual came out of the elevator and quickly ran up to the door his quarry had entered. Without hesitation, he pulled his gun from his jacket and waited for a few minutes to let the individual get settled before making his move. Looking at his watch and judging that now was the right time, he knocked on the door three times and cautiously stepped to the side so as not to give his identity away. The individual on the other side of the door answered abruptly in a harsh and anxious tone: "Who is it?!" This made it obvious to the man standing outside the door that this person did not want to be disturbed.

Hearing the response to his hard knocking on the door, the gun-toting man said through the door, "It's your landlord! Your time is up! I need the rent now! It's been a month already! I can't wait anymore!"

"Hold up for a second!" said the individual on the other side. The man outside the door heard dead bolts and locks clicking one by one on the other side. Without warning, the door swung open forcefully.

"Hey, dude! I told you that I would give it to you next ... Oh, shit!" Realizing who it was, the man tried to slam the door quickly, but he was unable to do so because the mystery man had blocked his path with his forearm and forced his way through as if he were a defensive linebacker playing a football game. He entered and grabbed the individual by his neck, forcing him down onto the floor while pointing his gun directly at the man's temple.

"Wait a minute, wait a minute! I know what it looks like! I wasn't trying to skip bail! I was trying to get some extra cash together so I could pay it off! I needed some time to get it!" he said to bounty hunter.

The bail enforcement officer replied,

"Yeah, you just happened to mistakenly skip out on a hundred-thousand-dollar bond for attempted murder! You knew damn well that if you didn't come up with 5 percent or 10 percent of that, you would be heading back to jail or would be going away upstate for a long time! So, you contacted one of your boys so he could get you out of the state or probably out of the country, all the while knowing you couldn't come up with the rest of the money! You were probably thinking about taking a trip to either Canada or Mexico, right?!"

Exasperated over the struggle, the man tried to explain himself yet again to the bounty hunter, who had him temporarily subdued.

"Come on, man! I can't go back to jail! Too many people know me there!"

"Don't you mean that you know a lot of guys you snitched on so you could stay out of jail? Yeah, I read your file, Damon. You're an unpopular fella in county. You turned over a lot of people up there so you wouldn't take the rap for a murder charge. That was real smart on your part. Maybe they'll put you in solitary—if you're lucky. Now, get up and put your hands behind your head."

The individual whom the bounty hunter had just referred to as Damon slowly got up from the floor and started to do what the bail enforcement officer had ordered him to do. With his gun still pointing at the back of Damon's head, the bounty hunter reached in with his left hand and pulled out his handcuffs.

"Now don't try anything stupid, Damon. If you cooperate and come along peacefully, I'll put in a good word for you with the BPD [Baltimore Police Department] and the DA, telling them that you were a good little boy all the way downtown. But if you try something, things are going to get really ugly and bad for you very quickly. So, don't try to grow a brain and think of something stupid to do."

"That's only if you can catch me, bitch!" Having said that, and without warning, Damon knocked the gun out of the bounty hunter's hand. He managed to get off a swing and hit the bounty hunter in the face, temporarily knocking him off-balance, which gave him a moment to make his escape through the front door. Surprised more than stunned, the bounty hunter jumped on Damon's back and knocked him down on the floor again. Damon tried his best to overpower him, but given the officers skill at apprehending and subduing assailants, he wrapped him in a submission hold and tossed him over his body, causing him to fall right back down to the floor again. Damon, struggling to get out of the bounty hunter clutches tried to grab an object nearest him, a glass ashtray, which he uses to hit the officer over the head. Temporarily stunned from the blow, the bounty hunter lets go, and Damon scurried from the floor and ran out the door. The officer quickly regained his composure and began his pursuit. Both men were running down the hallway, with Damon in front with a huge lead. He managed to go through the emergency exit and down the stairway with the bounty hunter close on his heels. The officer followed Damon down and jumped over the handrails, showing disregard for his own safety. Taking a huge leap from one level of the staircase to another, he successfully landed on Damon, knocking him down once again onto the floor, this time with a tremendous impact. Damon tried to fight his way out of the bounty hunters clutches, but again the officer was too much for him and too skilled in his grappling technique. The bounty hunter knocked Damon back against the wall with several hard blows to his abdomen and one across the face. The officer grabbed Damon's right arm and put it in an armlock, also holding his head down. Then he flipped Damon over in a maneuver that landed him on his back, leaving the culprit in pain and agony. For the fourth or fifth time, Damon was once again laid out on the floor, stunned and bruised, but this time he was not able to react as he had earlier.

The retrieval officer grabbed both Damon's arms and placed them behind his back so he could put the hand cuffs on him. As he did that, he sat Damon up against the wall and told him in a sarcastic tone not to move.

A little shaken by the physical ordeal, the officer gathered his senses and walked back up the stairs to the fifth floor. He made it to Damon's apartment, where he pushed the door open. Scanning the area, he found what he was looking for, his SIG Sauer, which was lying on the floor after Damon had attacked him and knocked it out of his hand.

The bounty hunter went back downstairs to grab Damon, who was somewhat out of it but still conscious. As both were exiting the building and walking toward the bounty hunter's car, Damon was still trying to carry out negotiations with the bail enforcement officer, hoping to worm his way out of the situation he was in.

"Come on, man, cut me some slack, bro! I told you I needed a little more time to get the money! All right, I'm sorry I called you a bitch back there, but I was scared at the time! I know how you are, and I would never disrespect you like that or in any other way. But you've got to listen to me, *Kill*: I can't go to county! Those motherfuckers will kill me down there!"

"You should have thought of that before you punched me in the mouth, called me a bitch, and tried to run. You know I can't stand it when you *assholes* run from me! That pisses me off even more! I told you that if you came along without giving me any trouble, I was going to help you out. But now, you fucked that up. You're up shit's creek without a paddle and now on your own. Now, get your ass in the car, Damon, before I change my mind and shoot you right here!"

He opened the passenger side door and threw Damon in the back seat. Then he slammed the door hard in frustration, soon going around to the other side of the car. He got in and started the vehicle up, looking in his rearview mirror at Damon, who seemed to be injured after their scuffle. He also appeared to be in agonizing pain from the handcuffs, which were tightly clamped around both wrists.

Just when the bounty hunter was about to pull away, he said one last thing: "And by the way, Damon, if you're going to say my name, then say it right. It's Killian, not Kill. I haven't killed anybody in a long time. And believe me, you'll be the next one I will consider if you continue to piss me off! Now sit back, relax, and enjoy the ride, because your ass is going back to jail."

Municipal County District Police Precinct and Bail Bonds Office, Baltimore, Maryland, 11:30 a.m.

Killian A. Milson arrived with Damon Harris at the Municipal County Police Department located in downtown Baltimore to surrender him into the system and get him booked. Milson led Damon through a crowded hallway, where many onlookers glanced at Damon's attire, which was in tatters because of the Milson techniques he had used in apprehending him. Milson went through several checkpoints to sign in and place his firearm in a lockbox for security purposes. He then took Damon up to the front desk to admit him for processing. Unexpectedly, two police officers came around the corner to assist Milson while he was busy signing the paperwork.

Milson took notice of the two men, who had attached themselves to Damon's side for the initial booking, and said,

"Hey, guys, do me a favor. This guy can't be in general population. He's high-risk. See if you can put him in a cell by himself for now. He ratted on a lot of guys in here, and if they spot him … well, I shouldn't have to tell you the rest. I'll have my boss notify your desk sergeant about his case and his capture."

"No problem, Killian. We'll take care of him. Did Mr. Harris give you any trouble?" said one of the officers, who was built like a semitruck and was just as tall as one.

Damon, who stood opposite the officer, just gazed in awe at the size and stature of the man, becoming more cooperative because he was intimated by this man with the huge physique. Milson, who was amused by the officer's question, looked over at Damon, who had a look of both concern and terror on his face because he had indeed given Milson some trouble.

"Nah, not really. He just had a hard time getting down the stairs when I cuffed him. He behaved like a good little bail jumper. Just see that he gets his own place until the DA decides what they're going to do with him."

"You got it, Killian. I'll inform the sergeant that you'll be getting in touch with him soon."

"Thanks, guys. I appreciate it." The officers escorted Damon around the corner to continue the process of booking him and getting him into a cell at county. Milson had just finished filling out the report on Damon's apprehension and was about to go upstairs to the bail bonds office, where he needed to give his supervisor forms, receipts, and documents pertaining to Damon's capture and arrest.

Just when Milson was about turn around and leave, he heard a loud and sultry female voice calling him from a corner of the hallway.

"Hey, Killian! Was I right?! Was he there?"

Milson looked over and saw a woman who was five foot six with brown hair, light brown skin, and a perfectly proportioned physique in the shape of an hourglass with long thick legs and a posterior to match, thin average waste and a voluptuous chest that stood out literally. She was a knockout, to say the least, from both far away and up close. In addition to being beautiful, she was wearing attire suited to the occasion—casual business clothes that complemented the atmosphere but were not too conservative or stuffy, more like laid back for comfort. Her clothes were appropriate for the surroundings but were also extremely sensual, delighting the imagination.

"Yes, ma'am, you were right. He came around the corner and entered the very place you said he would be." Milson walked over to the attractive woman and presented her with several papers. "Here you go, boss..." as the title of her position was surprising.

"I was about to come upstairs and give these to you personally, but since you're here already ..."

She took the paperwork from him and began to skim through the documents, her eyes moving from the top to the bottom of each page.

Obviously, this was Milson's supervisor and CO, Sarah Hawkinson, who was senior supervisor of Baltimore's Bail Enforcement Agency and assistant administrator in liaisons to the chief secretary of Municipal County Affairs with the Baltimore Police Department. "It saves me the time and effort it takes to chase you down, so you can pay me what Damon's bounty is really worth." Sarah looked at Killian for only a second, then went right back to reading the forms.

"Take a walk with me, Killian. We'll discuss it on the way up."

He knew where this was going. The tone of her voice said it all. His attitude changed the moment she had spoken with uncertainty and doubt. He walked next to her down the corridor, until they came upon an elevator, into which they stepped. As the door closed, and seeing that they were the only ones in the elevator, Sarah began to explain something to her employee that she hadn't wanted to convey out in the open. It was also something that he did not want to hear.

"Look, Kill, you know as well as I do that, you're only going to get 10 percent of Damon's mark and 5 percent for bringing him in. That's a good cut for now."

Frustrated by what he'd just heard, Milson replied,

"Goddammit, Sarah! That's barely enough from the bullshit I go through when chasing down these assholes! When are we going to see some real money for a change, especially for the work that we do around here?! We go after these scumbags more than the regular cops do!"

"Hey, watch your mouth, Milson. I may act like one of the guys, but I'm still your boss and a lady. Show some respect."

Milson looked at Hawkinson for a moment, then laughed silently to himself. Realizing his tone, he said,

"Hey, I'm sorry, Sarah. But I'm just tired of the shit sandwich that we have to eat around here. If I had known that I'd be going through this much shit each day, I would've stayed in the fucking army, or with my previous employer. This is ridiculous."

Understanding his frustration, Sarah tried placating him.

"I know, Kill. It pisses me off too. But unless the city council passes that new bill granting extra wages to independent contractors employed by city government agencies, as well as more money and higher wages for the Criminal Apprehension Enforcement Department and FRED [Fugitive Retrieval Enforcement Division], which is our group, we're stuck dealing with the same bureaucratic nonsense and low wages like everyone else. Hey, at least you get a nice chunk out of it. Eleven thousand dollars isn't half bad."

"Eleven thousand two hundred and fifty to be exact, but that's not including the taxes they're going to take out of it. After that, I'll be lucky to get half the amount. Then we have to account for the rent I pay on my apartment, my car loan, my credit cards, and the back taxes I owe to Uncle Sam. You know he's getting his share once I pay everybody else off. And I haven't even mentioned the alimony I owe to my bitch of an ex-wife in Texas. I'll be lucky if I see one thousand of that eleven go into my pocket. Wow! I never would've thought that I'd be trading the military and the company for this. Hell, maybe I should have stayed in and enjoyed a nice pension from both."

Hawkinson saw the disappointment on Milson's face. To ease his frustration, she made a surprising gesture. She stepped in front of him, gently touched his face, and said, "If you would've done that, then you and I would never have met and done this." She leaned over and pressed her lips against his while passionately embracing him.

Sarah Hawkinson and Killian Milson had been in a secret relationship for a long time. Just how long this relationship had been going on was a mystery.

Milson did not reciprocate. He invited the kiss, of course, acknowledging the passion that its host was eager to express, but he did not show the same enthusiasm as she did. He pushed her away abruptly, but not aggressively. He had to remind her of the position that they were in while, at the same time, explaining why he had rejected her advances.

"Sarah, you know we can't do this. Not now, and especially not here. For one thing, you're my boss. For another, I don't want to lose the only decent thing I have right now, and that's this job."

"Oh, so what you're saying is that I'm not decent?"

Milson quickly corrected himself as he noticed Hawkinson's expression and tone had changed. "No, no, that's not what I meant. You know what I'm trying to say. If people were to find out about us, we would both be in a lot of trouble—and out of a job. And I for one just got here, unlike you, who is next in line to become chief secretary assistant, under the county commissioner. You have a career. I, on the other hand, am starting all over again."

Hawkinson understood what Milson was saying. She released him from her tight embrace. With the elevator still in motion, she quickly steadied herself and straightened her posture as if she had been wildly rolling around in the elevator with her clothes in disarray, although such was not the case. She and Milson both made themselves appear professional. But that did not stop Hawkinson from flirting with Milson and saying provocative things.

"I suppose you're right, Killian. Well, since you rejected my advances, does this mean we're not on for dinner tonight?"

Milson looked at her with a warm smile and shook his head.

"Are you kidding, lady? I've been dying to taste your chicken lasagna for some time now. I can't wait."

She laughed softly, with a wicked sexual innuendo behind the laugh.

"Lasagna is not the only thing you're going to taste tonight, Mr. Milson," replied Hawkinson with a sinful, lustful grin on her face.

"Damn. You're a devious little mink, aren't you?" said Milson.

"You don't know the half of it, sweetie," Hawkinson replied. They both smiled devilishly at the thought of their date later tonight, but as soon as the elevator stopped at its destination and the door slid open, their romantically naughty attitude immediately changed to one that was more professional and businesslike.

"Killian, I need that paperwork on Damon Harrison ASAP in my office. Then I can contact the DA and the desk sergeant downstairs so they can figure out what to do with him. Understood?"

Milson responded in the affirmative as both stepped out of the elevator and came to stand in front of their respective offices. "No problem, boss. Let me make a phone call. I'll have it ready for you in a couple of seconds."

When Hawkinson was about to go into her office, something triggered her memory of a phone call she had fielded. "Oh yeah, I almost forgot. You received a call earlier today. Sounded like it was important."

"Well, who was it?" asked Milson. Hawkinson kept walking toward her office.

"I don't know, some sort of general calling for you. Probably one of your old army buddies from Iraq or Afghanistan. He left his number on your desk and asked that you call him. Sounded as if he was calling from DC."

Milson saw the sticky note posted on his laptop, positioned right above the screen. He looked at it and saw the name written on it, along with a short message that read,

"Chief Milson, call Admiral Cooper immediately. It's urgent. The number is (202) 555-8575." Milson thought that this was something strange and unusual, especially since whoever it was had used the title and rank from when he was in the service. Milson stared at the note for a moment, then thought to himself, *who in the hell is trying to get in touch with me from the military? And why now?* After thinking about it for a couple of seconds and contemplating whether to return the call or not, he decided at the last minute to find out. He picked up his landline and dialed the number written on the note. After the phone had rung several times, an operator came on the line.

"Department of Defense. How may I direct your call?"

"Hello? Yes, I received a message to call an Admiral Cooper. My name is Killian Milson."

"Yes, Mr. Milson, we've been expecting your call. Stay on the line, please. I will transfer you, sir."

Milson seemed a little uneasy and puzzled. He was wondering why in the world the DOD was contacting him, especially now. As he continued to wait, he heard several clicks on the other end of the line before a monotone voice made its appearance.

"Good afternoon. Is this Chief Warrant Officer Killian Milson?"

"Yes, it is. But I haven't been referred to that title for a long time now. Whom am I speaking with?"

"Forgive me, Mr. Milson, my name is Admiral Wayne Cooper. I am a correspondent for the Department of Defense. I was wondering if you might have a chance to speak with me today?"

"Uh, yes, Admiral, of course. What is it about?"

"Oh, this must be done in person, Mr. Milson, not over the phone. Security reasons and all that. You understand."

"Uh, yes, sir, I do. Where should we meet?"

"Are you familiar with the National Maritime Intelligence Center, located in upper Maryland?"

"Yes, I am. I know where it is."

"Good. I'll see you this afternoon around one o'clock, if that works for you?"

"Yes, I think so. It will take me some time to get there because of the traffic on I-95, but I will make it."

"Good. I will inform the guards at the gate to expect you. I will see you soon, Chief. Good day."

Milson held the phone for a while, wondering what was going on. He thought to himself that it was strange that a navy admiral would be calling him from one of the most secure facilities in the United States, next only to the Pentagon and Langley, the latter being his former place of employment. After going over it in his mind for a while, he realized that this was serious. He hung up the phone and ran to Hawkinson's office. Knocking on the door repeatedly, he went in without her having invited him.

"Sarah, I'm sorry to bother you, but I have to go. That message you put on my desk … I have to meet someone."

"Have you finished your paperwork on Damon yet?" Hawkinson asked.

"No, but I'll take it with me and do it tonight when I get home or when I get to the other place," he said, secretly referring to their dinner date later on tonight.

"Kill, I need that paperwork done today so I can send it up to the assistant district attorney. He needs the case file on Damon so he can determine whether to send him back to prison or not."

"I know, I know. I'll have it done by tomorrow. You know me. It's just for some strange reason, I have to meet with this guy today."

She stood up and walked over toward him in a curious way.

"Is this about that general calling you?" she asked with concern.

"*Admiral* is the correct term, and yes, it is. He wants to talk to me face-to-face about something. I can't tell you what it is because

I myself don't even know what's going on. But it seems important somehow." As Milson explained, there was curiosity in his voice.

"Does this have anything to do with your old job?"

Milson looked at her for only a split second, pausing for a moment before answering. "I don't know. Maybe. I'm not sure. But whatever it is, you'll be the first to know."

"Unless it has to do with national security."

"Well, if it involves that, then I know for sure that I won't be able to tell you anything about it," replied Milson.

She looked at him one last time and said,

"Okay, go ahead. I'll call the DA and tell him that his paperwork will be delayed until tomorrow morning."

"Thanks, Sarah. I owe you one."

"Oh, I know you do. You can pay me back tonight."

Milson smiled at her while shaking his head in approval. He stepped out of her office and went to his desk, where he gathered up most of his things. As he went dashing out of the office, Hawkinson, who was standing in her doorway, glanced at him one last time as he made his way through the glass doors and disappeared from her sight. Witnessing his departure and being smitten by his unique charm, she quietly turned around, adjusted her rectangular-framed eyeglasses on the bridge of her nose, and smiled a secret gleeful smile. While still thinking of her secret relationship with Milson, she readopted the demeanor of an adept supervisor and resume her managerial duties.

ONI Building, Suitland, Silver Hill, Maryland, 1:15 p.m.

Fifty-five minutes had passed since Milson left Baltimore. He was now arriving at Suitland, Silver Hill. Driving to the main gate, where two marine guards were posted, he rolled down his window to surrender his credentials and personal identification to the guards. The first, a lance corporal, waved his hand in such a way as to indicate to Milson that he need not explain the purpose of his visit. Even before Milson could produce his first name, the second guard, who was an E-5 sergeant and the senior NCO of the guard shack, came up from behind the corporal and made the same observation as his subordinate. "No need for explanations, Mr. Milson. The admiral has already informed us of your arrival. You may proceed, sir."

Somewhat hesitant, Milson drove ahead, looking at the two marines in his rearview mirror with speculation and worry as he made his way past the well-kept landscaping and a huge pond with an elaborate water fountain in the middle of it. He drove up to a nearly vacant parking lot and parked his Camaro. As he got out of his car, he took a long, hard look at the exterior of the facility, which caused him to fall into reminiscing about his years with the CIA. When he used to work for the company, he would coordinate with the other agents from different intelligence agencies who would flock to this place. The memories Milson was having now were both good and bad.

Milson walked up to the main entrance and introduced himself to one of the security officers. Strangely enough, the officers stationed there knew of him as well. The one he had approached asked him to wait patiently while he informed someone at the top of his arrival. Milson looked around at the mementos hanging on the walls; it reminded him of the Langley facility in Virginia. While he was distracted with looking at all the ceremonial plaques and naval guards within the place, one of the officers informed him that someone was coming down to meet him. After a short time of continuing to stand around and reminisce about his old days in the army and CIA, Milson was finally greeted by one of Admiral Cooper's subordinates.

"Mr. Milson? Good afternoon, sir. I'm Commander Dixon, analyst, supervisor of this facility. I'm here to escort you to Admiral Cooper's office. Here's your visitor's pass. If you would follow me."

Milson shook Dixon's hand and followed him up to the elevator. As they got in, Milson made a point to ask Dixon what he wanted to know.

"Excuse me, Commander, but do you have any idea why I'm here?"

"I'm sorry, Mr. Milson, I cannot answer that for you. The director and his guest will brief you on all the details during your visit."

"Oh, I see. So basically, this is a hush-hush meeting—need-to-know basis, keeping it on the down low and all that, huh?"

"Something like that, sir. I can tell you that you will be well-informed once we reach the director's office."

Milson gave a slight snicker, amused by the familiar cloak-and-dagger attitude he saw in Dixon. Once the elevator stopped, they both got off and proceeded down the long white corridor that led to the admiral's office. Milson took notice of Cooper's name painted on a glass door as he and Dixon walked through it. Dixon announced himself to the young officer who was Cooper's secretary. She pressed the button on the intercom to inform her superior that Dixon was here with Milson.

"Admiral, Commander Dixon is here with your visitor."

"Send them in, Ensign."

"Aye, sir." She got up from her desk and escorted them to the door, which she opened for them.

They walked in. Dixon introduced Milson. There were two other people, standing on opposite sides of Cooper's desk. The admiral stood up and said kindly, "Afternoon, Mr. Milson. I know I just got through talking with you on the phone, but let me again introduce myself. I'm Rear Admiral Wayne James Cooper, commanding officer and senior director of ONI. I'm sorry that I couldn't tell you my position and title over the phone. It was because of security reasons, which I know you are completely aware of."

"Yes, of course, Admiral," replied Milson with a peculiar look on his face.

"You've been introduced to Commander Dixon here, one of my senior officers in charge of counterintelligence." Once again, Milson gave a nod in Dixon's direction. "And over here is Director Robert Tyler, head of the NSA." Milson shook Tyler's hand and gave a nod of acceptance. "And over here is—"

Before Cooper could conclude the introduction of his guest, Milson, having recognized who he was said, "Assistant Deputy Director General Harold Richards of the CIA. My old boss and supervisor. So how are you doing, sir? Still sending officers off on wild-goose chases, are you?"

One could've cut the tension in the air with a proverbial knife between the two. It was obvious that Milson was not a fan of the director because of the sarcastic tone when addressing his former supervisor of the Central Intelligence Agency. Everyone in the room was aware of this, especially Richards, who was at first hesitant to acknowledge Milson at all.

"I'm fine, Mr. Milson. And that's senior director of the CIA." As Richards sneered at his former employee.

"So, how are things with you, Milson? Still employed as a common bounty hunter with no career incentives in mind?"

Hearing Richards's contemptuous remarks on Milson's occupation, the former CIA/CID agent replied,

"Oh, they're as good as can be expected, sir. Don't have to put up with a lot of bullshit as I did when I was with the company. A little, but not much. At least the city that I'm employed with has no problem telling their employees the truth every now and then. But at least they're honest with you and not sugarcoating the truth to save their own asses. I admire that in an employer, sir—straight to the point with no cutthroat rhetoric. You know, no backstabbing, no chickenshit rules that must be observed whenever a task is performed. I don't know if you're aware of this, Admiral, but Director Richards was my supervisor when I was at SAD. We didn't get along very well when I worked there, so to show his appreciation, he gave me a burn notice and a reprimand after I quit the company. I couldn't find work anywhere after that, not even as a rent-a-cop/security guard in a department store or mall."

The expression on Richards's face started to get more agitated every second that he remained in Milson's presence. Milson's demeanor and sarcastic remarks were becoming problematic for the former air force general who had fired him years ago. Cooper and the rest of the group bore witness to this and gave the two a wide berth. But to the admiral's mind, this kind of attitude and honesty was refreshing and useful to his goal. Thinking to himself,

"I think I found the right man for the job." The admiral asked everyone to take their seats as he began to brief Milson on why he was there in the first place.

Not feeling too comfortable with the present company of Richards, Milson obliged the admiral's invitation and took a seat in a distance away from his former boss. When Cooper realized that he had the attention of his audience, he started from the top, being direct and forthcoming so as to lighten Milson's attitude toward the DCI of the CIA. "I know, Mr. Milson. That's why today the burn notice has been expunged and cleared from your record."

Milson, who was surprised to hear this, turned his attention toward Cooper, who said,

"The reason I called you here is that we have a serious problem on our hands. Have you been listening to the news lately?"

"Not really, Admiral. My schedule, what with my being a "common bounty hunter", does keep me preoccupied." He looked over in Richards's direction with a smart-ass look on his face.

"Well, let me get you up to speed. Several months ago, the Department of Defense figured out that their archive of classified files was being hacked into and stolen from right under their noses. A severe security breach marked by many unauthorized downloads was being reported by every agency within the intelligence community: CIA, NSA, DIA, NIA [National Intelligence Agency], and military intelligence from all five branches of the arm forces. We did an intensive investigation into each department and reached a startling conclusion." Cooper stood up and went over to a sixty-inch-wide screen to use its projector. The screen lit up, and an image of Assad's face appeared.

"The man you see before you was an employee of ours. His name is Ad-dam Omar Assad, lieutenant commander in rank, and who was under our supervision until he went rogue and AWOL a few days ago. He's US-raised but is of Lebanese and Iraqi descent. He was an assistant analyst working in the Department of Counterintelligence and Foreign Military Affairs under Commander Dixon for three and a half years. We learned, unfortunately, a couple of days ago that Commander Assad is the one responsible for the theft of our classified materials. When we found out about his treachery, it was too late. Somehow he had managed to escape the authorities and possibly left the country."

Milson was surprised, but he said nothing, showing no response to what Cooper was telling him.

"Using tactics of espionage, Assad stole an incredible amount of information vital to the security of our nation and our military. He also took several items of weaponry hardware from an army weapons depot."

"What exactly did he take?" asked Milson, curious to know. Cooper was a little reluctant to say because the incident was an embarrassment, but it was necessary to provide him with this information since Cooper invited him in the first place.

"Information about research and development of secret weapons; schematics and blueprints for naval and air force vehicles such as fighter aircraft, ships, and drones; four highly advanced, high-powered, fully automatic rifles; and lastly, a list of the names of all undercover operatives within the federal government, including the intelligence community and the military, who are currently active in intelligence gathering, deep undercover operations in foreign countries, and special ops missions."

Milson did not know what to make of this. To him, it all sounded as if it had come right out of a spy novel or movie. But he saw the look of concern on everyone's faces, including Richards. He then decided to ask a most important question, one that Cooper was probably ready for.

"All right, Admiral, I see your dilemma, but what does this have to do with me?"

Cooper walked back over to his desk and, after a short pause, said,

"Mr. Milson, we want you to find Commander Assad and bring him back to stand trial for treason, espionage, murder and grand theft of classified US government intel and military materials."

Milson shifted in his chair as if he was uncomfortable.

"Wait a minute, Admiral, I don't understand. Why me? I'm just a bail enforcement officer who catches petty criminals who skip out on bails and warrants. This is not my department anymore. You have thousands of agents out there who are more qualified for this type of situation, better equipped to handle stuff like this—agents you already know and whose intel is solid."

"True, but our assailant does not know you or your previous skill set." Said Cooper.

"Assad has stolen a list containing all the information we have about every field operative within the intelligence community and within all federal law enforcement agencies from the FBI to the US Marshals. He has the names of all our sources, along with all the background info we have on every agent in the United States, as well as information about their relatives and who they associate with." Cooper continues.

"If he gives that kind of information to an organization or country that holds resentment towards the United States, it could spell disaster not only for our country but also for the men and women who serve under us."

"And their families and friends as well. They would be the proverbial sacrificial lamps to a slaughter house for whomever gets their hands on that piece of information." Director Tyler offered, assisting Cooper with his briefing.

"Okay, gentlemen, I see your point. But you still haven't answered my question. Why me of all people?" Milson asked.

"Because you yourself are not on that list, Chief Milson. Assad does not know who you are. He doesn't even know you exist." Still looking at Cooper with confusion, Milson let him finish.

"I looked up your file, Chief, and talked further with General Richards about your skills as a field agent. Your expertise in locating dangerous fugitives, international and domestic criminals alike, is very impressive. You've even brought in terrorists and organized cells. I even looked at your old service records from the army when you served as a CID agent in the MP Corps. You tracked down several notorious individuals who had been on both the army's and the FBI's Most Wanted lists, and you solved several of the CID's cold case files. You were even involved in coordinating the task force that helped locate and execute Osama bin Laden, showing that you are able to cooperate with both army and navy intelligence. And you did all of this at a very young age, in your early twenties to mid-twenties. You were even part of the army's ISA unit before joining the CIA. You speak four different languages—Spanish, Russian, German, and Arabic—and have been deployed several times to Iraq and Afghanistan. Along with that, you joined the CIA's SAD [Special Activities Division], where you became qualified to gather sensitive materials and intelligence on radical terrorist groups. In addition to doing these things, you have apprehended many foreign combatants who posed a major threat to the United States and our allies. It seems that your résumé speaks for itself, Chief. In my book, your career is very impressive. Your background and skills are extraordinary, to say the least, and I feel confident that you are the type of person we need, one who has the skills we are seeking. What we are asking of you now is in regard to your skills as a former operative. We also want to talk about your current occupation as a local apprehensions officer. The DOD, with direct authority from the president of the United States and the secretary of defense, wants to rehire you as a classified operative to hunt down and retrieve Assad, and also recover the data that he has stolen from us."

Milson was in awe. This was nothing like what he had expected or prepare for. All of this was coming at him so fast that he could not give an adequate response.

"So, let me see if I have this straight. You want me to track down and apprehend this Commander Assad, who has obviously gone rogue under your command? You want to hire me as a so-called GI bounty hunter to catch this analyst for you before he sells whatever intelligence he has to a foreign government or country?"

Cooper, Tyler, and Richards simultaneously nodded their heads in response. Observing that all three men remained silent, Milson continued his line of questioning.

"This apprehension that you want me to achieve, will it be considered an executive bounty, in place of an executive order from you and the powers that be, or is this all black ops–type stuff that needs to be kept under wraps?" Milson asked.

"Yes, to both questions, Chief. That's exactly what we want you to do. This is an executive mission that we want you to accept, but it is also a hush-hush assignment. We cannot afford to let something like this get out in the open for everyone to know about."

Milson, who was still baffled by what he had heard, could not believe this. He stood up and walked around his chair, contemplating the decision he had to make, while Cooper continued to brief him. "You'll be reinstated with your old army rank and title, as a reservist officer only, and you'll receive all back pay and benefits, in addition to your regular compensation. You will answer to me and to me alone. You will have top secret clearance and unlimited access to all intelligence files and materials related to criminal activity, domestic and international, in the databases of the FBI, DHS, DEA, ATF [Alcohol Tobacco, and Firearms], US Marshals, CIA, NSA, DCS, and DIA. You will also be briefed on all military activities and military intelligence involving surveillance and special ops. Commander Dixon will debrief you on the background of Assad and will suggest where he might have gone, and give you any other materials you may need. You will also—"

"Wait a minute, Admiral," said Milson, "this is a bit too much for me. I have not made up my mind to do this. I've been out of this particular game for quite a while, and here you're asking me to risk my life to track down a guy who was under your supervision because he stole some secrets from y'all? Pardon my language, Admiral, but it sounds as if you're trying to save your own asses before news of this situation gets out to the public and a real shitstorm develops. This reminds me of a similar situation that happened seventeen years ago, with Snowden. With all due respect, Admiral, I haven't yet given you an answer about taking this job. It seems that the CIA would likely call this job an 'expendable circumstance.' I don't know if I want to do this."

Cooper and the other directors went silent after listening to Milson express his apprehensiveness. They all thought that for him, this was a grand opportunity to finally grab hold of the brass ring—all except Richards of course. Cooper walked around to the front of his desk and approached Milson, coming to stand face-to-face with him. "Mr. Milson, I understand. This is a bit much and a lot to take in, but you must understand our predicament. This was something totally unexpected and unpredictable. We did not think that something like this could happen to us again, but it did, and we were not prepared for it. But you must realize that we are desperate. This man literally raped us, and we're embarrassed about it. As of this moment, he is probably thousands of miles away, out of the country, planning on distributing our most valuable secrets to a hostile foreign country or, worse, a terrorist organization that wants to see the demise of the United States. Terrorist groups, such as those in rogue countries that both you and I faced when in Iraq and Afghanistan, would love to see this happen. If Assad succeeds with his agenda, then I guarantee the United States and our partner countries will become vulnerable to terrorist attacks. And with the peace process that the UN and UEA are engaging in over in the

Middle East, something like this might destabilize the very thing they've been working so hard to build. We must not let that happen. The United States and the world must not fall into another conflict that would consume the planet. We have to find Assad and retrieve those materials now, before it is too late."

Milson looked at Cooper long and hard, considering what he'd just said. He did understand the situation and the consequences, but still he was not sure that he wanted to do this. "Admiral, give me the night to think about it. I have to go over this with my current employer."

"I understand, Mr. Milson. Think it over. And please get back to me with your decision as soon as possible. Don't think too long. The more we delay, the greater the advantage Assad will have over us. We must act now."

Milson understood the admiral's meaning and nodded in agreement. Cooper reminded him of another obligation. "One thing, Chief. You realize that you are not allowed to discuss what we have talked about today with anyone outside this office. Even though you're employed by neither the company nor by us, you're bound by the Secrecy Act to refrain from disclosing classified government information to anyone. If you do disclose such information to someone, the consequences will be—"

"Admiral, I know," Milson interrupted. "I was a field agent for six and a half years, remember. I know the deal on keeping things hush-hush and what will happen if I open my mouth. I promise you that I will give you my answer tomorrow morning."

Cooper gave a slight grin and a nod. Then he shook Milson's hand in appreciation and thanked him for coming. He told him that he would be looking for him to call tomorrow, then asked Dixon to escort him out of the building.

As soon as Milson left the office, Cooper turned to his colleagues to discuss their opinions of and reactions to the former CIA agent turned bounty hunter. "Well, gentlemen, what do you think?" Cooper looked over at the two directors, who remained silent in the face of the admiral's question, which caused Cooper concern. "General? Senator?" Cooper said in a tone that made his inquiry more forceful.

Richards, who was thinking deep thoughts, said, "Well, Wayne, you know my opinion of the man. Look at him! He's arrogant, disrespectful, and pompous. He has no respect for authority or supervision. I personally don't think he is right for this, and I still think we can find other agents to look for Assad. He's not that far gone from our radar that we cannot smoke him out."

"You don't know that, General. Assad was one of the smartest SOBs we had working for us. He was clever, crafty, and well trained. I think Milson is the perfect man for this assignment. He knows how to track people wherever they might be. In my opinion, he is the right man for this."

"You may be right, Wayne," said Tyler, "but are you sure that a man like Killian Milson, who has been out of the intelligence business for several years, has what it takes to go up against a younger, more intuitive, and highly skilled individual such as Assad, who, you have clearly shown, has had Special Forces training and has a superior intellect? Don't get me wrong, Admiral, I have nothing against Milson. He's probably good at what he does, but his current profession is to chase down lowlife petty criminals who skip out on their bail."

"That's exactly who we need, Senator, and that's exactly what Commander Assad is, a criminal—a criminal who has broken the law and has committed murder, theft, and large-scale espionage and must be brought to justice for these crimes. Mr. Milson is the right man and the right tool for the job. He specializes in catching criminals and bringing them in, no matter what infraction they may have committed, whether a misdemeanor or felony. They're all wanted by the law and must be accountable to the law. And in our case, Commander Assad is wanted by the United States government for espionage, treason, theft, and murder, even if it was murder of a foreign national. Milson is the man we want, gentlemen."

Tyler and Richards looked at each other as they considered the meaning of Cooper's words. They both stood up and shook the admiral's hand in respect for letting them be present for this interesting meeting.

"All right, Wayne. I hope you're right about him because, according to what General Dreyfus said to you last week, the ball is in your court. The president is going to want an answer by the end of this week or sooner," said Richards.

"I know. Even Secretary Miller and SECNAV want to know if Milson is going to be on board."

"I hope so for your sake, Admiral. We need for this to happen, like, right now," said Tyler. Then he and Richards walked out the door, leaving Cooper to himself with only his thoughts of what had just transpired.

The director sat back in his chair slowly and stared at the door through which Tyler and Richards had just walked out. Continuing to stare at the door, he whispered to himself, "I hope so too, gentlemen. For all our sakes, I hope so."

Sarah Hawkinson's Apartment, 3:30 a.m.

Milson's evening for the night was somber and quiet. He was sitting on the side of the bed with crumpled sheets laying across his bare lower torso, which was covering his genitalia. He was slumped over with his chin resting on his hand, sitting naked in a dark midsized room with only a small amount of light coming in from the bedroom window. As he continued his bruting posture, thinking of what had transpired earlier that day, a silhouetted figure beneath the bedsheets happened to roll over on the opposite side of the bed. The full-figured silhouette belonged to none other than Sarah Hawkinson, who happened to be in the same apparel as Milson. But in her case, her nudeness was sultry, sexy and extremely voluptuous. She happened to open her eyes and noticed Milson sitting on the side of the bed. Wondering what was going on, she rolled over taking up the remaining bed sheets on her side to cover her breasts while reaching against the night stand to turn on the lamp. The lamp illuminated half the bedroom which made it possible for them to interact with each other knowing how late it was. Milson, still unmoving did not flinch, even when Hawkinson herself moved closer to him to see what was bothering him. She spoke softly to him but still weary from her awakened state.

"Killian, sweetheart, what's wrong? Why can't you sleep? Is something bothering you?"

Still pondering his thoughts, Milson turns to acknowledged her.

"Yeah, kind of. I've just been thinking about yesterday."

"Yeah, I know." Hawkinson moved closer to him while leaning against the headboard.

"You were quiet at dinner tonight. And when we were making love, you weren't your usual self like before. What's going on?"

"Sorry, Sarah. It's just"—he paused—"that meeting I had with Admiral Cooper. It stirred up a lot of old feelings and memories. Things I hadn't felt for a long time." Concerned, Hawkinson asked,

"Feelings like what, honey?"

Milson paused again, but this time he was not hesitant to answer her.

"Feelings I had when I was a young man in the army. You know the stories I told you of my time and tours in the service. Especially that particular one that I don't like to talk about." She acknowledged with a nod of her head while listening and comforting him simultaneously. Submitting to the soft touch of her hand rubbing against his back, Milson continues to inform her of his past.

"Sometimes, I can't get that image out of my mind. Sarah, I saw firsthand what evil looked like and what it was capable of. When Cooper told me about this situation that they are up against, it brought back a lot of memories that I still want to forget."

"You mean that incident at Fort Hood you told me about years ago? And some of the things you saw when you were deployed in Iraq and Afghanistan?" Sarah asked, showing her compassion while still comforting him from behind.

"Yeah. At first, I thought I was over all that. But listening to the admiral talk about what this guy did just sent me back to that place."

Concerned for his well-being, she asked gently, "What did y'all talk about?"

Milson turned around and glared at Hawkinson for a minute.

"Babe, you know that I can't discuss this with you. The information he told me is classified and confidential. I can't say anything about it."

"You mean you can't tell me! The woman you've been seeing for the past three years, as well as having a long-lasting committed relationship with? You can't tell me anything at all about what's going on with you? Are you serious?!"

Calming her slight outburst, Milson explained his reasons to her in order that she would be compliant and understandable.

"Sarah, you know what I was before we met. Even after you hired me and did your background check, I had a hard time telling you who I was, and what I did. That's why I kept those bits of information out of my records and off my résumé, because I had sworn an oath not to disclose any information about my previous employment to anyone; family or friends. The company takes its secrecy and confidentiality very seriously. I kept only my army service record in my files for public usage."

Hawkinson sat back against the headboard hard. Both arms folded across her chest as if she were a pouting, spoiled child.

"I understand that you have trouble bringing up your past, and I know that there are certain things you can't tell me or don't want to talk about, but why are you letting this eat at you? Are you planning on going back to that life again and leaving what we have together?"

Milson shook his head.

"No, Sarah, of course not. I'm not going to leave you. You're the best thing that ever happened to me. But I am thinking about the offer the admiral made earlier. The person they want me to look for is extremely dangerous and could hurt a lot of people. I just don't want a repeat of what I witnessed at Fort Hood, that's all. Sarah, I must admit, when I first met you, I thought you were just like all the other women I've met in my past, including some with an entitlement attitude on their shoulders—mean, bossy, egotistical, self-centered women who thinks that the world owes them something. And since I'm being honest with you, I didn't like you very much from the start. But I needed this job after I quit the company. But as I got to know you and saw what type of person you were, I realized that you weren't half bad." Both of them laughed at each other's expense while Milson finished with his thought.

"But as I got my life back together, I noticed things started to turn around for me, or should I say for us. I've enjoyed our relationship together. Even though we're keeping it hush-hush from everybody else, I like what we have, and I don't want to lose it. But something in my heart and soul tells me I must take this job. Not just for my sake, but for the sake of everyone I knew who lost their lives to individuals that want to threaten our way of life. Babe, I think I should do this." Again, Milson paused, but only for a split second in order to conclude his final thought,

"No, I want to do this."

Hawkinson looked at him with so much compassion, warmth, and sensitivity in her eyes that she almost started to cry. Deep down within her heart, she felt a love for him that she had never felt for any man, but she did not want to express it so quickly, not now. So, instead of telling him how she really felt about him, she just leaned forward and embraced him in such a way that satisfied both their personal feelings. While she was still clutching his body, she whispered some comforting words in his ear to put him at ease.

"If you want to go ahead and do this, then by all means, you do it. You have my permission, sweetheart." They both released themselves from the embrace but stayed connected by their fingertips, locked in a mutual gaze.

"But you better damn well bring your black, Latino ass back here when you return, mister! It's hard to find another qualified experienced bounty hunter in this goddamn city! You'd better not get your ass killed over there to wherever the hell you're going. Because if you do, I'll have to go over there and find the son of a bitch who did it and kill him myself!" They both laughed knowing the implications of Milson's decision.

"Okay, listen. Tomorrow, I'm putting you on administrative leave of absence. I'll tell the assistant DA and the administrative captain that I had to put you on leave because of a family emergency. They will want to know the details, but I'll think of something to tell them. I know what you're doing is classified and, on a need-to-know basis. So, your secret is safe with me, sweetie."

"Thank you, Sarah. I appreciate it." Milson reached over and gave her a kiss on the lips with the intention of going back to sleep. But Hawkinson on the other hand had a different agenda in mind, one that did not involve rest.

"Oh, no, sir. You're not about to roll over and go to sleep on me. I did you a favor, so now you're going to do me one. You weren't up to par with your task earlier. So, come over here and finish what you started."

Milson, knowing exactly what she was talking about, gave a devilish smile and proceeded with the intent. He slid over in her direction, gently positioning himself on top of her, and started kissing and caressing her passionately as they began to make love for the second time.

Tuesday, ONI Headquarters, Admiral Cooper's Office, 10:00 a.m.

"Sir. Commander Dixon and Mr. Milson are here to see you. Should I send them in?"

Cooper wasted no time in answering his intercom.

"Yes, Ensign. By all means, send them in," the admiral replied. He got up from his desk, walked around it, and stood casually in front of it while anticipating Milson's arrival. Cooper was gratified to hear that Milson made his decision about taking the assignment. He had called the admiral early in the morning to accept the job and arrange to meet with him to be given the details of the clandestine mission. Standing in front of his desk with a self-satisfied grin, Cooper showed no hesitation in expressing his joy as he greeted his guest.

"Morning, Mr. Milson. I was pleased to get your call this morning. We can go over some of the aspects of your assignment and better familiarize you with the contacts you'll be meeting. You'll also be outfitted with some essential field equipment that you'll keep for the duration of this mission. Commander Dixon is going to be your adviser and your tech support, so talk to him about whatever hardware and software you need. He is also going to share Assad's profile with you and tell you where Assad may go next. Would you please have a seat?"

"No, thank you, Admiral. I'd rather stand. Sir, if you don't mind, I would like to talk to you about some concerns I have—in private."

Cooper, observing the unusual expression painted on Milson's face, which spoke of something very important he wanted to express, asked Dixon to step outside. The commander obliged and went into the lobby to wait.

"All right, Chief, you have the floor. What's on your mind?"

Milson took a breath and exhaled it.

"Sir, you've read my file. You know the ins and outs of my career. You know what I did before, during, and after my work with CID and Army Intelligence Support Activity—ISA. And I know you know what I did as a SAD operative. But I know personally that you are aware of my experience as a young specialist on November 5, 2009."

Cooper knew exactly what date Milson was talking about. He lowered his head for a moment and then raised it up again.

"Chief, I know that date very well. I remember it because I had just received my butter bars"—here he was using the military terminology for the rank insignia of a new ensign either in the navy or the coast guard. Or a second lieutenant in the army, air force, or marine corps—"for graduating from the academy, and was sent overseas to Afghanistan to train and lead some new SEALs at that time."

After hearing that, Milson continued, saying,

"Then you know exactly how I feel, sir. When you told me what was going on and the person that is responsible for orchestrating the security breach, I was at a loss for words. I was a bit apprehensive at first, but later I got over it. Still, I felt angrier than confused about why something like this had happened. I thought to myself after the meeting, *why are we letting this happen again?!* After what Major Nidal Malik Hasan did at Fort Hood twenty years ago, why would they allow someone like Assad to have classified information in the first place?! Have we learned nothing from 9/11 and the Fort Hood shootings?! Are we still so gullible as to think that we can let just anybody into our country, even into our military ranks, knowing the significance of the threats we face today?! Yes, we may have this new ideology from the United Earth Administration that is trying to send peace and love throughout the whole world, but in reality, Admiral, there are a lot of people out there who want to see America burn to the ground and fall to its knees! I have seen a great deal of hostility and hatred toward us in my short career as a soldier and an agent in the company, and I know you have personally seen it too!

Your experience as a SEAL operator and subcommander has given you some insight into what these people are and what they're capable of! Why are we still painting ourselves as the nice gullible guy who always forgives the girl who fucks him over every time?! Why don't we wake up from our fanciful dreams and realize that we have enemies who want to hurt us—and we have more internal enemies than external! It's the same thing that happened at Pearl Harbor in World War II! The navy saw the Japanese coming but didn't believe it until it was too late! The same thing is going to happen to us for the *third time* if we don't take off our blinders and see the world for what it really is!"

Cooper stared at the former CIA officer who had just made an emotional but compelling argument. He could tell that this man's past was deeply rooted, but he did not know the intricacies of Milson's personality or disposition of why he held so much animosity and bigotry toward individuals like Assad and anyone else of Arab or Islamic descent. After listening to Milson's judgmental ranting, Cooper decided to ease the tension with an intervention of his own.

"Okay, Chief. I see your point. Now let me tell you something I've learned over the years of wearing this uniform and responding to matters such as the ones you have raised. One, I would like to explain to you why we are so nice and forgiving as a nation, as you plainly put it. Yes, I've seen my share of violence and brutality. I've even seen the type of hatred that constitutes bigotry, racism, and xenophobia within individuals who've committed heinous acts against one another. During those times, I said to myself, *why are we here? No, more precisely, why am I here? And why are we allowing acts such as this to happen?* You don't know the number of times I've asked myself, *what are we doing this for?* And you know what answer pops up in my head every time I ask that question to myself? *Because we must do it, and we're obligated to do it.* If we allow ourselves to turn cold-blooded and heartless every time someone threatens us or commits acts of violence against us, then we are no better than that same enemy who wants to destroy us. We might as well become the Communist Party of old, such as that which held sway over Russia and China for so long. We would be dismissing our fundamental democratic ideals as a society, as a nation, and as a people. That would demoralize us to the point that we'd start functioning like a dictatorship, along with having a totalitarian brand of idealism, that would lead us to ostracize, repudiate, and ridicule people. People look at us as the last great hope of freedom, justice and equality. A prospect that is not easily available in many countries today. Yes, the UEA promotes an idealistic concept of peace and tranquility, but it is reaching out to people who are tired of the violence and pointless killing of others because they don't want to conform to their beliefs. People want to see a change in the world, Chief. They want to see democracy and freedom across the entire planet, for everyone and everything to enjoy. They want our world to be a peaceful one, without senseless and mindless violence that will lead us to a genocidal end. We all want to finally live free and be who we are without worrying about differences in skin color, ethnic background, language, religion, politics, and gender. The UEA is proposing negotiation talks as we speak between Israel and Palestine; two governments and countries that have been at each other's throats for over seventy-plus years."

Milson listened to what Cooper was saying. He found the admiral's views to be problematic. But the brash bounty hunter decided to consider his perspective and perception.

"We have to break the chains of violence and stop this vicious cycle of distrust and prejudice right now, or there won't be a planet for us to live or thrive on," Cooper went on to continue. "You asked earlier why we would allow someone such as Assad to have access to our secrets. Well, half of me asks the same thing. But are you perceiving things from a professional point of view given Assad's background and skills as a military official? Or are you saying this out of prejudice given his ethnicity as an Arab American? If we propose to have that type of mentality and attitude, and if we lose sight of what's important, then how are we as a people or a nation ever to grow into an evolved, more civilized society. We might as well go back to the fifteenth, sixteenth, seventeenth, eighteenth, and nineteenth-century practices of slavery, tyranny, and oppression. Because if we start to judge individuals based on the color, culture, ethnicity, and heritage, then we might as well throw the constitution and other civil right documents out the window. This country is based on diversity and opportunity. We live today because of those concepts that stands for freedom, justice, liberty, and equality. I've endured my own fair share of racism and bigotry, just like you and everyone else who doesn't meet the criteria of White America. We've seen individuals look at us with disdain in their eyes as they call us nigger, spick, wet-back, chink and kike. Does that mean we have to retaliate with equal hate and brutality? No. But sometimes it may feel good to react on that action." Both men laughed at the concept of satisfaction.

"Do you know why I was picked to be the director of ONI, Chief?" Milson said, No as Cooper continued. "I was appointed because of my qualifications as a "frogman" and submariner in the navy. I was picked to do this job because of my experience, my skills, and my knowledge as an intelligence gatherer and seasoned naval officer. Not because of who I was or what I was. The same reason why I picked you for this assignment. Because you are the best at what you do now, and what you did previously in the army and the CIA. I needed a tough son of a bitch to track, hunt down, and bring back another tough son of a bitch who is cunning and smart as a whip… I understand your feelings of the past, but don't let it control your morality or your ethical sensibility. What Major Hasan did back then was terrible and inexcusable, but don't let that be your crutch to what's morally right and just."

Milson gave a hard, long look at Cooper while considering the words he had just spoke. He hadn't realized until now that his prejudice was overclouding his rationality, his judgment, and his sense of ethics. Thinking about the subject matter at hand and the argument that the admiral so logically made against Milson's own views made him realize that he was wrong and politically incorrect. The bounty hunter, realizing his shortcomings, politely shook

Cooper's hand in apology. Milson not only saw the big picture but also realized the truth of what was important.

As soon as they made amends, Cooper ordered his secretary to tell Dixon to come back into his office. As soon as Dixon entered, Cooper started the briefing about Milson's objective.

"Over the weekend, the FBI picked up some interesting information that you need to know. It will be vital to Assad's capture. Commander Dixon?" Cooper pointed to his subordinate, insinuating he should start out where he had left off, while projecting several pictures of Assad, Kareem, and Gary Brown onto the wide screen. "You're already familiar with the image of Assad, but here are two other individuals whom we believe were his contacts. Unfortunately, they're deceased now. The man in the middle is—"

"Muhammad Kareem! I know him!"

Both Cooper and Dixon were surprised at Milson's eruption.

"Wait a minute. You know this man, Chief?" asked Dixon.

"Yes, sir. Years ago, Kareem was an up-and-coming dealer of heavy arms all around the Arabian Peninsula—Bahrain, Kuwait, Oman, Qatar, Saudi Arabia, Yemen, Iraq, and Jordan, even Syria and Iran. A few years back when I first started with the company, we kept tabs on him for running guns through Pakistan to the Taliban and insurgent fighters. We knew he worked for the Iranians, but we didn't have enough proof and couldn't catch him in the act. At that time, we didn't want to get a hold on him quickly because, at the same time, he was giving us information about al-Qaeda, ISIS, and Taliban leaders to save his own ass."

"You mean he was an informant for the CIA?" asked Cooper.

"Yes, sir, he was—to an extent. He knew we had a substantial amount of information about him and his dealings, including his shipping of weapons to both sides to make a profit for himself, but he couldn't afford for us to blow his cover and cause him to lose his clients' business. If they had found out what he was doing, they would have had him killed. So, he gave us intel about some of the people he dealt with to save himself from prosecution and subsequent federal time. And of course, we agreed not to give him up to the people he was selling weapons to. I'm surprised that Richards didn't tell you this."

"No, he didn't. I'm going to have to have a little chat with him about that," said Cooper, who looked at Dixon with irritation in his eyes. "Well, somebody finally punched Kareem's ticket. I knew it was only a matter of time before he would try to double-cross someone."

"Well, Chief, it looks as if the someone he tried to double-cross was Assad. Kareem was found dead in Assad's apartment last week—actually in an outside dumpster with a broken neck. We believe that he was one of Assad's contacts. The other one was found dead in Miami, Florida. His name is Gary Brown. He was an engineer for a chemical company as well as a contractor for the military. He dealt with military weapons and dabbled in biological weapons. When the police found his body, he had no sort of identification on him. The only way they could identify him was by his fingerprints and dental records. The authorities, including the FBI, searched his house and found a good deal of evidence showing he had dealings with Kareem through emails and phone calls, but Brown's ID was never found. We believe that Kareem killed Brown and took his identification for Assad to use."

"So, you think that Assad disguised himself to look like this Brown guy?"

"Yes," replied Cooper. "He knew sooner or later that we were going to find out about him and put out a BOLO [be on the lookout] for him, plastering his likeness all over the place. We believe he used Brown's identity to escape and leave the country. The FBI, with the help of the Department of Homeland Security and the TSA [Transit Security Agency], produced a log for a flight that left out of LAX. Assad, disguised as Brown, was one of the passengers on that flight. We believe that he traveled from Los Angeles to Hawaii, then probably either to the Philippines or Japan, and next to Saudi Arabia or Lebanon. He will try to deliver the secrets to his contacts in either one of those places, but I know that he will not stay there too long.

He will do his business, get paid by whomever wants the info he stole, and go to live in some secluded place in Southern Europe where he can remain undetected."

"Admiral, I know you have agents in those places. Have they come up with anything on him, or have they found any persons who might resemble him? Even a credit card purchase that he might have made?"

Dixon interjected, "No such luck, Chief. Assad is too smart for that. He wouldn't use one of his credit cards. But he might use Brown's. We do have several agents already positioned in different parts of the South Pacific, namely, Indonesia, Japan, and the Philippines. We have them there for"—he paused—"observational purposes."

"Don't you mean intelligence gathering for the Chinese and insurgent population? Come on, Commander, I know the drill. I know that after the blockade China set up years ago, the United States still wants to see if China is going to try to annex most of those little islands for themselves. But I know that the Micronesian government, along with the governments of Japan and Australia, will never allow that to happen, especially with the UEA looking down their throats."

"You're correct, Chief," replied Cooper. "Since they all signed the charter, no military occupation or facility may be established within their borders unless the Micronesians, the Filipinos, or some other South Pacific government grants them authority to do so. And its use must be for humanitarian purposes. But we have a feeling that Assad has traveled within those areas. If he has, our agents will BOLO him and let us know ASAP."

"So, you want me to go down there and get in contact with your guys to see if they've spotted him?"

"Yes, Chief," Dixon said. "He already knows what our people look like. If they try to capture him, they will only spook him, and he'll either go deeper into hiding or get away. They have strict orders not to apprehend him, just to watch him closely until you arrive.

They will record his movements and give this information to you only, no one else."

Milson gave a nod to both Cooper and Dixon and got up from his chair to get closer to the screen so he could study Assad's image. "Admiral, judging from his movements, he won't be too hard to track down. He knows that we will be looking for him, and you're right, he will be watching every move we make and try to sneak in below the radar. He may be an intelligence officer with high-level skills, training, and operational maneuvers under his belt, but all he's doing is acting like a common fugitive. His tactics are so elementary that the average criminal would be able to teach him a thing or two. I'll find him, sir. The question is, do you want him back alive … or dead?"

Cooper raised his eyebrows in response to the question. "Preferably alive to stand trial for a court-martial and prison time under UCMJ, Chief, and to recover the data and weapons he took. But if he gives you no other choice than to be brought in alive, Mr. Milson, then—"

"I understand, sir. I'll try to bring him back in one piece. All I need from you is a federal license to carry a firearm overseas and within foreign countries. The one I have allows me to carry within the Tri-State Area—Maryland, Virginia, and DC."

"That won't be a problem, Chief," said Dixon. "I took the liberty of looking up your old service record in the CIA database, and I reinstated the international federal license for your gun. You are now permitted to carry it anywhere on any continent, but don't think that you have a license to kill like James Bond. Your actions must be limited strictly to defensive maneuvers, and only if you think that your life is being threatened. I will supply you with the standard firearms you'll need out in the field, as I would for any other agent."

"That won't be necessary, Commander. I have my own tools for the job. I'll take my Beretta 96 FS, my SIG Sauer SP-2340, and my backup, a Glock 22. I'll be well equipped on my own. All I need from you is sufficient telecommunications, mainly a compact satellite phone with a high-powered GPS tracking system and a state-of-the-art cyber encryption interlink chip for counter disruption in case someone's monitoring me or tracking my movements. I will also need a reliable laptop for research and message sending, and to keep you advised of my current location, wherever that may be."

"That's covered as well, Mr. Milson. I will show you downstairs so you can see what you have at your disposal," Dixon said with an inviting tone.

Milson had a gleam in his eye that appeared to suggest he was impressed with the overall cooperation and sincerity of both Cooper and Dixon. He decided he would take advantage of their generous offer. Seeing that the sky was the limit in terms of any requests he might make, he freely asked for some more privileges, then made some inquiries to satisfy his curiosity about some of the finer points that were disclosed on a need-to-know basis only.

"By the way, Admiral, I need to know who I am working for. Since I'm hired as an independent contractor, and since you reinstated my rank and clearance level, am I contracting for the DOD, army intelligence, or the CIA?"

"None of the above. You work for me and SECNAV. Of course, we are all under the Department of Defense, but the jurisdiction I have over you strictly falls under the aegis of the Department of the Navy and ONI."

"So, will I receive a badge showing me to be an intelligence operative or a federal agent?" Milson asked.

"Yes and no, Chief," answered Dixon. "Your initial title will be official and will be made public, but your purposes will be classified and off the books. You will travel as a federal operative under the supervision of the State Department and the Justice Department, but you will not be identified as an intelligence officer even though you work for us. No one must know of your identity or of the fact that you're employed by ONI or DOD. Your status must be kept top secret, and you must seek to maintain plausible deniability. Your identification credentials will show you as a USFAO [United States federal apprehension officer] under the Justice Department and the State Department whose purpose is to locate fugitives who are wanted for felony charges and bring them back to the United States for trial, but they will not show you as an intelligence agent or official. We cannot afford to have someone looking up your status to find that you are employed by the Clandestine Service. That would jeopardize your mission and end our involvement with you."

Hearing all of this, Milson waved his hands in the air. "Okay, okay, so in other words, my cover is as a high-class federal marshal, but with greater leeway and more jurisdiction, better credentials, and more perks. I get it. And I do understand what you're saying. It would jeopardize the current practice of allowing US agents to operate inside the foreign countries named in the Intelligence Identities Protection Act of 2019 and recognized by the UN or the Geneva Convention, and would be in violation of the UEA charter regarding use of surveillance without permission from the governing country. I understand, Commander. This is not my first rodeo. Officially, I work for you. Unofficially, I don't work for you. And if I get caught, you never heard of me; it's my ass that's on the line, not yours. This is all familiar, gentlemen. Remember, who I used to work for, the Clandestine Service"—here he was speaking of the CIA "has the same type of playbook in its library." Under his breath, Milson added, "Some things never change.

"Okay, well, now that that's been settled, let's talk about my fee. What is the going rate for getting this guy, Admiral?"

Cooper pulled out a sheet of paper from his desk drawer and gave it to Milson. "You'll be receiving a lump sum of five hundred thousand dollars from the DOD and the State Department. Two hundred fifty thousand we'll pay you now. We'll pay you the other two fifty when you bring back Assad and the materials he stole."

"Even if I bring him back unresponsive?"

Cooper gazed at Milson with a portentous nod, wondering what his definition of *unresponsive* was, thinking that in this case he meant deceased or unconscious. "Yes, Chief, even in that state. But we prefer him alive, if possible, as I said earlier. We want to throw the book at him after having him stand trial. But it is of great importance that you retrieve the valuables he took. That is priority number one."

Milson had known the answer before he asked the question; he just wanted to be sure that he was clear on the admiral's intentions. He looked at Cooper and began reviewing the documents showing the amount of money he would earn by retrieving Assad. Looking up from the papers, he said, "Begging the admiral's pardon, sir, but that is not enough."

Both Cooper and Dixon stared at Milson in amazement, wanting to hear his explanation for asking for more money.

"Five hundred thousand is not enough, Chief? Well, I would like to hear your perspective on how much is enough." Cooper awaited Milson's response.

"Sir, respectfully, you're talking about me going after a high-profile whiz kid in intelligence who has the killer instincts of a skilled assassin and who has been trained by one of the best Special Forces units in our armed forces, along the lines of Delta Force, the Green Berets, and the Rangers."

Cooper smirked at Milson's remark, knowing the bounty hunter was being sarcastic by reminding him that Milson was loyal to the army, whereas Cooper was loyal to the navy and was a former SEAL.

"And he has classified documents and state-of-the-art weapons in his possession. If these were to get into the wrong hands, it could plunge our government and our allies into another unwanted war. Heck, the bounty for bin Laden was up in the millions until he got caught and killed. Sorry, Admiral, but you must raise the stakes higher than this if you want me to get this guy. I'm going to need a bit more than five hundred. I'm not trying to be greedy or disrespectful. With all due respect, sir, you called me; I didn't call you. You want me because you're afraid that this Commander Assad will be able to pick your guys out of a crowd. He doesn't know me, and he has never seen me. Because of that, sir, I need a little bit more money. Besides, Admiral, I'm damn near risking my life on a gamble here."

Cooper sat back in his chair and folded his arms across his chest as he stared at the young man who, he thought at the time, was egotistical and conceited to have made such remarks, although soon he would realize that the explanation provided was correct and to the point. In response to Milson's demands, the admiral shook his head, but he had some stipulations. "All right, Chief, I'll make you a deal. The offer still stands at two hundred fifty paid to you right now. If you bring back Assad alive—and he must be alive—plus the info and the guns, you'll receive one million dollars tax-free. But if you bring him back dead, the original offer stands, five hundred, no more and no less. Now is that suitable for you, Chief?"

Milson turned around and looked at Assad's picture one more time, then turned back to Cooper. "All right, Admiral. You've got a deal." As Milson stood to shake the director's hand, he said, "It looks like you got yourself a certified bounty hunter."

Cooper was pleased with the outcome. He got up from his chair and reciprocated by giving Milson a hard, gratified handshake. "Good. Now since we've got that cleared up and out of the way, you need to follow Commander Dixon downstairs to the basement area so he can get you tagged into our database. You'll be fingerprinted, photographed, and logged into our files as a covert operative working for ONI. You will not be polygraphed, but you will divulge all personal info about yourself and your next of kin, which will be entered into the database and run through the FBI's background check system. Commander Dixon will also be giving you your gear, identification, passport, and clearance status. As before, your ID will show you as a USFAO agent, if anyone asks, but really, you're a naval operative—sort of. He will also debrief you on Assad's background and personality. You'll be leaving first thing Friday morning around nine o'clock. We've scheduled a commercial flight for you. Dixon will give you your itinerary. You'll meet up with several agents, as I said before, one of ours, meaning from the navy, and one from the CIA. They will give you information about Assad's movements and his whereabouts if he shows up on their radar or if they get lucky enough to catch him. You will also be accompanied by the agents for backup and security purposes, only if you run into trouble. I'm giving you sole authority over this mission, Chief. You are the primary and the supervisor. I will inform my people of your status and title and will make them guarantee me that you will not run into any roadblocks or be subject to any misunderstandings."

Milson assumed that Cooper was finished with his briefing, but then the admiral gave a quick nod and started speaking again. "Oh, there is another stipulation I must add, Chief. SECNAV, under the authority of the president, is giving you seventy-two hours to find Assad and bring him back. If you go over that time limit, an executive order for Special Forces, namely, Navy SEALs or MARSOC [Marine Expeditionary Reconnaissance] units, will be put in effect despite your orders to apprehend the former lieutenant commander."

"Seventy-two hours? That's not enough time to find this guy, let alone figure out where he might be, sir. I need a little more time than that," Milson said.

"Sorry, Chief. That's all the president is allowing you to have. The administration is going up against the UEA and the UN on foreign policy, which involves stipulations on military actions in foreign countries. On that note, they will talk about the very thing that we do not want to do, but if push comes to shove, we will begin military and covert operations within those territories to carry out our agenda. If you don't retrieve Assad within seventy-two hours, then we'll have no choice but to send in Special Forces, before the president goes before the Foreign Council assembly. Oh, there's one other thing you should be aware of. They have also recommended that you be accompanied by both a CIA agent and an NCIS agent to help with the apprehension and arrest of Commander Assad."

Milson made a gesture as if he'd just gotten a crick in his neck in response to what Cooper had just said. He quickly reminded the admiral of his qualifications and his loner persona. "Admiral, with all due respect, sir, I don't need a babysitter or chaperone to do my job. I can get this guy on my own without the help of some snot-nosed rookie or a crusty old veteran agent who's going to be a pain in my ass telling me how to do my job," replied the retired warrant officer.

"I understand what you're saying, Chief. Believe me, I do. I argued my case with the president and the secretary, saying that my guy was capable of handling this on his own. But because this is a national security matter, and because I am outranked in this circumstance, the president wants assurance that you'll have the most competent help and adequate backup you can to find and apprehend Commander Assad. NCIS argued the facts, saying that since Assad is a naval officer and has committed acts of treason against the United States and the Department of Defense, he is basically under their jurisdiction according to the UCMJ and US criminal law. And Director Richards wants one of his men to back you up in case something goes wrong. But I did inform them that you are the primary on this case and that you have authority over all aspects of apprehending this man."

"Well, it looks like I don't have much of a choice then, do I, sir? Will these guys be coming with me, or will I meet them somewhere?"

Cooper again looked over at Dixon, insinuating that he should be the one to answer Milson's question. "They will meet you in Indonesia, as will the other supervisory personnel, one of whom is a naval officer who has been assigned as an NCIS agent under the aegis of the Department of the Navy, part of an exchange program operated by the DOD. He is also one of our liaisons officers."

"Great, a wannabe spy who is a cop and a squid," Milson said, using the derogatory term for navy personnel. "That's perfect. Admiral. I just hope that this guy knows what he is in for and doesn't get in my way. I would hate to bring back another body along with Assad's. What about the other guy? What's his story?"

Dixon answered, "The other individual is a company man with ten years on the job. He's former air force with a service rank of lieutenant colonel. He also served in intelligence in his branch of the service before he was recruited by the CIA."

Cooper caught Milson's expression of disapproval, so he thought to try to reassure him. "I understand your apprehensiveness in the face of these circumstances, but you of all people should know that we cannot take any chances on this. The capture of this man takes precedence over everything else. He must not be allowed to give our information to an enemy combatant; he must be neutralized immediately before such a thing can take place. Any other questions, Chief?" Milson shook his head and submitted to the admiral's orders. "Good. Commander Dixon, help Mr. Milson get squared away with regard to navy protocols and procedures. Oh, and by the way, Chief, welcome aboard." Milson saw a smug look come over Cooper's face just before the admiral smiled.

Milson followed Dixon out the door and into the hallway, where Dixon escorted him to a lower level of the building accessible only to authorized personnel. Meanwhile, Cooper picked up the phone and dialed a strictly confidential number. After waiting a bit, he heard the voice of an operator. In response, he said, "Yes, this is Rear Admiral Wayne Cooper, calling from ONI. I need to have a priority call with SECNAV and SECDEF [that is, Secretary Miller]. Security code: Romeo Alpha Whiskey Juliet Charlie, nine, five, three, one, one, seven, four, two, seven. Status, Tango Sierra [top secret]." The operator took down his message, delivered in the NATO phonetic alphabet, and put the call through.

"Morning, sirs. This is Cooper. Our predator has accepted the hunt. He'll be leaving Friday morning. … Yes, sir, that is correct. We will have backup for him if the prey strays off. He has been ordered to bring him back alive, assisted by other agents and by SF if necessary. … Yes, sir. We will monitor him at the MICROSCOPE facility in Langley—that's if he gets a feed on the target. … Yes, sir, I'm aware of the acronym and what it means. … I will inform Director Richards about this, sir. … Yes, sir. <u>Operation Executive Bounty</u> is under way. … Yes, sir. I'm sure that the president will be pleased that the mission is under way. … Will do, sir. Thank you. And good day, sirs."

Cooper hung up the phone and sat back in his chair. With ease, he swiveled around to look out his office window, where he gazed upon the distinctive landscaping surrounding the ONI building and began to think about the decision he had just made.

ONI, Ground Level, Strategic Defense Command Center

"So, Commander, if you don't mind me asking, what's the story on you and Commander Assad? Were y'all like best friends or something?"

Milson and Dixon made it to the basement level of the building. There was nothing to make it seem like a top-secret facility, such as special connecting rooms or enigmatic hallways. Instead, it was a large, brightly lit area, all white, filled with different clusters of people working on projects. In short, it was just a large room full of computer analysts and high-tech brainiacs or nerds working on specs, figures, calculations, and formulas, typing away on conventional laptops and holographic desktop computers with sophisticated instrument boards.

Before responding to Milson's question, Dixon took a moment to verbally enter his pass code and submit to a retina scan so he could gain access to the computer's security panel. Then it was time to answer.

"Yes, Mr. Milson, you can say that. We were friends. For three years, to be exact. I met him when he first came here to ONI. He was assigned to my division under my department. I've never had a bad word to say about him until now."

"What do you think would have made him do this? Did he ever talk to you about any kind of grievance he had towards the government or the country? Did he discuss with you any troubles he had, or past financial problems? Was someone threatening him or his family?" Milson asked.

"No, Chief, that's the thing. Ad-dam never had any trouble like that at all. He never complained about anything or anyone, not to me or anybody else I know. He was content and comfortable here. He was always the first one to get here in the morning and the last one to leave at night. He was proficient at his job and always did things by the book. Smart as a fox and just as clever as one. That's why I can't understand why he would do something like this. Within the next couple of months, he was going to be promoted to commander—full-grade status—and take over my job as senior analyst of counterintelligence. I, on the other hand was going to be transferred to the Pentagon and take over as assistant director of NECC [Naval Expeditionary Combat Command], working under the deputy or vice chief of naval operations. But that has to be put on the back burner since Ad-dam did this, and now my career goals are on hold because my services are needed here until we get him. But having to put my promotion and transfer to the side really doesn't bother me. The fact that Assad used us and betrayed my trust and his country—that's what bothers me. I hope wherever he is, he's enjoying himself and the money that he's being paid for to turn traitor… If you find him, Chief, give him my regards, and send him a little message from me." Dixon leaned over and whispered something in Milson's ear, obviously not wanting anyone else to hear. Milson drew back in surprise after having heard what Dixon related to him, also giving the disappointed commander a look of suspicion and curiosity due to what he conveyed to him. Dixon acknowledged the look and continued their conversation. As they continued their conversation, a petite and very attractive young woman walked up on Dixon's left side and interrupted both gentlemen.

"Excuse me, sir. Sorry to bother you, but here are the midmorning intelligence summary reports from the analysis department upstairs—"

Milson immediately took notice of her. She was very cute and young, in her mid-twenties. Her hair was an auburn color, pinned back in a bun due to regulations within the military. Her rectangular-framed glasses were sitting on the bridge of her nose, making her appear to be an intellect but also sassy. A pretty face with pinup cheekbones that made her look innocent and pure. Her physique was thin but very athletic and well balanced for her build. She was a looker to the opposite sex and Milson recognized it. He also saw something else: He notice right through her innocent, calm, geeky exterior lie dormant a naughty, promiscuous party girl with a hint of a nymphomaniac on the side. But that was just Milson's opinion. He could see that she was very needy and subservient in every way. Willing to please her superiors at every opportunity that was convenient to her cause and purpose. In light of all this, Milson being the trained observer that he was saw this in the way that most people would not recognize or care about at all. As he continued to observe the young lady's behavior, she persisted in jumping in while they were still engaged over Assad.

"Sir, here are the reports you wanted earlier on Commander Assad." Milson was attracted to her. But being wise and subtle in his compromising age, he showed no infatuation or desire towards her. And on that note, he was comfortable with that feeling. But he did notice the attraction she had towards Dixon. It almost seems as if she was making any excuse to get close to him at every opportunity she had. Not to say that Milson was an expert on how women behave or acted around men, but he was aware of the subtle things that women do when they are trying to get the attention or impress a man that they are attracted to. Milson knew this and snickered quietly to himself over the process without being noticed by either side. Afterwards, his train of thoughts began to concentrate on what was more serious and important. He caught several words of what the young officer was relaying to Dixon about the report and its continuity.

"They narrowed it down to several places where Commander Assad might have gone to."

"Thank you, Lieutenant," Dixon said as he glanced over the sheets of paper. Realizing that Killian was next to him, he promptly introduced them to one another without showing eye contact to either of them. "Oh, by the way. Mr. Milson, meet Lieutenant-junior grade Katherine Polanski. She's one of our junior engineers in encryption software and data mechanics. She will also be in charge of manufacturing your service identity. Lieutenant, this is Chief Warrant Officer Killian Milson, formally reinstated as an army CW2. You will run him through our database and classify him as 'Poppa Delta'—standing for 'plausible deniability'—for covert ops and retrieval missions. He is to be given classified materials and the highest-level top-secret clearance. Officially, he is working as a federal apprehension agent for the Justice Department and the State Department. Unofficially, he works for no intelligence agency but us. Understood?"

The vibrant officer replied with a solid "Yes, sir!" asking no questions afterward.

"If you would follow me this way, Mr. Milson, I will put you in the system and get you up to speed, sir." Milson watched Lieutenant Polanski step in front of him. She led him to a computer from which she would soon download identification documents and background information that will support his covert identity. Milson couldn't help but notice that when she walked, she shimmied a bit. The swaying of her hips suggesting pure sexuality and sultriness. He found it quite flattering and cute, but otherwise he did not think too much about it. He knew that the lieutenant was not doing it on purpose to attract his eye. He figured she probably had never even noticed how alluring or charming her walk was, especially to those of the opposite sex. She was probably as innocent as an adorable child with an angelic appearance plastered on a proverbial billboard. Milson saw how conservative and serious she was, especially when it came to her job. He assumed this because of the position she held and the responsibilities that went along with it. In any event, the whole time she'd been with him, she seemed to be suppressing her excitement and energy over current events. In other words, Milson saw in her a young woman who kept her sex life private—for the bedroom only. He figured her to be someone who acted like a lady in public but a sexual predator in private. As he kept his eyes fixed on her posterior, which was very round and tight, she introduced the components of his covert ruse.

"Let's get started, Mr. Milson. I will need your fingerprints, social security card, credit and debit cards, and any photo IDs you may have in your possession. I will also need to take several pictures of you to put in our database. A photo will also go on your new credentials. And we need a retina scan and dental X-rays, which will be used to identify you in case—"

"In case I'm captured or show up dead. I know the routine, Lieutenant. It's all familiar to me. Reminds me of my rookie days back at the Farm." Polanski gave Milson a strange look. She did not have a clue what he was talking about, and he noticed it immediately.

"The Farm, Lieutenant? Camp Peary in York County? Williamsburg, Virginia? The facility where they teach new recruits how to be CIA operatives and officers? The place where you learn how to be a spy?"

"I'm sorry, sir. I've never heard it called that before."

Milson shook his head in pity of Polanski's lack of knowledge and naive ignorance. She wasn't up to speed with what was going on in the intelligence community, but Milson paid it no mind as he continued to stare at her. Noting on her innocence and wholesomeness, he took advantage of her sincerity and simplicity while at the same time extracting the necessary info for the charismatic bounty hunter. In the meantime, he entertained himself by thinking about her last name as she took his fingerprints and gathered up his other belongings to be uploaded into the ONI and Department of Navy database.

"Your name, Polanski. Is it Polish or Lithuanian?"

"Both, sir. My father's side is Polish; my mother's side is Lithuanian. My great-great-grandfather emigrated from Poland to the United States."

Milson, his memory having been jolted, snapped his fingers.

"Wait a minute. You wouldn't happen to be related to—"

She stopped him in midsentence, knowing what he was about to say.

"No, sir, I am not. A lot of people have asked me if I'm related to him, but I assure you that that's not the case. Now that I'm finished with your fingerprints, would you stand right here in the center of the floor so I can get your picture?" Milson obliged the lieutenant's request and stood in the middle of the floor. There was a solid white wall for the background. He smiled at her as she operated the camera, centering Milson's features within the frame. Polanski, noticing the charming grin he gave her for his photograph, reciprocated with a smile of her own.

"You have a handsome smile, Mr. Milson. I'll bet your wife adores it."

Milson chuckled softly to himself, recognizing the ploy Polanski had used to try to satisfy her own curiosity.

"Well, thank you, Lieutenant, but I am not married. Girlfriend, yes. Wife, no."

"Lucky woman," Polanski said, staring at Milson, smiling sensually in such a way that it could only be interpreted as an invitation be seduced, while still occupied with uploading information about his new identity and background into the system.

Star City Hotel and Casino, Sydney, Australia

It was Sunday, October 14, at 6:59 a.m., at a luxurious hotel in downtown Sydney, Australia, overlooking the famous Sydney Harbor Bridge, which connects the mainland business district of Sydney to the North Shore. The hotel was on the outskirts of the city. Assad was standing in his room on the sixteenth floor, looking out the sliding-glass door. Holding a glass of red wine, dressed in nothing but black boxer shorts, and looking intensely out over the horizon as the sun rose over the beachfront area, he thought about the landscape design and what beautiful scenery it was. Content and comfortable in his surroundings while looking across the harbor, he was distracted by some strange noises coming from his king-size bed. He turned his head slightly to the right, not giving too much thought to the sounds themselves, as a wicked smirk spread across his face. What he was hearing were the soft moans of a woman. She was an extraordinarily beautiful woman who happened to be naked at the moment, with only a single sheet covering her body. She was lying on her stomach with her legs and arms stretched out, her blonde hair in a frenzy, covering half her face as it lay across the pillow. This was the same woman Assad had met on the plane from Los Angeles to Hawaii. She was currently in Australia on business, her area being real estate and construction projects in exotic vacation spots such as islands. The project she was working on in Australia involved the construction of upscale housing developments.

Assad gazed at the woman's splendid silhouette; the sheets fitted her form, showcasing her sexy physique as she lay in a seductive pose. He took one more sip of the wine and then set the glass down on the table next to the wide-open glass door that he'd been looking out of earlier. The door opened to a midsized balcony overlooking the harbor. As he was about to slip back into bed and invite his lovely companion to another round of passionate, unbridled sex, an unexpected beep came from a laptop that was sitting on the same table he had put his wineglass on. He'd purchased the laptop in Los Angeles prior to his departure, leaving his other one in his office at ONI.

Responding to the annoying chime, Assad turned around and flipped open the screen. The monitor flashed and booted to a screen saver with the image of a lion and a sea snake circling a pyramid with a hawk or some other bird of prey hovering atop it. Assad knew what it was. Immediately he started typing. Entering a series of codes so he could mask his trail and prevent both his emails from being traced and his location from being discovered, he checked his email inbox and saw a message with a live feed. He clicked on the URL to see the image of a person whose face was darkened out in the middle with only the outer portions of his facial features visible. Assad perceived him to be a distinguished gentleman with a conservative hairstyle that made him look politically involved and powerful. Assad switched on his visual link, also turning on his audio. He lowered the volume so the conversation he was about to have would be heard by him and him alone.

"Good morning, Mr. Assad," the mysterious figured said, his accent sounding like a combination of British and Arabian, "I see that certain things have gone well for you since last we communicated."

"Yes, they have. I managed to upload two-thirds of the data to your organization's database, as well as information on half our undercover operatives still in the Middle East."

"Does that include Israel, Turkey, Jordan, and the United Arab Emirates?"

"Of course. DOD, NSA, and the CIA have records of all foreign intelligence operatives, including manifests indicating where these agents are located 24/7, along with the reasons for they are stationed where they are."

"Good, Mr. Assad. This information will be vital to the organization and will help us strengthen our defenses against the Americans and their partners. When will we get the rest of the data and the weapons you promised?"

"As I told you before, you will receive the rest of it when I get to Saudi Arabia, at which time I expect the remainder of the money you promised me."

"Yes, yes, of course. That is a reasonable request. I would like to apologize for Mr. Kareem's having misled you. He was a valued associate of ours, but I knew that his lust for money and recognition would lead to his downfall. It is unfortunate that you had to kill him. We had other plans for Muhammad. He could've provided us services that would have benefited us in the long run, until we decided that he had outlived his usefulness."

"Well, I'm sorry it had to come to that. If he hadn't tried to double-cross me in the first place, none of this would've happened."

"Yes, I know, Mr. Assad. Maybe you could fill his shoes and serve as one of our agents. Your expertise and knowledge would be a great asset to this organization. I hope you will consider our offer." Assad said nothing. He just kept staring at the monitor as the figure continued the conversation. "I understand that you're having difficulty keeping up appearances."

Assad was hesitant to answer because he didn't want to disturb his female guest, who was still in the bed, supposedly asleep. "The Americans have issued a BOLO on me and are circulating my photograph. I can't be using my current disguise much longer. The authorities have already discovered the body of Gary Brown and have come to the conclusion that I have taken his place. I will have to come up with a new identity very soon if I am to leave Australia and enter either Kuwait or Saudi Arabia without being exposed. I have to hack into the hotel's computer files and submit a false ID to register so I can get out of here clean and safe."

"No need to worry about that, my friend. We have generated a new identity for you and have sent your room reservation to the hotel's computer for authorization. In fact, I am sending the information to you as we speak. Do you have a portable printer by your side?"

Assad jumped up from the table to go to the other side of the room. He pulled out one of his duffel bags that had one of the guns inside it. It was no coincidence that he had chosen to bring a portable copier/printer that he had picked up at the same time he'd purchased his laptop. He connected the printer to the port in his laptop, plugged the power cord into an outlet, and went into his email. There he saw that this individual had sent him a photograph and a packet of background information on his new identity, to replace his current one. "That is your new identification, Mr. Assad. You will take the role of a businessman on his way from Australia to Egypt, dealing in rare coins from the Far East. In fact, this gentleman happens to occupy the same hotel room as you. His identity will be permanent cover for you—a very discreet and unnoticeable person."

"A coin collector? That's the best y'all could come up with?" Assad said in a mocking tone.

"Mr. Assad, remember that you must keep a very low profile. This way, you will not raise anyone's suspicions or draw any attention to yourself. As you pointed out earlier, the Americans are looking for you."

Assad looked at the picture again as it printed out. He studied the facial features and the background of the individual he was to turn himself into. He nodded slightly at the photograph as if agreeing to take on this identity. "Okay, I suppose that this is satisfactory. I'm leaving later this week, say, Wednesday or Thursday. That will give me enough time to study my new identity and capture its essence. I will be in Saudi by next Sunday. First, I will have a stopover in India, and then I'll go on to Kuwait. I should arrive there no later than Sunday evening."

"That will be good, Mr. Assad. We look forward to meeting with you. Enjoy the rest of your day with your lovely companion, whom I hear in the background."

Astonished that this man had taken notice of the woman lying in the bed, Assad turned around and saw the fair-haired beauty staring back at him with her dark blue eyes and a gratified smile that made it obvious to him that she'd been awake the whole time he was talking to his contact on the computer.

"Gary, baby"—she stretched across the bed, still lying in a compromising position, and yawned softly—"who were you talking to?" Becoming acutely aware of her presence, he quickly turned off the laptop, took the printout from the printer, and put it in his briefcase, which was next to the copier. He stood up from the chair and went over to the bed with the intention of lying next to her.

"Nothing of importance, Charlene. It was one of my clients in Egypt wondering when I will next be in town."

"Oh," said the voluptuous vixen, who wrapped her arms around Assad's neck and pulled him close, planting several kisses on his face. "Because I could have sworn that he kept calling you 'Assad.'"

“No, Charlene, you were just hearing things. Remember, you had a lot to drink last night.”

“I know. That’s when you took advantage of me and got me back here to your room, so you could have your way with me, you handsome bastard. You’re lucky that you’re so good-looking and charming. I never sleep with anyone I’ve just met, especially a man on a business trip.”

Assad gave a slight smile to the woman who was clutching him hard.

“Well, since both of us are up, may I suggest that we get dressed and prepare to have breakfast downstairs? I heard the morning menu in this place is magnificent.”

Assad kissed her on the lips once and got up, maneuvering his body across the bed so he could get out on the other side. As he was about to head toward the bathroom to clean himself up, the woman who had identified herself as Charlene stopped him.

“Gary, sweetheart, we don’t have to get ready right now, do we? In fact, I already have your breakfast ready in bed for you.”

She flung the sheets off, exposing her naked body, a proposition to Assad to come back to bed for another sexual escapade. Pleased by what he was seeing, and also aroused, Assad, with no hesitation or second thoughts, accepted the invitation by slipping off his boxers and sliding into bed. He positioned himself on top of her and they had sex, which was pleasurable and satisfying for both of them.

CHAPTER 4

THE HUNT BEGINS

Soekarno–Hatta International Airport, Jakarta, Indonesia

At 5:25 p.m. on October 15, a chartered Lockheed Martin QSST was arriving at the Soekarno–Hatta Airport in the capital city of Jakarta in Indonesia. It made its touchdown at 5:27 p.m. and came to a stop at its terminal at 5:30 p.m. Standing within the waiting area were several men dressed in casual civilian clothing. From the looks of them, they were either military or CIA, which was obvious in the way they stood and carried themselves. They both stood silently and alone, observing the plane as the Jet Way attached itself to the doorway once the airplane had come to a complete stop. Airport personnel were opening the doors and offering assistance to the small number of people exiting the plane. Several couples with their children came out first, followed an elderly couple who looked as if they were celebrating their anniversary. Next to appear was a pair of college students who looked to be on a field trip or just vacationing. Last to emerge was Killian Milson, with a small carry-on hanging down to his side from the shoulder harness. The two men spotted

Milson and approached him casually. Milson saw them coming from the corner of his eye, but he made no moves to acknowledge them because he knew exactly who they were.

"Chief Milson?" asked the first gentleman.

"Welcome to Indonesia. I'm Lieutenant Commander Michael True of naval intelligence. I'm the US naval liaisons officer and attaché to the Indonesian Navy and their government." He showed his credentials to Milson before introducing the person next to him.

"And this is Operations Officer James Weaver, with the Special Activities Division of the CIA. We're here to take you to the US Embassy first, then to the Jakarta HQ naval base for debriefing."

Milson's attitude toward the agents was one of nonchalance. He perceived them to be rude and belligerent, so much so that he chose to ignore them and concentrate on his own well-being. At first, he looked at both men with contempt, but then he paid them no mind as he continued to gather himself together after he'd spent fifteen hours on an airplane. He nodded at them in response to the introductions and gestured to each to lead the way to the nearby carousel to retrieve his luggage.

Commander True, a tall man with an average build, was casual and relaxed, which meant he had a sense of ease about him. True took out some papers from his coat pocket and tried to give them to Milson. Weaver was another story. He was of average build with a slight bulge around his midsection, not your typical clean-cut US-bred CIA operative. Quite the opposite. He was of medium height with an ordinary look as if he were someone's middle-aged father who'd just fallen off the wagon in terms of drinking. His posture was slouched, which made him appear loose and carefree, like someone who didn't accept criticism or carelessness from anyone. Weaver looked almost sloppy, with a tiny hint of neatness to him. His hairstyle was not up to standards, but neither was it shaggy or mismanaged. To Milson, this was not the usual appearance of a CIA agent/officer. In the days he'd served as a field agent, he had fit and athletic associates who appeared to be endowed with professionalism, confidence, and sturdiness. Weaver's look was opposite this, nothing like what Milson remembered. But as Milson took a closer look at Weaver, he realized that this was his original contact whom Cooper and Dixon told him about. Milson was definitely not impressed.

While a judgmental Milson was sizing Weaver up, True began giving Milson some important information.

"Here's the dossier on Commander Assad's activities. We got it from our neighbors at Interpol. We did a dragnet around specific areas within the South Pacific. We think that he might be in one of several spots: Indonesia, Japan, or Australia. We can't confirm anything since we don't have agents or operatives at those sites, but Interpol and some of the foreign intelligence groups we partner with have been very cooperative, helping us to determine Assad's whereabouts. Reports says that he is likely in Australia, but we can't be sure."

Milson looked at the papers for himself as they continued to walk down the crowded airport walkway.

"You haven't told Interpol what Assad is suspected of, have you?"

Weaver, who maneuvered over to Milson's left side, answered first.

"No, Chief. The DCI and the director of ONI gave us strict orders not to divulge any information about Commander Assad, including his intentional crime. They don't want the international community or the world to know that we have a rogue US naval officer on the loose with vital military secrets in his possession ready to be sold on the black market. All that Interpol knows, and what *we* want them to know, is that the commander is wanted for murder in the States."

Milson nodded his head in agreement.

"Has he used any credit cards within the past couple of days around certain areas? Has he done anything unusual that might fit into his MO?"

"No, Chief Milson," said Officer Weaver, "but interestingly there has been a large amount of cash purchases around several high-class, very expensive hotels and restaurants, including here in the capital city, Sydney, Australia and Tokyo, Japan."

"So, what does that have to do with anything? Probably some rich high rollers on a spending spree, trying to impress their girlfriends or wives. What does that prove?" said Milson as his remarks came off a bit abrasive to Weaver.

"That may be, Mr. Milson, but my sources from Interpol say that they have files on all the wealthiest people in the region of the Pacific and Indian Oceans. The richest people on this side of the globe, who are either American or Northern European don't spend large amounts of cash loosely. If Assad is in this area, he's not going to be using credit or debit cards, as that might give him away. He's going to be using cash only, especially since he knows we're monitoring all financial transactions and looking for him."

Milson agreed with Weaver's conclusion as it made sense. Assad was not going to try to use his own credit cards or those of Gary Brown to make himself obvious to local or governmental authorities. Cash transactions are untraceable; therefore, using cash is less likely to get him flagged, unless he were to use it as part of a bribery scheme or counterfeit operation. But cash is reliable to make certain purchases, such as luxury goods, hotel stays, and automobile rentals.

As Weaver and True continued to talk secretly about Assad and where he might be, they managed to pick up Milson's one and only piece of luggage from the baggage carousel. Afterwards all three headed out the glass doors of the airport lobby into the outside parking lot. A gray sports utility vehicle was waiting for them at a pickup area. Milson got in the rear seat on the passenger's side. True took shotgun, and Weaver sat opposite of Milson.

Milson took notice of the driver immediately. To his surprise, the individual looked like an adolescent from behind, about seventeen to eighteen years of age, straight from high school or college. From Milson's perceptive, he was probably an enlisted sailor or marine obligated to undergo meaningless duties from superior officers and top brass. Reminding Milson from his experience and days as a young enlistee in the army, but given this young man's apparel and the fact that he was not in uniform, gave him more of an enigma to be questioned. Meanwhile,

True turned around in his seat to further his conversation with Milson.

"Chief, I know Admiral Cooper said that you would have an ONI field agent on this case working with you to get Assad. I would like you to meet Ensign James R. Sheppard. He works for us but is a liaisons officer for NCIS. He's one of ours but his temporary credentials, as well as his cover, shows him to be an agent."

Milson just stared at this baby-faced, adolescent-looking young man with disdain. Regarding him as worthless and unexperienced.

"*You've got to be kidding me! This guy is working under cover and is an agent? He's a freaking baby, for Christ's sake! Fresh out of high school or college from the looks of him!*" thought Milson as he shook his head in disbelief, an expression of "unbelievable" written across his face. "*It seems that the name James is very popular among certain individuals who are currently occupying this vehicle.*" Milson thought. Both the CIA operative and the young officer were named James. To Milson, it was kind of humorous. But to eliminate any confusion when identifying them, Milson decided just to call them by their last names. This would make things easier for both them and him.

The young ensign, who was the driver, turned around and gave Milson a heartfelt look.

"Pleased to meet you, sir. I'm looking forward in working with you on this case." He stretched out his hand to give Milson a handshake, but all he got in return from the former CID/ CIA officer was an empty expression and a nonchalant attitude that dismissed his gesture. Even though Sheppard was young and a bit naive, he recognized the salty exterior and coldhearted response of the age-old, seasoned veteran, who apparently disregarded him altogether. He did not take Milson's apprehensiveness personally; instead, he saw it as a clear message regarding how the young man should conduct himself around the hardened, callous bounty hunter. He chalked it up as a learning experience for now.

Coming to realize that Milson was not going to reciprocate the handshake, Sheppard turned around and continued to drive the deluxe-sized vehicle that he had signed out from the navy's motor pool. While speeding off from the airport's auto terminal and driving along a busy scenic route, Milson took another glance at the field reports on Assad's possible location that True had given him earlier.

"Commander, are you sure about these locations where Assad might to be?"

"No," said True.

"The intelligence from our Interpol friends has led us to conclude that if Commander Assad has gone rogue, he will most likely be in one of the areas I showed you, especially if his flight left out of Hawaii. The best guess is that he might be in one of these three places: Japan, New Guinea, or Australia."

Weaver interjected,

"CIA and the NSA think that he might have gone straight to Korea or the Middle East to negotiate the terms of his exile. But personally, I think he's taking a vacation or making a rest stop in one of those areas; preferably Australia. Hoping to lie low for a while before giving the goods to his contacts."

"Yeah, you might be right, Weaver," Milson replied.

"From my experience tracking down fugitives who want to keep themselves hidden from the public eye, especially if they know they're wanted by the law or they have a heavy bounty on their heads, they usually keep themselves secluded in faraway places where no one will discover their whereabouts or be able to easily identify them. At the same time, though, they can be creatures of habit. Wanting to be in comfortable and familiar surroundings that fit their personality. Sometimes they may have some kind of security net to keep them safe. Establishing a temporary dwelling spot until the time is right for them to start running again or have another safe haven some place. In other words, many of them have a well-laid plan before making their escape later. From the looks of it, Assad might be in Australia... Commander, take me straight to your TOC [Tactical Operations Center, or Ops Center]. I want to get an idea of where Assad's tracks are leading before his trail gets too cold."

Hearing this, True had to remind Milson of his stopover at the embassy to register, which was required of all foreign nationals arriving in the country on government business or government visa, especially if working for an intelligence agency like the CIA. But Milson did not want to hear that. In his unique way, he dismissed True's suggestion and came up with his own point view of argument.

"I don't have time for that, Commander. I need to get on this case ASAP, before Assad goes deeper. It is pointless for me to register with the local authorities and reveal my identity when I'm only going to be staying temporarily. I need to get started on tracking down Assad, before our window of opportunity to catch him closes. Besides, I'm here unofficially. This is a top-secret mission; our government wants no one to know about this. So, obviously it would be best if I didn't announce my presence here. I don't have time to play international bureaucracy games of accountability to a country that shouldn't be aware of my existence in the first place. I have a thief, murderer, and a spy to catch, Commander. I don't have time for this."

"I understand, Chief, but you have to realize that the US government, along with everyone else under the UEA act, has to go along with the new rules and regulations recommending that all foreign nationals representing their country's government must register as dignitaries of the foreign country they visit. This applies to the country we're residing right now. That goes for me, Officer Weaver, Ensign Sheppard, and all US servicemen that are deployed over here."

Stubborn and noncompliant, Milson was dismissive of the commander's remarks. Weaver, despite Milson's argumentativeness, cut into the conversation between the two, siding with the contract bounty hunter.

"Wait a minute, Mike. Milson may have a point. He's not obligated like you and I, who have orders to be here or have established permanent duty stations by orders of the State or Defense Department. His credentials show him to be a federal apprehensions officer on the hunt for a suspected criminal wanted by the United States. He is not legally obligated to register with the embassy because he has not been ordered to come here and does not fit the criteria for being a military consultant. What he appears to be is a federal law enforcement cop looking for a fugitive—nothing more, nothing less. The Indonesians do not need to know his reasons for being here or even his presence. To be honest, Mr. Milson has never set foot on Indonesian soil. In fact, Milson doesn't exist at all. To tell you the truth, Commander, I have never seen or heard of a man named Killian Milson. Have you?"

Milson and True looked at Weaver strangely, knowing what he was getting at. The commander turned back around in his seat, facing forward with a look of distaste and frustration on his face.

"You goddamn CIA guys. You and your cloak-and-dagger bullshit. Always wanting to pull the plausible deniability card out of your asses and throw it in someone's face. Especially if it'll help you achieve your own objectives and goals. All right, Jim, you win." Said True as he spoke loudly.

A wicked smirk broke out on Weaver's face, making him look both diabolical and satisfied. Milson just stared at the cunning yet clever agent with curiosity and caution. He did not know what to make of Weaver since he'd just met him. But he knew from his experience as a former spook not to let his guard down or trust anyone, especially a fellow company man.

Milson sat back in his seat and observed the scenery as the car passed by. Weaver said,

"Ensign Sheppard, or should I say Agent Sheppard, let's go ahead and take Mr. Milson to the naval yard."

"Yes, sir," said Sheppard, who accelerated in passing some of the ongoing traffic that was delaying their progress.

Star City Hotel and Casino, Sydney, Australia

It was Wednesday afternoon around one o'clock. In Assad's hotel room, Charlene was getting herself ready to leave to catch her flight to Tokyo, Japan, which was scheduled to leave that evening. Her and Assad's meeting had been only temporary since she had business obligations to attend to immediately. Specifically, she had a meeting with several executives in Tokyo about constructing hotels and business offices. She had to leave by seven o'clock to make her meeting with the executives early the next morning. She was alone, without the company of Assad, who was downstairs in the hotel lobby planning for his last stay before leaving for Saudi Arabia Thursday or Friday morning. He knew Charlene had to leave, so at the last minute, he arranged a little dinner. Little did he know that after a few hours of her being alone in his room, she would discover the truth about himself and his purpose.

As Charlene was putting the final touches on her makeup in the bathroom and looking for her other cosmetics, she heard several beeps coming from the center of the room. She thought it was her cell phone in her purse, which was over by the bed, but really it was Assad's laptop, which was sitting on a table unsecured. Hearing it chime a few times, she was apprehensive about going to check what the laptop was doing. Once the beeping had become a nuisance to her, she went over to the table to either shut off the computer or do whatever it asked so it would stop bothering her. As she opened the top side of the computer, she noticed that there was a notification of a new email message. Charlene did not want to pry into Assad's personal business, but her curiosity got the better of her. She pulled up his email account and looked at the message. It had been sent by the Alliance of Allah, and the message was encrypted.

Charlene moved the cursor and typed the address into the search engine. As the computer made the connection, a message emerged on the screen that shocked Charlene to the point of forcing her down onto the chair under her. With fright and horror, she read the message:

> We have most of the information you sent to us from the US Defense Department downloaded, but we are having trouble saving it to our database. It is encrypted in such a way that makes the downloading difficult. We need the original documents and the other data that you have on the two flash drives if we are to be successful in transferring this material to our systems. It is a shame that you were double-crossed and had to end Muhammad's life in order to bring us this information. As I said before, we do understand your reasons for making the decisions you made. We are not in the business of backing individuals who act on their own, as this is not good for the organization. That way of thinking is poisonous to our morale and antithetical to our objectives, beliefs, and goals. As stated before, we are looking forward to receiving the weapons you took from the American armory. We also look forward to benefiting from the knowledge and experience you've gained from being a skilled naval intelligence officer. This will be very useful when you join our private military force. We have already started planning attacks in several regions of the western world legitimized by the UN and UEA. The information you give us will interrupt peacekeeping missions in several Islamic countries that want to align themselves with the Americans and their allies. Once they realize that they've been deceived by the West and misled by its influence, they will retaliate against the Americans and anyone aligned with them. September 11 will be nothing compared to the damage and destruction we will inflict upon the West if they continue to ignore us and our cause. The world will soon know of our existence and will become aware of a new world order, one more powerful than any currently in existence on earth. And the old governments, such as that of the United States,

> the United Kingdom, Russia, China, and Israel, will be wiped out if they still refuse to repent and enter into a true alliance with God.
>
> We will see you soon, Ad-dam. Assalamu alaikum, my brother-in-arms, and to the organization to which we pledge allegiance.
>
> Oh, there is one more task you need to perform for us. You must fix an unpleasant problem that currently exists among us. We have found out that a certain individual has been embezzling money from us. The organization will not allow for this to go unpunished. When you see him, please be sure to terminate his contract. We know you have the means and the expertise to do this. Once again, assalamu alaikum, our brother-in-arms.

Charlene did not know what to make of this. She was beside herself with panic and fear, feeling as if she'd been slapped in the face for having assumed that the man, she'd been having a cordial affair with over the past couple of days was not who he had said he was. As terrified as she was, she pushed herself away from the table, knocking over the chair she'd been sitting in, and stood in the middle of the room feeling anxious and confused. Filled with disbelief and anxiety, she spun around the room in a daze, as if trying to make up her mind quickly about what to do next. She ran back to the bathroom to retrieve the rest of her belongings, with the intention of making a hasty escape before Assad returned.

After Charlene had grabbed her purse and several other things that she had left in Assad's room, she frantically pulled out her cell phone to make an urgent call to the airport to book a ticket so she could leave Australia right away. Frightened and terrified, she found she was scrambling her words as she tried to talk into the device. About to head for the door, still distraught over what she had discovered, and waiting for her phone to make a connection, she looked down and noticed Assad's black duffel bag sitting near the closet. Knowing full well the consequences of her actions and what was at stake if she prolonged her stay any longer, she quickly walked over to the bag. Filled with both curiosity and fear, she lifted up the flaps and looked inside. At first, she saw nothing but clothing—shirts, pants, and underwear—and a few hygienic products. But as she dug deeper, she discovered something else: the weapons that were mentioned in the message she had just read. Two of the four rifles were hidden under the clothing. The other two, which Charlene did not know about, were out of sight in the closet. She was instantly petrified. Rising up from her kneeling position with a sudden burst, she ran straight for the door without breaking her stride. When she turned the brass handle to open the door, a surprising shock came over her as she literally ran into Assad, who was standing directly in front of the door on the other side. Surprised by his presence, Charlene tried to act normally. But given the outrageous information she just read on his computer, she found it very difficult to remain composed. She quickly put her cell phone aside to hide it from Assad.

"Ah, Charlene, sweetheart. I'm glad I caught you. I want to talk to you about this evening before you catch your flight. I made dinner arrangements for tonight before you leave."

Terrified, Charlene just stared at Assad in horror. He was standing right over her. Finding it difficult to respond, she did manage to say, "Uh, wow! Great! That's wonderful. But I just remembered that I must show up an hour earlier to register at the gate. So, I can't make it, Gary. Sorry about that. Let's try to do it when we run into each other next, okay?" Nervous and eager to get out of the room and away from Assad, Charlene tried to make her way out, but Assad closed the door behind him while staring at her in a cold, malicious way. Charlene began to tremble in fright. Seeing that her hands were shaking, she tried to hide behind her back. But it was obvious to Assad what was going on. And it was obvious to Charlene what was about to happen.

"What's wrong, Charlene? You look nervous and tense. Is something the matter?" asked the former naval officer, who pretended to be concerned and understanding although he was really diabolical.

Jittery and trembling with fear, Charlene tried to hide her emotions from Assad and his piercing stare, but it was all to no avail; her distress and anxiety gave her away. She tried another excuse, hoping to fool the traitor who was acting as if he were concerned.

"Ah, no. Well, yes. I just looked at my email and found out that my boss has finally made it to Japan. He wants to see me right away with one of our clients who wants to finalize the construction plans and set a start date for the building project. He wants me over there to start the negotiations and begin building. So, I'm sorry, Gary, but I must leave right away. I'll take a rain check for later, when you're back in the States, all right?" As Charlene moved quickly, trying to make her way to the door, Assad stopped her again, blocking her escape.

"Wait, Charlene. You told me two days ago that your boss isn't arriving in Japan until the day after tomorrow, remember?"

Flustered by Assad's keen memory, Charlene tried another thing to worm her way out of the situation, wanting to get safely out of the room so she could notify the local authorities of what she had found on Assad's computer. Little did she know that Assad was way ahead of her.

"Yes, that's right. But he said in the email he just sent that it is now urgent and I should get there ASAP. So, I have no choice. I have to leave now." Frantic, but trying her best to get to the door, Charlene was dismayed to see Assad leaning back and continuing to block her passage. He locked the door from the inside while staring hard at the frightened young woman, whose white lies failed to fool him. He gawked at her contemptuously while coming closer to her.

"You know, Charlene, I don't think you turned in your ticket early today. In fact, I don't think you received an email from your boss at all. Instead, I think you looked at one of the emails on my computer."

Charlene's eyes grew wide with fright. Her body began quivering as if she were trapped in a freezing cold room. She began shaking her head back and forth and saying no repeatedly to his remarks.

But Assad, knowing the truth, continued his interrogation.

"You know how I know this? Because I have my email app linked to my phone." He pulled out his cell phone and showed it to her as proof, displaying the face with the message notification in a pop-up window. "Whenever I get a message on my laptop, it automatically connects to my phone, including if my mail has been opened and read without my consent. And judging from the looks of my duffel bag over there, it seems that you have taken more than just a look at my laptop. Am I correct in my assumption? Curiosity has been known to kill the proverbial cat, my dear."

Charlene's face turned white with fear. As Assad moves closer to her, she began to cry.

"Please, Gary, or whatever your name is, don't hurt me! I beg of you! I'm sorry I looked at your laptop! I'm sorry I read your email and looked inside that bag! I promise I won't tell anybody about this! Please, God, don't do this! I won't tell anyone about you! Please, I don't want to die!"

As Charlene continued to beg for her life, Assad took hold of her and gently wrapped his arms around her in a mock display of kindness and concern. This temporarily calmed her. He stroked her long blonde hair to quiet her anxiety and fear. Speaking softly, he said,

"Charlene, calm down. It's okay. I'm not going to hurt you. What makes you think that I would do something like that?"

Still crying with distress, Charlene answered Assad with stuttering and mumbling. Then she said, "Well, judging by the look you gave me, and according to the contents of that email, it seems to be"—she paused— "secret. I knew that if you found out that I had looked in the bag, you would not let me get out of here alive. I just panicked and didn't know what else to do. I'm sorry I looked at your email. I promise that I won't tell a soul about you."

"I know you won't, sweetheart." Assad continued to comfort her. Feeling less erratic and a little more comfortable now, she rested her head against his chest as he continued to stroke her hair. But to no avail, she had fallen into a false sense of security for which Assad had no intentions on letting her live that day. He pulled an object from his pants pocket, which appeared to be a small pocketknife. Peculiar in appearance, but most likely military grade. Moving the knife upward slowly without Charlene noticing it, he puts his other hand on the back of her head and pulls her towards him. Making as if he wanted to give her a sultry kiss for the last time for which he did. He pressed his lips against hers and wrapped his arms around her body into giving her a romantic-seeming embrace. With their lips still touching against his, and being preoccupied by the false passion that he was giving her, Assad continued the embrace. He then takes advantage of the situation without hesitation or second thought and thrusts the sharp instrument into the back of her neck at the base of her skull. Separating her spinal cord from the brain stem with accurate precision as if he was a surgeon conducting an operation. She suddenly grasped his shoulders as if she had received an electric shock throughout her body. Her eyes grew wide with surprise as she stared at Assad with disbelief and confusion, while still embracing him from the kiss earlier. As Charlene tried to hang on to the little bit of life that she had left as it was slipping away, Assad gave words to her that were cold and unfeeling.

"But I'm afraid you left me no other choice… I'm really sorry, my dear."

Charlene tried to speak but was unable to. She couldn't utter a sound non-the-less a single word. With the knife still stuck in the back of her neck, Charlene's appendages went limp very quickly. Seconds went by as she took her last breath from her mouth and exhaled it for the final time. Her deep-blue eyes that were full of life began to drain slowly as they stared at Assad, lifeless and unmoving. Assad's expression was coldhearted and unfeeling as he held the lifeless body in front of him with a clutching embrace of death. He continued to hold Charlene even after she expired. He took his right hand and felt for a pulse at her jugular vein, knowing that he would find nothing.

With the blood slowly trickling down Charlene's back, Assad gently laid her body across the bed. He gently closed her eyes by covering them with the palm of his hand. As he did so, he did not notice the cell phone that Charlene had hidden in her waistband had fell from her body and onto the floor for which it rolled under the bed, still active and working. He placed her arms beside her and straightened her legs as he lifted them upon the bed as if she was in a restful slumber of sleep. From her current appearance, Assad made Charlene to be at peace, giving her the illusion that she was sleeping and did not want to be disturbed. Her body laid still and motionless as he arranged her attire to show no evidence of a scuffle or the provocation of murder for which he committed.

Assad knew what needed to be done next. His first inkling was that he was satisfied that he didn't shoot Charlene in the head with the gun he had taken from Kareem. He had considered it but changed his mind because he thought that Charlene's official—albeit inaccurate—cause of death should not be something so brutal or barbaric. And death by way of gunshot was indeed violent. The quickest way to have killed her was the way he'd chosen. He'd been taught such methods in the Special Forces, along with close-quarter hand-to-hand combat. He knew that the quickest and easiest way to disable or incapacitate one's opponent in order to take them out of action or take their life was to either cut of their oxygen with a suffocating choke hold or separate their vertebrate by crushing or snaping their neck. This way, the victim dies quickly and quietly, without making a single sound or noise. Assad did not want to kill Charlene; he was quite fond of her. From the moment he met her on the plane, he found the time they spent together to be very enjoyable and delightful. He had really intended to have one last dinner date with her before she departed to Japan. Assad hated himself for what he had done, but it was necessary. If he would have let her go, she would have informed the authorities about him and his plans would have for nothing. Knowing she was a liability that needed to be dealt with, he had no other choice but to end her life so he could continue with his; along with his treacherous mission.

Now that Charlene was past tense, Assad set about the task of removing any possible evidence that would link him to the murder. He went over to his briefcase and pulled the items showing his new identity. He knew he had to change his appearance quickly and then leave the hotel. He had spent a few days familiarizing himself with his new identity, adopting the persona and characteristics of the individual he'd been ordered to portray by the organization. Again, he had all the tools and make up that required him to assume this new identity. The individual in the picture was an Arabic businessman and accountant; well-known in the Middle East by the name of Ahmed Shaula, surname pronounced "ash-Shaulah." He was a dealer of rare coins and ancient artifacts dating back to the Persian Empire; when Babylon ruled the southern regions of Europe before the Greeks, Romans, and English took over. The photograph showed the man to be common-looking. A Middle Easterner with jet-black hair, medium-dark olive-colored skin, and impressive Arabian facial features. The individual had a thick mustache that covered half his upper mouth, along with dark brown eyes and strong cheek bones. He appeared to be in his late forties pushing into his fifties with age lines across the upper and middle parts of his face, with a pair of eyeglasses that made him look conservative and older. His appearance spoke of professionalism and conservatism, which was the Muslim/Islamic way. This was the perfect disguise for Assad since he was of Iraqi and Lebanese descent. But he had to darken his complexion since his skin tone was as fair as an American or European Caucasian.

Sometimes as a child, Assad would feel ashamed of how he looked because his pigmentation appeared more whiter than Middle Eastern. But upon becoming into his adolescence, the saw his fair skin as an offering of unique advantages that he could blend in easily to adopted other cultures. As he scrutinized the photo, he realized that his time was short. Scurrying to the closet, he opened it to search for the other duffel bag. In addition to holding one out of the three rifles, the bag also contained his disguise kit to make himself look like Gary Brown. He pulled the bag out of the closet and opened it. Finding his kit, he rushed to the bathroom and began the process of adopting his new identity.

Assad laid out all the items on the counter that he needed to make himself look like the man in the photo, including hair dye, a fake mustache, a prosthetic beard, colored contact lenses, and a new addition, synthetic skin tone cream, which he had use to make his complexion look like Shaula's. The organization itself had deep ties to individuals of wealth, prestige, and importance, including people with the skills and knowledge the organization needed to further its goals of anarchy and dominance all across the world.

Assad took off his current disguise and washed his face to remove the makeup that made him Gary Brown. He applied the dye in his hair to change it from medium blond to jet-black. While allowing the chemicals to sit into his hair, he trimmed the mustache to make it match exactly like Shaula's. Removing the blue contact lenses, he replaced them with brown ones to match Shaula's eyes. Still waiting for the hair dye to take its course, he took the makeup cream and experimented with other colors and shadows to resemble Shaula's pigmentation. Once he had determined which shade of foundation to use to make his appearance match that of the man in the photo, he placed some into a small jar to use later when the time was right.

Minutes went by and the time was right to rinse out the dye. Once the chemicals were out, Assad was pleased to see that the hair color was an exact match of Shaula's. Now he needed to deal with the length; his hair needed to be a little shorter than previously, when he was posing as Gary Brown. He cut it evenly to match the photo, parting his hair on the left. Then applying the makeup to his face. After he was done with the cosmetics, he took the thick mustache and pressed it hard under his nose, applying the force needed to get the glue to stick to his upper lip.

Having finally accomplished his task, Assad now a dead ringer for Ahmed Shaula, apart from being a little younger. Assad was even wearing the same rectangular-framed glasses Shaula was in the photo.

Assad went to his laptop and started downloading the hotel's reservation records, which he had hacked into. He found Shaula's reservation. The organization had him staying in a room down the hall from Assad. The room number was 1615, down the corner and to the right of the exit stairwell, a good location from which to make a quick and easy escape. Assad quickly gathered his things and placed them in front of the door. When he was about to leave, he took one last look at Charlene's body and slowly walked toward her. He wanted to kiss her on the forehead one last time, but he hesitated, because to do so would leave DNA and other physical evidence behind, possibly to be discovered later by the Sydney Police Department. So instead, he whispered a soft goodbye and made a sweet and serene apology in Arabic. He picked up his bags and unlocked the door, opening it, not realizing that Charlene's cell phone was hidden under the bed. If discovered, the phone could provide evidence that Assad had stayed in his room for some time after the horrific event had taken place earlier in the evening.

Assad took the Do Not Disturb sign and placed it on the exterior door handle so that the cleaning personnel would not be so quick to enter the room the next day. Then, now transformed from Gary Brown to Ahmed Shaula, he began walking down the carpeted hallway to the room from which he intended to make his final departure. He knocked on the door with the number 1615 in the center of it and waited a couple of seconds for an answer. When the door opened, much to Assad's surprise, Ahmed Shaula was standing there.

Shaula was shocked beyond belief. There he stood looking at an exact replica of himself, a clone or twin as it were. He felt he was staring into a mirror of himself, a younger version to be exact. Shaula was speechless. He could form no words. Assad, on the other hand, was quite vocal and had no time to wait for an introduction or invitation.

"Move out of the way before someone sees us!" the former naval officer said abruptly.

Shaula, who was still amazed by his guest's appearance, granted his request by moving aside so Assad could step in. Overwhelmed by his uninvited guest, Shaula was confused about the sudden turn of events.

"Mr. Assad, what's going on? Why are you here so early? The plan was that you would take my identity several days from now, not today. What has happened?"

Assad dashed toward Shaula's table. He cleared the surface of Shaula's personal items and set up his computer, all the while explaining the reasons behind his actions.

"Circumstances have led to a change in our plans, Mr. Shaula. I must leave Sydney right away. As we speak, I'm hacking into the airport's database to book an earlier flight out of here."

"But I'm not prepared to hand over my credentials just yet. I still have some business to attend to with some local art dealers along with setting up a financial meeting with some executive bankers in Dubai. I've already informed the organization of this, and they said that it wouldn't be a problem, especially since we are trying to maintain our cover here."

"Well, I'm sorry, Mr. Shaula, but you're going to have to reschedule those meetings for some other day. The situation has surprisingly turned against our favor. The woman whom I was seeing unfortunately discovered my identity and my purpose for being here. I had no choice but to terminate our relationship."

Shaula's expression changed dramatically. He knew full well what Assad meant by that remark. "What?! You killed her?!"

"I had no choice. She read an email the organization sent to me a few hours ago. She knew about the list and the weapons I have in my possession. She even discovered my true name and knew of my previous employment in naval intelligence. I didn't want to kill her, but there was no other way. If I would've let her go, she would've called the local authorities and the Americans. Our plans would've been terminated. It had to be done."

Filled with regret, Shaula shook his head in agreement, taking a deep breath and then exhaling. He turned his back to Assad and began walking toward his bed and the small briefcase sitting next to it.

"I suppose you're right. She would've been a liability for us and our cause. I suppose individuals like that need to be dealt with immediately, even if they are innocent. Let's just hope that we show the same mercy to the guilty."

"Oh, you are so correct, Mr. Shaula." With no warning whatsoever, Assad shot Shaula in the back with his Walther P99. He had the silencer attached to the barrel to suppress the sound of the muzzle fire. Shaula's knees dropped instantly to the floor, making a loud thump, then the rest of his body fell forward. His body hit the corner of the bed, breaking the momentum of his fall, causing him to slump to the floor.

Finding it impossible to turn around because of the pain from the gunshot, Shaula looked up at Assad in disbelief just as Charlene had. He cried out in agony,

"What?! What is this?! What are you doing?! Why?! Why in Allah's name did you do this?!"

Unresponsive at first, Assad leaned over and, with the cold, merciless stare of an executioner, watching blood pouring from Shaula's wound, said,

"Why, you ask? You know why, Ahmed. Did you really think you would get away with stealing money from the organization? They sent me a message saying that they had caught you embezzling millions from their accounts and that it was up to me to terminate your employment. It seems now that you are the liability who needs to be dealt with immediately, don't you think?"

When Shaula heard this, he began to laugh with contempt and derision, the blood trickling from the corner of his mouth.

"You fool! You blind fool. You have no idea what the organization is or how they do things! You are ignorant of their true motives and what they really represent. Do you think you are doing them a favor by killing me? You are nothing to them, Ad-dam, nothing but a puppet for their amusement and their own pleasure—a pawn so to speak, a slave for use in advancing their so-called political agenda. After they have acquired your knowledge and used you for your skills, they will grow tired of you. Your life, your existence, your very essence, is theirs until they no longer have any use for you. Then they'll throw you away like garbage. I worked for them for years until I saw who they really are. Their politics are nothing more than deceptions and lies. They are no better than the very governments they're trying to overthrow or tear apart. Yes, I took some money from them, and I don't apologize for it! I did what I had to do for myself! I didn't do it for the organization or because I believe in what it stands for, because I don't—especially jihad. You will see what they really stand for, Ad-dam, and then you'll know. You will know!"

Assad continued to look down at Shaula, who was slumped against the corner of the bed, trying to hang on to life while suffering from the pain of the incapacitating wound to his back. Assad turned to the left, looking contemptuous at Shaula. As he looked down at him one last time, he spoke in Arabic to relay his meaning more carefully towards him.

"Maybe, Ahmed. But you will never get a chance to gloat about it."

Assad pointed the gun at Shaula and fired two more rounds point-blank into the center of Shaula's chest, finishing the job. Shaula's body collapsed with a slight thud onto the floor. His eyes were wide open, staring lifelessly, seeming to be looking up at Assad with pity. But in reality, his eyes remained as they were when he witnessed the final moments of his life, his executioner standing over him unscrewing the silencer from the barrel of his gun and placing it in his inside jacket pocket.

Assad looked around the room to see if there was anything peculiar to the eye, such as any items that were out of place and needing to be set right. He put his gun back in his jacket pocket and took out a pair of latex gloves. With the intention once again of removing any evidence, he placed the body on top of the bed and positioned it in such a way to make it appear as if Shaula was sleeping—the same Assad had done with Charlene. Assad cleaned the bloodstains from the carpet and removed the bullet casings from the floor, then arranged the room, restoring its original pristine orderliness. Opening Shaula's closet, he searched through the clothes, looking for Shaula's credentials and credit cards. Stumbling onto Shaula's wallet, Assad took out all the items he could make use of. Taking a second good look around the room, he caught sight of the small brown briefcase sitting between the bed and the nightstand. Even though Assad already had what he needed to make his getaway, he was curious to see what Shaula had in his possession.

He took the briefcase and put it on the table; along with latex gloves to eliminate fingerprints. Fortunately for Assad, Shaula's briefcase had no combination lock. After flipping open both clasps at the same time and lifting the lid, he was stunned by what he found. He had stumbled upon the contents of the briefcase that held a substantial amount of money; the sum of twenty-five million dollars, he would later learn. It was in US currency.

"*This is probably the money Shaula embezzled from the organization*", Assad thought.

"*This is a good enough reason for them to have wanted him dead.*"

Assad did not have time to sit and count how much money was there. He had to leave Sydney right away, before the bodies were discovered. He closed the briefcase, obviously deciding to take it with him. He looked around one last time to see if he had been thorough in his work. Satisfied that everything was in order, he took his own bags and Shaula's briefcase and exited the room. As before, he had taken the Do Not Disturb sign from the interior handle and put it on the exterior similar to Charlene's room. With a rolling suitcase, two large duffel bags—one on each side—and a briefcase filled with money, he stepped into an elevator car occupied by two other individuals and asked one of them to push the button for the lobby.

The elevator arrived at the lobby; the dooring opened for Assad to exit. He was preoccupied with dialing a number on his cell phone. As he walked casually into the lobby, taking his time to get to the reservation desk, he thought about what he'd discovered earlier.

"Hey, it's me," he said to the person on the phone. "I'm leaving right now to go to the airport. … Listen, I need you to do me a favor. Instead of meeting me in Holland as we originally planned, I need you to meet me in Dubai. … I know, I know. But some unexpected things have just come up. … I can't tell you over the phone, but believe me when I say that some things I've discovered will absolutely, without a shadow of a doubt, change our lives forever. Suffice it to say that our future has just received an upgrade. … No, I think you'll be pleased with this development. It will benefit the both of us, I assure you of this. … Good. Very good. My flight has a stopover in India, but it won't be a long one. The organization is expecting me to be in either Saudi or Kuwait by Sunday to give them the list and the merchandise. But now since my travel plans have changed, I will be there two days earlier than expected, and I will give you something that will truly surprise you. … Yes, of course, I know. It's a risk that we both agreed to take. I assure you that this is worth it. Trust me, we will be much better off than expected. … Okay, I must go. Remember, Dubai first, then after I complete my transaction, Holland, and after that, Greece, Amsterdam, or wherever we want to go. … I'll see you soon. Goodbye."

Assad hung up the phone when he reached the front desk. To address the customer service representative, he automatically switched gears, changing the tone of his voice, his accent, and his demeanor to imitate Ahmed Shaula. Noticing the surveillance cameras overhead, he did his best to avoid showing his full face when in range.

"Checking out early today, Mr. Shaula?" said the young receptionist, a native Australian woman on the other side of the registration desk.

"Ah, yes, yes I am," Assad answered, using a heavy Arabian accent to go with his disguise.

"I must make a flight tonight. It seems that my associates want me to be in Egypt a little earlier than we'd agreed."

"Well, we are delighted that you chose to stay with us again. Shall I charge this to your account as before?"

"No, no. I think I'll pay in cash this time. Will US currency do?"

"Yes, of course, Mr. Shaula." The receptionist took the money from Assad and completed the transaction, looking at her computer. She gave him a receipt, along with a pleasant smile. "Thank you again, Mr. Shaula, and do come back again to visit us."

"Oh, my dear, I probably won't be back here for a very long time, but thank you for the hospitality. Good day to you."

Assad turned around, not taking a second glance at the woman, ducked the security cameras as he made his way through the glass doors of the lobby and outside, where he hailed a cab and asked to be driven to the airport for his secret rendezvous with his mysterious counterpart.

Jakarta Joint Naval Base Headquarters, Indonesia

It was a late Thursday afternoon on, October 18th, at the Jakarta naval yard air station. Milson, who was already in a foul mood, was standing alone in the middle of a large conference room looking over some documents that Commander True and Operations Officer James Weaver had given to him a couple of hours ago. Trying desperately to learn of Assad's movements, which Interpol and a few other foreign intelligence groups were working on, aided by GPS data and manifests from flights within the entire South Pacific region, Milson had honed in on several FAA (Federal Aviation Administration) logs and flight plans for flights that Assad might have taken when he first left the States several days ago and flew into foreign territory. Milson had just narrowed things down to four commercial flights that departed from Hawaii around the same time, each going to one of the four locations he already suspected: Japan, China, Russia, and Australia. He looked over the crew's manifests to determine the names of the passengers on each of the four flights. He knew that it would be a long list, but he had to find the one name that would stand out from all the rest: Gary Brown.

As Milson was rifling through the papers, frustrated and tired, the young ensign James Sheppard, who was vibrant, energetic, and full of enthusiasm, stepped through the door to hand over some more travel logs and manifests from later flights. Milson was not feeling eager to look at these, but he knew he had no choice but to do so.

"Here you go, Agent Milson," said the young naval officer.

"These is the last batch of flight logs you wanted from Commander True. He had a difficult time getting them from the FAA, who wanted to know why an officer of the US Navy wanted flight information usually restricted to personnel from the FAA and ATO [Air Traffic Organization]. But he had a little help from Officer Weaver and his influence with the CIA, which of course sealed the deal. They just faxed these over to us."

Hearing the anxiousness and eagerness in the ensign's voice, Milson looked up at him for a moment, catching Sheppard's gleeful grin as he stared intensely at the hard-nosed bounty hunter, clearly admiring him. Milson shook his head twice, ignoring what he thought to be Sheppard's lack of maturity, given that the young man was fascinated with the type of cloak-and-dagger stuff one only sees in the movies or reads about in thrillers. Milson went back to scanning the papers, trying to dismiss thoughts of his present company. Overlooking Milson's rudeness, Sheppard, seeing that Milson was intensely focused on the task of finding Assad, felt that he should give him some assistance.

"Sir, if you don't mind, I can help you find out what plane Commander Assad took and where it was going in no time flat." Sheppard reached over and tried to take several papers from Milson, but the stubborn former CIA officer denied him of his request. Unwilling to yield his position, forcefully maintained his hold and snatched them out of Sheppard's fingers.

"Don't worry about it, kid. I got it. I've narrowed it down to these last three flights here. Hey, I've got an idea. Why don't you make yourself useful by getting yourself some coffee or help True and Weaver in the TOC? I'm sure they can use your 'expertise' for something."

Taking notice of Milson's sarcasm, Sheppard's disposition quickly went from excited and interested to confused, disappointed, and frustrated. He looked at Milson as if he were a fatuous asshole with a condescending attitude. Realizing that this was not appropriate military behavior, he stood up straight and tall with his hands behind his back in the posture of parade rest. He cleared his throat as if he was about to speak and stared hard. Blocking from his mind his opinion of the pompous bounty hunter, who was still looking over the documents.

Sheppard took a few seconds to gather his thoughts and search for the right words to say to the arrogant veteran who so far had been nothing but dismissive toward him. With a plan of what to say to Milson, he stiffened his jaw and said,

"Sir, may I have permission to speak freely?"

Milson lifted his head slowly from the papers and turned his attention toward Sheppard.

"Son," he said in a forceful voice,

"I'm not in the military. I'm not even an officer. I'm a freelance contractor hired by "YOU" navy boys. You can say whatever is on your mind." He straightened his posture and folded his arms across his chest, indicating that he was ready to listen to what the young officer had to say.

"Have I done something to offend you in any way?"

Milson shook his head.

"No, I don't think so."

"Well, have I given you any misleading information that has caused you to view me as incompetent?"

Again, Milson said,

"No, Ensign Sheppard, I don't believe you have."

"Then why have you taken every opportunity since you arrived here on this island to disrespect me and show a contemptuous attitude toward me? I've shown nothing but the utmost respect toward you, including respect for your endeavors as a former soldier and field agent. I've shown you nothing but courtesy and civility, which every officer or agent is due. Though you are no longer in the service or with the company, I have still shown you respect because of your profession and your position as the senior operative on this case. So, I don't know what it is you have against me. What is your problem with me, sir?"

Milson unfolded his arms and placed them on his hips, staring at the young officer, who was standing across from him.

"Listen, kid, I don't have a problem with you at all. To tell you the truth, I don't even know you. I'm not upset with you or pissed at you, and I don't have anything against you. But what I do have a problem with is your lack of experience as a field agent and your cluelessness about what's really going on here. I can't believe Cooper would send me a cherry—no offense—with no training in covert ops and no special skills to help me with an operation of this magnitude. From the reports I've read about this guy Assad, he's a smart and cunning SOB with the intellect of two mad scientists. Not to mention that he's highly skilled in the areas of killing people thanks to the training he received from Navy Special Forces." Milson paused for a moment but continued his opinion to the young officer.

"And I can understand Weaver's involvement. He's a veteran company man with years of knowledge and expertise under his forty-inch belt. But you, you look like you just came out of high school or the academy. Am I right?" Sheppard gave a nod, confirming Milson's suspicions. "Great! That's just great! I knew it. And on top of that, they decided to slap a badge on your chest and throw you out to the wolves so you can make believe that this is "cops and robbers" by you thinking that this is some two-bit petty scumbag. Well, it's not, kid. This guy is much more than that. He's smarter and much more dangerous than any other average criminal off the streets. I'm sorry, Sheppard, I don't have anything against you personally, but from my experience chasing after guys like this, I believe this is way out of your league, even if you are a legitimate agent working for both NCIS and ONI. Don't take it personally or the wrong way, kid. You're probably good at what you do, sniffing through computer files and hacking into encrypted databases to download secret messages. That sort of thing is probably your specialty, and likely you're a master at it. And you have probably accumulated plenty of stakeout time by keeping an eye out for any insurgent activity around here. But the work I'm doing here involves much more than that. It involves tracking down and pursuing dangerous individuals such as Assad who will not hesitate to kill anyone who gets in their way. For example, Assad's motive right now is to make a clean getaway and not get caught. He will use any means necessary to achieve his ends. It doesn't matter who or what he has to take out."

Once Sheppard was sure that Milson was through speaking, he said,

"Sir, I do understand the seriousness of this case, and to tell you the truth, I am quite capable of handling situations like this on my own. You may think of me as a clueless virgin with stringy pigtails on both sides of my head, but I assure you that I'm aware of what lies ahead for all of us. True, I don't have the skills that you or Weaver have. And true, I don't have the knowledge or experience to qualify as a covert operative, but I'm just as smart and cunning and sneakier than the next individual. I graduated top of my class at the Naval Academy and was the first to be recruited by ONI because of my knowledge and skills in cybernetic software and encryption. And to let you in on a little secret, I was trained in hand-to-hand combat by a marine recon sniper division unit, so I'm well equipped for combat scenarios and black ops missions. That's why I was given the opportunity to be a field agent working for NCIS, doing undercover work and investigation. And I was assigned here in Indonesia specifically to share with the Indonesian Navy and the Indonesian government any intelligence related to insurgent activity in which the Chinese are in some way involved. My father wanted me to follow in his footsteps by joining the FBI, but I chose the navy because I knew that here I could be something better than an ordinary field agent or an average beat cop. I can handle myself in a firefight, and I have enough common sense to get myself out of any situation I know I don't have the skills to handle. So, I might not be a cold-blooded killer, or a high-profile agent like you or Weaver, but I'm just as smart as one and probably cleverer than the two of you put together. I may look young and be young, but I promise you, I can outsmart you and outthink you at every turn. So, don't let the baby face fool you, Mr. Milson, and don't judge this book by its cover until you've read the contents of it, sir!"

Milson was surprised. He literally jumped back realizing that Sheppard had just shown the sharpness of his teeth. Milson had indeed underestimated the tenacity and competence of this young man who had just put him in his proverbial place. For the moment, Milson dropped his guard and spoke to Sheppard with sincerity.

"Okay, kid. I apologize for coming at you so strong. I should have given you the benefit of the doubt, instead of jumping to conclusions and thinking you were some dumbass kid trying to play cops and robbers. I made an ass out of myself by thinking that way, and I'm man enough to admit that I'm wrong. I'm sorry for making a mistake like that."

Sheppard could hear the sincerity in Milson's tone. He gave him a nod of appreciation, accepting his apology. Now that they had settled their disagreement, they went back to looking over the flight logs that Sheppard had just brought in. Soon Milson came across the very thing he was looking for.

"Got it! Sheppard, look at this. Flight number 308, from LA to Honolulu. Look at the name on the manifest: Gary Brown! Now look at this flight number, 254, from Honolulu to Sydney, Australia. Look who's on both the manifest."

Sheppard, looking at the paper in Milson's hand, said loudly, "Gary Brown! He's in Australia. We'd better inform Commander True about this, sir."

Just as they began to gather up the papers, Weaver burst through the door.

"Milson, Sheppard, glad I caught you both. Come to the TOC at once. I think we've finally got a hit on Assad."

Milson and Sheppard rushed out of the room, leaving behind the evidence showing Assad's whereabouts. Little did they know that their fugitive had already made another getaway.

CHAPTER 5

FOLLOWING THE TRAIL

Milson and Sheppard were right on Weaver's tail as the three of them entered the TOC. True was standing on one side of the room, looking at a seventy-inch flat-screen TV mounted high on the wall that was showing satellite images of Australia, including all major cities, with a sidebar indicating GPS coordinates and travel routes. Milson and Sheppard ran up to True while Weaver ran in the other direction, toward a petty officer who was operating the main computer that controlled the viewing screen.

"True! Weaver said you've got something. What's going on?" asked the former company man, a rough tone to his voice.

True looked over at Milson and crossed his arms over his chest.

"We've been monitoring Interpol's broadband communications for several hours. We intercepted one of their calls made on the NCIC [National Crime Information Center] telecommunications network. Two homicides took place at a luxurious hotel in Sydney, Australia, earlier today. The bodies were discovered by hotel personnel. Australian authorities, including the SPD [Sydney Police Department], are investigating."

"So? What does that have to do with our hunt for Assad? Commander, I don't have time for trivial pursuits," said Milson abruptly.

Once again True looked over at the hardened bounty hunter, this time with a look of indignation and frustration in his eyes, rather than an expression of mutual respect, having taken offense to Milson's last remark, which was spoken in a contemptuous tone with the disrespectful mannerisms to match. True went over to the operating station and hit several keys on the control pad, which brought several images up on the screen.

"The bodies you're looking at were found early this morning. The first is of a man in his late forties, and the other is a woman in her mid-twenties, possibly American. The gentleman is of Middle Eastern descent, a businessman. He's been identified as Ahmed Shaula, a historian who is also a museum coordinator and a financial consultant based in Cairo, Egypt. The woman is a high-class real estate agent who worked for a company in Los Angeles. Her name is Charlene Gardner. Her body was found in the hotel room registered to this man." True punched the enter button on the keypad to bring up the next bit of information. A photo of Gary Brown's identification came up on the screen, his information printed beside it.

Milson and Sheppard each fell back a bit to lean against the divider panel. Milson said,

"I'll be goddamned! It's him! It's Assad! The kid and I were checking the FAA's flight manifests and found Brown's name. He was on two of the flights from L.A to Hawaii, then Hawaii to Australia. That's where the bastard is!"

"Yeah, but even though he was there at one point, he's probably long gone by now," said Weaver, interrupting. "The FAA reported that a flight from Sydney left yesterday evening around seven o'clock and was scheduled to make a stopover in India, then fly to its final destination somewhere in the Middle East—Kuwait or Saudi Arabia. The passenger manifest shows that a Middle Eastern gentleman who fits the description of Ahmed Shaula boarded Flight 512 sometime after the bodies were found that morning."

"Goddammit! Assad killed Shaula so he could assume his identity to get out of Australia. He knew that we had our eyes on him, and he needed a new disguise to get out of there clean. This bastard is really crafty and slick," Milson said, looking at the screen with an image of Gary Brown's ID and one of Assad disguised as Brown.

"True, can you get me a flight to Sydney so I can go there to investigate?"

"I can. But it will take several minutes," said True.

"Great! Make it fifteen minutes. I must go there myself to figure out why Assad killed these two people and to discover what, if anything, connects the three of them. Were they his contacts, or were they simply impediments to his plan to get out of Australia quickly?"

"You know that you're going to get into a pissing contest over jurisdiction with the locals down there. It's a murder investigation on their turf, Chief. The Australians don't like outsiders interfering with things that happen in their own backyard, especially when it comes to matters such as this," said True.

"I know. That's why I'm taking Weaver and Sheppard along as backup. Weaver can show his CIA badge for purposes of intimidation, and the kid can show his NCIS badge in the event they question whether or not we have jurisdiction since Assad is still employed by the navy. We'll make up some story of a prolonged criminal investigation case that will throw them off the track temporarily. We'll impress upon them that this is strictly a US incident that must not be made public or turned into an international incident, as that would threaten our national security since one of the victims is a US citizen. Never mind that the fugitive we're searching for is a certified officer of the U.S. navy, but a man that is willing to sell U.S. secretes to a terrorist organization. By the way, this will give me a chance to unveil my USFAA credentials to the public and announce that my job here is to apprehend a suspected criminal who is a US citizen wanted by the State and the Justice Department of the United States."

"All right, Chief. I'll have a Seahawk ready for the three of you on the tarmac. Fully fueled within twenty-five minutes. You should reach Sydney within five-in-a-half hours from now." Weaver interjected,

"No, Commander. That's too long. We need a plane to get there ASAP. Possibly something that flies supersonic." True thought about it for a second and later came up with an alternative.

"You're in luck, Weaver. The U.S. navy just purchased one of its own privately owned jets in its aeronautic fleet. The *Cessna Citation X+*. One of the second fastest private jets in the world. She's only used for diplomatic purposes such as flying around admirals, generals and politicians like congressmen and senators. She can reach speeds of Mach 0.935 (1194 km/h) and can get you there in two-in-a-half maybe three hours tops. And probably run you a bill over a hundred thousand dollars." Milson looked over at True and said,

"Well thank God the navy is paying for the bill and not me." All four laughed at the notion as Milson continued with an approval.

"Good! We'll need something as fast as that to get there immediately. Along with plenty of time to get our stories straight for when the Australians start asking questions, which I assume will be numerous. Weaver, get your things. Sheppard, pack light. And I do mean light. We're not going down there to sightsee and check out the local beauties. Yeah, Sheppard, I can see right through you and tell what type of kid you are."

The young officer, appearing to be embarrassed, smirked, proving to Milson's mind that Sheppard was in fact still an adolescent horndog in an adult's body.

Making a wide gesture to everyone in the room, Milson said,

"Let's get ready, people! It looks like we're traveling to the land down under. Let's go!" He, Weaver, and Sheppard filed out of the control center, leaving Commander True behind to contact the aviation department to schedule a flight out of there and then call his superiors to tell them what was going on.

Star City and Casino Hotel, Sydney, Australia

Several hours had passed since the bodies had been found. It was still busy inside the hotel despite the gruesome discovery. The place was packed with people, including a large number of police officers and civil authorities who were there to look into the double homicide that had just taken place. Australia's New South Wales Police Force, along with local Sydney authorities, were cordoning off several areas of the hotel from the public so as to prevent people from using the stairwells or contaminating the crime scenes. Two separate groups of forensics investigators had set themselves up in each of the two rooms to try to determine both time of death and cause of death for both victims. One of these groups was the NSW's CSI team, which was heading the investigation into Charlene's death. The other group was made up of Sydney Police Department forensics specialists; they were working on Shaula. Each group was so preoccupied with their work that they did not notice that Milson, Sheppard, and Weaver had strolled onto the crowded floor and into one of the rooms. Milson first took notice of Charlene's body as the coroners and inspectors snapped photos of her lying motionless on the bed where Assad had left her. After taking a quick look around, Milson told Weaver to check out Shaula's room down the hall and report any findings.

As soon as Weaver stepped out, one of the NSW officers, noticing Milson and Sheppard, rushed toward them to stop them from coming any farther inside.

"Hey, mate, just what the bloody hell do you think you're doing? This is a crime scene; there's a police investigation going on here. How in the hell did you get past the constables? Actually, how did get up here in the first place?" The officer in charge had a thick Australian accent and spoke quickly, which made it almost impossible for Milson and Sheppard to understand.

Milson replied,

"I'm sorry, Officer, for barging in like this. I and my colleague were in the neighborhood and happened to hear a report of a double homicide on the police band. I assure you that we are not trying to stir up any trouble here or step on any toes, but it seems to me that what you have here is a murder that happens to be within our jurisdiction."

"Oh really?" said the officer, who quickly became irritated.

"Your jurisdiction? Well, mate, the last time I checked, this was Australia. And this building that you currently occupy is in fact in the middle of an Australian city called Sydney, which is within my jurisdiction! And the crime in this case was committed on Australian soil! So, if you buggers don't mind, you need to get the hell out of here and out of my way. I and my men are trying to do our jobs here in my city, *my jurisdiction*. Leave the premises immediately. And by the way, just who in the hell do you think you are?"

Before the officer could signal a constable to escort Milson and Sheppard out, Milson smiled devilishly and casually pulled out his billfold to show his identification and credentials to the Australian official.

"No, mate, I think we do mind," Milson said.

"I don't think we're going anywhere. And to let you know who we are, let us introduce ourselves, starting with me. My name is Killian Milson. I'm a United States apprehension officer working under both the US State and Justice Department. This is my colleague and associate Ensign James Sheppard, US Navy and special agent for the US Naval Criminal Investigation Service division, otherwise known as NCIS."

Sheppard pulled out his wallet as well. Milson continued, saying,

"These murders were committed by an officer of the United States Navy who went rogue and then went AWOL several months ago. He has already killed two high-profile individuals in the States and is suspected of committing several other murders as well. We've been tracking him for months, and it looks as if he has made his way down here to your lovely country. Now I have no problem sharing information with you and your superiors, seeing as this situation did, unfortunately, happen in your backyard. But this is in fact a case over which the United States has jurisdiction, because the victim over there happens to be a US citizen. The other victim down the hall happened to meet his demise at the hands of the same individual we're looking for. Now if you have a problem with anything I've said, I suggest you contact your commissioner or boss, and perhaps the US Embassy if you want information on jurisdiction over criminal procedures committed by foreign nationals in other countries. I'm sure they won't mind educating you in the area of diplomacy and professional courtesy among fellow law enforcement officials. Now, I'm not trying to be rude—nothing of the sort—but I, along with my associate here, would like to look at the body and see the room so we can get ourselves a better picture of what happened here. Oh, by the way, I'm sorry, sir, but I didn't catch your name."

Grinding his teeth in frustration and anger, the officer hesitated before saying,

"I'm Chief Inspector Frank Woodlouse of the Second Precinct of His Majesty's New South Wales Police Force [NSWPF]."

"Well, Chief Inspector, if you don't mind, I would like to look at some of the evidence you and your people have dug up. My superiors in Washington would like to find out what I've discovered here."

Woodlouse was very crossed. He snapped his fingers to signal one of his subordinates to assist Milson and Sheppard. Milson leaned over to speak one-on-one with Sheppard.

"Sheppard, go tell Weaver what's going on. And see if you can get in contact with True. I've got a feeling that Crocodile Dundee over there is going to try to contact not only his bosses but also Washington as well. I want True to intercept any calls this guy makes and also intercept any transmissions he sends. And ask if he will fabricate some sort of story to tell the police here to make us look legitimate, but without blowing our cover. I'm going to snoop around a bit and look for any clues that might give us an idea of what made Assad decide to kill these two people."

Sheppard gave a nod and ran out the door to find Weaver at the other end of the hall. Milson made his way around, never mind the lack of professional courtesy shown by the NSWPF officers. He leaned over to look at Charlene's body, noticing the deep puncture wound in the back of her neck. Judging by the size of the wound and the method used to kill her, he concluded that this was a type of mercy killing. Still, it was an execution-style murder that only someone who knew how to handle a knife and where to strike the victim so as not to cause any blunt force trauma that would be seen by an amateur or a person with no knowledge of forensics. To Milson, the actions spoke of an assassin, or possibly someone who'd been taught by Special Forces on how to kill a person inconspicuously and leave no evidence behind. This was Assad's handiwork. Only a trained combat killer would have known how to disable Charlene in this way.

After closely observing the corpse, Milson made his way toward the closet, then to the bathroom. Knowing he would contaminate the scene if he touched anything, he bemoaned not having latex gloves with him, which otherwise would have allowed him to touch anything indiscriminately. Next, he made a few more trips around the room, stepping between the investigators, to look for anything that might give him a clue. He was right on the verge of giving up when he saw something out of the corner of his eye. He glanced down at the corner of the bed, which was positioned against the wall, and saw what appeared to be a cell phone—Charlene's phone, the one she dropped just before Assad killed her. Milson was surprised that the investigators hadn't seen it. Doing his best not to attract attention, he bent down slowly and nonchalantly picked up the device. Woodlouse and his men showed no signs of having noticed. Quickly placing the phone in his jacket pocket, he set about pretending to be scouting the area close to the bed so as to make his counterparts think that he was still on a search.

Milson began to walk out of the room, the phone still in his possession. Later Sheppard came running down the hallway to tell Milson about what he and Weaver had discovered. "Mr. Milson, I've got something for you."

"Listen, kid, do me a favor. Call me either Killian or Chief, never Mr. Milson. Makes me feel like you're addressing my father." Sheppard grinned with Milson's invitation. It gave the young officer a confidence boost, which was in Milson's intention from the start.

"What do you have, kid?"

"Officer Weaver had to pull some strings to get permission to take a closer look at what the Australians found—and surprise, it's him. The victim is definitely Ahmed Shaula. Three gunshot wounds point-blank: two in the middle of his chest and one in his back. Caliber of the bullet casings were that of a nine-millimeter. Execution style, according to what Weaver and the police are saying. Weaver also interviewed some of the staff members of the hotel. They saw someone who looked like Shaula leaving the area with some extra bags and suitcases that he didn't have before when he checked in. One of the receptionists told Weaver and the police that Shaula always paid his bill with a credit card or else had management charge his room to his personal account for payment later after he returned from his business trip. This time he did neither. They said that the imposter paid cash for his room—US currency—all in crisp, clean hundred-dollar bills. The employees had never known him to pay cash for anything, not even his food. He was a regular here at the hotel."

"That's all fine and well, kid, but what is the connection between Assad, Shaula, and this woman?"

"I've got something for you on that, Killian." Weaver came from behind and explained in detail. "At the time, a man disguised as Gary Brown came into the hotel with an attractive blonde, who we now know is the deceased Charlene Gardner. She has an older brother in the navy, one Lieutenant Commander Bartholomew Gardner, who is stationed in Hawaii. And get this—he happens to be in naval intelligence." Both Milson and Sheppard raised their eyebrows.

"They took the same flight from LA to Honolulu, where Commander Gardner met his sister and Assad. She was on a business trip from her job in real estate. Her plan was to go to Tokyo, Japan, where she was going to finalize some deal with some executives over the construction of a new building. It looks like what happened between her and Assad was nothing more than a friendly hookup after having become acquainted on the plane," Weaver said as he continued.

"We also got the surveillance footage from the cameras mounted above the customer service counter. It shows a gentleman fitting the description of Assad disguised as Shaula leaving the hotel. The police are unwilling to turn the video over to us, but after I talked to some of the staff and disclosed that I was a federal agent, they were very cooperative and allowed me to take a peek. And, guys, in my analysis it's definitely Assad doing a damn good impersonation of Shaula, if I do say so."

Milson rubbed his chin and nodded.

"Okay, we've got Assad on film leaving the hotel disguised as our murder victim, but what was his motive? What made him kill the woman and then Shaula? There has to be more to this," Milson remarked faintly.

"The only thing I can come up with is that she was an innocent bystander. She probably didn't know anything about Assad or the missing weapons and stolen military plans. She must have accidentally stumbled across on who he really was, and tried to escape. He found out about it and killed her in order to keep her quiet." Weaver's conclusions were absolutely correct.

"So, you think it had nothing to do with her brother being a naval officer and being employed by the very agency he left?" Sheppard asked.

"No, I don't think so. Assad is too smart for that. He knew that there was nothing to worry about with this woman and her brother. And as clever as this guy is, he probably thought that it was a coincidence and didn't think there would be no consequences involved. I'm going with what you said earlier, Weaver. She unexpectedly came upon something that she had no idea about and found out later who Assad really was and what his motives were." said Milson.

"But what about Shaula? Why did Assad kill him? He had to be one of his contacts. Perhaps it was intended that Assad take Shaula's place. And I don't think that Shaula would have volunteered if he'd known he was going to be killed later," Sheppard said.

"What probably happened is that after Assad killed the woman, he figured he had to get out of there in a hurry. He knew where Shaula's room was, so he went there and told him what the situation was. This was not part of their original plan; the circumstances changed unexpectedly. They must have gotten into an argument or had a disagreement, and Assad eliminated Shaula and assumed his identity with the intention of leaving Australia right away," Weaver said.

"You may be right, Weaver, but now we've got to find out exactly where Assad is heading to. He may have gone to Kuwait or Saudi. We don't know if he has contacts in either of those places," said Sheppard.

"You may be right, kid. I think we may have some leverage to use." Milson reached into his pocket and pulled out the object he'd found in the victim's room, showing both Weaver and Sheppard. "I found this cell phone under the bed. I have no idea who it belongs to, but I have a feeling that it's linked to Assad. Sheppard, take this and put it in your pocket. Go somewhere quiet and contact True. See what you can pull up on the phone. Find out if it was the girl's or Assad's."

Sheppard quickly took the phone and placed it in his pocket as suggested. He gave Milson a slight nod before turning away. He began walking down the crowded corridor, ducking between the Sydney authorities to find a private place where he could contact True in Indonesia.

Weaver continued to brief Milson, saying,

"Killian, I just found out from some locals that Shaula had several business meetings with some high-class suits. An employee in charge of hotel security told the investigators that the men were all Middle Eastern and had their own bodyguards with them. From the description they gave me, these guys were professionals and were very serious-looking."

Milson crossed his arms.

"Hmm, they might have been members of the mysterious organization that both Assad and Shaula have ties to. You said that he was an art dealer and financial advisor? Why would a lowly businessman consort with individuals who bring their own security force?"

"Iranian secret service? Palestinian or Lebanese honor guard? Either of them could have a plan to use our stuff against us. Remember, it was an Iranian agent found dead in Assad's apartment," Weaver replied.

"Yeah, I know. But ONI and your pals from the CIA and the NSA found out that he was a double agent working for someone else. I knew the guy they found there. He knew that Shaula was going to meet Assad here and that the two were to exchange identities. But I don't think Shaula knew that he was going to be the sacrificial lamb."

Weaver said,

"Killian, I didn't want to say this in front of the kid, but he's right. If we don't find out where Assad is going and who his contacts are, the United States and our allies are going to be in a world of hurt. This guy has already killed three, possibly four people to achieve his goal of delivering those plans to whatever son of a bitch that wants them. If Assad can do this, then think of what the people he is in contact with might do if they get their hands on our secrets. I shudder to think of the damage they may cause. We've got to find this guy, and fast, before the situation gets out of control," said Weaver with concern.

"I know, I know," responded Milson.

"The admiral, along with the president, is giving me only seventy-two hours to sniff out this guy and take him back before they call in the trigger-happy SF [Special Forces] stooges to find him and punch his clock. We know that he's going to the Middle East, but where specifically is he going to make the drop-off?" Stopping a moment to think, Milson exclaimed.

"Wait a minute, Weaver! I have an idea where Assad might be heading. Get on the wire and see if you can contact any of your guys in Dubai."

"Dubai? Why there?" asked Weaver with curiosity.

"Dubai is the only logical conclusion. It may be Muslim, but it is politically neutral and invests heavily in tourism. And they have signed the trade agreements enabling business to partner with foreign companies, industries, and other governments. Dubai has no ties to terrorists and no political involvement with radical Islam. That's a for sure a sign that you want keep a very low profile in a country that is not looking for you or doesn't even know who you are. Such a thing is possible unless you're wanted for a local crime in that arca. Criminals think like this, Weaver. Cons and fugitives consider alternatives like that. They hide in areas where they think they'll never be discovered, preferably the last place the authorities would ever look. Assad's not going to Kuwait or Saudi Arabia; he's going to Dubai to lie low and probably meet with either his contacts or someone with greater pull who will meet his demands for immunity if the whole thing blows up in his face. He'll hang out there for a while until the dust settles enough for him to make his move and go someplace else, a neutral country such as Sweden, Holland, or Greece. That's where we'll find Assad, in Dubai," concluded Milson.

"I'm way ahead of you. I think I know someone there who can help us out. He's stationed there temporarily for the upcoming peace talks sponsored by the UN and the UEA. I'll give him a call right now." Weaver immediately got on his phone and made the call, using his earpiece. Milson turned around and was about to go back into the crime scene to search for more clues. Just when he was about to enter the room, he heard a loud and boisterous voice from the other end of the hall shouting his name. It was Woodlouse, with Sheppard following directly behind him. The inspector's face was marked with apprehension and aggravation.

"You goddamn Yanks! You think that you're so bloody smart, don't you?! I just got off the phone with my superiors! They told me that even though the murders took place on our turf, you have jurisdiction for this case! They contacted Washington, DC, to confirm who you are and who you work for in the United States, and it came back solid!"

"Did you think that I was lying about who we are, Inspector?" Milson asked with a condescending smirk on his face.

"Chief Inspector to you, you smug bastard! And yes, I would've enjoyed it if you were! It would've given me great pleasure to lock you and your colleagues up in my jail for obstruction of justice by interfering in a homicide investigation on Australian soil!"

"Well, *Chief Inspector*, I'm not trying to step on your toes, as I said before. All we're trying to do is discover any patterns that might help us locate our fugitive and figure out what his next move will be. As I told you before, technically this is your house and your investigation. All we want to do is take a look at the crime scene and share in what you find. That's all. Well, since this is your baby, and since I and my guys are through looking around, the investigation is yours to do with as you please."

As Milson and Sheppard turned around, about to join up with Weaver, Woodlouse stopped them. "Wait a minute, you bloat! What about the bodies?! Don't you want the girl and the guy since they were killed by your man?!"

Milson turned around slowly with a derisive smile and a derisive gesture in response.

"No, Chief Inspector. This is your case. The victims are in your custody to do with as you wish for now. But I must give you fair warning that the woman in there is the sister of a high-ranking official in naval intelligence who has a strong connection to our commander in chief, that is, the president of the United States. And that man over there? Since he's of Islamic descent, I should advise you to take great care when handling his body. Muslims don't take kindly to foreigners desecrating their peoples' remains. Using autopsy procedures that go against their religious beliefs are considered sacrilege in their religion. To do so is a sign of disrespect to all Muslims and could cause severe problems between the Arabian governments and your government. I suggest you call the appropriate embassy and find out what steps you should take in caring for the victims' remains. Take care, Chief Inspector. You have a pleasant day, and thank you for your warmth, generosity, and hospitality. Oh, and let me end this by saying good day, mate and take care!" Milson was taunting Woodlouse by mimicking an Australian accent, which made Woodlouse literally turn red with anger.

Satisfied that he had left the Australian inspector embarrassed and ashamed, standing in the middle of the hallway with an expression of inadequacy and anger written across his face, Milson caught up with Sheppard and Weaver. The three of them walked down the crowded corridor, leaving the crime scene in its present condition for the locals to handle themselves. They all sidestepped the constables who were still going back and forth to the crime scene and those positioned around the area for security purposes. They entered one of the emergency exits, which led them to a stairwell that opened onto the main lobby of the hotel.

As they made their way down the stairs, Milson said to Sheppard,

"Nice going, kid, blocking the call that Woodlouse made. I knew he was going to do that."

"Thanks, Chief. I called Commander True and told him about our situation. He intercepted the inspector's call by tying into his phone into the line and piggybacking on the frequency. The commander had one of our field analysts pose as a White House dignitary and throw him off. Surprisingly, it worked. The Australians didn't suspect a thing," said Sheppard, who was giddy and excited. "I also did as you said with the cell phone. I gave them the ID and registry number. Commander True is going to put a trace on it and also do an identification scan. He said that he'll send the phone up to ONI for further investigation. All I need to do is have one of the pilots who flew us here to take it back to base headquarters. The analyst there can dissect it and recover the information we need in order to find Commander Assad. But he said it will take some time to figure it out."

"Good," replied Milson. "I have a feeling that this phone belonged to the girl and that it was still active, meaning the battery hadn't died yet. This may give us some leverage to find Assad."

"Killian, you pulled a good bluff on the inspector back there when you said the woman was the sister of a high-ranking naval officer and said that you knew the president personally," said Sheppard.

"Who said I was bluffing? It might be true. You never know who has important connections in the type of business we're in, kid. You can never be sure who is carrying dirty little secrets that might either help or hinder them. That's one of the many perks of being in the intelligence business. Knowing things that other people don't know and keeping those things a secret from the people who do."

As Milson concluded his one-on-one with Sheppard, he was reminded of another situation that needed Sheppard's attention.

"Listen, kid. You'd better contact True one more time to inform Washington about Commander Gardner's sister. I think he and his family should be told."

Sheppard gave a sorrowful nod in response to Milson's request and went straight to his phone to contact the commander. Meanwhile, Weaver ended his call and began to brief Milson on what he had picked up.

"Killian, we're in luck. I got ahold of a guy I know there. He's attached to the British Embassy in Dubai. His name is David Fuller, of MI6."

"British Secret Intelligence Service?" said Milson with surprise. "I thought we were trying to keep a low profile on this case?"

"Come on, Killian, don't be naive. How long do you think the intelligence community can contain this story of Assad's treachery? Not long at all, especially seeing as we share many of our secrets and much of our intel with the Brits. I know this guy personally. He can be trusted, I assure you. He's former military, Royal Marines," Weaver expressed with strong admiration.

"Great! A James Bond wannabe," replied Milson in a condescending tone.

"Believe me, Milson, he's no James Bond. Far from it. This guy can get any info we need on anybody just like that," said Weaver with reassurance, having spoken under his breath.

Milson was a little apprehensive, but deep down he knew that Weaver was right. Data such as the type that Weaver had mentioned could have potential, yet possibly might also be leaked, especially when dealing with individuals who fabricate information. There were always serious repercussions when the transfer of classified information was at issue. But asking a foreign agency to help, and adding a foreign agent into the mix, was not exactly the plan that Milson and Admiral Cooper had in mind. The US administration, along with the military cabinet, wanted this matter to be rectified ASAP before it spilled out to the public via the world media. They did not want a repeat of what happened twenty years ago when a young Austrian entrepreneur distributed military secrets on a publicly accessible website. Now that one of the United States' own had sold secrets to the enemy, just as Robert Hanssen (a former FBI agent) did thirty years ago. And there was some similarity between Assad and Edward Snowden. Those three incidents were an embarrassment to the intelligence community and the entire US government. Milson knew that his role was to get this guy without drawing too much attention to himself or to the contract, which was a difficult line to toe given the trail of destruction Assad was leaving behind him. But Milson also knew that any little help would be useful, even if he did not want to have to deal with it.

Weaver continued his explanation to the salty bounty hunter, saying,

"If Assad is in Dubai or any other Islamic country, Fuller is the one who can sniff him out. He's an expert at covert and black ops, not to mention intel gathering. I know you're the primary on this, and you have authorization from Cooper and the president to do whatever it takes to get this guy, but I'm telling you, we need all the help we can get in finding him, and Fuller is the type of help we need."

"You're pretty sure about your man, aren't you, Weaver?" said Milson with a questioning gaze.

"Milson, I'm telling you, this guy knows what he's doing. David Fuller is one of the best agents MI6 has to offer, especially when it comes to stuff like this. In my book, he's the shit. No pun intended but I'm saying that in a good way."

Milson looked at Weaver strangely and said,

"Okay, I'm trusting you on this. But if something happens and this deal goes south and we lose our opportunity to grab Assad because you wanted to add another person into the mix, I'm going to hold you personally responsible. Got it?"

Weaver threw up his hands up and said, "No problem. If the shit hits the fan on this, I'll be the first one to take the hit."

Milson shook his head in approval, then turned to Sheppard, who was still talking with Commander True.

"Sheppard?" Milson said with authority,

"Do you still have True on the line?" The young ensign nodded with the phone pressed tightly against his ear.

"Inform him we need a flight out of here, like, right now—a one-way ticket to Dubai. And tell him to make it so we are not noticed by any onlookers."

Sheppard gave several nods while still on the phone. Then he looked over at Milson, still clutching the cell phone, and said,

"The commander heard you, Chief. He's getting in touch with one of our contacts stationed at the RAAF [Royal Australian Air Force] base headquarters in Richmond, near Sydney. He's going to set up an unmarked CIA C-5M Super Galaxy transport to fly us out of here. He wants to know our ETA from here to the base."

Milson looked at his watch and said,

"Inform him that we're leaving right now. Ask him to have that bird fully fueled and ready to go the second we arrive. We're going to have a long flight ahead of us, gentlemen, so let's prepare ourselves for it."

All three men made their exit, moving out of the emergency exit stairwell and into the lobby of the lavishing hotel to finalize their itinerary before leaving Australia.

Dubai International Airport, United Arab Emirates

Flight number 512 arrived in Dubai at a quarter after six on Friday evening. The Airbus A380 Assad was traveling on had made a smooth landing at the Dubai International Airport. While in the air between India, Kuwait, and his final destination, he had ceased posing as Ahmed Shaula and ditched the disguise, regaining his original appearance. He tossed off the fear and paranoia he'd felt earlier about revealing his identity, now feeling confident that he would not be seen as suspicious or be caught in a place thousands of miles away from the United States. Still, he knew that there were undercover CIA operatives and listening posts near to where he had just landed. He also knew about the wanted poster bearing his likeness that had been circulated to these agents. Assad took a few moments to consider the current circumstances, but he quickly dismissed any misgivings. He only had one thing in mind: delivering the plans and weapons to the organization that had promised to compensate him in exchange, and his upcoming meeting with the mysterious individual he had conversed with over the phone in Australia. To Milson, these were the only two things of any significance.

Assad exited the plane and proceeded to walk through the terminal, a spacious area congested with tourists. He took a look around at the lavish four-story airport. As he continued to make his way, looking for the carousel with his luggage, including the camouflage bags with the stolen weapons, he glanced quickly at his wristwatch, clearly a bit agitated and concerned. He was looking for someone of great importance, the individual he had been in nearly constant contact with ever since his departure from the States. Continuing to look at his watch, Assad was jittery. Still, he kept a cool appearance despite his compulsion to continually scan the crowd. Patiently standing by the luggage carousel, he finally caught sight of one his bags. Taking possession of the bag, he saw the others emerge, one right behind the other. He grabbed each of them and inspected them one at a time to see if he had the right bags without fully exposing the contents. Satisfied and relieved that everything had made it safely, he regained his composure and, picking up the three bags and the briefcase of money that he had taken from Shaula, started to walk away. But as he turned around to make his way through the crowd, he was stopped by a woman. She was average-looking and midsized with a sense of style that seemed European. Her body was very slender, yet curvy and well proportioned. She looked Caucasian, and her bone structure made her appear to be either European or Middle Eastern. Her long dark hair made her look mysterious. She was in Assad's way, hindering his movement, making not a sound. The two of them stared at each, although the woman was wearing black sunglasses, so it was impossible to see her eyes. After standing there awhile without saying a single word, the woman finally broke her silence.

"Lieutenant Commander Ad-dam Omar Assad?"

Assad made no movement and gave no response to the woman's question. He stood motionless in front of her. From an outsider's point of view, it might have looked as if Assad had finally been caught by the authorities with no chance of escape. This would have been a successful instalment if it had appeared to be true. That the information Weaver had given his contacts about Assad's arrival had finally reached the right people and the former commander was about to be apprehended. But in this case, it was the opposite of that. The casually dressed woman looked to be an agent—professional, strict, and with a hint of coldness to her appearance. But eventually, looks were deceiving. The mysterious woman took off her sunglasses. Slowly, a grin spread across her face, turning into a wide gleeful smile, then abruptly into joyful laughter. She began giggling.

"It's about time you got here, you gorgeous man. I've been waiting a long time for this." She lunged at him and put him in a full embrace, giving him a sensual kiss. Assad reciprocated by smiling a broad smile. Soon they managed to extract themselves from their fiery embrace.

"I am so happy that you're here. When I got your phone call asking me to meet you here instead of Holland, I didn't know what to expect," the woman said.

"I know, baby. It's been a long time since we last saw each other. But now, everything will be set right. I've got the plans and the weapons with me, along with something additional that will be of great benefit to our future," Assad said joyously.

"Ad-dam, are you sure about this? I know I've told you that I would stick with you through thick and thin and no matter what your decisions, but this thing you're doing is a little much, even for me to handle," the woman asked.

"Sweetheart, there's nothing to worry about. Trust me, we are in the clear. Absolutely nothing will come back on you. I've been waiting for the right time to do something like this. Really, I've been waiting ever since I was a kid and decided to join the military. The humiliation that my family suffered at the hands of the US government when we first arrived in the States was deplorable and disgusting. I've been waiting a long time for an opportunity like this to come along, and I'm not about to miss my chance to take it. The organization is our golden ticket. They're going to pay me double for what I know. We will have enough money to live out the rest of our lives in comfort and tranquility," boasted Assad.

"I know, baby, but what about the innocent lives you put in jeopardy because of this plan of yours? I'm no fan of the US government, but willingly giving up what you know to a terrorist organization that wants to take innocent lives in order to make a statement to the entire world and further its own maniacal purposes is not a good idea. And there is some evidence that this organization is not playing with a full deck. They sound like a radical group with an evil political agenda. Not to mention that if you get caught by the Americans, you could spend the rest of your life behind bars. And I don't even want to think about the other possibility, the death penalty, if they decide to hand that down as your sentence. I love you very much; I don't want to see anything happen to you," said the beautiful woman.

"Nothing will happen to me, sweetheart. I promise you. I've been careful in planning this and have covered all the necessary bases in order not to be caught by the Americans. And those innocent lives you speak of ... What about the innocent lives here in the Islamic world, the lives of thousands of men, women, and children who have suffered at the hands of the Americans' so-called democracy, which was supposed to bring peace, prosperity, and serenity? Instead, it brought nothing but death, destruction, and poverty, because the United States refuses to recognize Islamic rule and the fundamental Islamic values necessary for morally governing society. The Americans think that their way of life is better than that of the rest of the world. So, they force their views, their policies, their ideology, and their viewpoints, instead of understanding, and sincerely embracing, people from other cultures and backgrounds. The United States still believes that it is the savior of the world and that its policies and teachings are beyond reproach. No, this must be done. And I will see to it that the United States gets what it deserves. Now come on,

Desiree, I want to show you something in this briefcase that is going to change our lives forever."

The woman, now identified as Desiree, Assad's accomplice, picked up a couple of Assad's bags and walked with him to the airport exit. Once outside, they walked over to a parked vehicle, obviously a rental, and got in. Little did they know that while they'd been locked in their embrace inside, they were being watched. David Fuller, the British agent whom Weaver contacted earlier, was surveilling them from afar. He watched closely as they sped off in a two-door Mercedes-Benz that was white in color and very sporty.

Fuller took out his cell phone and speed-dialed one of the numbers in his directory. After waiting for the call to go through, he heard someone answer on the other end, and started speaking right away:

"Yes, David Fuller, SIS field op. ID number: 0-9-7-4, Iota, Gamma, Delta. Put me through to the CIA's liaisons department in the Special Activities Division in Langley, Virginia. I need to speak with Officer James Weaver. Code clearance: Omega, Alpha, 4-13-2-4." He waited awhile for the call to be connected. Once it had gone through, he began his dialog with Weaver immediately.

"Jimmy, hey, it's me. I think I have your man in sight. He just arrived in Dubai, like you said, several minutes ago. He left with a woman and was carrying three duffel bags and a briefcase, as you described. The car they left in is probably a rental. It's a white Mercedes-Benz SLK 700 class series. It won't be too hard to find around here. … Yeah, I received it yesterday; I already ran it through our database. … No problem. I'll put a tracker on him until you Yanks arrive. I'll also put surveillance on the car and find out who the girl is that's with him and where they're going. … No problem. I'll have one of my aides pick you blokes up. See you soon, mate."

Fuller walked casually out of the airport and over to his vehicle, which was not as luxurious as the Mercedes that Assad and Desiree had departed in, but it was enough to get him to wherever he was going.

CHAPTER 6

CONTACT

US Air Force Military C-5M Super Galaxy Transport

"Perfect!" Weaver said with enthusiasm.

"We just made it across the Indian Ocean. We'll probably have to make a pit stop at Diego Garcia [a US naval base located in the South Indian Ocean, in British territory] for fuel, then make our way toward the Arabian Sea channels! Our ETA will be five to six and a half hours from now, to the coordinates of N 25°3'56.52", E 55°10'16.61". Did you get the ID of Assad I sent you?! … Good. We'll be there shortly! Keep a close eye on him, Davy. He's a tricky bastard! … Good. We'll meet you at the embassy as soon as we touch down. Have a car ready to pick us up. … Yeah, same here. See you later."

Weaver got off the satellite phone with Fuller and headed straight for Milson who at the time was preoccupied with his laptop that was issued to him by Dixon and the ONI technicians. Milson was going over the background files on Assad, which he hadn't gotten a chance to look at during his stopovers on the flights. He sat alone in a seat between two vacant spots and probed through Assad's personal and military background in order to become familiar with the man. In his short time as a company man in the CIA, and now as a bail enforcement officer, Milson had learned to study the patterns and behaviors of fugitives or, as in this case, targets of retrieval. Concentrating intensely, Milson was going over Assad's files, page by page. Going all the way back to when he and his family migrated to the United States in the middle of the first decade of the 2000s and his enlistment in the navy.

Weaver could see that Milson was engrossed, but he interrupted anyway.

"Killian, I just got off the phone with Fuller. He says he spotted Assad just now. He arrived at the airport several minutes ago and left with a woman in a white Mercedes-Benz. Fuller is tracking the vehicle as we speak. I told him we'll arrive at the airport within five-in-half hours. I also informed him that we'll meet him at the British Embassy in downtown Abu Dhabi."

"Good. Have Sheppard call ONI, and tell him to speak directly to a Commander Sean Dixon of counterintelligence. Tell him what's going on and that we've got a positive lock on Assad."

When Weaver was about to turn away and inform Sheppard, Milson abruptly stops him for a moment.

"Hey, Weaver, look at what I found out about our guy. He and his parents came to the States after the toppling of Saddam Hussein's regime in 2003. From this file, it seems his father couldn't go back to Lebanon because he already had renounced his citizenship there. And his ties to Lebanon's military would've made him a substantial target for other Islamic groups that wanted to profit from his knowledge and expertise in political matters and his skills in chemical engineering. Assad's parents made an exodus out of the middle east, and landed in the States around the beginning or middle of 2004; that's when the Iraqi war started to heat up. Assad's father and mother thought it would be safe to live in the United States, away from the turmoil and political uprising over there. Assad was only ten years old at the time, but I think he was aware of the conflict that was going on in his country. When they came over from Iraq, his parents, especially his father, were interrogated heavily by the CIA, NSA, Homeland Security, and INS [Immigration and Naturalization Service's] because of the his history with the Lebanese government and Iraq's chemical engineering department. According to what I'm reading here, Assad's father was an assistant supervisor overseeing Saddam's energy development plants and oil refineries. Our agencies drilled him for weeks, seeking to learn of his knowledge about nuclear engineering and military weapons. They were suspicious that he'd had a hand in developing the new high-tech weapons that Saddam supposedly wanted to use against neighboring Iran. When our agencies figured out later that Assad's father was harmless, not having carried much weight at the time and likely not having known much about the development of any WMDs, or having any vital intelligence they could use, they cut him loose without an apology or explanation for the way he was treated."

"So, what you're saying is that as a child, Assad grew resentful because of what he and his family were going through." said Weaver.

"Yes," replied Milson.

"But it looks like it got worse over the years. Look at this: Around 2011, during the Arab uprisings in North Africa and other Islamic areas, Assad's father was called back for more questioning. The CIA at the time wanted to know why suddenly millions of Muslims were rioting and revolting against their own governments. They assumed that even though he'd been away from his country for many years, Almach Assad [Ad-dam's father] still had a strong political influence in that region. But of course, they found nothing. And once again, they threw him out like yesterday's garbage. They even questioned Assad's mother, Chafika Dina Assad, who was at that time an activist for Muslim women's rights, to see if she had any ties to what was happening over there. Assad, who was a teenager at the time, filed charges of harassment and discrimination against the State Department and the CIA, but the charges never stuck and they were dropped because again Assad Sr. didn't know anything and we had no evidence to back his claim."

"So, in other words, Assad started to manifest hatred for his adopted country because of the way his parents were treated by our government when they first came to the States." replied Weaver.

"Not only his parents, but also he and his siblings. Even though he graduated top of his class from Yale, he would get into fights with fellow students about his ethnicity and Islamic lineage. He would speak at public events and town hall meetings about the mistreatment and bigotry of Muslim Americans in the United States. He even protested against US military involvement in Libya amid the coalition air bombings that took place."

"Well, that's a good enough reason to turn traitor, wouldn't you say?" said Weaver, who was being condescending.

"I don't know about that, James. From what I've gathered on this guy, he had a legitimate beef with our government and it seems to me that his feelings go a little bit deeper than that. Something in his subconscious—something very deep and personal—had to be the thing that caused him to turn and do what he has done."

As Milson continued to stare at Assad's file on the screen, Weaver asked,

"Hey, do you still want me to tell the kid to call Washington?"

Milson jumped for a moment upon realizing what Weaver had said.

"Yeah, yeah," he said, as he was startled for a moment but continued his concentration on Assad's file.

"Have him talk to Commander Dixon like I said. He will inform Admiral Cooper and the president of what's going on."

"Gotcha. I'll let him know."

Weaver went back up front to tell Sheppard what was going on and to inform him about contacting Washington as per Milson's request. Milson turned his attention back to the computer and Assad's files. He stared at a photo of Assad from the navy's database. To the casual observer, it might have seemed that Milson was fixated on Assad's file, but his thoughts went much in-depth than that. He was reminiscing about his earlier days in the army in the late

2000s. It was obvious only to him that he was replacing the face of Assad's with Major Nidal Malik Hassan, the shooter at Fort Hood Army Installation in Killeen, Texas. Milson witnessed that massacre twenty-one years ago he was stationed there at the time. In his own mind, he was psychologically getting the two perpetrators mixed up due to the trauma he endured. He grew angry and restless, although outwardly he appeared calm and settled. Realizing that he was having an intense PTSD [Post Traumatic Stress Disorder] flashback, he quickly gathered himself together, and turned his attention to what was more important. Easing his focus away from the cross he felt he was his bearing at the time. He quickly put aside his past and aimed his full focus on what he was there for: to capturer Ad-dam Omar Assad—alive, if possible—and take him back to stand trial for what he has done.

British Embassy, Dubai, United Arab Emirates

It was early Saturday morning, and the C-5M transport has just touched down at the Dubai International Airport. The tower had cleared them to land earlier due to their US military identification and CIA credentials. As Milson and party were departing from the craft, they were greeted as soon as they made it down the exit ramp of the plane. The individuals who were there to meet them were definitely government officials, conservative in their apparel and very diplomatic in their attitude and appearance—professional to the teeth. It was obvious that they were from the embassy—both Arab and British nationals coexisting thanks to their respective countries' diplomatic partnership and cooperation. One of the officials walked up to Milson and introduced himself.

"Officer Weaver?" he asked with an affable smile.

Milson turned toward Weaver, looking for a response, but all he got from him was a snicker and a grin. Milson answered in an abrasive tone,

"No, this is Officer Weaver," as he pointed to his right.

"I'm Killian Milson, federal apprehensions officer with the United States Justice Department. I'm the one you're looking for, not Officer Weaver." Realizing his mistake, the government official apologized with sincerity.

"Oh, I am sorry, Mr. Milson. I was sent here by one of my constituents to pick up an Officer James Weaver of the Central Intelligence Agency, along with the party under his supervision," replied the mild-mannered official, who was overwhelmingly confused.

"No, I think you have that mixed up. Weaver is with me, as is Agent Sheppard, who's to my left. He's an officer with the Naval Criminal Investigation Service. They are under my supervision. I'm the leader of this group," said Milson with great irritation.

The agent was at a loss, and again very apologetic for his mistake.

"I'm sorry for the confusion, Mr. Milson. I'm Assistant Aide Sabin Farad, liaisons officer and consultant to the British Secret Service, from the United Arab Emirates government. I'm here to escort you to the embassy to meet with my supervisor and field officer, Agent Fuller. If you gentlemen would care to enter the vehicles, we will attend to your bags at once. Once again, my apologies, Mr. Milson. And welcome to Dubai." Agent Farad gave a complimentary bow to Milson, a gesture of cordiality. Milson reciprocated and followed the agent. Milson and his team got into the unmarked vehicles while the others secured their luggage. The cars sped off, leaving the tarmac of the airport and entering the congested streets of Dubai.

As they were being escorted, Milson and the others were taking by the sights of the beautiful city of Dubai and its remarkable landscapes. As they were mesmerized by the city's magnificence, they did not realize that they had arrived at the embassy. Milson and party were impressed by the huge facility. It was a skyscraper of magnificent engineering. Tall, made of glass and steel with a hint of American ingenuity but had been constructed by Arabs, having been designed by Arabian architects. The cars stopped in front of the main entrance, where David Fuller was waiting for them.

Fuller was not your typical British national. Indeed, he was the opposite of what one may expect an MI6/SIS agent was supposed to look like. He was neither dashing nor devilishly handsome like the typical Ian Fleming hero. No, he looked more like Crocodile Dundee, but with a look of disdain on his face. Rugged with sturdy features and a huskiness that made him appear outdoorsy and scruffy. He did not resemble your typical bureaucratic field agent. He wasn't muscular or bulky, although he was strong. He was dressed casually in attire suited to the warm climate—very different from what his colleagues were wearing when they'd picked up Milson and party.

As the visitors got out of the car, Weaver, noticing Fuller right away, headed straight toward him as if they were long-lost brothers finally reuniting.

"Davy, you old British bulldog! How the hell are you?"

"Better than you, you Yankee bloke! You've packed on some weight since I last saw you. What's the matter, the bloody CIA hasn't been giving you enough field work lately? Pushing too many pencils, you old bastard? Looks as if you've been sitting around on your fat lazy ass collecting government paychecks I see."

The two men laughed as they traded insults at one another. Milson and Sheppard, not part of the reunion, came up from behind and made their presence known, with Milson nudging at Weaver from the back, seeking to be introduced.

"Davy, this is the guy I've been telling you about, Killian Milson, former CIA and US army intelligence. He's working with ONI to capture Commander Assad. He's the primary on this and the leader of our group. His cover is as a USFAA officer right now."

"Pleasure to meet you, Agent Milson." Fuller stretched out his arm to give Milson a handshake. Milson reluctantly reciprocated. Weaver turned to Sheppard.

"And this is Ensign James Sheppard, also with ONI. His cover is as an NCIS agent."

Fuller shook Sheppard's hand as well.

"Glad to meet you too, mate. Come on in. There's some interesting stuff that I pulled up on your guy. Follow me."

All four gentlemen, plus Farad and his colleagues, walked down a somewhat crowded corridor as Fuller began to brief them.

"As I told you over the phone, I was about to wait for you to show up before I put a tail on your man, but I didn't want to lose the opportunity of losing him so, I put one on anyway, and this is what I came up with. When Assad got here, he was met by this woman at the airport." Fuller showed Milson and Weaver the photo he had taken of Assad and Desiree.

"ID recognition identifies her as Desiree Asherah. She's a US national, but she was born in Iraq. She has a degree in political science and finance from Yale University. She resides in Holland, where she works as an accountant in a financial firm. She moved there a two-in-a half years ago to take the job. I put an ID tag on the car they drove off in. It's a rental registered in her name. She arrived here several days before Assad." Fuller gave Milson the picture and some other information about Asherah as they arrived at a very spacious luxurious stateroom occupied by other governmental officials.

"I also traced her financial and credit card transactions. She's staying at the Emirates Towers in downtown Dubai, a very classy, very expensive hotel."

"How long has she been staying there?" Milson asked.

"About two days now. She arrived here late Thursday afternoon. Your man must have contacted her and asked her to meet him here."

"That sounds about right, Killian," replied Weaver.

"Remember, he booked a flight that Wednesday night after he killed Shaula and Gardner. He must have called Asherah in advance and told her to meet him here. From the looks of it, given their educational background, it seems that she and Assad knew each other from the same university that they attended."

"Yeah, an old college sweetheart," replied Milson in a low rough tone.

"That makes perfect sense, Mr. Weaver. Who else can you trust when you know that the government you used to work for is after you? A loyal friend from your past. And I'll bet you that Assad is going to get ahold of his contacts and tell them to meet him and this woman here so he can give them the plans and weapons in exchange for whatever he is asking for." said Sheppard.

"You're right, kid. But for him to do that, he would have had to change his entire plan in order to make this transaction successful. There has to be another reason, other than the lavish scenery of this place, why he chose to do the exchange here." Milson and the rest of them began wracking their brains, trying to figure out why Assad wanted to come to Dubai.

After thinking about it for several seconds, Weaver came up with an answer.

"Killian, I remember something you said earlier when we were in Sydney. You said Dubai was a logical choice for Assad because here he could blend in and not be conspicuous. He knows that he can do the trade here without being discovered. No one around here knows him. And if somehow he does get caught by us—"

"Then he'll have an easier way to hide out by blending in with the local population," Milson said, finishing Weaver's thought.

"He speaks fluent Arabic and knows the culture very well because of his background. Not to mention the intelligence that he has gathered over his many years of being employed at ONI and attached to a SEAL unit stationed in areas like this."

"You're right, Chief! Then he'll wait for a few days until everything has settled down to make his move. And when the opportunity presents itself, thinking that everything is clear, he will slip out the back door and go to another country that is not bound by any extradition treaty and has no ties to the United States. At the same time, this terrorist group or organization that he's doing business with will have in their possession our weapons and secrets. This bastard is really smart, Chief!" exclaimed Sheppard.

"If you guys are right about this, then we have to raid that hotel immediately and arrest this Assad at once," Fuller said.

"No," said Milson.

"Sending a bunch of agents or a tactical team in there will just tip him off. Assad knows your protocols and strategies for undercover operations and surveillance. He's got a list of all US intelligence agents and their allies who are deep under cover in foreign countries. Sending a bunch of bloodhounds into the woods to chase after the fox is just going to make him go deeper into the woods or underground. He needs to be caught off guard, and I'm the only one that can do it. He doesn't know me."

"What do you mean, Mr. Milson?" asked Fuller with curiosity.

"I was hired to get this guy because my name does not appear on that list of undercover agents on covert op missions, unlike yours, Weaver's, and Sheppard's. I quit the company years ago, and the data that Assad stole doesn't include my name or any of my information. He doesn't even know I exist."

"Well, you still should have backup ready just in case he tries to run. I can create a special response team to assist you when needed," suggested Fuller, who was quite adamant.

"No, Fuller, that will only spook him. He'll see your guys coming from a mile away. I need to catch him in the act, take him by surprise. If I do need any assistance, Weaver and Sheppard will be my backup. But the real issue here is going to be getting close to him without him knowing it. And I think that his girlfriend is one of my ways in. If I can get closer to her and develop some familiarity with her, I will be increasing my chances to get Assad."

"How in the hell will you be able to do that, Agent Milson? Do you speak bloody Arabic? And are you even familiar with the locals here, or their culture, mate?" Fuller asked.

Instead of blowing up at the British agent who was questioning Milson's knowledge and expertise in handling foreign affairs as well as apprehending runaway criminals, Milson just sneered at him while indulging to his question.

"As a matter of fact, Agent Fuller, yes I do. I speak four different languages, and one of them happens to be Arabic, which I am very fluent in. I spent a year and a half in Iraq and two in Afghanistan when I was in the army. I did a total of five tours for the CIA in the Middle East: one in Libya, one in Saudi, two in Syria, and one in Egypt. That's not counting my other tours in Western Europe. And to be honest with all of you, I'm the likeliest candidate to blend in around here since my complexion is darker than any of yours. I can pass myself off as a Middle Easterner or African national better than any of you guys ever could. Assad will not see me coming until it's too late. Oh, and by the way, Agent Fuller, I know more about this culture and its history than you know your own. Don't ever question my abilities or skills as a professional. You have no idea how skillful I am in reconnaissance and how capable I am as a tracker."

Fuller's eyes were ablaze as he glared at Milson. It was plain that he wanted to knock this arrogant, cocky American on his ass. But given the number of spectators around them, such a thing would not be possible if Fuller wished to maintain his reputation as an Englishman and an intelligence officer representing the government of the United Kingdom.

Seeing the tension developing between Fuller and Milson, Weaver intervened.

"Okay, you guys, why don't we cool our jets and continue this tomorrow? We're exhausted and hanging on by a thread after our long flight over here. Agent Farad, if you don't mind, will you show us where we are going to be staying for the night?"

The Dubai official humbly nodded to Weaver and asked Milson and Sheppard to follow him to the accommodations that they had set up for them. As Milson and Sheppard walked away, following Farad and his men, Weaver stayed back to talk more with Fuller and calm him down.

"The bloody nerve of that wanker, Jimmy! Where the fuck did you get this asshole from?!" said Fuller, who was outraged and still steaming.

"Calm down, David. I know he's cocky, egotistical, and arrogant, but he knows his shit. To tell you the truth, he's been right about our man's patterns so far. If it weren't for him, we wouldn't have gotten this far. Just follow his lead on this so we can get this guy."

"I don't know about this, Jimmy. You know how I was when I was in His Majesty's Marine Corps. I didn't take shit off of anybody back then, and I'm bloody hell not about to start now! And that includes arrogant pricks like him!" Fuller said strongly.

"I know. But you've got to chill out on this one. He's the primary on this mission. The president, along with SECDEF [Secretary of Defense] and SECNAV [Secretary of the Navy], wanted this guy on the case. So did my boss and the director of naval intelligence, who is the one calling the shots, Davy. And Milson has been given the authority and the green light to do as he pleases." Weaver said, trying to steady the already displeased Fuller.

"I don't bloody care if King Charles himself hired him. If he gets in my face one more time like that and throws his cheek at me again, I'm not going to be responsible for what happens to him. Do you hear me, mate?"

"I got you. But for now, relax and let things take their course. Now, do you have eyes on Assad and his girlfriend?" Weaver asked.

"Yeah, I've got electronic surveillance on every corner of every block around the hotel. He can't make a move—can't go in or out—without us knowing about it."

"Good, because it's important that we get this guy, Davy. We can't afford to let him slip through our fingers. This guy knows too much and can give up a lot of info to this radical terrorist group that wants to put us in the ground. The information that he has is vital to both our governments, yours and mine." Weaver paused for a second to look around.

"Hey, by the way, do you have a bar in this place? I think I need a drink after that long flight," he said.

"Wait a minute, I thought you were off the sauce, you drunken bloat. You told me that you quit after your divorce from your second wife," replied Fuller, surprised by Weaver's request.

"Hey, if you were in my place, having to deal with a bitter old ex-army spook and a wet-behind-the-ears navy brat on a flight that takes almost seven hours, you would be running to the barrel yourself. And besides, you know that *air force* doesn't associate with army or navy. They're beneath us in every way."

"Oh, but you'll hang out with an old English marine now, won't you, you goddamn Yankee braggart?" replied Fuller, hysterical.

"Hey, do I have a choice?" he asked. "At least you're not as tight-assed as Milson is." he said under his breath as started walking down the main corridor, laughing and reminiscing about the days they'd spent together doing jobs for their respective clandestine agencies.

Emirates Towers Hotel, Downtown Dubai, United Arab Emirates, 12:45 a.m.

It was late at night. Assad and Asherah laid naked together, side by side, caressing each other in a comfortable bed in their suite located on the tenth floor of the luxurious Emirates Towers, which overlooked downtown Dubai. It was obvious by their appearance that they had just finished having intercourse. They were locked in a passionate embrace. The soft, tantalizing sounds of mild Arabian music playing in the background as a gentle breeze blew in through the open glass balcony doors. They looked into each other's eyes with compassion devotion and desire. Showing their deep love for one another and the commitment they have for each other. To Assad, Asherah was magnificent and beautiful. She was glowing as a sultry angel as she laid on top of him, the sweat from her body glistening in the moonlight, beading on her caramel-colored skin. She had a perfectly toned physique, Assad thought, as she wrapped her arms around his torso and buried her face in the center of his chest, then stared up at him intensely. They had spent hours in the hotel room conversing about their future plans. Asherah had brought up Assad's intricate plan to surrender the disc, the flash drive, and the weapons to his contacts within the organization. He'd decided to keep the money he took from Shaula in Sydney knowing the consequences if he were to get caught by those same terrorists.

"Ad-dam, I know we've been over this, but are you sure that this is the right thing to do? Aren't these people going to want their money back after it was taken from them?"

Hearing her concerns, Assad gently rubbed her face and produced a smile to comfort her, saying, "Sweetheart, you worry too much. They have no idea that I took the money from the man who stole it from them in the first place. If they ask about it, I'll just tell them that I didn't find it. Once I hand them the data and the guns, we will be three hundred million dollars richer. That's not including the twenty-five million that's in the briefcase. We will spend the rest of our lives in luxury and comfort, living wherever you want to live—France, Greece, Italy, Spain, or Sweden. We can even go back to Holland if you so desire. But we don't have to stay in Europe if you don't want to. We can go to the Caribbean, or a South Pacific Island of your choice. It doesn't matter. We are going to live like kings and queens for the rest of our lives."

Asherah grinned at the notion, but her smile soon faded as another concern came over her.

"Ad-dam, I know you and I have been through a lot together. From the time you and your family left Iraq to the time we first saw each other on the Yale campus, I've been in love with you. I've been in love with you since we were kids in Baghdad. After you left, my heart crumbled because I thought I would never see you again. You are my life, and I love you very much. I will be at your side through thick and thin, no matter what, but I want you to be honest with me. Throughout everything that has happened, from the time you left the States up till now, have you hurt anyone in the process of accomplishing this plan of yours? I want you to be honest with me because I love you dearly." She paused to gather the courage to speak the next question. "Tell me the truth: have you hurt anyone?"

Assad sat up momentarily. His expression changed slightly because he did not know how to respond to the question. He could not see his way of telling her the truth about what he'd done in the past forty-eight hours between leaving the states and arriving in Dubai. She knew of his occupation at ONI, but she was unaware that he had special training with special forces and had skills equivalent to those of a trained assassin. These aspects of his life and career remained hidden to the woman he loved. He purposely kept those portions of his life secret from her. In his mind and to his defense, Asherah was too innocent and too fragile to know of such things.

Assad turned his head away from Asherah, hoping to avoid her gaze as she lay waiting for his answer. Knowing there was no escaping this awkward situation, he turned back toward her and said with conviction and false sincerity,

"No, Desiree. I have not hurt anyone. I swear it." He gazed into her light-almond-colored eyes as they filled with tears of relief and satisfaction. Knowing that he was deceiving her, he found the thought of exposing her to a psychological trauma objectionable. Figuring that it would emotionally devastate her if she knew the truth. To him, Asherah's naivete was what that kept her innocent and pure. She moved closer to him, resting her head on his chest once more as if she was about to go to sleep. Simultaneously wrapping her arms around his torso for comfort and security. Assad reciprocated instantly. He held the woman whom he claimed to love very much, while strangely thinking about Charlene Gardner and the life he took from her in Sydney. It was tragic that she found out the truth about him and his intentions that terminated her life. But he felt that he'd had no choice but to kill her if he wished to safeguard his identity and secret. He knew he could not tell Desiree about Charlene, who would have been shattered to learn that he'd had an affair with another woman, no matter how brief it was.

Assad feared that not a day would go by without his thinking about Charlene and the violent way in which he had taken her life. He obviously didn't have strong feelings for Charlene as he had for Asherah, or any emotional bond with her, but he had enjoyed her company very much, even if she was only a temporary distraction at the time. Sometimes he would flash back to the expression of shock on her face as he stabbed her in the back of the neck, killing her to keep his plan a secret. It was something he knew he'd never forget, looking into the eyes of a person with whom he'd been intimate with. The memory of her face still haunts him as he was the catalyst of witnessing her life essence leave her body prematurely.

In another way, though, Assad had no problem killing, no matter the circumstances. He had been trained for it, and when it came time to use his training, he showed no hesitation, weakness, or remorse, at least not where Kareem and Shaula were concerned. But killing an innocent person with whom he had a relationship with, even if it was brief and meaningless, did not sit well with him. Yes, he was a man filled with pent-up anger, frustration, and rage, a man who was highly opinionated and very political. But deep within his psyche, he did feel compassion and regret, especially when considering that Charlene did not deserve to die in such a horrible way. Still, he was certain that he had done the right thing. If he would have changed his mind and let Charlene go, then he would not have gotten as far as he has now. Because of this, he confirmed to himself that it was necessary to execute Charlene in order to finish what he had started. Dismissing any further thoughts of his past aggression, Assad continued to lie comfortably with Asherah on the twisted bedsheets beneath them. They both fell into a deep, soothing sleep, the two of them holding each other and daring not to let go.

Little did Assad know, several miles away at the British Embassy, the group of people who were determined to capture him by any means necessary were making a plan.

British Embassy, Dubai, United Arab Emirates

At six o'clock Sunday morning, Milson was wide-eyed and ready to go. He'd gotten up an hour earlier than everyone else to get his equipment squared away for the initial plan to take Assad at the hotel. Milson was loading both the handguns he had brought with him, namely, the SIG Sauer, which was his primary, and the Glock, which was his backup. When he was about to stash them away in his holster, a knock came at his door.

"Yeah?!" as he shouted through the door, inviting whoever to come in.

Surprisingly, it was Sheppard. Barging in without introduction.

"Chief, Weaver and Fuller are ready to go. They've got video surveillance on the hotel where Assad and the girl are staying. They're waiting for us in the TOC."

Milson gave a quick nod while finishing his business. He followed Sheppard out the door with a quick pace. They proceeded down the corridor to meet up with the rest of the group. As they were walking, Sheppard handed Milson a sheet of paper that had some important information on it.

"Chief, I should have given you the heads-up on this last night, but I was so tired that I completely forgot about it."

"No problem, kid. What is it?" Milson asked in a low tone.

"Remember you asked me to look up the information on the cell phone back in Sydney? Well, I got the results. You were right: the phone did belong to the girl. More importantly, it was turned on the whole time she was there. Commander True had send it up to one of our analysts, and they found out that when Charlene Gardner made a call that evening, her phone automatically recorded the entire conversation. The SIM card in her phone happened to store not only specific information about messages and contacts but also any downloads, text messages, and voice mail communications between the subscriber and the person she talked to. On here it says that Ms. Gardner found out about Commander Assad by looking at an email that was sent to him on his laptop. When she read it and found out who he really was and what he was about, she tried to call the airport to book an earlier flight to get out of there. But it was too late because Assad already knew about the message from his cell phone prior to her reading it on the computer. His email app informed him prior of receiving the message."

"And when he discovered she'd looked at his email, he did the only logical thing he could've done: he killed her. So, the girl was innocent after all and had nothing to do with Assad other than having a sexual relationship with him." Milson paused for a moment to read the report. "What I don't understand is why he would keep his phone when he knows that we're going to track it. Why wouldn't he replace it with a prepaid one? And second, why haven't we been able to track his movements using his personal phone or pick up transmission calls that will track his whereabouts when he calls out?"

"That's easy, Chief," Sheppard said.

"Even though Commander Assad is a dangerous individual, he's still a tech wizard just like me, and a one clever if I say so myself." Milson snickered at the young officer, who was trying his best to impress him, but paid it no mind.

"Assad knows that we are going to monitor his every move through his only means of communication—his phone. Somehow, he managed to get his hands on a scrambler chip that blocks all caller ID, GPS signals, tracking devices, and frequency locators within a thousand-mile radius. Remember, Chief, he was assistant supervisor of counterintelligence and had access to all top-secret hardware and software. There is no need for him to use a disposable phone when he has the latest telecommunications software and knows how to disable his phone without getting caught or compromised. It wouldn't make any difference to him at all, Chief. He knows how to play the game." Sheppard stated.

"This makes him even more dangerous than I thought. We must get this guy before it's too late. Good job, kid. I really underestimated you. You know your stuff, despite you being a squid and all."

Sheppard grinned at the sarcasm but realize it was Milson's way of complimenting him. It seemed that this was Milson's way of being grateful, even if it was derogatory.

Continuing down the hallway, they arrived at the briefing room, where Fuller and Weaver were waiting for them.

"Bout time you made it, Killian," Weaver said loudly.

"Everything is in play for us to make our move."

Milson and Sheppard walked to a table where Weaver was giving a briefing on the surveillance of the hotel.

"Fuller has cameras positioned all around the hotel on every block. He also has lookouts stationed in those areas. All we need to do is to position ourselves along those areas to catch Assad and the girl when they try to leave and make contact to whoever he meets with."

Milson looked over the printout of the plan.

"Weaver, I thought I told you that we don't need lookouts. That's only going to spook Assad if he sees them. If you're going to put some guys in place, it's going to be us."

Fuller interjected.

"Chief Milson, with all due respect, I think it will be a good idea to have some people there just in case your man tries to run. I can have my men cordon off any areas that look like potential escape routes for Assad. He won't even know they are there."

"Agent Fuller, I appreciate your help and the services of your men, but setting up guys in those areas is not going to help us at all. Assad doesn't realize that we're here. He knows that the US government is looking for him, but he doesn't know who exactly it is. We know the man is smart. His job was counterintelligence, and from the reports given to me by his former supervisor, this guy is not dumb, stupid, or complacent. He has knowledge of all foreign personnel working with different government intelligence agencies, including MI6 personnel stationed in the embassies of foreign countries like this one. He's been trained to spot covert operatives, suspicious activity, and anything out of the ordinary. He's going to spot your men in a matter of seconds, even if they are locals. Assad does not need to be tipped off. He doesn't have actual knowledge of me or my crew. We can get him by doing it my way." argued Milson.

"If you're so sure that he'll spot my guys right off the bat, what makes you think he won't get a good look at yours? No disrespect to you, Weaver, old chum, but you and Ensign Sheppard don't exactly fit in with the majority around here. You two blokes will stick out like a pair of sore thumbs in these parts. You guys are whiter than I am. What makes you think Assad won't pick your guys out from the crowd?"

"Fuller is right." Thought, Milson. There had to be another way to smoke out Assad without being conspicuous and out of place. Contemplating on their current objective, he thought long and hard on how this was going to work out and fall into their favor. After looking around the room at his present company for which they did not have an answer, Milson humbly asked Fuller for a solution that would help them solve their predicament.

"Good point, Fuller. You may have something there… Do you have anything that would keep us off his proverbial radar so he won't spot us out?"

Fuller's left eyebrow raised as he pondered an idea that might help them in the surveillance over Assad.

"Dubai has a huge tourist population, right? And most of the tourists are Europeans or Americans who fit the Caucasian profile. Am I correct?" Everyone nodded at Fullers questioning. "Well, all we have to do is disguise you three as tourist who are new to the country."

Milson thought about it and agreed with the notion. The idea was sudden and last minute, but it was valid and made sense. The expressions on their faces indicated that this idea was logical and reasonable due to the time frame of their objective.

Weaver expressed his opinion by saying,

“Killian, I think Fuller has got something. Dubai is a big tourist attraction with many people from other countries coming in and out to visit. Assad would never suspect a thing.”

“Yeah, I think Fuller has something here, but we need to act quickly if we’re going to get him. From Fullers sources, they believe that he and his girlfriend may be checking out of the hotel very soon.” Milson replied.

“And on his way to meet up with his contacts to hand over the plans and weapons.” continued Weaver as he finished Milson’s statement.

“Well, gentlemen, if that’s the case, we’d better get started right now.” said Milson, who turned his attention to his team as they further discussed their plans to catch Assad. Fuller turned to Farad, who was standing beside him requested that he gather up his tactical team as a last-minute deterrent if the original plan goes south. This was at that time the moment of truth. After days of filtering out leads, locations and man power, Milson and his crew were finally at the pinnacle of capturing Assad and finding out who his contacts were along with discovering the identity of the mysterious terrorist organization that he had been affiliated with for more than three years during his service with the navy. This by no means was going to be the highlight of the operation, or so they thought.

CIA Headquarters, Langley, Virginia

On the other side of the globe, hours before the plan to capture Assad was to commence, Admiral Cooper and Commander Dixon, the latter serving as aide to the former, were making their way to Clandestine Headquarters within the CIA building, walking through the glass doors at the front entrance. They were on their way upstairs to meet Director Richards, who was not aware of their presence there. The reason they were there was obvious. They had information about Assad's whereabouts and wanted to relay it to the director in person.

The first to notice Cooper coming through the door was Richards's secretary. She had just finished uploading documents related to the current CIA caseload to their electronic files. When she saw the admiral had made his way through, she automatically jumped from her computer and greeted the ONI director with graciousness and pleasantries. After leading Cooper and Dixon to Richards's office, she knocked on the door. Richards, who was startled at first, shouted in an abrasive tone, which led his secretary to crack open the door and pop her head in through the narrow space.

"Director, sorry to disturb you, but Admiral Cooper from naval intelligence is here."

Richards waved his hand, saying,

"Send him in, Ann."

She opened the door wider so Cooper and Dixon could make their entrance. Richards stood up to shake Cooper's hand, but instead of reciprocating, Cooper began immediately, saying,

"General, we got him."

At first, Richards was dumbfounded. But later he regained possession of his faculties and came to realize what Cooper was talking about.

"Wait a minute. You found Assad?" he asked in a surprising tone.

"Yes, we did. He's in Dubai right now. Milson and his team tracked him from Australia. He's now in central United Arab Emirates, in Dubai. Commander Dixon received a call from one of our junior officers who is with Milson. Right now, they're at the British Embassy which is located there."

"How in the hell did he know he was there, let alone where to find him?" asked Richards, who was skeptical at first, but curious as well.

Cooper turned to Dixon to answer the director's question. "Somehow they found out that Assad was in Sydney due to a murder that took place there. There were two victims involved. One was an American female in her mid-twenties, and the other was a Middle Eastern male in his late forties. The young woman happened to be a relative of an officer within our ranks, and the gentleman was an Egyptian businessman who dealt in finance and historical artifacts. They were both killed by a man familiar to them who had disguised himself as the deceased Gary Brown."

"Assad!" said Richards as his voice raised an octave.

"But wait a minute, Wayne. How do you know it was Assad? And why would he kill two more people, knowing full well that he would only draw more attention to himself?"

Dixon answered,

"From our agent's report, Chief Milson picked up a cell phone at the crime scene that belonged to the woman he killed. They sent the phone to Indonesia, where some of our ONI specialists are stationed. The analyst there deciphered a conversation that had taken place over the phone. Fortunately, it was recorded by the phones SIM card. It appeared that Assad was having a relationship with this woman, who found out who he was, and what he was planning by reading a private email on his computer. She tried to book a flight out of Sydney to escape, but unfortunately Ad-dam found out—and the consequences for her were severe and tragic. Later, after killing the woman, he took on another identity. This time it was an Egyptian businessman who was later identified as Ahmed Shaula. We gathered some interesting intelligence on Shaula, but we also believe that he was one of Commander Assad's contacts and might have had dealings with him in the past."

"So, Assad kills the woman that discovers his identity, and later kills the guy who happens to be his contact. But why would he do that?" Richards asked, thinking the situation is a bit peculiar.

"Isn't it obvious, Harold? He needed a "patsy" to get out of the country before he was found out. This Ahmed Shaula was the perfect scapegoat. Assuming the identity of this individual would be a sure thing, especially since he had killed two other people. Chief Milson, along with one of my operatives and one of your officers, has been working with MI6 who spotted Assad arriving at the airport over there." Cooper relayed.

"British Secret Service?! I thought we were trying to keep this under wraps! How in the hell did they get involved?!" Richards asked abruptly while confused.

"Well, it was suggested by one of your men named James Weaver. Somehow, he coaxed the chief into letting one of their agents help them subdue Assad." Cooper replied.

"Weaver… I know of him. Good man, but too damn impulsive," replied Richards as he shook his head in disapproval. "Reminds me a lot of Milson and his bad habits. But if that's the case, the Brits are definitely going to want a piece of this."

"Not to worry, Harold," Cooper said, trying to calm the retired general.

"I contacted MI6 and spoke to their director firsthand. I informed them about our situation and told them that we are the primary on this. I had gotten approval to contact them from the president, SECDEF, and the vice chief of naval operations [Admiral Taylor]. It seems that our president is chummy with the prime minister and King Charles."

"Well, that's reassuring, Wayne. But I think we need to look at this more cautiously and collectively, don't you think?"

While still showing concern in a opinionating tone, the director stands up from behind his desk and walks around it to approach Cooper and Dixon.

"I know this is a silly question to ask you, but do either of you have top secret clearance above grade level?"

Both of the naval officers look at each other strangely by Richards peculiar inquiry.

"Director," Cooper replied with a sarcastic inflection in his voice.

"If we didn't have that type of clearance, then neither of us would be having this conversation with you in the first place, now would we?"

Richards chuckled.

"Good point." he said as he asked them to follow him out of his office. As they were leaving, Richards told his secretary that he would be out for a while and hold all of his calls. The three men exited the office and went to an elevator down the hall. When they stepped into the car, Richards pulls out a key from his coat pocket and placed it in a keypad console that operated the lift. He then looked over at Cooper and asked,

"Wayne, what do you know about MICROSCOPE?"

Cooper looked back at him and said,

"If you're asking me if I'm aware of its existence, then yes, I know a great deal about it. But I've never seen the actual facility."

Richards looked over at Dixon.

"What about you, Commander? Are you familiar with it?"

"Yes, sir," replied Dixon.

"I know of its history and the content of its meaning. MICROSCOPE is the acronym for Military Intelligence Counter-Response Objectives for Strategic Covert Operational Procedures and Efforts. It was created after 9/11, sometime between 2005 and 2011. It's funded by the DOD and the intelligence community. Only a few people know of its existence. It's somewhat similar to the Situation Room beneath the White House, but a bit more elaborate than that. It is much more technical and highly sophisticated than your normal surveillance area. It's well concealed from the public eye and very secluded. Only military personnel above rank of O-8 through O-10 knows of its existence. This isn't counting those other special operations personnel who have special, top-secret clearance, with ranks between O-3 and O-7 knows about this. No offense or disrespect to you, Admiral." Cooper gave a nonchalant gesture to Dixon, showing his appreciation and respect from his subordinate.

Dixon continued,

"It became operational when the Middle East started to destabilize, around the same time the crisis in North Africa hit and launched the Arab Spring—2010. Its sole purpose is to monitor, survey and gather information and intelligence on foreign countries and their governments that may go rogue during or after a civilian or military coup. Another purpose of MICROSCOPE is to monitor the activity of suspected terrorists and to aid in determination of whether groups or organizations are developing radical ideology to foreign nationals. It was the key tool to use when surveilling terrorist cells and groups such as al-Qaeda, the IRA, and ISIS, among others, operating within the borders of rogue or combative nations. MICROSCOPE is also used for strategic planning and execution of covert operations to neutralize any threats against governments that are friendly to the United States. This requires intelligence operatives (CIA, DIA, NIA, and NSA) and Special Forces units (army, navy, air force, and marines) to operate strategic operational procedures. As well as all classified black ops missions."

Richards glanced over at Cooper in astonishment, clearly impressed by Dixon's knowledge. He was literally blown away by how much the young commander knew about MICROSCOPE. "Damn, Wayne. I'm impressed. I could use a man like him on my staff," Richards offered.

"No, Director, he's not for sale. Commander Dixon is one of the best counterintelligence supervisors I have. Without the intel and background on Assad he collected, I don't think we would've ever gotten this far. No, sir, I'm keeping him—unless he has other intentions for furthering his career."

Dixon did his best to maintain his stone-faced demeanor in the presence of his superiors, but it was difficult for him given the overwhelmingly positive compliments they were barraging him with. Inside, he was as giddy as a five-year-old boy who'd just gotten a piece of candy or a brand-new toy.

"Well, Commander. I can't speak for the admiral, but if you change your mind when your commission in the navy is over, look me up. I'll be happy to get you a job with us."

Dixon nodded, saying,

"Thank you, Director. I appreciate the invitation, but after we apprehend Assad, I'm planning on staying in the navy for a little while longer. I'm due for a promotion very soon, and I'm about to take a new position and a new assignment at the Pentagon, sir."

"All right, Commander. Suit yourself. But I don't give out invitations like that too often."

The elevator came slowly to a stop, having arrived at their floor. The doors slid open. Cooper and Dixon concluded that they'd just arrived to the basement level of the building. Richards, Dixon, and Cooper exited the elevator and started walking down a long well-lit corridor, crossing paths with two CIA agents who were stationed as armed guards at a secure entrance. The two agents immediately recognized their director but had to ask Cooper and Dixon for their identification and entry passes. Richards vouched for them, telling the two guards that they were there with him. One of the agents typed in his security code, went through the voice recognition protocols, and submitted to a retina scan. The shiny steel doors opened, and all three men entered the room. As they approached another secure entrance, Richards took out a pad and began to read out several letters from the NATO phonetic alphabet into a computer interface on the wall next to the entrance. The interface beeped several times in acknowledgment of Richards's security code. Next came the voice recognition and retina scan. Once Richards had submitted to those protocols, the second door opened. To Cooper and Dixon's amazement, the door opened onto a huge, wide-open, two-story area occupied by an abundance of personnel dressed in both civilian and military attire.

"Admiral, Commander, welcome to MICROSCOPE. Americas last line of defense after NORAD [North American Aerospace Defense Command] and the NMCC [National Military Command

Center, located within the Pentagon]. Let's see if we can get Dubai on the map and get satellite confirmation of the area. Follow me, gentlemen."

Richards walks across a mezzanine and downstairs to the lower level. Cooper and Dixon followed him, still amazed by the place. It was as sophisticated as its sister facilities NORAD and NMCC but was more elaborate. As the three men walked through the congested area, looking into every nook and cranny of the huge facility, something unexpected occurred. Cooper happened to run into someone he knew, an old friend.

"Frank?! Frank Roberts?!" Cooper said as he instantly recognized one of his old acquaintances. Two-Star Major General Franklin Roberts of the US Army Forces Command [FORSCOM] Division. A tall, robust man with the appearance of a rugged outdoors man, but the personality and attitude of a gentle giant.

Before receiving his commission as a submariner, Cooper was a young lieutenant commander supervising a USSOCOM (United States Special Operation Command for Navy SEAL Units) unit. During that time, Franklin Roberts was a liaisons officer (lieutenant colonel in rank) and attaché to the navy's SOCOM division from army intelligence. He has personally worked with special warfare groups such as Seals, Marine Recon, Air Force Special Expedition Forces, Delta Force, Rangers, and Green Berets. Roberts, who is a former Green Beret himself, had worked with Cooper on a number of occasions, even serving as his supervisor on several black op's missions—classified and off the books. Roberts is now the commander of USASOC [US Army Special Operations Command], which oversees various operation forces for the US Army and other elite ground forces. And is an adviser to JSOC [Joint Special Operations Command], which controls and supervises the organization itself.

"Wayne! Wayne Cooper! You old sea dog! How the hell are you?! I see that they finally gave you a star on that collar. I guess the navy is running short on admirals these days. Is that it? What the hell are you doing here?"

Seeing that the two old compadres were clearly poised to dredge up old times and wax nostalgic remembrance of their early days, which likely would have led Cooper to tell Roberts why he was there, Richards abruptly intervened.

"Admiral Cooper is with me, General Roberts. He and his aide are here to disclose the location of the traitor and fugitive Lieutenant Commander Ad-dam Assad."

"Assad? That's your guy, Wayne?" Roberts asked.

"Unfortunately, yes. He was one of my senior counterintelligence officers, under the supervision of one of my senior aides." He points in Dixon's direction.

"We found out he went rogue several weeks ago, after it was discovered that a number of our files and data had gone missing. He's the one who's responsible for their absence. He also stole a cache of weapons from an armory in Hartford."

"Wait a minute, you're in charge of ONI?" Roberts asked, surprisingly.

Cooper, who was reluctant to give an answer, nodded his head.

"Yeah, I'm the director and chief supervisor of special intelligence for all naval operations. I was the one who was accused by your boss General Dreyfus of having dropped the ball, because all this shit hit the fan on my watch."

"Ah, Wayne, don't worry about Dreyfus. From what I've heard, that old bastard is on his way out to pasture. He'll be retiring three months from now, and guess who's in line to take his place according to SECARM [Secretary of the Army] and the army's chief of staff?" Cooper made a gesture by pointing his finger in response to Roberts newly appointed position in the future along with a hug of gratification and solidarity.

"Hey, speaking of your branch, I heard you have a guy on the case, a former CIA man who used to be army CID and Intel. Good choice, Wayne. An army bloodhound can sniff out a navy squid any day." said Roberts as he laughed at Cooper.

"Very funny, Frank. And for your information, I don't consider him as part of my navy. He's a traitor and a disgrace to the uniform in every way, shape and form. The man has no honor or integrity about himself. And I will see to it personally that he spends the rest of his life in Leavenworth or some other military prison for what he has done. And besides, you know I always like to help out the army when they're in need of a job. We navy squids are always trying to keep the world safe, while you army "knuckle-draggers" sit around all day with your thumbs up your asses, waiting for something to pop off." As Cooper shot back with a retort of his own.

"Whew! That's harsh, Wayne," Roberts said, chuckling.

"You still know how to cut deep with those remarks of yours you conceited, dirty son of a bitch. It sure is good to see you after all these years." Roberts laughed.

"It looks like we're going to be doing this type of stuff again after all these years, old friend." replied the two-star general, grabbing Cooper's shoulders from behind in a gesture of unity and friendship.

Seeing that the two flag officers were about to start reminiscing again, Richards interrupted by clearing his throat and raising his voice higher than before. "Gentlemen, I hate to break up your little heartfelt reunion, but we do have more important things to concentrate on, like finding our fugitive who is bent on crippling our nation." With that, Coopers and Roberts quickly got down to business and started discussing their plans in capturing Assad.

CHAPTER 7

PURSUIT OF THE HUNTED

Emirates Towers Hotel, Downtown Dubai, United Arab Emirates, 10:30 a.m.

Three cars were parked outside, several yards away from the hotel's main entrance. Milson was in the first car, along with Fuller and Farad, the latter of whom was in the driver's seat. The second car was occupied by Weaver, his driver, and two of Farad's men from the embassy who were tagging along as their undercover backup. Sitting in the last vehicle were Sheppard and his driver, along with three other operatives as well. Each of them had their eyes set on the hotel and surrounding areas just in case Assad tries to sneak out from the rear of the building. They were communicating with each other by short-range radio and listening devices that were concealed as earpieces and mini microphones. As they waited patiently for several hours, Milson broke the silence by communicating with his people. "Sheppard, Weaver, do you copy?"

"Read you, Killian. Loud and clear," replied Weaver.

"Same on my end, Chief. We've got eyes all over the hotel including its rear." said Sheppard, who was anxious and giddy.

"Very well. Keep frosty, guys. Fuller's cameras may have a twenty-four-hour watch on this place, but we know how sneaky Assad is. If he makes out one of us, he's going to go rabbit. And I'm not particularly in the mood to go running after him, so stay hidden until the time is right. It's a shame that we don't have eyes inside the place to know if he's leaving or not."

"On the contrary, Mr. Milson, we do." The British agent pulled a tablet from his jacket pocket.

"There's no way this bugger can get past without us knowing about it," Fuller said belligerently. "I've got eyes not only all around the exterior but also inside the hotel. The hotel's interior security cameras are linked secretly to our systems at the embassy. I have patched a live feed from the cameras through this pad. There's no way he's getting past us."

"I hope you're right, Fuller. Because my time for catching this guy is running out."

As they waited, Fuller got a call from the embassy. It looked like the connection between the hotel's cameras and the embassy's surveillance system was strong. It was someone from the embassy calling to inform him that Assad and Desiree had left their room and were heading toward the lobby.

"Are you sure? … Roger that. Thanks." Turning to the others, he explained,

"That was the TOC. They spotted a couple who match the description of Assad and his girlfriend leaving their room and heading for the lobby. We should see them any minute now." Fuller held up the pad so everyone in the car could see.

To their surprise, the information turned out to be correct. Milson and the others watched on the tablet as Assad and Asherah walked through a hallway and into an elevator.

"Identification confirmed, people. It's them. They're heading down right now. Stand by," Milson announced through his microphone.

"Perfect, Chief! As soon as they come out of the door, we'll grab them." said Sheppard.

"It's not that simple, kid. Assad is going to make his play when meeting with his contacts today. If things work out to our advantage, we may have a chance to catch him in the act and discover who his cohorts are. We have the chance of killing two birds with one stone," Weaver said, speaking over the open mic.

"I hate to say this, but it looks like I'm forced to agree with you again, James. The orders of my bounty are to bring Assad back alive if possible, along with the stuff he's stolen. But my instincts, and previous training as a former CIA spook, tells me to find out the identity of the people that he's been dealing with." said Milson.

"So, you're saying that we should follow him to wherever he's going so he can lead us to his contacts? I knew I should have brought more men as I wanted to do in the first place," Fuller said pretentiously.

Milson just rolled his eyes and shook his head at Fuller.

As they continued to watch the entrance, one of Fuller's men spotted something out of the ordinary.

"Sir, there's a car coming around on your side. It's a white Mercedes-Benz. I think it's the same one the girl's been using."

"I got it, thanks," Fuller replied. "Looks like you're right, Milson. They're planning on going somewhere. The valet is bringing their car around to the front entrance."

"All right, people, this is it. Heads up. Our boy is about to come out." Milson announced. He and the other occupants of the car straightened up quickly and craned their necks, looking for Assad and Asherah to exit the hotel. With their anticipation growing, they noticed two individuals, who appeared to be bellboys, came out with several bags of luggage while putting them into the trunk of the vehicle.

"Killian, you see that?" Weaver shouted.

"Yeah, I see them. Must be the weapons in those bags. Assad is definitely going to meet with his contacts now since he's moving the weapons out."

Everyone in the cars stared even harder as they watched the hotel employees load the contraband into the car. Just when the employees finished, out came Assad and Asherah through the glass doors.

"There they are!" Fuller announced loudly. He's the one who had the best view since he was in the front seat.

Everyone, including Sheppard and his team, who were parked in the back, was wide-eyed and alert. Finally, they had a visual on the man they saw as public enemy number one. Milson was especially relieved seeing his target in motion.

The stakeout team continued observing the couple from afar. Even though it wasn't possible for Assad to see them because of the huge crowd of people walking by, and the large capacity of automobiles zipping back and forth on the busy street. Milson and his team remained motionless and out of sight as they watched him and girl vigorously. They watched him tip the bellboys and the valet for their services, which seemed to please the employees very much, if their facial expressions were any guide.

Assad got in on the driver's side, while Asherah took the opposite.

"Sheppard, go ahead and come around. They're about to leave… Okay, everybody, we're going to follow them. Stay at least fifty yards away from each other. We don't want to spook Assad and make him think he has a tail. We're going to follow him to see where he takes us." Milson said anxiously.

"Gotcha, Killian" replied Weaver.

"Aye, aye, Chief," Sheppard announce, letting everyone know he was a navy man.

The Mercedes-Benz pulled out of the carport and into the stream of traffic. After waiting a few seconds, the driver of Milson's car pulled into the traffic as well. Weaver's vehicle was right behind Milson's, followed by the car Sheppard was in. The Benz was cruising at a speed of forty-five miles an hour along one of the more well-known highways in Dubai. Milson and his convoy kept their distance but were not too far away. It looked as if Assad was driving the posted speed limit, not in a rush, but also not too slow. He kept peering into his rearview mirror to see if he was being followed, but he saw nothing to indicate that such was the case. He was totally unaware of the situation that awaited him and was ignorant to the possibility that he was going to be nabbed right off the bat.

Milson knew what he was doing. He had been in this business for a long time and knew all the tricks of the trade that it offered. He knew exactly how criminals think and act, especially when money was the issue. To Milson, money was a criminal's Achilles' heel. It was the most common reason for the mistakes made by people with unlawful intentions and greed-driven aspirations. "*Doesn't matter how smart or educated they are,*" Milson thought, "*when money is involved, they all get dumb, stupid, and careless.*" Regardless, Milson was not about to underestimate Assad. He had already seen that this guy was clever and good at covering his tracks. He'd been one step ahead of them this whole time. But then he made the fatal mistake of killing Charlene Gardner at the hotel in Sydney and not noticing that she had dropped her phone beneath the bed. That one simple mistake made Assad vulnerable. A chink in his armor, you could say. Once Milson saw the body of Gardner, he knew right then and there that he had to get this guy who'd killed her. Not for the obvious reason, namely, espionage and thievery, but for taking the life of an innocent person for nothing. For Milson, this assignment not only was a crusade against Islamic extremists but also was a matter of bringing someone to justice and having him pay the consequences for the crimes he committed.

The three cars continued to tail Assad for about five to seven miles. Still within Dubai city limits, amid the elaborate landscape, they were traveling on Route E-311, a very famous and heavily populated highway that resembled many roadways in the United States and other well-known expressways around the world. Milson and party were getting a little anxious. They kept wondering where Assad was going, to what his next destination would be. After several more miles, Farad noticed that the Mercedes was about to exit on a ramp that led to another road, E-11, a heavily populated scenic route within the city limits. While continuing their pursuit but staying back as requested, they noticed the Benz was heading toward a parking garage next to a deluxe building with pedestrians coming and going. Farad, who was with Fuller and the others, knew this place. It was the *Dubai Galleria Mall*; very elaborate, very distinguished and very popular. As they saw Assad pull in, the rest of them parked outside at a corner of the building. There, they talked together about their strategy to get him and confiscate the guns.

"Okay, people. He pulled into the mall's parking garage. I, Fuller, and Farad are going to drive in to see where he is. The rest of y'all stay out here until we give you the signal to come in. Leave your cars outside just in case he tries to make a run for it. When we spot him and the girl, Weaver, you and Sheppard, along with your guys, come inside so we can rally and corner him when the opportunity is ripe, okay?" Milson said. The others, having heard him through their earpieces, agreed and responded as much. Farad put the car back in gear and drove into the garage. They circled the levels slowly, using caution, so they would not be spotted by Assad too easily. After a few seconds of looking for Assad and his companion, Fuller saw the Benz and what looked like Assad and Asherah, standing at an elevator door waiting for the car to arrive. Farad, who happened to see an empty parking spot, drove into it inconspicuously. All three sat in the car motionless as they continued to watch the couple waiting for their elevator. Milson happened to notice Assad taking a moment to scope out the area. All three in the car ducked their heads so as not to be seen by him. When Milson thought it was safe to look up, he peeked out from the rear window of their automobile and saw Assad and Asherah get into the elevator. When the doors closed, that was their opportunity to depart from the vehicle and give chase.

"Weaver, Sheppard, the target is in play. They're on foot and mobile. They're on an elevator right now, going down to the first floor—the main lobby. They'll be entering the building's main entrance very soon. We're in pursuit. Get ready to come in on my signal," Milson said.

The men followed Assad and Asherah, taking the stairs down to the lower level that ran into the main entrance of the mall. When the doors of the elevator opened on the ground floor, Asherah came out first, holding Assad's hand. They both exited the elevator as if in a rush to get out. Asherah, who was as giddy as a schoolgirl on her first date, was leading the charge. She sprinted to the entrance with Assad close behind her. As the couple made their way in, Milson and party rushed down the stairs. They followed but remained distant so as not to blow their cover.

Entering the mall, they saw the couple walking casually in a crowded area, looking in store windows at the advertising displays. Milson gestured to Farad and Fuller to split up, signaling that they each go in a separate direction while keeping close to the couple, urging them not to lose sight of them. Later, he signaled Sheppard and Weaver to come in from outside, each from the opposite direction. They acknowledged Milson and split up. Weaver came in on the north side of the mall with his men while Sheppard and his guys entered at the east end. Each of the group gave off the appearance of a clueless group of tourists seeing the sights of Dubai's elegance for the first time.

Milson followed Assad and Asherah very closely without giving himself away. Speaking to his team through their earpieces and microphones, he gave accurate reports of his distance from the couple and what they were doing. He noticed Asherah was trying to persuade Assad to look at something that caught her interest, but it seemed that his attentions were preoccupied at the time, appearing to be looking around for something else. Milson, feeling that he was getting a little too close to them, stepped into one of the neighboring stores, where he acted as if he were a customer. He told the others where he was and advised them to stay close but out of sight. When he thought that it was clear to move again, he cautiously walked out of the store and continued his surveillance of the couple. Later, he witnessed them having a slight disagreement with one another. He could not hear the conversation, but he knew that something was wrong in paradise. Moving closer to the couple, Milson bore witness to their difference of opinion. They were speaking in Arabic, which he could understand but most of what they were saying was very difficult and vague to hear amid the noise of the surrounding crowd. Milson, wanting to know what they were talking about, took the chance to get a little closer than was advisable. He walked right past them as they were bickering inside the store. Once again, Milson pretended to be a customer, looking around at the furnishings, acting as if he were interested in the merchandise. He whispered into his mouthpiece that he was close to them and was trying to hear what they were talking about. Knowing full well that Assad was not going to recognize him, he managed to get a little closer to the couple without them suspecting a thing. Still pretending to be a customer, he continued acting in a nonchalant way, observing them as they continued talking about something that seemed to be very important to them.

"Desiree, I have to do this. The people I'm looking for are here somewhere in this mall. I must find them to complete my business with them. It will only take a few minutes, that's all," Assad said.

"Why does it have to be now, Ad-dam? I thought that this was our time to spend together before we went back to Holland?" Asherah said adamantly.

"Listen, sweetheart, we discussed this back at the hotel before we checked out. I must meet with my contacts to give them the flash drive, disc, and weapons as promised. Then they can give us the rest of the money. I'll only be gone for thirty minutes, twenty if everything goes well."

The look on Asherah's face was a mix of disappointment and concern. Assad, taking notice of this, right away began to comfort her by rubbing the palm of his hand across her cheekbone. "Look, Desi. Go ahead and do some shopping for the both of us. Spend whatever you want, honey, I don't care. Just be patient for a little while longer. I'll meet you in the food court in thirty minutes. If I'm late, call me on the cell. Listen, don't worry. Everything is going to be fine. I promise. And besides, I have a little protection if something goes wrong." Assad patted the left side of his leather jacket, presumably carrying the Walther that he had confiscated from his slain victim Muhammad Kareem back in the States.

Assad's words seemed to soothe Asherah's anxiety for now, but she still showed a little aggravation. She inhaled and exhaled slowly in relief as she hugged him tightly around his waist, seeming not to want to let go of him. Assad kissed her on the forehead and said, "I'll be back. Food court, thirty minutes, okay?" He began to walk off with Asherah still holding on to his hand. She nodded in a faint sign of acceptance and gave a slight wave as he walked away from her and into the hustle and bustle of the crowd.

When Milson saw Assad leaving without Asherah, he began to follow him without breaking a stride.

"Heads up, guys. Assad is heading somewhere to meet his contacts. He's leaving the girl behind. I'm going to follow him."

"What about the girl? We can't lose sight of her. Where is she?" asked Fuller.

"She's still here. She's inside the clothing store I just left. I think Assad is about to make the switch. Fuller, you and Weaver back me up. Follow my six, but keep your distance. I don't want to tip him off. Sheppard, you, Farad, and the others watch the girl. She's located on the 2nd floor of the mall in a women's clothing store between the south and the west entrances, near the food court area."

"Gotcha, Chief. Fuller's men says he knows exactly what store you're talking about. We'll be there in two seconds."

"Okay, I'm heading out."

Just as Milson was about to follow Assad and give them more information about where he was going, he unintentionally bumped into Asherah, knocking the apparel she was carrying from her hand. Trying not to lose sight of Assad while also attempting to seem hospitable toward the young woman, he quickly helped her to pick up the clothes, apologizing for his blunder.

"Excuse me. Sorry, ma'am, for bumping into you. My mistake. I'm just in a hurry. Let me help you with this."

Asherah smiled, saying,

"That's quite all right. It's my fault. I should pay more attention to how I handle things. Thank you very much."

As Milson helped her with the items, he apologized again, then rushed out of the store in the blink of an eye so he could catch up with Assad. Even though Asherah was grateful for Milson's assistance and hospitality, she gave him a peculiar look that suggested something was very wrong. But in her ignorance of what was really going on, she dismissed the uneasy feeling and went on about her business, continuing to shop.

Milson, having caught up with Assad, was traveling down an escalator to the mall's lower level. He made his way through the crowd, managing to keep his cover while still following him. Weaver and Fuller were yards away, but they saw Milson chasing after Assad. They kept their cover intact too, knowing that it was only a matter of time before the opportunity would arise and they'd be able to apprehended Assad and his cohorts. Milson was right on Assad's tail. He wanted to grab Assad right then and there but knew it would be premature to do so. He also considered what was at stake as he looked at the big picture.

Assad was walking with a purpose. His eyes looked straight ahead, his focus intent, as he kept circling the mall as if looking for something or someone. When it seemed to Milson that he was about to give up his frantic search, he spotted something.

Assad noticed two well-dressed men standing apart from the crowd at an exit door to his left. He recognized them, and they recognized him. Each man gave a gesture to Assad, one that only he would recognize, meaning that he had their permission to approach. Milson, seeing this, fell back immediately. He reported what he'd seen to Weaver and Fuller and told them to stay back. Then he witnessed Assad approaching the two gentlemen. The three had a brief conversation. Milson could not tell what they were saying, but it was obvious that the two men were Assad's contacts. Milson stayed hidden amid the crowd, but he knew he had to make a move sooner or later. While still observing the three men, he saw that the two newcomers were escorting Assad to an exit door. Milson had no choice: he had to follow so as not to lose them. "Hey. They went in through an exit on the left side, near one of the stores. I'm going in."

"Wait, Milson. We're coming with you," Weaver replied.

"Negative! That will give us away. Assad's contacts might have people watching over him as we speak. We might not be the only ones who have eyes on him right now. We can't blow our cover, not right now. I'll go in unnoticed and see what's going on. You guys stay back until I call for you."

"All right, mate. Be careful. Just remember, if this goes south, I'm calling my guys in to intercept. I've got a tact team on standby just in case," said Fuller with anticipation.

Milson, shaking his head in dismay, an apprehensive grin across his face, said, "Okay, Fuller. You win. If my bounty goes rabbit, then unleash the dogs. Until then, keep them on their leashes. Understood?"

"Gotcha, mate. Good luck."

Milson took a deep breath and went in. Moving through the large crowd that temporarily blocked his passage, he finally managed to get through and enter the same doors that Assad and his contacts went through. Upon entry, Milson saw that he was standing in a long grayish corridor that seemed to go on forever. There were long light fixtures overhead that flickered on and off. Milson did not like this. Knowing that he had to catch up to Assad and the two other men, he walked cautiously down the hallway, pulling his SIG Sauer from the holster concealed inside his jacket. He continued at a careful pace, not exposing himself or making his presence known. As he trekked along the empty corridor, he heard voices. Faint at first, but then became louder as he moved closer. He turned several corners of the corridor when he came upon a dark secluded area that looked familiar to a large basement cavern or a structured subterranean level garage. The location was dark, musty and extremely wet and humid with puddles of water on the floor that appeared to be coming from leaky, unresolved pipes. This was definitely the text book scenario of the proverbial secret place that you don't want anybody to know about but yourself. After Milson arrived, he began relaying the information back to the team, but had to whisper it in order that he would not be discovered.

When he finally came to the source of the voices, he saw, in the distance, Assad and several other men: five to six total, with one in particular standing out from the rest. To Milson, it seemed that this single individual, who was conversing to Assad, was probably the leader of the group. From his perspective, this person was cold, calculative, devious, malicious and mischievous. Not to mention enigmatic and mysterious in such a way that it seated his persona and appearance as a black silhouette shadow figure that was only visible to the naked eye; along with secluding himself from the light to be identified. Judging by the sound of the person's voice, Milson surmised that he was extremely intelligent and very knowledgeable and clever. It happened to be the same voice with whom Assad had previously been speaking with on his laptop in Australia. From Milson's point of view and conclusion, this was a dangerous man who was not to be taken likely, and extremely serious about his convictions.

The area where they were having their secret meeting was of course dim, dark, and stale, with a hint of light shining through from one of the overhead lamp fixtures above. Milson could not make out the appearance of the dark figure who was doing most of the talking, but he could of course distinguish Assad from the rest of them. Trying to hear bits and pieces of the conversation, Milson took out his cell phone and started recording the meeting as it happened. Hoping to get definitive proof of Assad's treachery and to learn the identity of the terrorist that he's involved with. While doing this, Milson happened to overhear some very interesting exchanges between Assad and the mysterious figure who was dominating the entire conversation.

"You have done well so far, Mr. Assad. Despite all the obstacles you've encountered in your travels this past week. You have shown a tenacity that I am very impressed with. You are indeed a man who is worthy of joining us in our future endeavors. I was surprised to hear from you in the last communiqué I received. I found it intriguing that you wanted to meet here in Dubai, instead of Saudi Arabia as we had agreed upon. But no worries; we have connections here as well. I believe you have the data and the weapons we require?"

"Yes, I do. But you're not getting them until I see the money. As I said to you over the phone and through emails and text messages, I'm having a hard time trusting you and your people because of the number of mishaps I have dealt with on account of your employees' misdeeds and mistrust." Assad said.

The dark figure laughed somberly at Assad's statements.

"You are right, of course, Assad. It is a shame that we do not screen our people thoroughly when it comes to matters such as these. Sometimes we recruit individuals on the merit of their instincts, expertise, skills and passion, rather than on their honesty, loyalty, and trust. We do this especially when we have outlined certain objectives, purposes, and goals that fit our satisfaction. I for one hope that you are a man whose character encompasses the latter set of traits I just mentioned. While at the same time being constructed of a small percentage of the former set of traits that I have just pronounced."

Assad, nodded and said,

"My views on these matters are of my own devising, sir. I'm doing this not because I agree with your political viewpoints and opinions, but because I am seeking something for myself, a sort of compensation for the hardships that I and my family have endured for the past thirty years. Now, if you don't mind, I would like to get this over and done with. I have something to get back to."

"Oh, yes. Miss Desiree Asherah. Beautiful-looking girl. Very affable and very attractive. I assume that the two of you will have a prosperous future together once our business is complete?" the mysterious figure said.

Shocked that this man had knowledge of his girlfriend, Assad fell mute.

"You act surprised that I know about your female companion who is waiting for you upstairs, Mr. Assad. As I told you earlier, we know everything about you and your private life. The organization I serve did not get to where it is today by being ignorant to whom or what we have a personal investments in. Especially when it comes to mold and entice certain individuals to come into our fold. I hope that my disclosing this piece of information to you doesn't sway your opinion of us or hinder the transaction that we are about to make. My job is to compensate you for everything that you've done for us and to persuade you to join us. Are you in hesitation about our proposal?"

Assad started to grow nervous and irritated. He was overwhelmed by the surprise thrown at him by this person, especially his contact's knowledge of Asherah and her present location. He thought that if they knew about him and her, then they probably knew about the money he took from Shaula when he was given the contract to terminate him. Such were the thoughts that were racing through his mind. He thought if they knew that he'd taken the money for himself without returning it to them, he would be dead right there on the floor, along with Desiree, who was innocent despite Assad's dealings and involvement. But there was no way for him to know for sure at that moment if they had known about it or were on to him from the start. Thinking on this heavily, Assad kept his cool, waiting for the outcome. He answered,

"No, I am not. But as I told you before, I need to take care of some other things before I make a decision about joining your group. That's all."

The dark figure crossed his arms over his chest and nodded his head, saying,

"Understandable. The organization can wait for you to make your decision. But don't take too long to think it through. We do have other applicants whose expertise and skills match yours. And I would hate to waste such talents as yours when they could be used to the utmost to benefit us. So, let's not waste any more of each other's time and get down to the business at hand, shall we?"

The figure snapped his fingers, and one of the four gentlemen instantly appeared and gestured towards two leather briefcases sitting on a concrete slab. The leader ordered the other man to open them. To Assad's astonishment, they held an abundance of money, the bills stacked neatly together. It was US currency—hundred-dollar bills. Assad went over to inspect it for himself, but the dark figure interrupted his approach by putting his hand in front of the briefcases.

"No need for you to count it, Assad. All three hundred million dollars are there. Accountable, clean, and ready to be disbursed to you—once you give us our merchandise as agreed."

Assad looked at him.

"Okay. It's in my car in the parking garage upstairs, all four weapons, one thumb drive and one data disc you need to encode the rest of the information in your database. We can go get the items right now."

"Good, Mr. Assad. Very good. Let's end our business on a high note. You may lead the way," replied the mysterious individual who was calling all the shots. After he had ordered one of his associates to close both briefcases and follow Assad down to the garage level, he stopped for a moment, realizing there was another issue that needed to be addressed. "Oh, by the way. Did you happen to take care of that little problem we had in Sydney?"

This was it; the topic Assad had been anticipating and worrying about: the killing of Shaula and the taking of the $250,000,000 dollars. Knowing he was in a tough spot; Assad had no choice but to answer the question. And he knew he had to answer it right.

"Yes, I did. One in the back, two in the chest. Shaula didn't even see it coming. He was a little surprised, judging from the expression on his face when I shot him. But like you said, it needed to be done. I'm surprised you didn't hear about it sooner."

"Oh, but we did, Assad. As I told you, we have people everywhere. Did you happen to retrieve a certain briefcase in his possession when you disposed of him?"

This was another moment of truth for Assad. He could go either way on this, but he knew the outcome if he were to choose the wrong one. Still, he felt confident of his ability to swing the pendulum in his favor.

"No, I did not. I didn't see a briefcase in his room when I killed him. Was I supposed to?"

Though Assad could not see the expression on the figure's face, because it was shrouded in darkness, it was obvious by the man's body language and posture that he was a bit perturbed by the answer given to him by the former commander. He paused for a moment and tilted his head to the left to show his uncertainty. Because he was still hiding his features from public view, it was difficult to make out his reaction.

After giving a slight, condescending laugh, the man said,

"No, probably not, Commander. How could you have known? Knowing Shaula, and the kind of man he was, probably did not take in account that his misdeeds would be discovered due to his arrogance and self-entitlement. Thinking that he could've gotten away with it only prolonged the inevitable to his demise. I'm concluding that he probably invested it in one of his offshore accounts... But no matter. I assure you that the organization will find its whereabouts soon, especially if someone like him is bold enough to have taken something that does not belong to them and spend it without thinking of the consequences that will lie before them. But this is of no concern at this moment. The organization's treasury can afford to lose a small sum as two-hundred and fifty million dollars. It is just unfortunate that someone like Mr. Shaula, who cared more about the money instead of the cause that we're creating, had to be disposed of. Don't you agree, Commander?"

Assad did not have any words to convey at that moment. He was preoccupied with his own well-being and with the safety of Desiree, who was unaware of the real danger that surrounded her.

As the group started to travel once again toward Assad's car, not realizing that Milson had been watching them the whole time, the mystery man stopped once more to relay another bit of important information to Assad.

"Oh, I almost forgot to tell you, Commander. I don't know if you are aware of this, but you have been followed."

"What?!" Assad shouted in disbelief.

"What are you talking about?!"

The mystery man stood his ground while his entourage surrounded him for protection as he continued to explain his statement.

"No need to raise your voice, Ad-dam. I can hear you quite well from where I'm standing. You didn't realize that you were being followed?" Assad was in a state of confusion and disarray after the announcement that he'd been surveyed and followed.

"The Americans have been following you for quite a while. Ever since you left Sydney, they have been watching you for some time now. And unfortunately, they know about the homicidal act you conducted with the young woman at the hotel. It is unfortunate that you did not dispose the body properly, as you should have done."

Still in shock, Assad could not believe in what he was hearing. Amazed by his detailed cognition of Gardner's death. The mysterious figure continued to present his knowledge to Assad in great detail.

"You mean to tell me that you didn't sense the presence of federal agents tracking your every move since you arrived in Dubai?"

"No! How could they? I've been covering my tracks carefully! I know every protocol and every intel procedure the Americans use for covert operations and undercover surveillance. There's no way I could've been followed here! I know how many agents are assigned to different areas of the world and where they are located! That's why I chose Dubai, because there's no US presence and no US covert operations here! I made sure of that! And especially given the events that have occurred, I didn't leave any trace of evidence behind!" Assad, who'd been calm and cool a second ago, was now nervous and rattled.

"Well, you haven't been doing a very good job of that, have you, Commander? And you haven't been keeping up on your intelligence as well as you think you have. We found out from one of our sources stationed here along with working for the UAE government that a small CIA team has been shadowing you ever since you left the United States. We have an operative planted in the British Embassy who informed us of the arrival of this team two days ago, also telling us that they were surveilling you."

Both Milson and Assad were stunned by what they were hearing, especially Milson. *"Jesus!"* Milson thought to himself. *"If we've got a mole, then they know we're here!"* Even though he knew that his cover and operation might be compromised, he remained hidden and carried on with the surveillance.

"Right now, at this very moment, there are American and British agents here in this mall looking at you and your beautiful girlfriend right now. Isn't that right, Mr. Milson?"

Milson's expression fell hard in disbelief. Not only of the proclamation announced by the dark figure, who obviously knew he was there, but also the surprising sound of a hammer clicking back on a gun that was now pressed against the backside of his head.

"You may come out from under the shadows, Mr. Milson, so I can properly introduce you." The man who was pointing the gun at Milson made him get up slowly and took his pistol from his hand. He then pushed him toward the group so Assad and the others could get a better look at the man who had been following him from the beginning.

"Now, I think introductions are in order, gentlemen. Mr. Milson, you already know Lieutenant Commander Ad-dam Omar Assad, but I don't think the commander knows who you are. Assad, meet former US Army chief warrant officer Killian Antonio Milson. A bounty hunter by trade who is now working for naval intelligence under the US government, your previous employer. Oh, did I fail to mention that he was formerly an employee of the CIA as well? He has been ordered to take you back to the United States dead or alive. That's the bounty hunter creed/motto that you go by, is it not, Mr. Milson?"

Milson said nothing. Temporarily incapacitated, he wondered how this person had come to know so much about him and subsequently his undercover identity.

"I found this on him, sir. He was recording everything on his cell phone." said the henchman who caught Milson, as he handed Milson's phone to the mystery man.

"Oh, shame on you, Mr. Milson. Recording private conversations between two people is sacrilege. We are not in the position to let prying ears of the public know of our plans… Not just yet. Don't you agree, Commander?"

Assad could not say anything. He was still in shock over the current situation.

"That may be your opinion, whoever you are. But treason and espionage are not so sacred as you think. The American government will not let you get away with this. They will see this as a threat to its democracy and a declaration of war. Stealing military secrets for your own personal agenda is not only criminal, but its suicidal. Contemplating on this objective is wrong, especially when it involves the loss of innocent lives—people who have to pay the ultimate price because of your malicious intent of destroying the world. You may have me right now, but there are hundreds of agents around this building waiting on my signal. If they don't hear from me within the next couple of minutes, this whole place is going to be locked down. You might as well give up and surrender yourselves right now."

The figure laughed sarcastically and maliciously.

"Oh, Mr. Milson. You do have a sense of humor after all. That speech you made was quite entertaining. I almost took you seriously for a moment, but unfortunately, I don't have the luxury to indulge your dogmatic view of morality and righteousness…" As the figure paused for a moment, he recanted on what Milson said prior to the building being surrounded by international agents.

"By the way, Mr. Milson. I cannot fathom the idea that you are that naive? Don't you think that I'm aware of your tactics for subduing Commander Assad? As I told him before, we have people all over this area. My intentions were clear from the start. We were going to complete our transaction and afterward dispose of you and your little covert band. The plan was for the agents who are with you to meet with unfortunate demise on account of false intel. And I and Mr. Assad were going to depart from this scene safe and well satisfied. Your feeble attempt to capture us would have been a useless gesture, no matter what type of information or intel you've gathered today. You are obviously outnumbered and outgunned, bounty hunter. What can you possibly do to change the outcome or improve your circumstances?"

Milson looked around and said,

"Not much from where I'm standing, but I can do this." Without warning, Milson who was being held at gunpoint from the rear, elbowed his captor in the face, breaking his nose in two places. Afterwards he twists the man's arm forward and flips him over his back, leaving his captor temporarily disabled and unconscious. Witnessing this event taking place, the others pull out their firearms from beneath their garments and proceeded to discharge their weapons at Milson. Assad, along with the shadowy figure and his cohorts, quickly took cover behind several concrete barricades while the exchange of gunfire took place. Milson, having managed to retrieve his gun from the injured man, reciprocated immediately, shooting back at the opposing forces who were bent on terminating his life. After having to take cover, he managed to hit one of the terrorist's henchmen several times in the chest. He also hit several of the others in the shoulders and arms.

As the chaos continued, Assad managed to make an escape through one of the exit ways. Milson saw this and wanted to go after him, but the crossfire from the opposite sides made it difficult for him to pursue. Witnessing the terrorist leader and his aides escape, Milson was unable to go after anyone amid the intense gunfire that continued against him. He had no choice but to hold his ground while concentrating on his marksmanship by staying alive. While still engaged, he managed somehow to call for assistance and support, relaying to his team what had transpired.

"Weaver, Fuller! Get down here now!"

Hearing the despair in Milson's voice, Weaver answered,

"Milson! What's going on?! Is that gunfire I hear?!"

Condescending as Milson was, he responded sarcastically,

"No, James! I'm cooking popcorn down here with some of my new friends I just met!" In the grip of mortal combat, the bounty hunter added,

"Of course, its gunfire, you fucking idiot! I'm getting shot down here! They've got me pinned down, and Assad is getting away! We've been compromised! They know we're here! Tell Sheppard to hold the girl. And get Fuller's men down here fast!"

"Already called them, mate!" Fuller cut in.

"Weaver and I are heading to your position right now! We're on our way!"

"Hurry up! I'm losing the chance of getting Assad. They've got me trenched in! I can't go anywhere!"

The gunfire continued without ending. Even though Milson had killed two of the assailants and was able to injure at least three others, not including the one lying on the floor unconscious with a broken nose, he was still in the crosshairs of ricocheting bullets shooting across his path by two of the remaining terrorist's. When it seemed that Milson was about to run out of ammo, and as he was trying to retrieve his backup gun, Weaver and Fuller, along with two other agents, came up alongside on his rear and gave him assistance. Weaver hit one of the individuals in the chest, knocking him forcefully to the ground, while Fuller capped one in the head, killing him instantly. With a temporary break in the standoff, Milson knew he had to go after Assad. He jumped over one of the barricades and started running in the same direction Assad had gone.

"Milson! Where are you going?!" shouted Weaver.

"I'm going after Assad! He went this way! He's going after the girl!" Milson shouted while running in the same direction.

"We're going with you!" shouted Fuller, while at the same time ordering his men to stay behind to canvass the area and collect evidence from the shoot-out.

Milson, Weaver and Fuller ran down a corridor that led up to a steep ramp which in turn followed into the interior entrance of the mall. As they bust through the doors with the intent of looking for Assad, they came across an abundance of people who were obviously customers and merchants of the mall. Frantic in their search, Milson and company had to literally fight through the crowd in order to catch a glimpse of where Assad might have gone to. Feeling the adrenaline in his body, Milson ran through the crowd abruptly in an attempt to spot him out. As he pushed everyone aside leaving a wake of confused people behind him, Weaver and Fuller were trailing in the distance as they too were searching for the fugitive officer. Not realizing that he was causing a disruption within the crowd due to his overbearing physicality, Milson did not see Assad sprinting up the escalator until seconds later. When he realized that Assad was not downstairs, he quickly looked up and spotted him right away.

"There he is!" Milson shouted to Weaver and Fuller.

"Assad! Stop where you are!" yelled Milson. All three ran to the escalator that carried him to the second floor. Driven by anxiety and anxiousness, Assad pulls out his Walther and starts shooting into the crowd. In an instant, pandemonium and chaos came into play.

The discharge of Assad's gun echoed throughout the mall. Panic and disarray rushed over the crowd as the sound of gunfire spread through the atmosphere causing everyone to disperse immediately. Confusion and disorder were the theme to Assad's actions. People were shouting and screaming as they ran for cover, afraid of the gunfire that was being displayed amongst them. This course of action provided Assad with enough cover to get out and retrieve Asherah. But to his surprise, the respite had come too late. Sheppard, along with Fuller's men, took charge of apprehending Asherah. Witnessing this event unfold in front of him, Assad was unable to do anything about it. He just watched helplessly as they detained her and took her into custody.

He yelled out her name in an attempt to get her attention. She reciprocated by turning around to look in his direction. When Asherah saw Assad, she screamed frantically by saying,

"Ad-dam! What is going on?! Who are these people?! And why are they grabbing me?!"

When Sheppard realized that Assad was only yards away from him, he drew his pistol and ordered him to surrender as well. Over whelmed by what was going on, Assad paused for a split second to comprehend his situation. But in that same moment, he regained his composure quickly and noticed Milson and party engaging in his direction. Realizing that he was in a tough spot, he had to make a drastic decision quickly. When he knew he was out of options, Assad had no choice but to make the only logical but detrimental decision he had. He realized that this course of action would jeopardize his current situation. As he looked at Asherah being detained by the authorities, he gave a loud outcry in her direction hoping that it would calm her hysteria.

"Desiree, I'll be back for you! I promise!" Not giving her a chance to respond, and also not wanting to leave her behind, he saw that he didn't have much of a choice. In another attempt to escape, he discharged several more rounds from his gun, aiming at Sheppard and Milson. He did this only as a temporary distraction, hoping to secure his getaway. His intentions were not to kill the two men;

instead, he wanted to cause more pandemonium among the already confused crowd.

Although his bullets missed Sheppard, Assad was able to hit one of his men in the leg, leaving him incapacitated. Witnessing this, Sheppard took immediate action and returned fire. Soon, Milson, Weaver, and Fuller joined in. As the bullets ricochet across the area of the mall, Assad ran through the food court and into a nearby department store, knocking over bystanders who got in his way. Seeing this, Milson gave chase. Leaving Weaver and Fuller behind. While Assad continued his run, toppling over merchandise and other store materials as a distraction to delay his pursuers, Milson was not far behind—only a few feet away and closing the distance. If this were a track-and-field race, Milson would come in second, right after Assad.

Assad did everything he could to throw anything into Milson's path so he could extend his lead. When he was able to get away from Milson's reach, he managed to exit the mall by leaving through the main entrance from which they came from and headed to the parking garage to which their car was located. He ran upstairs to the upper level to find the Benz that he and Asherah had arrived in. Milson knowing where he was going, chased after him in haste. Running frantically and almost out of breath, Milson managed to tell his colleagues through his microphone of what was going on during the chase.

"Listen up! Assad is heading for his car, the white two-door Mercedes-Benz. Block the entrance and exits so he can't get out! I'm still in pursuit!"

"Gotcha, Milson! I've got some people on their way now!" replied Fuller.

Assad made it up several stairs. Finding the level where the Mercedes was located, he dashed toward the vehicle without breaking a stride. Milson was right on his heels as he managed to close the distance between them. He saw Assad running to the car and continued his chase. Knowing that Milson was close, Assad shot several more rounds from his gun at the bounty hunter. This time attempting not to distract or deflect, but to injure or kill him. But Milson managed to move out of the way of the deadly projectiles that were intended to cause his demise. When he saw Assad getting closer to the car, he shot three to four rounds of his own. Several of the bullets managed to hit some neighboring vehicles, but one or two came dangerously close to Assad's head. Realizing how close he was to getting shot, Assad quickly got into the car and started the ignition. Milson, meters away, ran up to the car, still firing his weapon. Assad wasted no time putting the vehicle in reverse as it moved backwards. Each tire screeched upon the pavement, leaving smoke and debris, as it made its way from the lot. The Mercedes ran into several other parked cars, leaving scrapes and damages in its wake. As it pulled off, Milson ran behind it, aiming and shooting precariously without giving a thought. He knew he could not chase the car on foot from where he was. Looking around, he saw some distinctive opportunities that might help his situation. The design of the garage was similar in many ways to that of mall garages in the United States, with openings and spaces between sections. Milson could see down and onto other levels of the lot very easily. Without hesitation and only going on instinct, a wild idea came into his mind. He didn't have time to rationalize or give it a second thought. It was all adrenaline and motivation that took control of his thought process and senses. Milson looked at his objective closely and took a deep breath. And within seconds, he catapulted his body between each level of the lot, maintaining control as he spiraled downward in an attempt to catch Assad. The scene itself looked as if it was conducted out of an action movie. Milson was running, jumping, and vaulting in and out of several floors of the garage and over several barricades that were made of concrete and steel. From a spectator's point of view, he looked as if he was a "Parkour" stuntman establishing his skills professionally. The word "*Parkour*" is a French term used to describe free running or excessive movement training. Parkour entails swift, non-stop jumping, climbing, vaulting, rolling, and swinging through man-made obstacles and urban terrain—along with wall scaling of buildings and permanent structures. Showing no regard for his own safety or well-being, seeking only to catch Assad, he jumped onto several other automobiles to cushion his fall after having leapt from level to level. Seeing the Mercedes whipping viciously around turns to make its escape, Milson, with incredible luck and absolute determination, somehow managed to jump across and land on the hood of the Mercedes as it continues to speed away. Assad, surprised by this course of action, began to turn the steering wheel violently from side to side in order to throw Milson off of the vehicle. But Milson, relentless and resolute, was far from surrendering. He held his ground on the hood of the car as it violently swung him from side to side, speeding through the tightly crowded garage. Assad grew agitated at the bounty hunter's persistence. He even shouted some obscenities at Milson to show his frustration.

"Get off the fucking car, you bastard!" he screamed, trying to throw Milson off. But Milson could not respond. He was too busy concentrating on holding on while the car tore through the garage. Approaching the exit, thinking he was about to be free; Assad glanced over Milson and saw two to three vehicles blocking his path. These were Fuller's men, who were dressed in tactical gear and had blocked the entrances and exits. Milson took notice of this as well. He managed to utter some colorful invectives of his own at Assad while banging on the windshield.

"Stop the car, you son of a bitch, or I'll shoot you myself!"

Not heeding his warnings or threats, Assad pushed the envelope, increasing the vehicle's speed even more. Fuller's SWAT team drew their guns and pointed them at the oncoming Benz with Milson still on the hood. Knowing that they could not engage, they stood their ground, never mind that an oncoming vehicle was about to collide with them. Milson knew in his mind that Assad was not going to stop. Assad revved the engine even more to attain a higher accelerated speed, moving closer and closer to the SWAT team and their barricade of vehicles. Milson had a hard time hanging on. He knew he could not last much longer, never mind physically getting his hands on Assad. With a hard decision to make, and knowing his life was in jeopardy, he lets go, saving himself from a head-on collision and possibly death. As he let go, he was thrown from the car ferociously, which caused him to hit several vehicles on the side, leaving his body bruised and battered from the violent impact.

Assad was able to break through the barricade, leaving behind debris and mangled metal. Fuller's men, who had gotten out of the way of the collision, opened fire on the twisted front end of what used to be a lavish luxury automobile as it continued onto a road congested with heavy traffic. Onlookers and pedestrians were startled. They stared at the wrecked vehicles and also at the tactical-uniformed men, who still had their weapons raised toward the long-gone white Mercedes-Benz, which had disappeared into the ongoing traffic. The events were shocking to the public, who were not used to such excitement in their modest city. But all of that had changed due to the corruption and depravity of the terrorists.

While the crowd remained in awe over the events that had just taken place, Milson was a bit groggy due to the impactful event that nearly took his life. One of Fuller's men helped Milson get to his feet, while another retrieved his firearm. Milson was hurt, but the pain in his body was nothing compared to the one his pride was feeling. He regained himself but remained angry over the outcome. As he gathered himself physically and thanking each of the SWAT members for assisting him, Fuller, Sheppard, and Weaver came storming out of the mall looking for him to find out what had happened.

"Milson! Are you all, right? What happened?" asked Weaver.

"What do you think?" shouted Milson. "The bastard got away! He rammed right through the cars and made it into the street! I had to jump on top of the car to catch him. If I hadn't let go in time, you three would be scraping me off the pavement right now. That son of a bitch tried to run me down!" Still shaking the cobwebs out of his head, he thought about Asherah and if Fuller's men still had her in custody.

"The girl! Did you get the girl?"

Sheppard answered,

"We got her, Chief. Farad has her apprehended. She's on her way back to the embassy for questioning."

"Good. I want to interrogate her myself. Assad will try to finish his business, but he won't leave here without her."

"Are you sure about that? The bugger just sprinted through here like a bat out of hell without giving her a second thought. He's on his way out of the country now that he knows we're on to him," said Fuller.

"I don't think so. Just before he went rabbit, he shouted that he'd be back for her. He's not going to leave her behind. Trust me, guys. I know how these assholes think. He's coming back for her. The question is when, where, and how." Milson replied, still gathering himself after his physical ordeal.

While the four men continued talking about what had transpired, one of Fuller's men ran toward him to give him an update. "Sir, we've got a problem. The police are on their way. They heard about what happened here on their scanners. Someone must have called and told them about it. They'll be here within twenty minutes."

"Bloody hell! That's all we need now is for the locals to start snooping around and asking questions. Listen up," as Fuller began to bark orders to his entourage of men.

"Have one of our guys stay behind to be the poster boy for us. Have him cook up some cockamamie story for the locals to throw them off. Say it was a robbery or carjacking—anything but the truth and what really happened. The police must not know that this was a terrorist job. If the government were to find out about this, they would lock this city down in a heartbeat."

The agent acknowledged Fuller's orders and ran back to his colleagues to informed them of the same. Later that moment, Milson remembered what the mysterious figure had said to him when he was seized by them.

"Hey, guys, we've got another problem on our hands," Milson called out.

"We were lucky that Assad didn't give up the weapons or the plans to the terrorists, but now that situation is the least of our worries." Milson looked right at Fuller to tell him the news.

"Fuller, when I was down there, I caught a glimpse of the top guy who was doing most of the talking. He was too hidden for me to get a good look, so I couldn't ID his face. But he did say that they knew about us and our surveillance on Assad. He said that they have an operative planted in your ranks at the embassy. They knew we were coming and knew about our arrival. The bastard even knew me by name. We're dealing with a group of terrorists that are not playing around and mean business. And from what I've heard, they will stop at nothing to achieve their goal. You've got a mole in your department, Fuller. And he or she is buried somewhere very deep inside your house."

Fuller got angry rather than being shocked or surprised. For months, he had suspected that something in his department was not right, due to intelligence leaks and mission compromises, but he could not put his finger on it. He was aware of the number of new employees who had been hired by the United Arab Emirates state department without official background checks, and the number of digital reports and information that mysteriously disappeared from the data files in their electronic archives. He was also aware of the number of new interpreters and agents being hired by the Dubaian government and not from the MI6 agency itself from London. This fragment of information got Fuller's juices stirring.

"Goddammit! A bloody leak?!" Fuller shouted.

"You didn't happen to catch the name of the person he was talking about?"

Milson shook his head and said,

"No! I was too busy keeping the bullets out of my ass! Unfortunately, he didn't say. But it has to be someone close, someone in your department or division."

Weaver interrupted.

"David, you were the only one I told we were coming. I know you didn't have much of a choice about contacting your bosses in London and telling them what's been going on, but I know you had to tell some of your colleagues that we were on our way. Otherwise, you wouldn't have had Farad and the others pick us up from the airport. I agree with Killian on this, Davy. It has to be someone who works with you or next to you," Weaver replied.

Fuller bowed his head and started rubbing his face. The accusations put him in deep thought as he probed his brain for several seconds thinking about who the person or persons might be. As he stood there contemplating on this difficult conundrum for several more seconds, a surprising conclusion came over him as if he was struck by lightning itself.

"I'll be damned!" replied the British agent.

"You just said the magic word, Jimmy boy! I think I know who it is, but I've got to prove it before I name the individual. I just hope I'm wrong about this, and for God's sake, it isn't who I think it is."

After that, Fuller called over one of his men to tell him something in private. They both stood there for only a minute as Milson, Sheppard, and Weaver observed quietly. When they were finished, the agent gave Fuller a gesture that resembled a salute and ran to one of the nearby vehicles that they came in. Afterwards, Fuller's man drove off in a flash, leaving them behind. Weaver grabbed Fuller by the shoulder wondering what was going on.

"David, what are you doing?" Fuller replied,

"Don't worry, mates. I have a hunch about who the person might be. But now we need to get you blokes out of here, before the bloody locals show up. They don't know that you Yanks are here. And if they find out about you guys, it won't be only my ass on the line; my superiors in London will be in hot water too. Not to mention that all the heads of all the advisers who are permanently stationed at the British Consulate will be on the chopping block because of this unsanctioned operation conducted jointly by the United States and the United Kingdom. Our involvement in this will jeopardize our relations as ambassadors of the UK, and will damage our trust and cooperation as mutual international partners in the middle east."

"Wait a minute, I don't understand. Why are we running away from this? What do the police have to do with our being here? This is our case and our call," Sheppard said.

"Listen, kid, David is right." Explained Weaver.

"We must leave here or the local authorities will fry our butts. Under the United Earth Administration charter, whenever a foreign operative intends to visit a member country for either business or pleasure, the operative's government must contact the host country to inform them that said operative will be spending time there on international business. We didn't follow this procedure or protocol because ours is a covert op to catch a high-value target and extradite him to the United States. And we're trying to keep this on the down low because we don't want anyone to know of our country's involvement here. And we don't need a repeat of what happened in Sydney, with the locals asking a lot of questions," Weaver said.

"That's right. And you Yanks are here illegally—never mind that your government has sanctioned your mission, and the Emirates knows nothing about your presence here. We've got to get you guys out of here now!" said Fuller. He and his men rushed Milson and party to the remaining cars so they could make a clean dash before the Dubai police arrived on the scene.

CHAPTER 8

THE HUNT COMPROMISED

British Embassy, Dubai, United Arab Emirates, 7:15 p.m.

Milson and the others made their way back to the embassy in less than thirty minutes. Fuller's men had Asherah sitting in what looked to be an interrogation room, with an armed guard present at her side. She appeared to be nervous and scared. Her body was trembling from the excitement and her hands were shaking profusely. She did not know what to think or say at that moment. Puzzled and confused, she kept asking the guard who stood watch over her why she was there and what she had done. But the sentry kept quiet throughout her questioning. One could see that she was agitated and overwhelmed, but her demeanor was more a result of fright and terror than anything else. Even though she was fidgety and jittery, she remained seated on the cold steel chair that supported her lightweight frame. Obviously, she was being observed on the other side of what looked to be a large two-way glass mirror pane. Weaver and Sheppard, along with a stenographer, were positioned on the other side ready to observe and take notes as they watched the frightened young woman before them. Sheppard was getting a little anxious himself. He kept asking Weaver where Milson and Fuller were.

"What the hell is taking them so long? Why aren't they in there questioning her? Every moment we wait, Assad gets closer and closer to getting away."

"Relax, kid. They'll be in there soon to get the answers we need. Right now, they're trying to figure out who the leak is and where that person is currently hiding. Fuller is going over all the email messages in the embassy's database and is looking at all inbound and outbound communications—landline, wireless phone calls and text messages—from the past forty-eight hours, since our arrival in Dubai. Finding whoever tipped off those terrorists and thereby blew our chance to catch Assad is just as important as questioning Ms. Asherah. So, take it easy. If Milson's right that Assad has not left because of her, then we know that he's not going anywhere anytime soon. He still needs to make the switch with his buyers to get paid, and his girlfriend here may be our only link to help us find him. Again, don't worry, Ensign. He is not about to leave the country while we have his girlfriend in custody. He's going to want her back."

Sheppard realized that what Weaver was saying made sense. As the two men continued to observe the frightened woman, who was still bewildered, a door next to Sheppard suddenly burst open with Fuller and Milson making their way inside.

"Chief, how are you doing? Are you all right?" asked Sheppard, concerned about his ordeal in the garage.

"I'm fine, kid. One of Fuller's doctors checked me out upstairs. All I got were some bruised ribs and a shitload of scratches. Other than that, I'm good. Now we can concentrate on that lovely young lady in there. How's she doing, James?" Milson asked.

"She's as scared as a church mouse surrounded by a pack of hungry stray cats. She has no clue what's going on or why we snatched her. But she knows that somehow her boyfriend is involved. She just doesn't want to admit it out loud."

"Well, she's going to have to. If she knows what's best for her, she'll give him up, unless she wants to spend the rest of her life in prison for harboring and conspiring with a suspected murderer, spy, and terrorist." replied Fuller, who was already annoyed after finding out that he has a mole in his unit.

Milson, looking at Asherah closely through the glass, determined that she was terrified due to her posture and demeanor that was taking place.

"You're right, Fuller. And I think I may have an idea that just might work in our favor. It's far-fetched, but I think it could help us. Weaver, you and I are going in there. I want you to back me up on what I'm about to do," he said.

"What's your plan of attack?" asked Weaver.

"We're going to do the old-fashioned good cop, bad cop routine. From the looks of her, she's never been in a situation like this before. This will be a perfect opportunity to squeeze her into a false sense of security—scare the living crap out of her, to put it bluntly. Submit her into confessing where Assad might be or where he's going. If one of us scares her in just the right way, we may get our answers and finding him—and also figure out what his next move is going to be."

"Wait a minute, Killian, do you actually think this is going to work? She's not some hardened criminal off the streets. Her file tells us that. She just got herself caught in a bad situation without realizing what was going on. Wrong place, wrong time type of scenario," said Weaver.

"I know, James. That's why we're going to do this. I have a feeling it will work. Look at her; she's scared out of her mind right now. As you said, she doesn't know what's going on, besides the fact that Assad left her to be apprehended by us on purpose. She's terrified about what's going on. But I have a feeling that deep down, she's pissed at her boyfriend for hanging her out to dry. I think we can pull off what you suggest and use this to our advantage."

Weaver and the rest of the crew decided to go along with Milson's idea.

"Okay, I'm game. So how do you want to play it? Do you want me to portray the bad cop or the good cop?" asked Weaver.

Milson said, "I'll let you have the fun of playing bad guy. I can see it in your eyes that you want this role because you come off as a certified asshole. And everybody knows that the CIA are just government douchebags in disguise—well, them and those IRS scumbags."

Both Sheppard and Fuller laughed.

"Oh, you're funny, Milson. Have you forgotten that you were once a company douchebag yourself for four years, you pompous-ass son of a bitch? So don't think that your shit doesn't stink either my friend. And to think I've been defending your sorry ass all this time."

"Oh, have you now. That's so sweet of you, James," Milson replied facetiously.

"I didn't know you felt that way about me. I'm so sorry cup cake." Replied Milson as he extended his witticism on Weaver's behalf.

"But really, all jokes aside, I figure that you have better interrogation methods than I do. I have been out of the game for so long that I'm better at catching these assholes than questioning them. But if we can persuade her to get on our side to give up Assad, I know that she'll open up and tell us everything we need to know to grab her boyfriend. This is what you'll do: you play at her rough and hard with threats of prison time and any other thing you can think of to rattle her cage. I on the other end will console her. Using words of comfort and understanding while promising her restitution and reward. I figure that once she feels safe around me, she'll definitely give up Assad, even if she doesn't want to."

All of them were in agreement as they started to put the plan together. Fuller told the stenographer to start the recording as soon as they walked in the next room. When they entered, Weaver went over to the guard and asked him to leave. The individual gave a nod and made his exit. Milson sat down in front of Asherah, who recognized him from the department store when he purposely bumped into her.

Her eyes grew wide with surprise, but they also showed suspicion and cautiousness.

Weaver, on the other hand, paced back and forth over the young woman like a predator stalking its prey before the kill. He also had an odd-looking folder tucked under his left armpit which was probably Asherah's file records of some kind. She did not know what to think of this. She was already nervous and scared, but the presence of Milson and Weaver in the room just made it more unbearable for her to handle.

With Weaver standing at the far corner, Milson initiates the interrogation by saying,

"Ms. Desiree Asherah? My name is Killian Milson. I'm an apprehension officer working for the US government."

Hearing that, she wasted no time in saying,

"I know you! You were the one that bumped into me at the clothing store in the mall!"

"That's correct, Ms. Asherah. I'm a federal agent who has been sent to take custody of an individual you know personally who is wanted by the United States for espionage and treason. Unfortunately, you have been brought in for questioning because of your association with such person. This is my colleague, Mr. James Weaver. He's also a correspondent for the US government. He represents the Central Intelligence Agency. I know you're confused about why you're here, but as I stated before, we have some important questions to ask you, ma'am."

She looked up at Milson, who reciprocated a look to her of compassion and understanding. With tears flowing from her eyes, she immediately began pleading with Milson for her freedom and absolution.

"Please, Mr. Milson, let me go! I didn't do anything! I don't understand what's going on! Why am I here?"

"Oh, stop with the dramatics, Ms. Asherah!" Weaver shouted with an attempt to scare her even more.

"You know damn well why you're here! You've been caught aiding and abetting a criminal who's been attempting to sell highly classified US military software and hardware to a hostile terrorist organization!"

"What?! Are you crazy?! I have no idea what you're talking about!" Asherah said hysterically. "Besides, I know my rights! You can't do this to me!"

"Rights?! You have no rights lady! Your rights were forfeited when you were caught colluding with a man wanted by the United States! A fugitive who has stolen military secrets from the US government and selling them on the black market to a terrorist group! That, my dear, makes you an accomplice and an accessory in an espionage ring set up by your acquaintance, who ran out on you in the mall today!" Weaver exclaimed by yelling directly in Asherah's face.

"Look, this is insane! I and my boyfriend were just—"

"That's right, your boyfriend, Lieutenant Commander Ad-dam Omar Assad! The very person you've been affiliated with and the one we want. Yes, Desiree Asherah, we know all about you and your association with Commander Assad. I've read all about it in this file that I'm holding here." Weaver took the folder out from his armpit, slammed it on the table and began adlibbing the contents of it out loud as he read it to her:

"A naval officer whom you've been having a relationship with for the past several years. The same individual you've been friends with since you were a child growing up in Baghdad, Iraq. The same person you attended Yale University with ten years ago. The same man who was employed by US Naval Intelligence for three and a half years as a counterintelligence analyst, and now suddenly is a thief and traitor of stolen military intel from our government's archives. You do realize that you can go to prison for a very, very long time for conspiracy by association, don't you? And not just that, Ms. Asherah. Not only will the US government will bring you up on charges your boyfriend has committed, but they will extradite you to the US to appear before an American court of law with bipartisanship of a military tribunal for association and ties to a terrorist's organization. In fact, you will be tried as a coconspirator for such terrorist activities. Not to mention breaking the laws of this country [that is, the laws of the United Arab Emirates], as well as the laws of your own homeland of Holland, where you currently reside. Oh yes, Ms. Asherah, we know about your citizenship there. Remember, this file tells us everything about you and your life partner." Weaver did not let up as he continued his intimidation tactic.

"If I'm not mistaken, Holland doesn't take too kindly in finding out that their citizens have ties to terrorist activities. They consider themselves as a neutral state opposed of terrorism and its ideology. You might lose your job, your citizenship, and your freedom all at the same time, as well as serve consecutive prison terms if you're sentenced by either of these countries I just mentioned. You may do hard time with hard labor, who knows. In other words, you will either die in prison or become eligible for parole by the time you reach your ninety-ninth birthday. So, what is it going to be? Help us find Assad and tell us what his next move will be, or go down by yourself for collaborating with him and the terrorist group he is affiliated with? The ball is in your court, lady. What's it going to be? Help us out or spend the rest of your life in either an American or foreign prison?" Weaver continued hovering over the distraught Asherah.

At first, she was at a loss for words. Her emotions were running high; she was confused and terrified. She felt that she was under a great deal of pressure, especially because she had no idea what was going to happen next. But after realizing the seriousness of her situation, she began to break down. She was literally at a loss, physically, mentally, emotionally, and probably spiritually. She was still crying after Weaver's proclamation of punishment. Just when she thought there was no hope of a solution that fell in her favor, Milson gently grabbed hold of her hand and began speaking in a softer and more relaxed tone than Weaver had used.

"Ms. Asherah, listen to me. I know this is hard for you, and I know it's a lot to take in, but honestly, we don't want you. We want your boyfriend. Everything that Officer Weaver said to you is true. If you don't help us find Assad, then you will be accountable for all those charges. I know you're innocent and personally you had nothing to do with what he was planning. But if he ends up handing over those classified materials to this terrorist organization who wants to kill thousands, probably millions, of innocent people for their own gain, then you will be involved in a catastrophe beyond belief, unlike anything the world has ever seen. Assad could eventually start a third world war or, even worse, a nuclear one. We must stop him from doing this. You must understand the gravity and validity of our situation, and how serious this is. We need your help, not just for our sake, but also for yours—and the sake of the entire world."

The strategy was working. Milson had reached her rationality. Having made his appeal to her sense of moral obligation by being comforting and understanding. Still holding her hand, he gave her a tissue so she could wipe the tears from her eyes and face. Hoping to calm her down by gaining her trust so she could open up even more. Weaver, still in character, stood back in the corner and observed. He realized that Milson's plan was actually working. Asherah was being more relax and comfortable around him.

Milson continued with the affable/mild interrogation.

"Desiree, do you have any idea who Ad-dam's contacts were and where they might have originated?"

"No. He never told me anything about them. All he said to me was that they were highly connected and very influential in the middle east. He even told me that they have connections within some parts of Europe, Asia, and South America. He also said that the amount of money they were going to give him in exchange for the plans was in the millions—two to three hundred million to be exact. But he never told me about their identity or where they came from."

Asherah was calmer with this type of approach. She starts confessing more in remembrance of what they were going to do after Assad had received the money.

"Our plans were to go back to Holland and stay there for a little while until everything had blown over. Then we were going to settle down in either France, Greece, Italy, or Spain for a short period of time. Ad-dam was even considering one of the Micronesian or Solomon Islands in the South Pacific."

"Ms. Asherah, didn't you know that what he was doing was wrong? And that if he got caught, the consequences for both of you would be severe and damaging to your lives?" Milson asked the already guilt-ridden young woman, who now realized the seriousness of the situation she was in.

"I knew it was wrong, Officer Milson, and I told Ad-dam the same thing. But he insisted on doing it anyway. He wanted to teach the government a lesson because of what they did to his family and other Muslims who were treated unfairly and harshly. I told him that this was not the way and that it wasn't right. I said that this sort of action was not the way to solve his problem with the Americans. But he had made up his mind; he wanted retribution. He wanted revenge for what he and his family went through all those years ago. That's the reason he joined the navy, to learn everything about your military and how it operates from the inside out. And when he found out that the government kept its secrets stored in a database, he decided to use those secrets against you. He was obsessed with this. So, he decided to punish the country that discriminated against him, his culture, and his ancestral homeland."

"So, what you're saying is that his motives are more personal than political?" asked Milson.

"Yes. When we were kids, he didn't want to come to America. But when the war started and the Americans invaded, his parents lost everything. His father was a special adviser to Saddam Hussein, and part of his political party. When Saddam fell from power, Assad knew that he and his family could stay in Iraq no longer, especially due to the warring tribes of the Shiites, Sunnis, and Kurds. He knew he couldn't go back to Lebanon because of his renunciation of citizenship. So, the only logical place for Ad-dam's family to go to was America. Ad-dam blamed the Americans for the start of the war and for having to leave his homeland." explained Asherah, who was still in tears.

"So, let me see if I got this straight," said Weaver, who was still in character.

"Assad has been orchestrating this whole thing ever since he was a boy just to show his profound hatred against the very country that adopted him? Well, I'm sorry, but all of this just shows me that not only he's a traitor to his country but also a bona fide terrorist with deep political resentments, delusions of grandeur, and tyrannical egoism."

"He is only doing this because of what you people did to him and his family!" Asherah screamed as she stood up and confronted Weaver face-to-face.

"You Americans have treated Muslims and Arabic people like shit ever since 9/11! You people thought that the entire Islamic world was behind that terrible plot thirty years ago! You blamed the entire Muslim community for what only a handful of radicals did back then, and we've been paying for it ever since! You invaded my country because your previous president, George W. Bush, thought that Saddam and his regime had taken part in that attack or had some foreknowledge of it! Not to mention the ignorant thought that he had weapons of mass destruction in his arsenal, which your government never found, only to realize later that he never had any in the first place! But what it all comes down to is that you so-called mighty Americans with your self-righteousness did not want to admit when y'all were wrong and made a mistake! There was no reason for you to invade Iraq! Yes, Saddam was a brutal dictator and he killed thousands of people, but he was no different from the others in power around the same time. Some of whom your government supported and helped to put into power! Just because a country fails to follow your democratic ideology doesn't mean it's primitive and backward; it's just a different type of society with a different way of thinking. And just because the Islamic ideology has taken hold all over the world does not mean Islamism is evil or presents a threat. But still, you Americans think that you have the right to police the entire world by subjugating the authority to do so!"

Weaver looked at her and said,

"Are you finished?! Are you finished with the bullshit now?! Are you through with your outburst and tirades?! Spare me your sanctimonious views that you and your people are the victims here, lady!" Condescending in his role of bad cop, Weaver added,

"Because no matter how you define or characterize it, Assad is still a traitor and a terrorist! So, you can drop the act. The whole thing of putting the blame on others and saying it's because your boyfriend has issues from when he was a child doesn't fly with me! Assad is going down, and you are going down with him!"

The debate between the two started to get heated and out of control. It was too much for Asherah to handle. When Milson saw that she was emotionally compromised, to the point of having physically lunged from her seat to get at Weaver, who stood opposite of her was the breaking point. Milson who was stunned by her reaction stood up and got between the two.

"All right, Ms. Asherah, calm down. I know you're upset, but you must understand the severity of this situation. No matter the reasons Assad had for doing this, it's still wrong and criminal. He must be stopped and brought to justice before the unthinkable happens. He has already committed several murders in two countries and must not be allowed to hand over the,"

"Wait a minute, what did you say, Officer Milson?" Before Milson could finish his statement, Asherah cut him off in midsentence because of what he said. She was bewildered and shocked to hear the word "murder" come from his mouth. When Milson realized her reaction to what he said, he knew right then that he had struck a nerve by mentioning Assad's murder conviction. Right at that moment, he thought to himself that she was ignorant of the event and did not know of the two killings that Assad had done earlier prior to his rendezvous with the terrorists. Taking advantage of this, Milson played to her vulnerability.

"I said, he must not be allowed to hand over the weapons and—"

"No, before that, you said murder. Ad-dam hasn't murdered anyone. He's not a murderer," Asherah said with sincerity.

Milson leaned forward, hoping to portray sympathy and comfort because of what he was about to tell her.

"I'm sorry, Desiree, but unfortunately he is. Our investigation and his whereabouts has led us to conclude that he committed three murders within the past two weeks. One was in his apartment the day before he left." Milson took a photo from a folder he had brought in and showed it to her. "This gentleman, now deceased, was a known arms dealer named Muhammad Kareem. He worked for the Iranian government and possibly had ties to the terrorist organization Ad-dam was doing business with. The FBI found him in a dumpster near his apartment. His neck had been broken intentionally. We know that Assad is responsible."

"This doesn't prove anything! Ad-dam couldn't have done that! He's not capable of doing that!" Asherah cried hysterically.

"There was a witness who said she saw him carrying a huge trash bag to the dumpster. It was determined that this bag had Kareem's body in it. I'm sorry, but the evidence shows that he is responsible, Desiree. Another murder happened in Australia, where I and Officer Weaver went to investigate. Assad took two more lives at a hotel in downtown Sydney." He showed the pictures of Gardner and Shaula, then placed them on the table.

"This one is of an innocent woman by the name of Charlene Gardner. She was found dead in the hotel room with a knife wound to the back of her neck, which caused severe spinal trauma, killing her instantly. The second is of an Egyptian businessman named Ahmed Shaula. He was also found by hotel staff in his room, several yards away from Ms. Gardner, with three gunshot wounds, one in the back, two in the chest. We believe he was another contact of Assad."

Automatically a light bulb flashed in Asherah's head. She instantly remembered the phone conversation she had with him when he contacted her from Australia. She remembered that he said that something had come up and he had to leave Sydney right away. She had forgotten until now.

Milson continued to tell her about her boyfriend's secretive, malicious lifestyle.

"As for the woman, we think she was an innocent bystander who was in the wrong place at the wrong time. Assad was having a casual sexual relationship with her."

Milson knew he had pushed a button when he said that. So did Weaver, Fuller, and Sheppard. Asherah looked at him with confusion and dismissal. Once again, she rose up and stared across at him, saying with emotion and stress,

"What are you talking about? He didn't have a relationship with this woman—or any other woman for that matter. He's been with me for a long time."

Milson silently inhaled and exhaled. He saw the denial in her face, but he had to continue, even though it was going to cause her more emotional damage. He cleared his throat and went on to say,

"I'm sorry again, Desiree, but he did. After his treachery was discovered, he assumed the identity of this man." Milson showed her Gary Brown's photo.

"His name is Gary Brown. He was a chemical engineer who resided in Miami, Florida. There was a connection between him and Muhammad Kareem, as evidenced by emails and phone calls to each other around the time we've been investigation. Brown was also found dead with a gunshot wound to the head. We assumed that Assad wasn't involved in this killing, thinking that Kareem may have been the culprit. Before Assad left, he took the identity of Gary Brown. Then he fled the country and went to Australia. Our investigation and surveillance led us to conclude that Ad-dam met up with Ms. Gardner between the time he left Los Angeles, to the time they arrived in Sydney. They were on a plane together at each moment, and several eyewitnesses said that they were together each time, including their stopover at Honolulu, Hawaii. One of the eyewitnesses is the brother of the deceased. His name is Bartholomew Gardner; he's a lieutenant commander in the US Navy, stationed at Pearl Harbor, Hawaii. He was the last person to see his sister alive, with Assad at her side. He identified him immediately when we sent word of his sister's demise along with the photo of Assad in disguise. Commander Gardner also told us that his sister described their relationship as"—he paused— "a romantic interlude. The hotel staff also observed Assad with Ms. Gardner several times. They even dined together on many occasions and shared a room."

Asherah shook her head frantically. She did not want to accept what Milson was telling her, let alone the notion of Assad being a murderer, and having a secret affair with another woman.

"I don't believe you. I can't believe you. It's not in his nature to do such things. Ad-dam would never try to hurt anyone, let alone kill somebody. He is the sweetest man I've ever known. And he would never cheat on me. He's been faithful to me all these years! He loves me!"

"Oh, for Christ's sake, lady, wake up!" Weaver interrupted, lashing out again at her.

"You're living in a fantasy world if you believe that crap! Your boyfriend is an expert at what he does! And what he does is keeping secrets from people! He worked as an analyst in naval intelligence for three and a half years—counterintelligence and espionage! He did black ops missions for both the navy and CIA after graduating from the academy. And he was a member of one of the most elite Special Forces units the navy had to offer. He specialized in counterintelligence and counterinsurgency because of his skills, expertise, and background. He was trained to kill with accuracy and proficiency! Look at these pictures. Do these people look like they've been killed by hoodlums or thugs off the streets? *No!* They were killed by a professional! A professional who knows how to kill with precision and efficiency. Your boyfriend is a professional killer no matter how you look at it!

He was taught and trained by us to do such things under certain circumstances. He's been lying to you, Ms. Asherah. He's probably been lying to you for a very long time, perhaps throughout the entire course of your relationship and his career. Haven't you been curious to know exactly what he's been doing during the past couple of years when you two haven't seen each other for a long time? Haven't you wondered about that?"

Hearing this, Asherah broke down, crying harder than ever before. The woman who earlier had seemed so attractive and vibrant was now a stressed-out shell of derailed emotions and extreme distress. She was face down on the table, sobbing heavily, without any attempt to wipe her face. Dismissing the fact that Weaver was still hovering over the young woman in an attempt to intimidate her some more, Milson, playing the sympathizer, intervened by giving Asherah some tissues so she could wipe the tears from her face. He reached across the table and gently took hold of her hand.

"Desiree, please, you must be honest with us. We need your help to find him. He's going to hurt a lot of people if we don't stop him. Please help us so we can help you."

With those words, Asherah slowly raised her head. She took the tissues from him and began to wipe her face. After composing herself, she looked over at Milson and said,

"Okay, I will help you. But promise me that you will not hurt him."

Milson looked over at Weaver, who looked back at him. They gave each other a glance recognizable only by fellow spooks or law enforcement agents in recognition of their true motives. To try to ease Asherah's worries, Milson shook his head and said,

"Desiree, if he gives himself up peacefully without retaliating or resisting, then you have my word that he will not be harmed."

Asherah squeezed Milson's hand in appreciation and gave a hint of relief as she sighed softly. She nodded in Milson's direction, making eye contact, a gesture of thanks for his understanding. But in reality, she was more disappointed than relieved. Milson knew this deep down. He felt a little sorry for the young woman, but he knew he was not in that room to console her. His purpose was to extract the information he needed from her and persuade her to help him catch Assad. That was his first priority. Everything else that went on in there was just the means to get the job done. This was the way of CIA covert operations. Use any means necessary to achieve the goal, and finish the mission, even if it means acting in ways that are unprincipled or illegal. Milson knew this, and so did Weaver. But fortunately, they did not have to make use of any harsh tactics. In this case, their task was much easier to perform.

Milson stood from his chair, still holding Asherah's hand.

"Desiree, we're going to need you to get in contact with Ad-dam. We have your cell phone in our possession. We know that he is going to try to get ahold of you and possibly meet up with you. You're going to use your phone to get in contact with him. We're going to advise you on what to say to him and how to say it. I will personally coach you on everything, understand?" She shook her head yes, still looking sad and somber.

"One of the guards is going to take you to another room so you can get cleaned up and relax for a bit." Milson helped her up.

"Listen, everything is going to be fine. You help us, and you're in the clear. And I promise you, no one will get hurt."

Asherah shook her head again and followed Milson to the door, outside of which there was an agent waiting for her. He instructed the agent to take her somewhere comfortable so she could get herself together. After she left the room, Milson and Weaver retreated from the area to return to the room next door where Fuller and Sheppard resided as they observed.

"Well, Davy boy, how was that for good old American interrogation?" asked Weaver, who was rubbing the back of his neck, although it looked more like he was patting himself on the back for his performance.

"Not bad for a couple of Yanks. You two almost had me believing in your farce. But I think you two should brush up on your knowledge of Arabian laws and UAE policies. They don't have extradition policies or treaties in this country. If she had known that, I doubt she would have dared to give up Assad so easily. You two really scared the piss out of her, especially you, Jimmy boy," Fuller said.

"That was the plan from the start," Milson said, crossing his arms. "I had a feeling that she didn't know too much about the laws over here, even though her file shows her to be highly educated in International law. You did a good job throwing that bit in about the prison time she'd face if she didn't cooperate, Weaver."

Once again Weaver smiled as he boosted himself up.

"I had to go with what I know, fellas. You and I both know that the UAE doesn't hold individuals accountable who have committed crimes in other countries. In the event they do have in their custody a terrorist or group of terrorists who have committed heinous acts in the UAE, they automatically send them back to wherever they came from. But if such individuals have committed crimes on UAE soil, the UAE will have them stand trial and, if a guilty verdict is delivered, execute them without hesitation. It's been a long time since I have done the good cop, bad cop routine. Once more you were right, Killian. Asherah really didn't know about Assad's affairs and had no clue of who or what he really was."

"And that's exactly what we're going to use, guys. She is more afraid for his well-being than she is afraid for her own self. This is the perfect opportunity to coach her into saying whatever we want her to say and push her in the right direction so we can catch this guy. I guarantee that he is going to get in contact with her sooner rather than later," Milson said with assurance.

"I like how you played the sympathy card with her, Milson. You were so convincing that I almost cried. You had her eating out of the palm of your hand, you sly, cheeky devil," Fuller said with a snicker.

"That was my intention. She had to feel safe with me to know that I am here to help her. And by playing into it, she will definitely help us to get him. I know how these scumbags think; he will definitely come for her."

"That may be, Chief. But he knows that we've got her, and he knows that we've interrogated her. Do you really think he's going to take the risk and try to get her back, knowing that we know his entire plan, and also knowing the information we've already gathered from her? If I were Commander Assad, I would think that she's a liability and leave her. Not worth the time or effort to extract her," Sheppard said over the intercom.

"You're probably right, kid. But I don't think you've ever been in love before. Assad said on the balcony level of the mall that he'd be back for her. He knows we've got her, and he knows what we're doing to her. But this guy has it deep for this girl. Remember, they grew up together. They've known each other ever since they were kids. Trust me, fellas, I know how these guys think and act when it comes to money and women. It's not in their nature to leave either behind, especially when the have an investment. No, he's coming back for her, and he knows that we're going to be waiting for him. It's as I said before, just a question of when, where, and how he's going to do it, while trying not to get caught. Remember, he's a sneaky, clever SOB. We're going to have to stay one step ahead of him."

While they were still contemplating what Assad might do next, one of Fuller's men entered the room to whispering something in Fuller's ear, simultaneously handing him a piece of paper—a logbook entry with names and numbers. Fuller's expression turned immediately after he looked at the paper and heard what his man had to tell him. "That bloody bastard! Hey, gents, I just received a report from one of my men. It looks like we may have found that mole." Fuller stormed out of the room with Sheppard right behind him. Milson and Weaver joined in as they followed them. All four walked in sync down the corridor with a collective purpose in mind. To find out the identity of the infiltrator and the info if any they have passed to their source.

Undisclosed Facility on the Outskirts of Sharjah, United Arab Emirates, 9:30 p.m.

Persistent of the speed he was traveling, Assad drove for fifty miles outside the city limits of Dubai. Exceeding the speed limit of 80 to 90 mph, Assad did not slow his momentum on the road, nor gave a thought about police or any other local law enforcement agencies that may have been around the area. His thought process at the time was concentrated on the fiasco in the galleria and how close he came to being captured by Milson and his crew. He was upset by the outcome but more enraged about leaving Asherah behind to take the fall. He did not know how to deal with the guilt that he felt and how much it was eating away at him at the time. All he could think about was Asherah's face and how she looked at him when he left her. For a few seconds, he was in a comatose state as he relived that moment, but later, he regained himself and subconsciously returned to his normal state of mind. Traveling ferociously down the Dubaian highway, Assad was passing up town after town until he came upon a populated UAE city named Sharjah. The third-largest metropolitan area in the region after Dubai, located on the southern coast of the Persian Gulf near the tip of the Arabian Peninsula. Assad had been instructed by the leader of the terrorist group to go there immediately after the botched meeting in the mall earlier that day. He was told not to go within the city limits but to meet at a secret location outside of Sharjah.

He drove another couple of miles north until he was close to the waterfront coastline. As he drove along the beachfront area for several minutes, he happened to catch a glimpse of something out of the corner of his eye. It appeared to be a small privately owned harbor or port facility. It was in fact the very place where he had been instructed to go to. He was to meet them there to finish the transaction, or so he assumed. Assad followed the directions showed by his GPS. He came upon an unsecured gate that he went through, then traveled several yards down a dirt, graveled road that led him to a wide-open pier with several empty docks. He noticed a well-constructed concrete shack to his left that was next to the pier. From his observation the building was vacant with no occupancy inside. Assad looked around, noticing that there was no one in sight, while driving closer to the empty pier. Not one living creature or soul was to be found anywhere. It was as if no one knew that this place existed or its existence. It did not appear to look run down or old, but it seemed as if it had not been used for quite some time. Assad was leery about this location, but given the circumstances of what happened earlier, he figured it made perfect sense that they wanted him to meet them there at this secluded spot. The area was desolate, far away from public view, with no distractions and no onlookers. Still, Assad remained cautious and skeptical because of the emptiness of the location which was disconcerting to him.

He drove up to the building and parked in front of it. He got out of the car slowly, but did not exit all the way. His Walther was clenched in his left hand as a precaution if something were to arise. Preoccupied, constantly looking around the dark, empty pier, and halfway out of the car, Assad did not realize that his cell phone was ringing. He snatched it quickly from the center console and answered it without hesitation. To his knowledge it was the individual who had arranged the meeting in the basement level of the galleria, the same man who had advised him to show up at this current location.

The conversation between the individual and Assad became quite volatile. Assad began screaming at the top of his voice to the person on the other end.

"Why didn't you tell me back at the hotel that I was being followed by the CIA and this bounty hunter?! If you knew that I was being shadowed by the Americans, why in the hell did you want to meet at the mall in the first place? I thought you people were smarter and more reliable when it came to things like this!" Assad continued his rant into the receiver.

"First of all, Mr. Assad, lower the tone of your voice when you speak to me. I am not a common hoodlum with whom you grew up in the ghettos of Baghdad, so I am not to be talked to in this manner. You may possess the knowledge and skills we want, along with the merchandise we asked for, but don't think that you can disrespect me whenever you want. Do you understand my meaning?"

"Are you threatening me?!" Assad asked, not letting up.

The dark voice over the phone showed no reluctance in saying,

"I don't make threats, Mr. Assad. I make promises. You see, in my line of work, I and the people I represent don't make threats; we make guarantees and assurances. Guarantees that what we say will do will be carried out efficiently. And assurances that everything we say will be done precisely and perfectly without question or delay. So, the next time you feel the need to disrespect me or talk to me in an unflattering way that I might find offensive, think twice. You may find that your tongue will be responsible for your demise. Have I made my point clear to you?"

Assad immediately went silent. Perplexed by what he'd just heard, but not surprised, he paused for a few seconds, still infuriated about what had transpired earlier. Though his frustration was coming to the surface, and though he blamed himself and felt guilty for having left Asherah behind, he managed to calm himself for the time being. He knew what type of people he was dealing with and was aware of their reputation as a dangerous establishment. Also, knowing that his chances for success were now limited because of what had happened, he was afraid he had nothing left in his arsenal to fall back on. Assad, feeling helpless, decided to take the malevolent remarks of the mysterious individual seriously and refrain from showing aggression and hostility towards them. To humble himself, Assad literally had to swallow his pride, gulping through his throat in order to resume the conversation, but this time in an apologetic tone.

"I'm sorry for the outburst, but you have to understand my dilemma. Not only did we fail to complete our transaction, but also the circumstances have changed dramatically. I've been compromised. Now, the CIA knows that I'm here, as do ONI and MI6. It will be impossible for me to get out of here, especially now because they've hired someone to come after me. I know the SOPs [standard operating procedures] and general tactics of the CIA and MI6 and how they work, as well as their protocols for covert operations and retrievals, but I have no clue who this guy is or how he operates. And none of this is taking into account the fact that they have my girlfriend in custody. Everything has turned to shit now!" Assad said, hysterical.

"Do not worry yourself, Mr. Assad. We have contingency plans in place for situations such as this. Our man inside knows all the details about Killian Milson and his little band that he has conjured up. All you need to do is just sit there and wait for your transportation to arrive. We can settle our business very soon after you get to the destination we've arranged. There, you will find a boat we charted. It will pick you up within the next couple of minutes. Do you still have the flash drive and weapons in your custody?"

"Yes, I do, but I cannot leave Dubai without Desiree. It's because of me that she was arrested. I will not leave without her," Assad said, concern and passion in his voice.

"I'm sorry for the unfortunate capture of Ms. Asherah, Commander, but I'm afraid that she cannot be helped at this time."

"What?!" shouted Assad.

"I am not going to leave her! I'm responsible for putting her in this situation in the first place! I must find a way to get her out of there!"

"What are you going to do, Assad? Walk right through the front door of the embassy and force them to let her go? Don't be naive and stupid! She's a liability. You cannot afford to go back for her. Your obligation is to us and us alone. It is a shame that she was apprehended, but you cannot help her now. She is considered collateral damage now. She has made a sacrifice for the organization and our cause. You must take responsibility and realize that you are the one, not us, who brought her to this point. Our business goes forward first and foremost; everything else is secondary. You knew the consequences and the risk when you contacted us several years ago, and you're the one who had the idea of launching this endeavor. Our contract must go forward. If it does not, well, I don't have to remind you of the consequences that lie ahead for you."

Again, Assad stood silent. Squeezing the phone even tighter, indignant about what he had to adhere to, he was at a loss—no comeback, no argumentative remark, nothing, not a word. All he did was continue gripping over the phone and listening to the contemptible tone of the voice in his ear. Feeling distraught and full of blame, he looked across the pier at the horizon, the Persian Gulf in the background.

"Yes, I know. And I understand," Assad said with anger, discomfort and grief.

"All is not lost, Commander. Our agent inside is monitoring Ms. Asherah as we speak. From the information he has given us, it appears that she has told them nothing about her involvement with you, other than to say it was a cordial relationship. She said she had no knowledge of your plans or your partnership with us. She claimed ignorance of the entire situation. They will hold her no longer because they have no evidence. They have acquired limited intel from her."

"So, she will be let go without any repercussions?" Assad asked with astonishment.

"I do not know. But what is important is that we conclude our business at once. The yacht that is coming for you will be accompanied by two small gunships that we acquired from one of our constituents. These will escort you to the designated area as scheduled."

"A yacht? I'm impressed," said Assad with surprise.

"Don't be, Commander. Any material goods we have access to are just things we use to further our aims. The real reason we use such things is to establish power and control throughout this region. Our possessions are especially helpful when we seek to extort our greedy enemies. That is why we need what you have."

"This place where I'm going, where is it?" Assad asked, curios.

"You'll be traveling to Iran."

"Iran?" said Assad with surprise.

"Why there?"

"Because Iran is one of our many safe havens, along with a prospering partnership. The Iranian government is unaware of our existence, but we do have operatives inside many of Iran's government departments for the purpose of persuading them to aid in our cause. Muhammad Kareem was one of these operatives, until you terminated his contract with us. But Iran is a haven to us now that our previous meeting place has been compromised. And in Iran, we don't have to worry about further US involvement or any disruptions to our gathering since the United States is prohibited from intervening in Iranian affairs and entering Iranian territory.

"You'll follow two channel routes along the coastline. You'll travel to the port city of Bandar Bushehr, which will be your first stop. Your next stop is the city of Khorramshahr, in the Khuzestan province, where we will meet you personally and do our exchange."

"Bushehr. I've been there before, when I was attached to a SEAL unit several years ago. A group of Somali pirates tried to set up a temporary FOB [forward operations base] there to hijack privately owned boats and commercial ships entering and leaving the gulf through the Strait of Hormuz. The SEAL unit was sent there to stop the pirates' operation. Bushehr is also the location of one of Iran's main nuclear power plants," said Assad, who was obviously familiar with the location.

"Extraordinary! Now, I am impressed with your geographical knowledge and your intel of the region. You will indeed be a unique asset to us if you can control your emotions. We will conclude this conversation later, along with our business, when we meet again. Assalamu alaikum, Mr. Assad."

Assad hesitated to return the greeting, but he figured it was necessary to do so.

"Wa-alaikum salaam," he replied quickly, pressing the button to end the call. Still feeling disgruntled, he slammed his hand onto the roof of the car, feeling frustrated about the whole ordeal and feeling impotent to save Asherah. After that, he walked to the back of the vehicle and opened the rear trunk. Looking down at the contents—the duffel bags containing the weapons, and his own suitcase—he reached to pull them out, but then caught a glance of several other pieces of luggage through the rear window. The items were Asherah's. She placed them in the rear passenger seats behind her. They were lavished with decorative print and made of leather. At that moment, Assad experienced a vivid remembrance of her due to the site of the suitcases, which caused him to get emotional once more. Again, he blamed himself for leaving her to make his escape. He felt so guilty that he started thinking out loud to himself.

"Goddamn you, Ad-dam! You shouldn't have left her! You should've gone back and grabbed her when you had the chance! It was stupid of you to do that!" He was filled with so much regret, that yet again he ignored his cell phone ringing for the second time. At first, he thought it was the terrorist leader calling him back to remind him of something, but when he looked at the caller ID, his mood and expression changed dramatically. The number was foreign and he knew it was not the terrorist leader that he spoke with earlier. Assad was cautious to answer it because he knew it would be traced to his location from the people that are looking for him. He thought for that moment in his decision to answer, but his instincts hesitate him to do so. But at the last moment, he throws caution to the wind and taps the answer button on the phone. Being reluctant not to say anything on his end, Assad waits for a reply from the caller so they can identify themselves first. As both receivers were quiet for only a second, a soft but shaken tone of a female's voice broke the silence immediately. Assad recognized it instantly and said, "Oh my God! Desiree, is it you baby?!"

British Embassy, Dubai, United Arab Emirates, 9:59 p.m.

Fuller's people were trying to trace Assad's location, but as a reminder, he installed an anti-tracking chip that blocks individuals from tracing/tracking his phone. Earlier, before Asherah made the call to Assad, Milson had coached her to say certain things to him in order to maintain the illusion that she had been freed by the authorities and was no longer in the embassy. She was nervous, of course. Still frightened and confused about what was going on and uncertain of the situation she was involved in. She was obviously subjected to close observation from Milson and the others, but it was Milson who was coaxing and consoling her throughout the conversation. The exchange between Assad and Desiree was being recorded, and Fuller's tech people were trying their best in tracking the signal to figure out where Assad was located.

After his outburst of delight upon hearing her voice, Asherah answered, "Yes, it's me, Ad-dam. They let me go several hours ago because they didn't have anything on me. They dropped me off at this cafe next to the hotel that we checked out of. Ad-dam, I'm so scared right now. Where are you?"

"Baby, I am so sorry that I left you. I never should have done that, but I panicked when I saw those men chasing after me. I didn't know what to do. Are you safe and sound, sweetheart?"

"Yes. I'm sitting alone in the cafe. Ad-dam, I don't know what to do. I'm alone and scared, Ad-dam. Tell me what's going on and where you are?"

"Baby, I can't tell you that right now, but I can tell you that I'm coming back for you. I want you to listen to me very carefully, because what I have to tell you is extremely important. Do you still have money or credit cards on you?"

Asherah looked over at Milson, who gave her the signal to say yes. "Yes, Ad-dam, I still have my cards and a little money left over. What are you asking?"

"I want you to book a flight to Kuwait."

"Kuwait! Why?" Asherah asked, startled.

"Listen, the organization is picking me up tonight and putting me on a charter to Iran, where I will meet my contacts to do the switch. The exchange is going to take place in Khorramshahr, Iran. That's only a hundred or so miles from the Kuwaiti border. But first, I must travel through Bushehr, which is a port city along the Iranian coast. Once I give them the plans and weapons, I will meet you at the airport in Kuwait. I promise, baby."

"Why can't you come and get me now? Ad-dam, I'm so scared about what's going on. They told me that I could serve life in prison because of my involvement with you and because of what you've done. They also said if they catch you, I will never see you again. Baby, please give this up. I changed my mind about the whole thing. It's not worth it anymore. All I want to do is to be with you and spend the rest of my life with you. Please, Ad-dam, let go of this and come back to me. Forget about the plans. Forget about the money. Just come and get me so we can be together," Asherah said, frantically crying over the phone.

"Desiree, baby, I'm so sorry I put you in this situation. I never wanted to involve you in this. But, sweetheart, I'm doing this for us, you and me. After I make the exchange with the organization, we are going to go so far away that nobody is going to know where we are or how to find us. Be patient with me, Desiree. I assure you that this will be all over soon. I promise. Now, you need to go to the airport and book yourself a flight to Kuwait. Stay in Kuwait until I call you. Oh, by the way, do you still have what I gave you earlier?"

Asherah hesitated for a moment, knowing that Milson and the others were listening to every word she and Assad were saying to each other, but she decided to answer anyway.

"Yes, I do," she said, giving no more details.

"Good, good. That's perfect. We are going to need it after the exchange. You did good, sweetheart; you did good. Baby, I love you.

And I promise that after all of this, we will be free of everything. I'm so glad to hear your voice again, baby. I'll see you soon."

"Wait, Ad-dam! There's something else."

"What is it, sweetheart? Make it quick. I know that they're tracing this call. They probably planted a bug in your phone that you don't know about."

Asherah stood mute and motionless. Once again, she looked over at Milson for support, knowing that what Assad was saying was absolute. But this time the reason for her pause was not her reaction to his comment; it was her desire to find out if Assad really did kill those people and have an illicit affair with the woman in the picture that Milson showed her. Asherah's earlier reaction to this news hadn't abated; she was still in denial. Not able to grasp the concept that her boyfriend was a killer and that he was unfaithful to her, she was in emotional turmoil, which was apparent to Milson. She was grasping at straws, trying to keep it together and not give herself away, hoping to keep Assad from finding out they still had her in custody and had been listening to the whole conversation. Milson coached her through the difficulty. As she remained silent, contemplating asking Assad the volatile question, Milson waved his hand at her, urging her to either continue or conclude the conversation. Asherah, taking notice of this immediately, said to Assad,

"Nothing. It's nothing. I'm still shaken up by all of this. I'll go reserve a plane ticket right now. I'll see you in Kuwait."

"I'll see you too, baby. I love you, Desiree. Bye."

Without warning, Asherah slammed the phone down on the table, not caring if she broke it or not, and starting crying profusely again. Milson walked up and tried to console her. While comforting her, he looked over at Fuller, Weaver, and Sheppard to find out if they had been successful in tracing the call. "Well, guys, did we find him?" Milson asked, still holding Asherah.

"No, dammit!" Fuller said with frustration. "We couldn't pinpoint his location or get an accurate lock on his signal link. The bastard probably has a scrambler chip or blocker in his phone."

"But we're in luck. We did record everything he said. I downloaded the audio file," announced Weaver.

"Yeah, but that's not going to do us any good. We still don't know exactly where he is," said Milson.

"Wait a minute, Chief. He did say that he was being picked up by a charter. Obviously, a boat or ship is coming to pick him up. He has to be at some sort of harbor or port," Sheppard said.

"Yeah, but where? There must be hundreds of ports and harbors on the Emirates coastline. He could be at any one of them," Weaver added.

"You're right, James. But I don't think that's relevant now. What's important is that we know where he's going: Iran!" Milson said.

"Iran. That's typical. I suspected from the start that the Iranians might be involved in this. Iran, the one place we know we're not welcomed. Even though the Persian Gulf is free of international shipping routes, we, and I mean US Naval ships, cannot travel within Iranian coastal waters or cross its borders unless it's for purposes of commerce and trade. That's one of the stipulations Iran is proposing to the UN and UEA right now," Weaver said.

"True, Weaver. But we must get in somehow to intercept Commander Assad and stop him from making the switch. If he gets to either Bushehr or Khorramshahr, we won't have a chance of getting him then. And then our secrets will be in the hands of the Iranian government or, worse, this terrorist organization that keeps popping up. We have to figure something out!" said the young and eager ensign, who was very adamant and passionate as he spoke.

Hearing all of this and taking it in, Milson stood there pondering something. He thought to himself,

"*There is a possible way to get around all of this without starting an international incident with Iran*". He looked over at Sheppard and said,

"Hey, kid, do me a favor. Contact ONI. See if you can get Admiral Cooper on the line. I want to talk to him about something.

Weaver, why don't you call Langley and get your boss too. I want to see if I can set up a virtual conference call between Cooper and Richards. I've got an idea that just might work in our favor."

"What's brewing in that head of yours, Killian?" Weaver asked, curious about Milson's intentions.

"I think we're going to go with the covert objective after all. I'll explain everything to you in more detail in a few minutes. Right now, just see if you can get them on the horn."

Both Weaver and Sheppard nodded their heads and went straight to their cell phones. While they were occupied, Milson turned his attention back to Asherah, who was still upset about what had just happened.

"Desiree, you did good. Listen to me. I know you feel betrayed and confused. But you know deep in your heart that this is the only way. Ad-dam must be stopped. I'm very sorry that it has come to this."

Still emotional, with tears running from her eyes, she looked up at Milson and said,

"I know. I just can't believe that he lied to me. We were going to get married and spend the rest of our lives together, but all that has changed now. Agent Milson, please promise me one thing: don't hurt him when you do catch him."

Milson gazed into her light brown eyes and said,

"Ms. Asherah, the one thing I do when I catch these guys is make sure I keep them alive and bring them back unscathed. I promise you that I will not to hurt him, or try kill him."

Even though she was saddened by the circumstances, Desiree was able to offer a glimmer of a smile to the bounty hunter who had comforted and supported her in this difficult time in her life.

Later, a thought entered Milson's head. He went back to ask her about something he heard while they were talking to each other.

"Ms. Asherah, Assad asked you if you still had something he gave you earlier. Will you elaborate on that?"

Asherah instantly turned her head counterclockwise to avoid the question, but she knew she had to give him something—either the truth or a fabrication. So, hesitating no longer so as not to cause suspicion, she answered his question by saying,

"Oh, it was nothing. Just something he gave me after we left the hotel. The information for his bank accounts in Switzerland. He wanted to make sure that I had the account and routing numbers so he could log on after making the switch and verify that they transferred the money to him. That's all."

Milson looked at her suspiciously and said,

"Okay. We can use that to our advantage. Trace the account and the money if the deal goes through." Milson did not want to press the issue because he knew that Asherah was hiding something more. He put it aside for when the time was right to bring it up again.

With Milson and Asherah still conversing, one of Fuller's men dashed into the ops center to give Milson some startling news.

"Sir, we've got it. We traced the emails and phone calls and were able to pinpoint the source. We also ran several transmissions and communications through our data logs, backtracking to various email and text messages. The messages were encrypted, but we were able to crack them. It's conclusive, sir: here is the mole." Fuller saw what he already knew and responded explosively.

"Where the hell is he?!" as he shouted loudly.

"We found him, sir. He's downstairs in the cyber encryption computer lab. I don't think he knows we're on to him."

"Good. Let's keep it that way. Send some guards down there on the double, but advise them not to enter or apprehend him. Wait for my arrival instead. I want to see that bastards face when we bust him." Fuller ordered. His associate moved to carry out his command.

"Davy, what's going on?" asked Weaver.

"Remember earlier when I told you that we probably found our mole? Well, we did, and we've got him. I'm going down there now to tear him a new one!" Fuller responded in aggressive tone. He then told some of his men to follow him, with Weaver, Milson, and Sheppard walking right behind them.

Fuller was leading the charge downstairs to the lower levels of the building. As he made his way to the floor that he was looking for, he saw two of his men standing outside a closed door marked "Cyber Encryption Communications Area—Authorized Personnel Only." As he approached with Milson, Weaver, and Sheppard at his back, Fuller signaled his guys to draw their weapons, but to stand clear to the side. He pressed his ear against the door to find out if anyone was in there. As he had suspected, there was someone there. Making a gesture to his men to ready themselves as he was about to enter the room, Fuller drew his weapon, which was the same make and model as Assad's pistol, while gently turning the door handle. As he slowly opened the door, he could see the person he suspected as they sat in front of a computer outlet typing away. Again, he signaled to everyone behind him, then made his way through as he barged through the doorway, surprising the individual.

"Hold it right there! Don't you dare bloody move or I'll blow your head off! Turn around slowly and step away from the computer!" The individual raised his hands and did exactly what Fuller had told him to do. As he turned around, everyone was taken off guard upon seeing who it was, except for Fuller, of course. It was none other than his own assistant, Sabin Farad. Farad was the mole and double agent the terrorist leader had mentioned earlier to Assad and Milson when they were in the basement level of the galleria. Fuller was so enraged that he lunged at Farad, slamming him violently against the wall with the intent of putting him through it.

"Son of a bitch! It was you all this time?! How long have you been doing this, Sabin?! I trusted you! I trusted you, goddammit! Why?!"

Noticing Fuller's aggressive tone and physicality, Sheppard and Weaver tried to pull him off of Farad. But the way he held him up against the wall made it tougher for both men to pry Fuller's grip away from Farad's collar and exposed neck. But Milson suggested that they stood back until the British officer got the answers he wanted out of him.

"Why?" Farad said.

"You ask me why, you pathetic English puppet. I'll tell you why. The Islamic world is tired of the West involving themselves in affairs that do not concern them. We are sick of your deluded sense of morality and your political interventions, which have disrupted Arabia and Islam for years. You have been a thorn in our side for decades, a ravaging disease that has plagued and poisoned the Islamic community for more than sixty years. Leaving us with nothing but your false ideas of democracy and independence. From the time of the revolutionary uprising in Iran in the late 1970s to the time of turbulence in the Islamic/Muslim world—Iraq, Afghanistan, Pakistan, and the entire Arabian Peninsula—in the mid-2010s. There has been nothing but total chaos and confusion about who and what we really are as a people and as nations because of your egocentric ideology. You Americans, who are aligned with the Russians and the Europeans, and now with the Asians, have invented this sanctimonious new world order body called the United Earth Administration, which is another deceptive ploy by the West and the UN to destroy our culture, our traditions, and our way of life. The organization to which I have proudly pledged my life and that I have served for more than three years is fed up with your interference, and now they are going to show you how truly tired of it they are. They represent the true ideology of Islam, and they want the entire world to know what they're capable of. You think of us as a fly-by-night terrorist group who hides in caves, shacks, and compounds, but you are ignorant of who and what we really are and what we're capable of. We are well-off financially and well organized, more organized than all your intelligence agencies combined. We can infiltrate you whenever we want, as you can plainly see. We've been around for at least a decade, and you haven't even been aware of our existence until now. We have people everywhere. Some of us look like you, and some of us are you, but you will not know which ones, my friend, until it's too late."

The British agent was really at his end. Fuller, desperate to give Farad the beating of his life, had to restrain himself from smashing his clenched fist, which was locked and loaded in preparation to be deploy, right across the jaw line of his face. He wanted to strike him so badly that he almost gave in to the temptation, nearly disregarding the consequences and disciplinary action that would befall him if he were to assault the man, who had surrendered himself to UAE government authorities on charges of espionage and terrorism. Weaver, with the help of Sheppard, managed to talk him down, then suggested that Fuller's men take Farad into custody immediately so he would not be subjected to the horrendous beating that Fuller wanted to deliver.

"Get him out of my sight. Put him in interrogation room four. Lock him down with two agents standing guard. I will be up later to question him. No one is to see or talk to him but me," Fuller ordered.

As they put the handcuffs on Farad and were about to escort him upstairs for more questioning, Milson stopped them.

"Wait a second," he said, directing his gaze toward Farad.

"What were you doing down here before we came in? Were you informing your superiors about the girl and how she helped us? Or were you telling them that we know where Assad is and where he's going?"

Farad looked at Milson and said,

"Wouldn't you like to know, Mr. Milson? It is a shame that you'll never succeed in your mission to catch Assad. As I said before, we have people everywhere. Think about that." He smiled at him with a devious grin, a conceited tone in his voice.

"Get him out of here before I change my mind and shoot him!" Fuller said with great tenacity.

At that moment, the agents literally pushed Farad out through the door and escorted him upstairs as ordered. As for the rest of them, they turned their attention toward the computer where Farad had sat only moments before. Milson wanted Sheppard, who was computer literate, to see if he could pull up the information that Farad had been looking at.

"Sheppard, do think you can find out what Farad was doing?" Milson asked.

"I can try, Chief. But it's going to take a while. He probably installed some booby traps in here, such as encryption blockers, data scramblers, and virus enablers. It's going to take some time to get around them and decipher what he was doing here. For all I know, he put in a cyber bomb so the program, and probably the whole system, would crash instantly if tampered with. But I think I can figure it out," Sheppard said.

"Well, time is wasting, kid. Go ahead and get started so we can find out what he was up to," Milson replied.

Sheppard sat down and started to play with the computer. He started off by typing in encryption codes and sequences that looked like formulas. After that, he brought up the embassy's mainframe security system and disabled its lockout program so he could look at the hard drive. Then he began to pull up all kinds of sensitive materials—data records and log entries that were stored in the embassy's electronic filing system. Each bit of data had a firewall to stop anyone who tried to hack in. Somehow, Sheppard got around that as well, and was able to penetrate the system's defenses. After performing his tech-savvy feat, which took him only a few minutes, he managed to pull up something interesting on the screen.

"Chief, Officer Weaver, Agent Fuller, I've got something. Look at this." Each one of them went to stand near Sheppard to see what he had found.

"I went in, bypassed some of the encryption protocols, and deciphered the sophisticated algorithm he had set up. Farad was definitely up to something here. Check this out. He was sending an encoded message with these two emails. One is called 'Crimson Swords of Allah,' and the other is 'Alliance of Allah.' They appear to be two different email addresses, but personally, I think that they're one and the same."

"Hold that thought," Milson said. Something had jogged his memory.

"I distinctly remember hearing something about one of those names when I was at ONI. Commander Dixon, Assad's supervisor, briefed me on how they discovered his treachery. One of their analysts broke into Assad's secure files and personal emails. She happened to find a reference to the Alliance of Allah in several of his backlogged files, going back to two years ago. That must be the name of the terrorist organization he's been dealing with."

"Could be. But how do we know which is the right one? For all we know, Farad could have slipped in a decoy or a dummy address to throw us off," Weaver suggested.

"Maybe, sir. It's going to take a little more time to figure out which is the real one," Sheppard answered.

"Well, we don't have time for that, kid. We need to find out what Farad sent them—and fast. Sheppard, is there a way you can find out where these addresses originate? I mean, I know that each one has its own IP address to identify the sender and the receiver. Can you find out where exactly those emails are from and who's receiving them? That might tell us the identity of this terrorist organization," Milson said.

"It's possible, Chief. But you must realize that the sender or the receiver can use anonymous proxy servers to keep his or her identity a secret. I'm talking about private networks on their servers, and about misrouting IDs and other info, either to different URLs or possibly another system. This doesn't even take into account IP address spoofing, the purpose of which is to conceal the identity of the sender and/or receiver or to impersonate another computing system with a different program or address. I can do it, but it's going to take a lot more than just the few seconds it took me to hack into this. But again, I can do it," Sheppard explained.

"Okay, maybe later. But for now, can you dig into his history or messenger files to see what he wrote?" Milson asked.

"Yes, I can, Chief. Give me a second."

Sheppard was a whiz kid when it came to stuff like this. He managed to hack in to every electronic file that had a self-diagnostic security blocker that otherwise made it impossible for individuals to perform an electronic breach and engage in cybertheft. As he was punching numbers and letters on the keyboard to access Farad's file, he happened to stumble across the very thing he was looking for. "Chief! I've got it! Check this out. These are all syntax messages that were encoded to go to the addresses shown. I had to reroute the messages and reformat the program so I could see the plain text and read it. These are the actual messages Farad was sending to his contacts. I've got to give Farad his props. He put a lot of bugs, flags, and firewalls into this system so it wouldn't be compromised or tampered with. But I don't think he ever counted on someone like me trying to break in," Sheppard said, proud of his own performance.

Milson, Fuller, and Weaver were amazed by his knowledge and skills at the console. He brought up a list of emails and messages that went all the way back to when they first arrived in Dubai. Included were the names of the senders and recipients, as well as why these people were in Dubai to begin with. The messages also described the surveillance detail that Milson's team had set up at both the hotel and the mall. When Fuller read all of this, he started to get aggravated again. But it did not stop there. They also read a message explaining how Asherah would help the Americans to capture Assad and how they knew of his next destination. Continuing to look through all the messages Farad had sent; they finally came to a piece of intel they needed to know: Assad's current location.

"Hey! Look at this! Farad just gave us the location where Assad was calling from, a port outside the city of Sharjah," Weaver said.

"Wait a minute, I know where that is. Sharjah is forty to fifty miles from here, but there's a little harbor several miles outside the city. It's privately owned, used for fishing and lodging purposes.

Hardly anyone is ever there, unless it's for business or recreational purposes. It's pretty much secluded and isolated," Fuller replied.

"That's the idea. They want to pick him up from an area that is empty. No prying eyes, no witnesses. It's the perfect spot," Milson replied.

"Well, since we know where he is, let's go get him!" Weaver said with excitement.

But Milson put a halt to his enthusiasm. "Not so fast, air force. We don't know if he's still there. He's probably long gone by now. And with Farad having given them all that info about us and our intel on him, there's no way he would have stuck around this long. We're just going to have to get him at either Bushehr or Khorramshahr. And that's where my plan comes in."

Fuller and Weaver both looked at Milson strangely, trying to figure out what this so-called plan of his was. He finally explained his plan of action to them, adding how he wanted to implement it. Fuller gave a nod of approval, as did Weaver and Sheppard, who were both smiling at the idea. "That's going to be a real gutsy move to make, Killian. Especially inside Iranian territory. This is not going to be easy at all," said Weaver.

Milson replied, "That's why I need you to get on the horn and contact Cooper and Richards for me. I need their approval and their permission to do this. If it were just me, it would not be a problem, but since Assad and his new pals are upping the ante on this, we might need some more help after all—like navy and Special Forces help."

MICROSCOPE Facility, CIA Headquarters, Langley, Virginia, 6:40 a.m.

"Director, I have an incoming call from Officer James Weaver. Location, the British Embassy in the heart of the United Arab Emirates, Dubai. Priority code, Alpha One, sir," announced a young female air force lieutenant, who had rushed out of her cubicle to give Richards this news.

“Pipe it through here, Lieutenant,” Richards requested, waving his hand in his own direction.

The officer ran back to her station and transferred the call. Richards picked up a phone in an area manned by an E-7 army sergeant and started talking into it immediately.

“Richards here. What’s going on, Weaver?”

“Sir, we may have struck gold. We’ve found Commander Assad, but unfortunately he was able to elude us.”

“What! You called me for that?!” shouted Richards, whose tone caught the attention of Admiral Cooper and Commander Dixon, who were on the other side of the room talking to General Roberts.

“I don’t need to hear that you almost had him! I need to hear that you do have him! Alive or dead!” screamed the DCI.

“Understood, sir. But this is the reason why I am calling you. We have pinpointed Commander Assad’s exact location, and we know how to apprehend him. It’s just that we’re going to need some assistance from military personnel to get him, namely, army and navy personnel, sir.”

“What?! Hold on a minute, Weaver!” Richards made a hand gesture to Cooper and Roberts to get their attention.

“Admiral, General, come over here please.” Both Cooper and Roberts, along with Dixon, walked over to Richards to find out what was going on.

“What is it, Harry?” Cooper asked. Richards pressed the hold button on the phone and hung up the receiver. He then ordered the sergeant to transfer the call to a six-foot overhead screen sitting in the middle of the ops center inside MICROSCOPE. As soon as the sergeant transmitted the call and created a sight-to-sight linkage on the monitor, Weaver’s image flickered on the screen. The director wasted no time in asking why he was requesting this type of assistance.

"Weaver, I have you on a video conference call with Admiral Cooper of ONI and General Roberts of ASOC. Now tell us, why are you requesting help from the army and the navy?"

Just when Weaver was about to explain, Milson interrupted by stepping in front of him.

"I can tell you why we're asking for help, Director. Assad is moving into Iranian territory to give up the plans and weapons. I think we're going to need some seaworthy transportation, along with some covert ops expertise from Admiral Cooper's Navy SEALs and backup assistance from General Roberts's Delta Forces."

CHAPTER 9

ENGAGEMENT OF THE HUNT

Operations Center, British Embassy, Dubai, United Arab Emirates, 10:45 p.m.

"Iran? Are you sure about this, Chief?" asked Cooper, as he stepped in front of a screen.

"Yes, sir," said Milson.

"We caught up with him at a mall in Dubai several hours ago. He set up a meeting with his contacts to exchange the list and weapons for a sum of money that totaled up to three hundred million dollars. We intercepted him before he could make the exchange. Unfortunately, he got away, but we were able to get some valuable intel from a unique source: his girlfriend."

Cooper along with Richards, Roberts, and Dixon looked at each other in bewilderment while Milson continued.

"Her name is Desiree Asherah. She's a childhood acquaintance of Assad along with knowing each other intimately. We brought her back to the embassy for questioning to find out what she knows.

While she was aware of Assad's dealings and the stolen items in his possession, she had no idea of the seriousness of his intentions or motives. We persuaded her to help us find him, and fortunately, it paid off. The commander is meeting with a dangerous group of terrorists who can infiltrate any government or political agency anywhere around the globe. Just now, Agent Fuller of MI6, who is the chief supervising officer here, found out that one of his aides was a spy working undercover for this organization. We apprehended the aide earlier; he's in custody right now, waiting to be questioned. We were also able to crack a coded message that he sent to this organization detailing Assad's current whereabouts and where he's going. Admiral, Director, he's traveling up the Persian Gulf, through Iranian waters, and rendezvousing with this group in the city of Khorramshahr, on the Iranian border."

"Jesus! If the Iranians or this terrorist group gets their hands on those secrets, it will indeed be disastrous to our national security! If this is so, Milson, why do you need both army and navy resources to do it?" Richards asked.

"Because, Director, we're going to need military assistance to get Assad, especially if we're going to cross into Iran," Milson said.

"Sirs, that's going to be impossible. It will also pose a major problem," Dixon said, politely interrupting.

"We all know that Iran is classified as an unfriendly nation to us at the moment. Their dislike of the United States goes all the way back to the mid-1970s. If we send a squad of troops, especially military Special Forces, along with several undercover agents, this will definitely become an international incident, especially if our guys get caught by the Iranian government. Not to mention that we're also crossing into Iranian airspace, which they have tightly secured with sophisticated radar and GPS tracking systems. It will be somewhat of a repeat of the Iranian hostage crisis of 1979–81, when we sent Special Forces to Iran to rescue US hostages. And if the UN and UEA find out about this, we'll be looking at numerous sanctions and huge penalties—economic, military, and financial—along with an international investigation into covert operations without proper authorization or consent from our allies, the UEA, or NATO. If our guys are caught, they will be tried. If found guilty, they'll be executed as criminals and spies under the laws of the Iranians, the UEA and the International tribunal courts. And we all know that they will not be extradited under any circumstances." Dixon's explanation was sound and logical. The consequences of their entering Iran would be horrendous and would put a heavy political strain on both the United States and the UEA in terms of foreign relations.

But the others, especially Cooper, did not see it that way. He commented,

"Noted, Commander. But personally, I think it's worth the risk. Twenty years ago, I was involved in another high-stakes operation to neutralize a high-value target in a place that we had no authorization to enter, and it worked out perfectly for us." Cooper was referring to the operation he took part in to kill Osama bin Laden in Pakistan.

"We need to get Assad right now before this gets any worse," said Roberts, who was standing next to Cooper.

"Gentlemen, I for one understand our predicament. I will agree with whatever decision you make. But I also agree with Commander Dixon's warning. We all have to take this into consideration. You realize that all of you, as is the case for us, have to have undeniable proof that this man is traveling into a hostile sanctioned country such as Iran. This intel must be verified to prove beyond any reasonable doubt that Assad is in Iran and providing US military secrets to the enemy. We all must look at this decision seriously and exercise caution. We simply can't carry out a plan of attack on our own authority. The decision and the order must come from our commander in chief, and or SECDEF, if this operation is to go forward. Not to mention that National Military Command must be in the loop, along with the chairman of the Joint Chiefs. If we proceed with this operation without getting permission, it will be like launching a pirate campaign with no senior authority or hierarchy to sign off on it. It would be as dangerous as the Bay of Pigs Invasion of

1961. The president must be advised that we're going to do this." said the two-star general, reminding them of a pivotal moment in history that happened seventy years ago.

The moral implications started to sink into the psyche of each senior official, especially Cooper, who heeded the words of his old friend, then looked over at Richards for a final resolution.

"He's right, Hank," Cooper said.

"Even though I'm all for getting Assad and doing whatever it takes to achieve that end, we must do this by the book. No matter if it's right or wrong, secretive or out in the open, we must inform them of our proposed course of action. It's not like we're crossing over the border of Canada or Mexico. This is Iran we're talking about. And I hate to say it, but Dixon made some interesting points. If we do this without an executive order, we will likely lose our jobs."

Richards turned around and said,

"True, but remember what the president said to us earlier: 'by any means necessary' and 'at all costs.' The president did give us total autonomy in this operation. Whatever it takes, remember?" Richards gave Cooper a hard stare, which the admiral returned decisively.

Cooper turned his gaze towards the viewing screen and said,

"All right, Chief, let's hear what you've got. What's your plan for carrying out this operation? What do you have in mind?"

Milson, giving a gratified grin, said,

"Admiral, Director, General, this is what I propose: an aircraft carrier positioned in the gulf, off the coast of Saudi Arabia, near the Kuwaiti shore. The Saudis and the Kuwaitis are already our allies, and we all know that we have several embassies and naval ports in those regions. This will give us the perfect cover if the Iranians start asking questions about a US Navy ship traveling in Arabian waters. We'll assemble two Special Forces teams, SEALs and Delta Force. The SEAL team along with Weaver, Sheppard, and myself will travel by helo under cover of night right to the border between Kuwait and Iran. The Deltas will be our QRF [quick reaction force] backup and will provide support cover. I'll go in, find Assad, and extract him, the plans, and the weapons all at the same time. We'll head back to either the Kuwaiti border or the aircraft carrier in no time flat, getting away scot-free. Admiral, this can work. I know it can work. I know that you and the president have given me only seventy-two hours to find Assad and bring him back before you unleash the dogs of war on him instead. If that's the plan, then why don't I use those dogs as my backup in order to get him? Especially since I'm going to a place where wise men fear to tread. This is the perfect opportunity, sir. We won't get another chance like this ever."

All four gentlemen looked at each other with uncertainty and concern. In their minds, they already knew that this was going to be a high-risk move. But with the deck stacking up against them, they knew that they had to make a choice sooner or later. In this case, it would have to be sooner—much.

Richards was the first one to speak, his image superseding that of the others.

"That all sounds well and good, Milson, but how are you going to know where he's at exactly? And how will you get out of there in one piece, son? When the Iranians discover that you are in their backyard, they aren't going to give you a welcoming greeting. Your chances of getting out of there are between 25 and 50 percent at best, no matter how many SEALs or Deltas you have watching your six. And if you're right about this new terrorist organization that has dibs on Assad, this whole operation that we're signing off on is going to be doomed from the start."

"Not necessarily, Director," Weaver replied.

"If you remember, sir, we do have allied operatives in Kuwait and Iraq. They can give us the intelligence we need to find out exactly where Assad is within the city of Khorramshahr. And we can find out if they have any knowledge of this terrorist organization. That's if we share our intel with them, meaning both the Iraqi and the Kuwaiti SIS," he said, speaking of the Security Intelligence Service.

Again, Richards glanced back at Cooper with an unsure look. But this time the admiral did not reciprocate it. Afterward, Richards turned his eyes back toward Milson, wanting to ask him an important question. "Let me ask you something, Milson. Why do you think you need double backup from the Deltas? You're already requesting assistance from the SEALs. What's the deal with the extra support?"

"Director, I feel that if we go in there with a small squadron of SF troops, sooner or later we're going to be overrun by a much larger opposing force. Having Deltas at my rear evens up the odds. And quite frankly, I feel safer when the army has my back. Army special ground forces make for better support and better handlers than all the others, especially Admiral Cooper's boys. We know that those navy lifeguards need some additional help from time to time."

Milson saw the somewhat irritated, but also somewhat amused, expression on Cooper's face. He'd known that the admiral, a former SEAL, would get a kick out of his facetious remark. For purposes of amusement, not ridicule, Army Special Forces sometimes referred to Navy SEALs as "decorated lifeguards," but SEALs were still respected and honored in light of the military code and the warrior ethos.

After that lighthearted remark, Richards turned his attention back to Weaver.

"All right then, we'll give it a shot, Milson. Agent Weaver, you know which people to call. Get both SIS agencies on the horn and tell them what's going on. But do not, I repeat, do not, tell them the whole story. Do not under any circumstances mention the stolen plans or guns. Cook up some other story about Assad, for example, that he killed several VIPs—anything but the truth. Give them only things that we can plausibly deny. Feed them with a long-handled spoon, son," the DCI said to his undercover operative.

Cooper whispered to Richards,

"That's really not that far from the truth, Hank. He did kill three people, possibly four if he had anything to do with Brown's murder."

"I know, but if a foreign intelligence agency finds out Assad's true intentions, we'll be the laughingstock of the intelligence community all around the world, Wayne, not to mention an embarrassment to our own government and a threat to its security. They'll think that we can't keep our shit together in our own house. It's bad enough that the Brits and Interpol know about our situation, but if other governments come to know, it will be catastrophic for us. We can't afford to let something like this circulate. We've got to keep this information under lock and key, and make sure no one but our own people know about this screwup over here."

Even though Milson did not get along with Richards, he had to agree with him on that.

"I hate to say this, Admiral, but the director's right. We've got to keep this hush-hush. Even though we've been able to contain it so far and keep it from the public, it is more likely that this will get out in the open if political entities are notified or involved. Here I'm speaking of the UN and UEA. We absolutely must not let them find out about this. News like this will definitely pique their curiosity, and it will take us months to years to explain everything, especially to the UN Security Council and the House of Representatives' Armed Services Committee. It will circulate across the globe and cause more damage than has already been done."

Richards was a bit surprised that his former employee was agreeing with him, knowing that the two of them never got along in the past. Milson knew the repercussions if something like this were to get out. There could be lasting effects for the US government. But Richards's surprise was short-lived after hearing Milson's next statement.

Milson said,

"I'm going to have to get myself checked out when I get back, Admiral. I just agreed with the DCI. Now I know something's wrong with me."

Weaver, Sheppard, Cooper, and Roberts found Milson's anecdote amusing, but Richards did not share into Milson's sense of humor too well.

"Admiral," Milson replied,

"Is there a BSG [Battle Strike Group] fleet around the gulf, or a lone carrier?"

Dixon answered,

"Yes, there is, Chief. Admiral, Director, we do have a battle strike group off the coast of the UAE, between Qatar and Bahrain. It's the Fifth Fleet, gentlemen. Their purpose is to patrol the Indian Ocean and the Strait of Hormuz in the Persian Gulf." Dixon signaled his intentions to an E-6 air force technical sergeant, who pulled up a map of the Persian Gulf on a separate screen, simultaneously revealing the type of naval ships stationed there.

"The lead carrier is the USS *John F. Kennedy*, CVN-79. She's commanded by Rear Admiral Galen Palmer (two star) of the Fifth Fleet. His group is made up of two destroyers, two cruisers, one dock lander, and one Virginia-class attack submarine. They're currently performing battle maneuvers with the Royal Saudi Navy. Oh, and there's one other thing, sir. There is a SEAL attachment stationed aboard the carrier, SEAL Team Six, under the command of a Lieutenant Commander Josef Marin," Dixon said.

"Well, isn't that ironic, gentlemen? The team to which Assad was assigned five years ago is going to be the very team to bring him down," Richards replied in a condescending way.

"You think you could give Admiral Palmer a call and give him a heads-up on what we're trying to do, sir?" Milson asked.

Cooper, rubbing his chin, said,

"I think it could be arranged, Chief. Commander, get National Military Command Center at the Pentagon on the line. Also get me NAVCENT [US Naval Forces Central Command] right now. I need to speak with Vice Admiral Taylor immediately. He's the VCNO [vice chief of naval operations] and the COMSUBLANT [commander, Submarine Forces Atlantic] of that fleet. Advise his staff that this is an urgent call; say that the director of ONI needs to speak with him ASAP. Also, place a call to Rear Admiral Richter, also at the Pentagon. He's in charge of SOCOM and DEVGRU.

Tell him I need to use one of his SEAL teams aboard the *JFK* for a spec-op mission."

Dixon gave an "Aye, aye, sir" and sped off in the opposite direction, disappearing from the monitor.

On that note, Milson brought up another point, this time directing his remarks to General Roberts.

"General, sir, if I may? Are there any Deltas within Saudi or Kuwait that I can use?"

Roberts went over to the same screen that Dixon had used to show the battle fleet.

"You're in luck, Milson. There is a unit stationed in Kuwait, training their SF teams over there. If I'm not mistaken, the squad leader supervisor is Major Christopher Troy of Bravo Squadron. And it just so happens that I am the commander and supervisor of USASOC. I'll give them a call and have them advise First SFOD–D [First Special Forces Operations Detachment–Delta] to stand by and be ready for deployment. I'll also have to give General Dreyfus of army intelligence a heads-up about this and let him know that his services and the services of his team are going to be needed," replied the two-star general.

"Thank you, sir, I appreciate it. Admiral, Director, we're going to get this guy, I promise. And I'll make sure we bring him back to stand trial for what he's done. I made a promise to someone that I'd take him alive, and I also give you my word that I'll do just that."

Cooper stepped closer to the screen and said,

"I know you will, Chief. That's why I picked you in the first place. I know that you and your team are going to fulfill this mission no matter what and find out who is responsible for turning Commander Assad against us. Be careful, gentlemen and God Speed."

Milson gave a gesture that showed his utmost respect for the rear admiral. This was the first time in his career, both in the past and present, that he felt a certain degree of respect and admiration for a commanding officer such as Cooper. Right there he knew that this man was behind him all the way, and would support any decision that he made. Despite his views and opinions of officers, Cooper alone was in a class by himself.

"Thank you, sir. I'll definitely keep that in mind, and I will find out who these people are."

Fuller signaled to Milson that he had some more important news to share.

"Admiral, Director, we're going to sign off. I'll give you a sitrep within the next six to seven hours to advise you of our progress."

"Understood, Chief. We'll get in contact with the Fifth Fleet and Delta Bravo Squadron to let them know of your arrival. I'll even inform the president and SECDEF about your operation and what all is involved. Good luck and good hunting, gentlemen," Cooper said to Milson. The screen went black instantly as Milson's image vanished.

Milson turned to Fuller, who just finished conversing with Cooper on the screen.

"Milson, while you were talking to your admiral, I had a chance to look up MI6's summary reports on naval exercises in the gulf, and it seems that you Yanks were right. Your USS *John F. Kennedy* is traveling away from Bahrain and is heading straight to a port on the coast of Kuwait to dock. The battle group is going to remain at the Bahrain harbor until the *JFK* returns. I had a chance to talk to my superiors about this, and they said they will arrange a bird to transport us over to the *JFK* while she's still under way. One of our flag officers from the British Admiralty who is familiar with your Admiral Palmer and his fleet said that he's going to give him a call about us coming aboard. So, it looks as if your admiral is going to get two calls about our arrival," Fuller said.

"Good, that's perfect, Fuller. Can you have them pick us up in an hour?" Milson asked.

"No problem. I'll make it thirty minutes," Fuller said.

"I informed them that we're carrying tactical gear on this mission. The crew is going to try to accommodate all four of us on the bird. It'll be tough with all the extra equipment we're carrying."

"Wait a minute. Hold up," Milson said. "What do you mean, all four of us? It's just going to be me, Weaver, and Sheppard. You're not going with us."

"The hell I'm not! I'm coming, mate," announced Fuller with passion.

"My government and I have just as much at stake in this as you do. We also need to find out who these people are and how far their influence reaches. And besides, I want to get back at those buggers for planting a spy in my house."

Milson pondered it. At first, he was not sure. But soon he gave in to the idea, and welcomed the British agent to tag along.

"Okay, you win. See if you can get our gear up here ASAP. All of us need to be ready when that bird touches down. Make sure they have the precise coordinates of the *JFK*'s location."

"Gotcha. I'm on it," Fuller said. He dashed across the ops center to inform his people of the situation and to get the gear from the armory below. Milson advised Sheppard and Weaver on the same situation, then instructed them to get their stuff and prepare to head out within the next hour.

While everything was going according to schedule, Milson, making preparations for this operation, negligently forgot about Asherah, who was standing to the far right, unsupervised and alone. She saw the hustle and bustle of around her, but her eyes were fixed only on Milson. Walking through the shuffle of people going by, she headed toward him while his attention was on the capture of her boyfriend. She approached him from the back and, because he was not aware of her presence, startled. He acknowledged her but also realized that something was wrong. "Ms. Asherah, I apologize. I almost forgot you were here. I had Agent Sheppard set you up with a flight that is scheduled to leave tomorrow afternoon for Kuwait. We've arranged a hotel for you to check in to the moment you get there. I will contact you on your cell phone as soon as we arrive in Kuwait. I also made preparations for you."

"No, Officer Milson," Asherah said.

"I'm not going to Kuwait. I'm coming with you."

Milson's head literally snapped back from her reply.

"Excuse me? What did you say?" he asked sharply.

Asherah said again, this time firmly,

"I said, I'm going with you." She was not going to budge.

"No, you are not. You are staying here and later getting on a plane tomorrow to go to Kuwait," Milson said.

"Mr. Milson, I know Ad-dam. Or I thought I knew him. But independent of that, I need to find out the truth from him. I need to know, after all these years we've spent together, telling each other how we felt about one another, if everything that he said to me was a lie. Or was there some speck of truth somewhere within all that deception? Especially now since I found out he had a relationship with another woman. I must know this for myself. I want see his face for the last time before … before you take him away from me."

Milson drew a breath then exhaled it. He knew where this was going. But he could not or would not say what he really wanted to tell her. The truth would be too damaging for her. She was not emotionally ready to know everything about Assad, including his past. For the first time, Milson could see it in Desiree's eyes that she really did love Assad and did not want to let him go. "Ms. Asherah, listen to me. You're not going to do us any good by endangering yourself, which is what you'll be doing if you tag along with us on this extremely dangerous mission. I'm not going to threaten your well-being by letting you tag along with us. Desiree, I know that you're hurt, confused, and angry about all of this, but the best way for you to help us is to stay clear and let us do our jobs."

But Asherah was adamant. In an effort to change Milson's mind, she said,

"Well, Mr. Milson, if I show you this, will it change your decision to let me come with you?" She reached into the front of her pants and pulled out what appeared to be a compact memory device.

Milson was stunned by where she had hidden it.

"What is that?" he asked with a baffled look.

"This is the flash drive that contains the list of names and undercover operatives from your intelligence agencies that Ad-dam stole from your governments archives."

Milson was overwhelmed.

"Wait a minute," he said, as his voice jumped an octave higher,

"These are the plans he took?!"

"Yes, they are, but these are only the second half. Ad-dam has the first drive which contains the blueprints of all newly develop military weapons and vehicles that your government has created. What he told me is that those blueprints are advanced technological specification created by a department called DARPA [Defense Advanced Research Projects Agency]. He didn't get into much of the specifics with me, but he did tell me that the thumb drive he has contained a lot of advanced vehicles that are being developed for the Space force and other military branches." Still in awe, Milson was in shock over the details that Asherah knew. When she finished, she saw the look of confusion on Milson's face and became slightly amused by it. Pausing for a moment, she continued with her explanation.

"I've had the drive on me for a while, ever since he and I left the hotel together. I was going to give it back to Ad-dam when we were going to depart from the mall."

"So, you mean to tell me that you've had the drive hidden all this time down in your—" Milson felt too embarrassed to name the area out loud where Asherah had stowed the small device. He just let his imagination speak for itself, which caused an awkward and uneasy development between the two, but it sparked a devilish grin across his face.

Asherah, who noticed the expression right away, said,

"Why don't we just say that it was in my underwear and leave it at that, Mr. Milson?"

Milson shook his head in amusement. But the circumstances were anything but funny. She had in her possession the very thing that he had been hired to retrieve, along with the capture and arrest of her boyfriend. "Ms. Asherah, didn't they pat you down and search you when you were taken into custody?"

Asherah's expression was a mirror image of the one previously on Milson's face. Though she was in love with Assad, and despite the psychological turmoil she had experienced of late, she was a little smitten by the handsome middle-aged bounty hunter who had helped her out during her emotional turmoil, not knowing it was all a ruse from the start because they needed her help. She responded flatteringly and flirtatiously,

"Well, Mr. Milson, you of all people should know that when it comes to searching individuals, women have the best hiding spots—much better than what men have."

After hearing that, Milson literally had to step back and clear his throat. He feared he might be blushing. He also had to dismiss the fact that physically, Asherah was very attractive and extremely sensual. This temporarily fogged his perception. But soon he composed himself and returned to what was more important.

"Okay, let me see if I can get this straight. While you've had this the entire time in your"—he paused and made a facial expression to indicate his meaning— "Assad has been carrying the main drive that has all US secret military weapons along with the stolen guns?" Milson asked with astonishment.

"Yes, but that's not all. He has a backup compact disk that holds the same information as the first one, but he needs the two drive to integrate with the disk in order to transfer the information to a digital file and give it to his contacts. The only thing is that the disk cannot work without the two flash drives. He gave me this for safekeeping in case something happens, like if they renege or double-cross him," Asherah explained.

"So that's the reason he said what he said. Knowing that we grabbed you, he knew that you had the main drive in your possession and tried to come back for you."

"No. No, you're wrong, Agent Milson," Asherah admonished.

"Ad-dam loves me. He wasn't coming back just for this; he was coming back for me."

Milson looked at her and saw the conviction in her eyes. To him, she was blindly misguided and deceived by Assad's motives. He felt kind of sorry for her because of what she had gone through and because of her naivete about the whole situation, but he could not entirely blame her for thinking Ad-dam loved her. Her passion and her undeniable loyalty toward this man was truly incredible, even when she was now aware of the whole truth. All Milson could do at that moment was to give her a grin of understanding and a short nod of his head to make her feel a little bit better about everything.

"Of course, he was... Wait a minute! That's what he was talking about over the phone with you. He was asking you if you still had the drive in your possession. Son of a bitch! Why didn't I pick up on that before? You lied to me, lady!"

"I'm sorry, Mr. Milson, but I wasn't sure about you or your intentions. At that time, I didn't know if it was the right thing to do. I didn't know whether to trust you or not. So, I kept it secret until I knew for sure that you were on the level, not like your partner over there," she said, pointing at Weaver with contempt.

Despite being surprised by her actions, Milson shook his head in a way to show that he understood her cautiousness and trusted her judgment. "I understand what you're saying, Ms. Asherah, and frankly, I don't blame you. But unfortunately, you're still not coming with us," Milson advised.

"Well, if I can't come with you, then you're not getting this." She clutched the flash drive in her hand and began to put it back into the confines of her pants.

Milson shook his head.

"You know I can get that myself since you've shown it to me. I just have to ask for some help from a female officer."

Asherah, staring back at Milson with a devilish grin and said, "Yes, you could, but I don't think you want a threesome in this case right now. You look more like the type of man who wants a one-on-one challenge without interruptions. Am I right?"

Again, Milson was uncomfortable at the innuendo made by Asherah, but also chuckling softly afterwards.

"Wow, lady. You are something else. Do you always get what you want?" he asked in a cool tone.

"Sometimes, Agent Milson. Especially if I like what I see."

Milson drew back once more, taken aback by the seductive remark. At that moment, Asherah did not seem like the terrified woman they had brought in hours ago. This was a completely different person with a devious agenda, almost a Jekyll and Hyde scenario with a hint of seduction mixed with it.

"Mr. Milson, all jokes aside, I know you have your doubts about me. And I don't blame you. If I were in your shoes, I wouldn't let me go either. But in all seriousness, I must find out the truth for myself from Ad-dam. I have to look at him in the face to see if everything he has told me has been a lie from the start, including what he said about our relationship," Asherah said.

"And if you do find out, what are you going to do? Is this going to be a situation where you seek revenge? Are you planning to replay this entire event over and over again in your mind and focus on how much he hurt you, just so you can feel satisfaction when we do catch him? Are you hoping to see that he suffers and goes through the same pain and the same type of ordeal that you are going through right now? Or are you going to go the route of self-pity, bemoaning what you've lost or what could have been? What do you think would be the alternative to knowing? What are you trying to accomplish by coming with us?" Milson asked.

Asherah lowered her head and raised it up again with an expression that showed her pain and anguish.

"The truth, Mr. Milson. All I want to know is the truth. Is that too much to ask from a man whom I was deeply in love with for a very long time? The truth, that's all. Can I please find out the truth?"

Once again Asherah showed her sensitive side to Milson. He looked at her and rubbed her face as several tears ran down her cheek. His mind was telling him that it was not a good idea for her to come along on this mission, but his conscience was telling him something else. Milson rubbed his own cranium three or four times, trying to figure out if this was the right thing or the wrong thing to do. He turned his head and gritted his teeth in frustration, trying to make sense of it all, while at the same time having to make a difficult decision. When he turned back around and looked at Asherah, she was still staring at him, her eyes fixed on his, waiting to see what he was going to decide, either yes or no. Milson shook his head and chuckled to himself as he looked at her for the final time. He had made his decision but was still questioning it in his mind.

"All right, Ms. Asherah, you win. You may come. But only as an observer and a key witness whose help has led to our capture of your boyfriend. But I swear, if you get in the way at any time and ruin our chances of getting him, I will personally bust your ass for interfering in a federal investigation and botching the operation to apprehend a wanted fugitive. All that stuff that Officer Weaver said to you about prison time, I will personally make it stick. Do I make myself clear?" Milson spoke with seriousness in his voice, but at the same time he had a look of concern on his face.

Asherah looked at Milson with a smile of gratitude and said,

"Yes, Mr. Milson, I understand. And by the way, call me by my first name. I would feel more comfortable if you'd do that." She batted her eyelashes and gave him another alluring smile that almost caused him to drop to his knees.

While they were still talking, Fuller and Weaver came up on Milson's side to inform him of the arrival of their transport. "Milson, I just got word from the tower. A fully fueled Black Hawk is coming our way in twenty minutes. They've made room for all four of us to get on board. They even contacted the USS *JFK* and notified them of our pending arrival within the next several hours," Fuller announced.

"Great, but tell them to make one more seat available. We're bringing Ms. Asherah with us."

Fuller and Weaver looked at each other with surprise. "What?! Are you serious, mate?!" Fuller said loudly, with Weaver backing him up.

"Wait a minute, Killian. She can't come with us. She's in collusion with Assad!"

"As well as being a potential witness to his dealings with a terrorist organization and having substantial proof of his espionage," said Milson.

"Desiree, show them what you showed me."

Asherah took out the flash drive and showed it to them.

"Is that what I think it is?" Weaver asked.

"Yes, it is," Asherah answered.

"The thumb drive containing the files that Ad-dam downloaded from your archives. All your military secrets and records are on here. And I will only give it to Agent Milson because he is the one who agreed that I could come with all of you."

"Milson, are you insane? This is a mistake!" Fuller said.

"She has no business going on a black ops mission like this. She's a liability, a civilian without the military experience, the training, or the background to handle something like this. In fact, she was in cahoots with Assad, for Christ's sake!"

"I agree with Fuller, Killian. This is not a good idea," Weaver said.

"Fellas, I understand where you are coming from, and I agree 100 percent, but I think she can help us get him. I know that it's a big risk I'm taking, but given the circumstances, we don't have much of a choice. Assad is on his way to Iran right now to give up our weapons and the first drive which contains undercover operatives to a terrorist group that we know nothing about. We need to get to him before that happens. I hate to say this, but Ms. Asherah is our only key to success here."

They all looked at each other again with disapproval on their faces, disliking the decision made by Milson.

"Listen, guys, we've been through a lot today. And I know I've been acting like a real asshole by throwing my weight around and saying that I'm the primary and the decision maker for this mission. But this time I'm asking for your help and your permission. If she can help up catch this guy, then let's drop the rule book for once and take a chance by taking her along with us. I would be the first one to agree that this is a bad idea, but she literally has in her hands the intelligence we need to capture him. I'm asking you guys on this one, not as a supervisor or leader, but as an equal and a fellow agent." They could see that Milson was sincere. His voice, his mannerisms, and even his expression were of a quality that they were not used to. But they knew that he was being genuine and honest in his remarks, not arbitrary or superficial as they had come to know him to be.

Fuller was the first one to address Milson.

"All right, you bloody Yank, you sold me. I'm in." He raised his hand in a show of shaking Milson's to agree with his plan.

Weaver did the same. Then he said, "Milson, when I first met you, I thought you were arrogant, self-centered, and egotistical—a know-it-all prick with an ego the size of Alaska. But so far, everything that you've said and predicted has turned out to be true and right on target. I still think that the girl's tagging along would be a bad idea for us, but I will stand by you in whatever decision you make at any point in the mission, Killian. Let's go in there and get this guy, and get the hell out of there."

Milson and Weaver slapped each other across the shoulders. But Weaver had to get one more point across. "I just hope that this doesn't backfire and blow up in your face. If the director and the admiral find out you took a civilian on this mission, they're going to hand you your nuts for breakfast."

"I know, but I hope it doesn't go down like that. Like you said, I'm taking a big risk by taking her. I just hope that I don't regret it later," Milson replied, one more time contemplating his decision.

After everything was said and done, Sheppard came up.

"Chief, Officer Weaver, Agent Fuller, I just received a call from Commander Dixon at Langley. He said that Admiral Palmer has been notified by the VCNO and is expecting our arrival sometime soon. He also said that the SEAL team and Delta Force group have been alerted and put on standby. The president, SECDEF, and the chairman of the Joint Chiefs have been informed, and they've given us the go on everything. We've been given the authorization to go forward, Chief."

Milson, pleased by the news, told everyone to get their things together right away. Fuller and Weaver went off in the opposite direction in order to retrieve their stuff. Sheppard was about to do the same and go gather his belongings, when Milson stopped him in midflight. "Ensign Sheppard, I need you to do me a little favor."

"No problem, Chief. What is it? What do you need?" asked Sheppard, who was eager to please at that moment.

"I'm glad you asked that, kid, because I need for you to gather some gear up for Ms. Asherah. She's coming with us."

Sheppard's eyes lit up. "What? Are you serious?" Milson gave Sheppard a look to suggest that he was very serious and did not want to explain himself for the second time on why she was going with them. After taking heed of the look, the young ensign humbly nodded his head and said, "Yes, Chief, no problem. I'll get her stuff squared away right now."

Milson slapped Sheppard on his back and said,

"Thanks, kid." Then he sped off to get Asherah her equipment.

As Milson stood there in the middle of the ops center, looking around at everything, he glanced over at Asherah, who was standing by herself, observing the people who were passing by. Milson was having trouble believing what he was doing in light of the decision he'd just made. He knew that he was putting this woman's life in danger, but he realized that one individual was not as important as the thousands lives that Assad was putting into jeopardy by helping a terrorist group accomplish the slaying of millions of people around the world by using their own technology against them. To Milson, this was the most important factor of the mission. It was his job not only to make gut-wrenching decisions and sacrifices to get his man, but also to save lives and protect the innocent. That was what mattered; everything else was insubstantial.

As Milson continued to stare at Asherah, she had a feeling that he was glaring at her. She turned around and looked over at him. Their eyes locked. It was no secret that Milson thought she was stunning and attractive, but this was the farthest thing from his mind right now. He was still pondering his decision to let her come with him. One side of him was telling him that this was a bad idea. The other side was saying that this was the only way.

Milson did not realize that he was staring at Asherah so hard. She gave him a slight grin that suggested gratitude, not a full-blown smile that would have been flirtatious, meant as an invitation. It was more of a *Thank you. I appreciate this,* less a coquettish gesture.

When he finally came around, he snapped his head forward and started concentrating on the task at hand. As he started to put his own things together, his crew came up to inform him that everything was ready and that the helicopter was waiting for them on the landing pad.

"All right, guys, have we got everything?"

Fuller, Weaver, Sheppard, and even Asherah nodded their heads and gave a thumbs-up, indicating that everything was good to go. Milson made sure that Sheppard had prepped Asherah for this long-haul trip they were about to make. Sheppard told him that she was set and had everything that she needed to go on the flight. Milson gave the okay and said, "All right, gentlemen and lady. We have a rendezvous with a flattop. Let's go."

The five of them dashed out of the ops center with all their gear as if they were Special Forces. They went up several floors to exit the building from the rooftop, where the Black Hawk was waiting for them. It was a British military craft, a Royal Army or Royal Air Force S-70A-9 Black Hawk with the same features and modifications as its US counterpart. The rotors were so powerful that they almost blew Asherah away with her petite frame. Milson had to literally grab her and put her in front of him so she would not fly off the platform.

As all five got into the helicopter, the pilot and copilot told them to buckle themselves in tight and standby for takeoff. Again, Milson had to assist Asherah with her harness. Again, he thought to himself, *Have I made the right choice after all, or am I going to regret this decision later?*

As each of them was secured in the seats, the pilot informed them that they were ready to take off. Fuller, Weaver, Sheppard, and Milson were accustomed to this type of atmosphere because all four of them had served in the military and were used to traveling this way, but Asherah was visibly uncomfortable. This was her first experience flying in an aircraft that did not have first-class accommodations or flight attendants waiting on her hand and foot. This was indeed a military aircraft with strict protocols and procedures that needed to be followed. This was in fact not her cup of tea. Milson and the others took notice. As the Black Hawk started to lift off and the noise inside and outside the helicopter started to become even louder, the pilot again got on the horn to make another announcement.

"Ladies and gentlemen, this is your pilot speaking. We are departing from the embassy's platform and heading straight for the open waters of the Persian Gulf. Our destination is the aircraft carrier USS *John F. Kennedy*, whose location is between the Bahraini coast and Manama. Our ETA will be two and a half hours, with an arrival time of zero one hundred hours (one o'clock in the morning). As you Yanks say, sit back, relax, and enjoy the ride! Take naps if you want. This is going to be a long flight."

They all sat back as they felt the helicopter lift even higher, then moved forward and flew off from the building into the midnight sky.

USS *John Fitzgerald Kennedy* (CVN-79), Persian Gulf, 1:15 a.m.

"XO, I have an inbound bogey from the southeast. Range, twenty-three thousand yards, traveling at a speed of 170 mph or 147.72 knots. It's a registered bogey with identifiable markings, sir. Identification is a British military aircraft, helo class. It's an S-70 Alpha series, a Black Hawk, sir," announced the radar operator, a young third-class petty officer positioned in an area called the primary flight control center, which controlled aircraft launches, landing procedures, and radar detections, with the radar equipment being positioned at the very top of the control tower of the ship.

"Understood. Seaman, get me the flag bridge!"

The sailor got on the radio and contacted what was called the "flag bridge," which hosted either a superior or senior officer (such as an admiral or a captain), along with his or her staff to oversee all ship and flight operations. Once the sailor signaled to the XO that he had a linkage, the senior officer aggressively picked up the telephone receiver and started speaking into it.

"Skipper, XO. Our guests are arriving. … Yes, sir, understood. I'll meet them on the deck personally and bring them up to you. … Aye, aye, sir, will do." The XO hung up the receiver and turned toward one of his subordinates.

"Commander, you have the pri-fly. I'm going down on the deck."

The junior officer gave him an "Aye, aye, sir" and proceeded with his task as ordered. The superior officer exited the control center with a junior officer trailing directly behind him. He traveled downstairs, passing through the flag bridge, then the captain's bridge, and ended up on the flight deck as he exited the tower. He saw the daily operations of the flight crew as they usually performed their usual routine around this time. There were groups of aircraft directors and handlers running up and down the deck, securing or positioning aircraft for either launch or maintenance detail. Air bosses, aviators, and flight officers were going over flight schedules and midnight patrol runs, punching things into their keypads. Some signal officers were going over landing procedures and practicing hand-to-sight signals for incoming aircraft. All these activities were a daily regular thing aboard this Gerald R. Ford–class aircraft carrier. They were not to be taken lightly or misused. Any changes to the operation of the mammoth-sized vessels were not to be tolerated because of the importance of the crew's primary directive. The function of an aircraft carrier must be above standards always, whether in peacetime or during war.

As the XO was busy looking around the flight deck, his aide gave him a discreet nudge on his shoulder to communicate that he had spotted the incoming helicopter through a set of small binoculars he had in his possession.

"Sir, I see the Black Hawk coming in on our south vector." The junior officer, pointing in the direction of the helicopter, handed over the binoculars so the XO could get a look for himself. The bird was far away, but the XO could identify it easily. He told his aide to contact the pri-fly control center and have them inform the deck crew of a helicopter coming in for a landing. The officer got on the phone and dialed upstairs to relay the message. As soon as he did so, the call came down from the control area. Several LSO (landing signal officer) personnel scrambled to get to their positions to signal the approaching Black Hawk. Even though the night was very dark with only the moon giving off some light, the running lights on the helicopter became more visible the closer it got to the ship. The handlers and LSOs were signaling to the craft to suggest a potential touchdown on a certain area of the deck. The air bosses and their assistants, the mini bosses, had radio contact with the Black Hawk so they could guide the crew and tell them where to land. As the helicopter's silhouette became more prominent as the bird got closer, the flight crews started to guide the helicopter down to the spot where they wanted it to land. The Black Hawk came in slow and easy, like a bee approaching a honeysuckle. She was steady without one hint of heavy vibration or turbulence to her chassis despite the wind shear from the overhead and rear propellers. As the LSOs were signaling her to touchdown, the Black Hawk finally made her landing permanent, her wheels touching the steel deck plates of the *JFK*'s flight deck. When the XO and his junior officer saw this, they headed right away toward the helicopter. As they approached, one of the handlers opened the starboard-side door of the helicopter, where Milson and his party were visible. The XO waited until one of them got out—Milson, of course, was first to disembark—and then made his introduction.

"Which one of you is Chief Warrant Officer Killian Milson of ONI?!" asked the XO, shouting over the loudly roaring engines of the Black Hawk.

Milson raised his hand. "That's me, sir!" Weaver, Sheppard, Fuller, and Asherah exited the helicopter right after him.

"Welcome aboard, Chief! I'm Captain Ronald Cartwright, first executive officer and senior CAG [Commander Air Group] of the *John F. Kennedy*! This is my aide and third officer, Lieutenant Commander Benjamin Sloan. I'm here to escort you and your party to Admiral Palmer and Lieutenant Commander Marin, who are upstairs on the bridge. Grab your gear and follow my six, gentlemen! We're looking forward to hearing your briefing."

Milson and party did as Cartwright had asked. Each of them grabbed their duffel bags, which were holding their tactical equipment, except for Asherah, who had no military items in hers other than tactical attire. All five followed Cartwright and Sloan up to the flag bridge, where Palmer and Marin were waiting for them.

Flag Bridge Control Center, USS *John Fitzgerald Kennedy*

They traveled up through the steel railing staircase and entered the bridge. With Milson's military and clandestine service record having been only midterm appointments throughout his career, he had never been on a naval ship before, let alone an aircraft carrier. This was a new experience for him. He found it exciting, but at the same time knew he was not there to sightsee. As they stepped through the hatch, they saw only a few individuals working around the bridge, probably because this was the midnight shift and the duty operations required only a skeleton crew to maintain a fraction of the ship's performance and operations unless an emergency were to arise. Milson, following Cartwright a bit farther, broke away by himself to approach an individual who happened to be sitting in the captain's chair, looking outward from the observation window, with another officer standing at parade rest right beside him. Milson knew this was none other than Admiral Palmer and Commander Marin, the latter being the SEAL leader. The admiral turned his chair clockwise to get a better look at Milson and his group, with Marin already staring at them as they entered. Cartwright proceeded with the introductions, even though it was not necessary to do so. "Chief Milson, Rear Admiral Galen Palmer, senior commanding officer and captain of the *John F. Kennedy*."

Palmer got up from his chair and stretched out his hand to shake Milson's.

"Welcome aboard, Chief." Milson reciprocated. "So, you're army? What outfit did you serve in?"

"I was an MP with the Eighty-Ninth MP Brigade for three and a half years during my enlistment at Fort Hood, sir. Then I went to the army's CID for a while, where I served in the intelligence department, until I was recruited by the CIA. Now I work for Admiral Cooper with ONI as a freelance contractor," Milson replied, giving his entire résumé to the two-star admiral.

Palmer was impressed but was still a little shaky about what his unfamiliar guests were doing aboard his ship.

"So, you're working for Wayne Cooper?" he asked Milson.

"Hell of a sub captain back in the day. We were at Annapolis together. We both got our commissions at the same time, before he went back to SOCOM to be a SEAL leader and instructor. Speaking of SEALs." Palmer turned to the SEAL commander. "Chief, this is Lieutenant Commander Josef Marin, squad leader of DEVGRU, otherwise known as SEAL Team Six."

Marin also stretched out his hand. "Good to meet you, Chief."

"Likewise, Commander," Milson said, drawing attention to his team standing behind him. "Admiral, Captain, Commander, these are my associates." He introduced them one at a time with Weaver in front.

"Special Agent James Weaver, CIA liaisons and air force reservist. His rank and title are lieutenant colonel."

"Ah, a flyboy," said Palmer with curiosity and amusement.

"What was your MOS [military occupation specialty], son?"

Weaver answered,

"Intelligence, sir. I served with the Eleventh Intelligence Squadron Wing at Fort Bragg, North Carolina, for eight years as a first lieutenant and captain, until I was picked up by Langley when I made major."

Palmer shook his head and said,

"You too? Hmm, I should have known. You looked like a company man the moment I laid eyes on you." Weaver did not know how to take that, but he humbly and graciously accepted the remark. It gave everybody the impression that Palmer was an outspoken, uncensored type of man. He did not hold back for anything or anyone and was very vocal about speaking his mind. To Milson, this man's attitude was old school through and through. To him, it was refreshing to see someone behave like this, but the admiral's abrasiveness did throw him off a little.

Milson went and stood beside to Fuller to introduce him.

"Sir, this is Agent David Fuller, British intelligence and prior military, Royal Marines—a major in rank. He's the one responsible for getting us here."

"MI6? Wow, this is more serious than I thought. One of your superiors in the Royal Navy happens to be a friend of mine, Major.

He called me five hours ago to tell me you were coming. You know Eddie Oswald, son?"

Fuller responded,

"Yes, sir. Vice Admiral, Sir, Edward Oswald. Commander in chief of His Majesty's Naval Maritime Amphibious Forces in the Atlantic and Mediterranean. I spoke with him personally, sir. He said he knows you from his trips back and forth to London and Washington."

"Yes, I know, Major. That's why I allowed you to come aboard, as did Cooper, SECDEF, the chairman of the Joint Chiefs, the VCNO, the commander of the British Navy, and the entire goddamn armed forces." Fuller also gave a nod and accepted the comment.

Milson went to Sheppard next.

"Sir, this is one of yours. Ensign James R. Sheppard, also naval intelligence."

"Damn, another one?! How many spooks do you have working under you, son?" Palmer said, using the word *spook* to mean a spy in the intelligence community. No one took offense to it, including Milson, who snickered at the comment.

Palmer looked over and stared at Sheppard for a couple of seconds.

"Jesus, son! You're young to be an ensign, let alone work for navy intel. How old are you?" Palmer inquired.

Sheppard snapped to it when the admiral addressed him.

"Twenty, sir!" announced the young officer in a tone that made it seem as if he were back in boot camp as a recruit and Palmer was his drill instructor. In Sheppard's short naval career, this was the first time he had ever seen a flag officer. To him, it was incredible, something to be in awe about.

"Twenty? Jesus!" said the twenty-five-year sea veteran, who towered over the young man.

"I have cigars older than you. That's way too young to be so responsible and serious, son. You're not even of drinking age yet. So, you work for Cooper too?"

Again, Sheppard answered with assertiveness and alertness in his voice.

"Yes, sir. Sort of. In a way, sir. I was stationed in Indonesia under the command of Lieutenant Commander Michael True, senior supervisor of the Intel and Tactical Command Operations Division and liaison to the Indonesian Navy and their government."

"Ah yes, that's right," said Palmer as he looked over toward Cartwright, signaling that the CAG should finish his statement.

"The Defense Department wants us to hold hands with foreign military advisers and personnel down in the South Pacific to show friendliness and partnership with the native folk. It's to show the UN and UEA that we can get along and be one big happy military family. In my opinion, it's all a ploy by the brass at the Pentagon and the bureaucrats in Washington to show the Chinese and North Koreans that we still have some pull in the area." Even after the sarcastic comment made by the two-star admiral, Sheppard stayed stiff and motionless, until Weaver nudged him in the side to relax.

When it came to Asherah, Milson was a bit hesitant to announce her presence. But Palmer, having noticed her right away, was eager to find out who this young woman was.

"Chief, aren't you going to introduce your fourth colleague?"

Milson turned around nervously.

"Yes, Admiral. This is Desiree Asherah. She's my"—he paused— "assistant, sir. She has vital intelligence and information about our target package, sir."

"Pleasure to meet you, Miss Asherah. Do your credentials match those of your colleagues?"

Asherah looked at Milson for help and reassurance. But all she got from him was an expression indicating that she should do her best to improvise. She looked back at the admiral, his stare meeting hers. There was a noticeable gulp from her throat as she swallowed.

"On the contrary, Admiral. My previous employment is with the Holland government in the accounting and finance department.

I was recruited by Mr. Milson because of the intel I have and my unique relationship with the target package, so to speak."

Milson looked over at Asherah with surprise. Fuller, Sheppard, and Weaver had the same look on their faces as well. Palmer, who did not think too much of it, gave a smile to Asherah and said with glee,

"A civilian? Well, that's refreshing to hear. I thought you were another spy, but a pretty one at that." He continued in a condescending tone, saying,

"A beautiful but easygoing pencil-pushing accountant surrounded by four roughneck field spooks. You don't see that every day, do you, Ronald?" He nudged Cartwright while laughing at his own remarks. But Milson and the rest of them did not share Palmer's humor, probably because they knew the real reason for Asherah's presence.

After all the introductions had been made, Palmer waved his right hand at Milson.

"Okay, Chief, let's get down to business. From what I have gathered from Cooper and Vice Admiral Taylor, it seems that we have a real situation on our hands. My deck is yours. Tell me what's going on and why you need my ship and the assistance of my crew to do this."

"Thank you, Admiral. But I must request that the information I'm about to tell you be kept in this room. Top secret and all that, sir," advised Milson.

"Ah, jeez, the cloak-and-dagger routine, son? Well, all right, Chief. I understand." Palmer took a breath and sighed with exhaustion, plopping down into his captain's chair to hear whatever Milson had to say. He looked over at Cartwright while crossing his arms over his chest. "Ron, get rid of the bridge crew. Have all of them go down to the CIC [Combat Information Center] until called for."

"Aye, aye, sir." Cartwright went over and stood in the center of the bridge. In a loud commanding tone, he announced,

"Attention on deck! All nonessential personnel, evacuate the bridge! You're relieved until further notice! All essential personnel still on duty, report to the CIC under Commander Smith [who was the second officer and third in command]. Dismissed!"

The remaining crew members began to leave via the numerous exits. As the last one left, Cartwright closed the hatch doors behind them to give the senior officers and their guests some privacy. Cartwright, who had seen the last person leave the bridge, signaled to Palmer that it was secure.

"All right, Chief, there's no one here but us officers and the lady. The floor is yours," said the two-star admiral, who was agitated and tired from having stayed up all night for the meeting with Milson and party.

Milson and the rest of his group set their duffel bags down simultaneously. Milson pulled several copies of Assad's picture from his bag and passed them around to Palmer and his senior staff. "I'm sorry, Admiral, but it's important that we keep this to ourselves. Direct orders from Admiral Cooper and SECDEF. The mission that I'm on has been designated as Operation Executive Bounty, under the direct orders of the president and Admiral Cooper. I am to retrieve a naval officer who has gone rogue and AWOL. This is a picture of the target whom I'm after. His name is—"

Marin interrupted, having recognized the person in the photograph.

"Ad-dam Omar Assad?!" the SEAL leader said.

"You know him, Commander?" Cartwright asked. It was obvious that everyone else was intrigued by Marin's outburst.

"Yes, sir. Nine years ago, when I was a lieutenant JG and first serving as a SEAL, he was attached to our unit. He acted as an interpreter and an intelligence officer for us when we were sent out on missions. We trained him in combat ops and intel gathering so we could be more proficient at communicating back and forth with SOCOM, with the intention of having a reliable source at our disposal. Assad was used for that purpose under a direct order from the chief of naval operations at the time. Last I heard, he was working for ONI as an analyst."

"Well, you heard right, Commander. He was working for ONI, but he doesn't work there anymore since he turned traitor." Milson turned his attention back to Palmer and Cartwright. "Commander Assad is now wanted for conspiracy, espionage, and treason. He stole military secrets from the DOD archives and four experimental weapons from an army depot in Hartford, Maryland, two weeks ago. I and my team have been tracking his movements ever since, from the time he left the States to now in the Emirates. Judging from the intel we gathered, he is on his way right now to the Iranian border to a city called Khorramshahr to give the secrets and weapons to a terrorist organization in exchange for a cash payment in the hundreds of millions of dollars."

Palmer, Cartwright, Marin, and Sloan were all stunned by this news, especially Marin, since he knew Assad personally. Milson continued,

"Our sources say that he's traveling along the Iranian coastline between Bushehr and Khorramshahr. Commander Sloan, do you have a GPS Nav-Map (Navigational-Global Positioning System-Map) I can use to show you, his route?"

"Yes, we do, Chief. With the Admiral's permission, of course." Palmer gave a nod to Sloan, granting him the request.

When Sloan was about to activate the GPS navigational system located near the communications area, Marin respectfully interrupted.

"Excuse me, Admiral, Captain, and Chief, but I think we need to bring another individual into this briefing." Palmer looked at Marin strangely for a few seconds, then realized what he was talking about.

"Oh, that's right. I almost forgot about him. Good call, Commander. Get him on the line right now. He needs to hear this as well."

Marin went over to the NCS (naval/net communications station) and typed a sequence of numbers and codes into the keypad. Having managed to get through to the area he was trying to contact, he linked the transmission to the relay system so the composite picture would be displayed on the overhead monitor, giving them a chance to make a confirmation. The screen was a little fuzzy at first, but it cleared up very quickly. The image that appeared on the viewer was of a man in his early to mid-thirties with a full dark beard and a mustache. He looked scruffy but had a professional aura about him. From his neck down to his waist, he appeared to be dressed in military fashion: army-issued combat uniform—ACU—but with no rank, insignias, or identifying name plates. As the picture became clearer and the individual became easier to identify, Marin opened a dialogue with the person on the other end of the transmission. "Chris, can you hear me? I've got you on a secure closed channel, so we can use names!"

"Read ya Lima Charlie [loud and clear], Josef! You're coming in crystal!"

Marin looked over at Milson and said,

"Chief Milson, this is Major Christopher Troy, leader of Delta Force Squadron Bravo."

Milson acknowledged the Delta leader right off the bat.

"Pleasure to meet you, Major, although I wish it were under better circumstanccs."

"Same here, Chief. I already got the call from both General Roberts and General Dreyfus about you and your mission. And if I may speak freely, I'd like to say that what you're planning to do is no walk in the park. It's damn near suicidal. It's going to be a shitstorm if the Iranians find out that we're playing in their backyard and trying to retrieve someone. This is not going to be an easy hit-and-run type of operation, Chief. In my opinion, this is definitely a suicide mission."

"Don't worry, Chris, you may speak freely on your end." Marin replied sarcastically given to Troy's honest opinion. "We may be using a satellite uplink belonging to Kuwait's SIS, but I have this transmission encrypted through our network. Nobody will be able to tap into our conversation, not even if they seriously want to. Both our mics are safe and secure," Troy acknowledged.

Milson looked over at the view screen to answer Troy. "That's good, Major, because what I have to say to you and Commander Marin is definitely for your ears only, plus the ears of everyone in this room. Admiral Cooper and the director of the CIA do not want the Kuwaitis to know too much about this operation. Neither does the president or SECDEF. All SIS needs to know is that Commander Assad is a fugitive wanted by the United States for murder in the first degree, nothing more and nothing less. And what you said earlier, Major, about this not being a walk in the park: you're absolutely right. This is not going to be easy. The Iranians have their entire militia spread across several of their major cities, including the one I must gain entry to. And if I get caught by the Iranian government, it's going to be downhill from there. That's why I want to use your team and Commander Marin's men as backup, in case I happen to get caught up by the Iranians when taking my target out of there. My plan is to catch him in the act of selling the secrets to this terrorist group he made a deal with and bring him back, along with the weapons and the plans, over either the Kuwaiti or the Iraqi border—alive."

"And how are you going to accomplish this, Mr. Milson? What is your plan for getting yourself, the SEALs, and the Deltas over there without being detected?" Cartwright asked with curiosity.

Milson looked over toward Weaver, hoping he would answer the captain's question. Weaver gladly obliged.

"Sir, you may be aware that you have the Combat Craft Medium Mark One (CCM Mk1) speedboats in your inventory," Weaver said.

Cartwright and Palmer looked at each other in dismay and disbelief. Palmer said without hesitation,

"Jesus, son! How in the hell do you know about them? Those boats are strictly classified, and no news of them has ever been circulated among the public. Hell, I was even kept in the dark about them until Marin told me later, when we were out to sea."

"I'm sorry, Admiral, but the CIA has known about them for quite a while. We acquired several of them for our own black ops missions some time ago. Some of our engineers helped designed them in partnership with the navy and marines Civil Engineering Corps, and with NAVFAC [Naval Facilities Engineering Command] for the SEALs and other amphibian special forces for stealth and clandestine purposes. These boats have been around for almost twenty years. Since then, there have been predecessors—the Mark V, VI, VII, VIII, IX, and its latest one the Mark X SOC [Special Operations Craft] which were constructed years ago have all been replaced by the new CCM Mk1."

Palmer asked,

"Well, why do we call them top secret when they really aren't? It just goes to show you that words like *intelligence* and *classified* are really ironic terms used by the stuffed-shirt bureaucrats at the NMC [National Military Command] and those pencil-necked Pentagon desk jockeys who probably have never served in their lives. Well, Mr. Milson, Mr. Weaver, since you know a hell of a lot about those boats and what they can do, why don't you enlighten us about your plan for using them?"

Milson went back to have Sloan turn on the Nav-Map so he could show them what he had in mind with regard to entering Iran without being discovered.

"Sir, at first I was thinking about using some helicopters for the mission, but Weaver and Fuller persuaded me against doing that since the Iranians have sophisticated radar detection. We will be spotted way before we reach the mainland. So, we came up with an alternative. Our plan is to use those boats for transport since they have stealth capability and are able to reach seriously high speeds, both of which will prevent them from being spotted by Iranian radar. We'll need two of them, one for my group with the SEAL team, and the other for the Deltas. We can travel up this route along the coastline on the border between Kuwait and Iran. There's a canal river at this junction that leads into the city of Khorramshahr—

the Karun River. It's miles long and easy to navigate. We can go in under the cover of night and have the SF teams set up a temporary perimeter along this side of the border, which the river runs along. This will give us a tactical advantage when I retrieve Assad. I'll go in under cover with the assistance of one of my people, namely, Ms. Asherah, since she knows the target personally and can speak fluent Arabic, just like yours truly. I'll track him down, identify him, pick him up, and bring him back across the border."

"One thing, Chief Milson," Cartwright said, stepping in front of the map.

"What if he isn't willing to come back?"

Milson, who obviously knew what the captain was implying, looked over at Asherah to gauge her response to this question. In answer, she looked across at Milson, but only for a second, before turning her head to hide her disappointment and regret.

"Well, I'll just have to persuade him otherwise, sir," Milson answered Cartwright.

Cartwright, liking that answer, gave Milson an approving slap on the back. Then he asked, "Okay, Chief, after you catch him, what is your game plan for getting back across? You can't use the stealth boats for a second run, unless you're planning on hiding them out there. And even if you do that, the Iranians are going to have their own shore patrol or coast guard running up and down that river canal. You'll be discovered way before you can snatch your man."

"You're right, sir. That's why I'm only going to use the Mark 1's, and only one way—for the trip there. They'll be returning to either the *JFK* or the nearest Kuwaiti naval port after they drop us off. I was hoping to be granted extraction by helo. Either Black Hawks or Seahawks, it doesn't matter. If they have stealth capabilities and are able to get in and to get us out, then we'll be in the clear as long as they continue to fly under the radar. They must come in without the Iranian air force spotting them, much like the maneuver we did nineteen years ago in Abbottabad, Pakistan." Everyone in the room knew what Milson was talking about: the joint task force effort by the CIA, US Military Intelligence, National Military Command, and USSOCOM to send in a Special Forces team, including SEAL Team Six, and two stealth Black Hawks to find Osama bin Laden and terminate him. They were successful despite having lost one Black Hawk to mechanical failure and having to destroy it so the Pakistanis would not use it for reverse engineering. After Milson mentioned that little piece of history, he thought of something that could improve their chances of getting out of there in one piece.

"Admiral, I know you're scheduled to arrive in Kuwait tomorrow evening. But do you think you can delay your heading out by just a bit and stay out beyond the coastline? Will it be possible for you to do that, sir?"

Palmer rose from his chair and walked over toward Milson.

"I'm not sure I'm following you, son. What are you asking?"

Milson had everybody's interest piqued. He asked everyone to gather around the map table. Then he repositioned the view screen with Troy's image on it so that Troy could grasp the intricacies of his plan.

"Sir, there is a strong possibility we can make it out of there, but there's also a chance that this terrorist group, with the help of the Iranians, will launch a counterstrike against us with ground troops, and probably order an air assault as well. Now, if that happens, our chances of getting across the border in one piece will be slim. But with helicopter support, I feel we would have a better chance given that we'd be flying over open water instead of engaging in a land pursuit. Now the plan remains to cross into either Iraqi or Kuwaiti territory, the latter being closer, but I don't want the Iranians to think that the Iraqis or Kuwaitis are helping us. That would destabilize the relationship between the countries. But of course, we know the truth here. It would be too risky to reveal the truth. And we definitely don't want to cause an international incident with all three countries going at each other's throats just because of us. Sir, I was thinking, if you can position the *JFK* here"—Milson pointed to a certain area of the gulf— "along this channel right at the northeastern end of the gulf, right at the edge of Iranian territory but still within Kuwait's waters, we can get the helos to you easily, in no time flat. Now, as I said before, they might launch their birds at us, which I think they will do because of our aerial escape route, but they'll think twice about it once they realize they must go into international waters and international airspace—considered neutral by the Iraqi, Kuwaiti, and Saudi governments—to get us. I have a feeling they'll do that anyway. But after they do, they'll be facing a squadron of your F/A-18's and F/A-XX's—our support group and welcome wagon. Even though the Iranians don't like us very much, personally I don't think they will want to tangle with a US fighter group outside their airspace." Palmer and everyone else looked at the spot where Milson was pointing.

The admiral took his glasses from his shirt pocket to get a better look.

"Damn, son, that's a tight spot right there, latitude twenty-nine-point-seventy degrees north, longitude forty-eight-point-thirty degrees east. Hell, I might as well park right up on their shore, I'll be so damn close," Palmer said with a pessimistic tone.

"Admiral, I know it's a little too close for comfort, but this is just a backup if plan A doesn't succeed. We will have the advantage of surprise either way, sir. I guarantee this will work for us."

After looking at the map closely, Palmer took off his glasses and gazed around at all present, including the leader on the viewer, to take in their reactions to Milson's proposal. Everyone had just about the same look on their faces, a look of confidence and assurance. No one had a problem with this plan, not even Troy, who was hundreds of miles away, listening in from a satellite projection.

Palmer went to his XO for a second opinion.

"Ron, what do you think? Does this sound like a feasible plan?"

Cartwright folded his arms and said,

"Sir, you know me; I'm just a fighter pilot. But after looking at this and hearing Chief Milson's proposal, I think it's solid, and has a good chance of being successful. Even if we miss our hookup at the Kuwaiti port and swing off course somewhere in the range of seventy-five to a hundred miles to the east, we will still be on our side of the border. That area of water is international, belonging to both the Iraqis and the Kuwaitis. The Iranians have no claim whatsoever to those waters. But if they do ask us why we're out there, we should tell them that we're doing air and sea exercises with the Kuwaitis and Saudis, which isn't that far from the truth."

Palmer shook his head and grinned at the idea. He looked over at Marin.

"Commander, what's your thought on the chief's plan?"

Marin bent down and looked at the map more closely than Palmer did.

"Sir, tactically, we might be able to pull it off, but it's a toss-up—and a huge gamble." Milson was stunned by Marin's answer.

"The chief has a good plan for getting us in, but it is sketchy to rely on air support because it doesn't always come through. Now I'm all for the plan to have backup from Troy and his guys, but if we do run into resistance, which I know we will, and the shit really hits the fan, we're going to need some other plan to follow besides extraction by bird."

"What are you suggesting, Commander, a plan C?" Milson asked, his tone both abrasive and relaxed.

"Chief, you misunderstood me. Your plan is right on target in my opinion, but honestly, I don't think we should rely on just one way to make our escape. I don't know if you're aware of this, but the Kuwaitis built several underground tunnels that stretch for miles between Iraq and Iran. Back in the 1980s and '90s, when Saddam Hussein declared war on Kuwait and Iran, the Kuwaitis constructed these huge subterranean tunnels so they could move back and forth between the two countries to resupply the troops fighting against Saddam's military. They also used these tunnels to escape from his tyranny when he temporarily took over Kuwait. Now these tunnels are located right along this area, which is approximately five miles from our setup point. It's also very close to Khorramshahr, about ten to twenty miles outside it. The Iranians are not aware of the existence of the tunnels, so they're perfect for an escape route. If we can't get to the border on the surface by foot or get out by helicopters, I think our best chance is to use those tunnels as our third option."

Milson objected to that idea.

"I'm sorry, Commander, but I don't think so. I know what you're talking about, but your idea is not plausible for this type of mission. Those tunnels have been obsolete for almost three decades. Ever since we liberated the Kuwaitis from Saddam's rule in the early nineteen nineties they haven't been used since. For all we know, the Kuwaitis probably filled them up or dismantled them when they were no longer needed. No, Commander Marin, our best bet is to go with the helicopters. We will have a better chance of getting out of there by air than by a string of underground tunnels that probably don't exist anymore. With all due respect, Commander, what you suggest would be better for another scenario, but not this. Again, the best alternative is to use the helicopters to get in and out."

Marin was still adamantly against Milson's idea to use the helicopters. He refused to budge. Both men were so stubborn with regard to their difference of opinion that an intense argument erupted. Palmer intervened quickly to resolve the dispute, taking advantage of his authority and rank.

"All right, gentlemen, let's settle down. There's no need for this to turn into a pissing contest between the two of you. I'm not going to sit up here and watch you two get into a fistfight to determine which idea will work best. Each of you gave compelling arguments, both being logical and sound. What you need to do now is create a plan of attack using these elements to your advantage. Chief, I know that this is your baby and you have operational control, but you need to look and listen to the alternatives brought to your attention and consider one in case your first plan falls apart."

Milson agreed with the admiral.

"Yes, sir. You're absolutely right." He then looks over at Marin.

"And you, Commander, you are a squad leader with an elite spec-op group at your disposal. You of all people should know the consequences of faulty intel. On some occasions, the intel is reliable and trustworthy, but in some circumstances such as ours, it isn't worth spit. You need to be objective, reasonable, and open-minded when it comes to any information that may be pertinent to your goal and mission. Don't be so quick to judge when you first hear an idea or when an order comes your way, even if it's not yours to convey or carry out. We all balance each other out one way or another, even if we don't like the other alternative being proposed."

Palmer said,

"Let me tell you why I have Captain Cartwright as my XO. He keeps me grounded and levelheaded. I can act like a stubborn bastard sometimes. But he's the only one who has the ability to center me—one of the privileges of being the SIC and my first officer."

Marin replied, chuckling, "Aye, aye, sir. Understood." He placed his arms behind his back and stood at parade rest showing respect and military protocol to his commanding officer.

Palmer went over to the monitor to address Troy.

"Major, you've been quiet throughout this whole discussion. I want your opinion on this. What do you think of Mr. Milson's plan?"

Troy cleared his throat.

"Sir, the chief's plan for infiltrating the area is a good one, and it can be carried out with accuracy. But getting out of there in one piece will be a problem. It's going to be touch-and-go no matter how you dice it. A helo extract is the most logical way to get out of there, but I must give credit to Commander Marin for his proposal to have a fallback if the aerial pickup is compromised. Still, I must side with Chief Milson on this. A helo pickup would work much better than a tunnel extraction, but I don't want to rule out an escape by tunnel, sir. I would like to suggest that when we touch down and set up our perimeter, my guys put up a GPDU [Ground Penetration Detection Unit, commonly known as GPS (Ground Penetration Sonar)] in and around the area. These devices will allow us to detect any underground area between several meters in depth and one mile below sea level, sometimes deeper. We use them for finding high-profile targets, such as caches of weapons and other black-market items used by terrorists. We can program the GPDU to detect any subterranean passageways. That might help us navigate the area, sir."

"That sounds good, Major. I like that."

Palmer turned to the group to give his final say.

"Okay, gentlemen, I think you've got your go-ahead. Chief, we're going to go with your recommendation, but I want you to use Commander Marin's suggestion as a backup in the event those tunnels still exist. Understood?"

"Yes, sir," Milson replied with appreciation.

"Commander, go get your team ready, and prep those boats for deployment. Take as much ammo with you as needed. I have a feeling that you and the chief are going to need a lot." Palmer turned to Cartwright.

"Ron, set us on a course to reach the area the chief suggested. Also, prepare four Seahawks with stealth equipment. They're going to be the chief's way of escape if it is needed. Oh, by the way, contact the Kuwaiti navy and their harbormasters. Inform them that we are going to arrive a little later than expected. Make up something if they ask questions. For example, tell them we're doing naval exercises as ordered by our fleet commander, or underwater geological research to survey the depth and width of the gulf floor—any obscure tale you can tell them to buy us some time."

Cartwright chuckled and said,

"Aye, sir. I'll have Commander Smith in the CIC make up an explanation to give them and send it. I'll give the order to change course immediately, and I'll ready four birds with stealth capabilities for deployment. I'll also put some fighters on standby alert as suggested by Chief Milson, just in case the Iranian air force wants to get a little froggy with us."

As Cartwright turned to go to the communications center, Palmer continued his briefing with Milson and the others.

"Chief, I want to say this to you and the rest of y'all. I'm an old sea dog. I've been in this navy for twenty-some odd years now, and

I'm set in my ways. I'm not used to this espionage type of stuff that you kids find so fascinating. I'm just an old-fashioned admiral with old-school ideas in a new and modernized navy of the digital age that relies on computers, satellites, and all the other thingamajigs and doohickeys you kid's today are used to. But I want to say this to all of you: you be careful out there. I know that all of you are aware of the risk and the dangers involved. If you weren't, you wouldn't be here in the first place, taking on a suicidal assignment such as this one. That goes for you too, Major Troy! I'll do my part to get you there. That's what I'm here for, and that's what I've been ordered to do. You just do your part by getting this guy and coming back in one piece. Is that clear, people?"

All five of them, including Troy, gave out a boisterous "Yes, sir!" Even Asherah, who was not military, gave the same response as the others.

Palmer gave a nod to everyone and said,

"All right, people, you're dismissed. Major Troy, we will contact you upon the arrival of Chief Milson's team and Commander Marin's group to have them pick you up!"

"Understood, Admiral. Me and my guys will be ready and waiting, sir."

Troy's image disappeared from the screen once Palmer disconnected the transmission. Afterward, he sought the attention of Milson to remind him of something else.

"Mr. Milson? You and Commander Marin need to put your heads together and determine what time you guys will be leaving tonight. We're still far from Kuwaiti waters. I know you two need to depart ASAP so you can get a line on your target."

"Yes, Admiral. My ETD [Estimate Time of Departure] is two hours from now. I estimate that Commander Assad has already left, having gotten a head start on us, and will reach Bushehr within the next hour or so. It will take us at least two hours to reach the channel, which we'll likely do after he does," Milson said.

Palmer rubbed his face and looked at the map again without putting on his glasses.

"I'll tell you what, I'll have engineering increase our speed to forty knots. That's our top speed. If she can give more, I'll give it to you so you can beat him there."

"Thank you, sir." Milson appreciated the offer.

"Also, I want you to coordinate with Commander Marin to establish radio contact with us when you touch down in Iran, which I'd like to remain constant. Get with one of my officers in the CIC so we can be electronically tethered to each other at all times. Understood?"

"Yes, sir. I'll have Ensign Sheppard get on it ASAP, Admiral," replied Milson. The group walked off and headed for the exit hatch of the bridge.

Palmer told Commander Sloan to retrieve the rest of the bridge crew from the CIC so they could finish out their duty shift before the next group comes to relieve them. When everybody was going down the rail ladders to get to the lower decks and prepare themselves for the mission, Marin stops Milson, pulls him to the side and talks to him in private.

"Chief, may I have a word with you over here?" Milson turned to Weaver and Fuller and told them that he would catch up with them later. They both walked off ahead of each other leaving the two gentlemen to discuss their private conversation.

Marin opened the dialog by saying.

"Listen, Chief, I hope you didn't get the wrong idea up there. I wasn't trying to take over or step on your toes. All I was trying to do was provide another perspective. I've had more experience in aerial combat and retrieval missions than anyone here: aerial jumps from C-17's, C-130's, and C-5M's, and air assault missions from Seahawks, Black Hawks, CH-53E Super Stallions, and CH-46's and -47's—Sea Knights and Chinooks. I have experienced both good and bad retrievals using these vehicles, and I can tell you that most of them didn't pan out well. When I read your file, I knew you were the type of guy who—"

"Wait a minute! You read my file?" Milson said with shock.

Marin, a bit surprised by the reaction, continued his explanation.

"Yes, I did, Chief. I had to find out what type of person you were before going on a mission like this. I wanted to know for sure if you had ever participated in an operation of this magnitude before, and would put myself and my men in harm's way to a man that is not familiar with combat tactics such as this. Wouldn't you do the same if you were in my shoes?"

Milson was irate at the audaciousness of the young officer. Again, he thought, here was someone questioning his professionalism and his skill as a former agent.

"What gave you the right to look into my file in the first place, Commander? On whose authority did you do so?" Milson asked abrasively.

Marin tried to explain his intentions respectfully to Milson, but the angry bounty hunter kept cutting him off.

"Let me explain something to you. I may be out of the game, but I've been doing this type of thing for a long time. I've spent many years developing my skills, both in and out of the CIA. Tracking down individuals like Assad is nothing new to me, and I've made a pretty good profession out of it. I've spent my life putting guys like him where they belong, either in jail or in the ground. And I've never once lost a fugitive from my radar, ever. It's because of people like him that we are in this mess in the first place. Radical individuals who think that just because the people of the world don't agree with their ideology or religious beliefs should be eradicated from the face of the earth. I know this from firsthand experience. If it weren't for Assad and the many others like him who have the same traits that he recently displayed, you and I wouldn't be having this conversation right now. And you wouldn't have to hire people like me to bring people like him down or look in my file to see if I'm qualified to do a job such as this. If you have questions or doubts about me or my qualifications, just ask. I'll be happy to tell you anything that you want to know about me. But don't be sneaking around, digging into my past to see if I'm the right guy for the job. Do I make myself clear, Commander?"

Milson's tone was abrasive, harsh, and unpleasant. But for the sake of argument, his reasons were justified along with his reaction.

The SEAL commander replied,

"You made your point, Chief. And I understand. Now let me tell you something. When it comes to the safety of my men when carrying out a dangerous assignment such as this, you're damn right that I'm going to check the background of the individual who is leading me and my men to a no-win-scenario, especially when I think it's a suicidal one. Now I have no problem with you, but it seems that you're looking to have a problem with me. Or are you just looking for an opening that you can squeeze through to show your true colors, given what you said earlier?"

"What are you talking about, Marin?" Milson asked, intrigued by Marin's question.

"Oh, you know damn well what I'm talking about, Chief—your bigoted views on Muslims and the event that took place at Fort Hood twenty years ago when you were an MP. You remember the situation. An army officer shot up the whole damn place when you were stationed there, and he happened to be Muslim. And the fact that Assad, a naval intelligence officer who happened to be working for ONI, as well as being a Muslim, got away with stealing classified information from one of the most secure facilities in the United States and is trying to sell it on the black market to a radical terrorist group that is bent on global domination and genocide. That must really bother you, doesn't it, Chief? It all makes sense now. You're using your personal feelings, along with your biasness and prejudicial perception, as an excuse to get Assad because of what happened in your past."

Milson started to get aggravated again as he replied bluntly.

"You don't know what the hell you're talking about, Commander. My views and personal feelings don't have a damn thing to do with this. Neither does my personal history. I'm hunting a traitor, plain and simple, a man who betrayed his country, his ethics, and his morals to help a sinister organization that wants to annihilate us because of our independence and freedoms. I am bound by a code and an oath to bring such individuals to justice. And I will not let anything or anyone get in the way of that, not my past, not my feelings, and especially, as you so kindly put it, not my political views or perception of people of certain religions or beliefs. Assad is a wanted man who is extremely dangerous and threatens the United States. I will either apprehend him or execute him."

Milson was about to walk away, but again Marin stops him in his tracks.

"Do you think you're the only one, Chief? I also swore an oath to defend my country against all enemies, foreign AND DOMESTIC. To achieve that end is the reason I became a SEAL. I wanted to look for fuckers like him who want to threaten the security and stability of our country, along with the freedom and the democracy that the UEA and the UN are trying to establish across the world. So, I am also bound to defend the Constitution and the right to religious belief it protects, because *I* too am a Muslim."

Milson's eyes almost shot out from his head when he heard that announcement from the SEAL leader.

"Wait, you're Muslim?" the bounty hunter asked, a surprised and astonished look on his face.

"Yes, I am, Chief. I may not have Middle Eastern features, but I am Islamic. My father is Caucasian, and my mother is Arabic, Saudi Arabian to be exact. My father is a retired sergeant major from the marine corps, and my mother was an accountant for the Saudi government. They met when he was stationed there at the US embassy. They fell in love and got married. I was born in the States, as were my brothers and sisters. My father, who was a hard-core marine jarhead, was a devout Christian, but he wasn't concerned about marrying a Muslim woman. He loved my mother very much and wanted to be with her despite their religious differences. He wasn't concerned which way I and my siblings chose to go, whether toward Christianity or Islam. If we were satisfied and comfortable in our own faith and with who we were, then so be it. He wasn't even concerned when I chose to follow Islam, even though I don't practice it much, but he did get pissed off when I joined the navy, instead of the marine corps as he wanted me to follow in his footsteps. When I joined the service, the US government didn't care what my religious background was. All that mattered was that I had volunteered to defend the Constitution and what it stands for: freedom, justice, and *equality*. Now, my opinion is that what Assad did is inexcusable and downright intolerable and disgusting, but I won't let that deter me from doing my job as a SEAL and a citizen of the country I love. Assad and I may be of the same faith and may have similar backgrounds, but our intentions are different. His intentions are evil, selfish, and deplorable. I will do everything within my power as a naval officer and a SEAL to help you track him down and catch him—even neutralize him when the time comes, if need be. But don't use our religion as a tool to justify your own prejudice. That right there, Chief Milson, is unprofessional and shows a lack of discipline on your part. It's also a mark of a distasteful, revolting and racist human being that you have become. Which I can clearly see that you are not."

Milson stared at Marin for a moment. He gave a low, humorous chuckle, acknowledging Marin's overwhelming but mawkishly banal statements. Realizing that he had seriously misjudged this person, he was apprehensive to acknowledge it. Marin's sense of duty, honor, and purpose was authentic and sincere to Milson. In a way, Marin was a carbon copy of Milson, especially their family traits. Although his last comments were a bit corny in Milson's opinion, Marin seemed genuine and honest.

Although Milson tried to hide his laughter, Marin caught sight of it and became curious as to its meaning.

"Did I say something funny, Chief? If I did, I would like to know what was so humorous."

Milson shook his head and tried to wipe the sarcastic smirk off his face by literally wiping a hand across his mouth.

"No, Commander. It's just that for a split second, you reminded me of somebody I used to know a long time ago: me." Marin, looking at Milson, tilted his head in confusion, not sure of the meaning of that comment, which he chose to take as both a compliment and an apology.

Milson had one more anecdote to share with the young naval officer.

"By the way, if I may ask, what is it with you navy squids anyway? Admiral Cooper gave me a similar pep talk weeks ago in his office right before I left, talking about the very same thing. Do you SEALs have some kind of special code of honor that y'all go by to persuade people to go along with your sappy rhetoric? Or is it that all of you SEALs are just full of shit?"

Marin snickered and turned his head, thinking that Milson was unbelievable, but not taking what he had said as an insult to him or his profession. He turned back around and answered him in a way that only Milson would appreciate:

"Well, Chief, let me say this. If it weren't for us navy squids doing the jobs that you army pukes punk out on, we would still be looking for bin Laden right now. As for the code of honor we adhere to, we take that very seriously. We don't seek to persuade anyone; it's all voluntarily. And for your information, just in case you didn't know, Admiral Cooper was a member of this team. He took part in several of the operations that you mentioned earlier upstairs, so he has been a tremendous influence on me. Oh, and another thing. From my personal experience, I think ex-CIA agents are full of shit than anyone else, apart from the army's CID and intelligence department."

Milson just stared at Marin hard and stiff without moving. Then, without warning, he broke out into hysterical laughter. This surprised Marin a great deal. He hadn't expected Milson to have a sense of humor or any humor at all in what Marin had previously said. Being the attentive person that he was, Milson stretched out his hand as an invitation of reconciliation. Marin accepted the gesture.

"I misjudged you, Commander," Milson said.

"In a way, you and I are alike."

"In what way, if I may ask, Chief?" Marin said.

"We both had fathers who were mean and ornery bastards; we both have dangerous occupations; and we both adhere to the same bullshit rhetoric that got us here in the first place: duty, honor, country."

Marin laughed. He and Milson turned to walk down the crowded corridor filled with sailors, marines and officers, who passed them by as they continued to talk with one another, making their trek to meet up with their people to execute their plan for getting into Iran and catching their objective, Assad.

Bushehr Province, Iran, 2:35 a.m.

Two speedboats, heavily armed and with a yacht traveling between them, had made their way into the harbor of the Iranian port city. Each of them docked alongside the pier, where there was a line of men armed with Russian-made AK-47's waiting for them. As the men helped to tie up the boats and secure the lines, Assad, who was on the yacht, made his way topside on the forward deck. Several other men who were on the pier made their way onto the boat as it was secured against the dock. As Assad was walking up the scaffold ramp with the duffel bag of weapons in his hand, he was greeted by one of the men who was obviously a member of the terrorist group.

"Mr. Assad, welcome to Bushehr. I presume that your trip here was uneventful?" the mysterious individual said.

"On the contrary. We had a hard time getting past the checkpoints along the coastal borders set up by the Iranian navy.

It seems they don't want any unauthorized ships to cross into their waters. That made it a lot harder for us to get here," Assad said, complaining about the ordeal.

"Well, you won't have to worry about that again, Mr. Assad. The next transport you take, you'll have your identity cloaked. We made arrangements to have you travel on an Iranian coast guard vessel. It is something that we"—he paused meaningfully— "acquired from the Iranian navy. I assure you; they will not be looking for it amid their inventory." He looked down at the bag that Assad was carrying.

"Are those the items?" he asked.

"Yes, along with the flash drive. The other one is not with me. It is in a safe place, where I will pick it up later and give it to your superior when our transaction is done."

"Excuse me, Mr. Assad, but that was not a part of the agreement. My supervisor told me that you should have all three of the items we agreed on, including both the flash drives."

"Well, after the fiasco in Dubai, I wasn't about to take any more chances. One of my contacts has the drive and will give it to me as soon as they know that the deal has been successfully carried out. I have on me the other drive, as well as a backup disk that will secure the upload of the intel you need. It has all the information about the Americans' defenses and their undercover agents, just like the second one does," said Assad.

"But it is only one of the two. We cannot integrate it into our systems unless we have both drives in our possession. This is very disappointing, Mr. Assad. My superiors are not going to like this. I must inform them about this change immediately." When the individual took out his cell phone and began to use it, Assad stopped him by putting his hand over the device.

"Listen, you will get the other drive after our deal has been made. I promise you; this is not a subterfuge. My contact will be in Kuwait by tomorrow morning. I will arrange for them to meet me in Khorramshahr to give me the other drive after you and I complete our exchange. I assure you that there's no double-cross here. I'm just taking extra precautions to satisfy the both of us; my needs as well as yours."

The individual looked at Assad very peculiarly and nodded his head.

"All right, Mr. Assad. It looks as if I have no other choice but to go with your"—he paused— "plan. But I must warn you, deceiving the organization would be an unwise move on your part. If they discover any sort of deception, they will greatly disrupt your future endeavors and find some arbitrary means by which to dispose of you."

Assad, intuitively understanding what that meant, did not need for it to be interpreted or defined. He nodded his head and went with the circumstances that lay ahead of him. As he and the other man began to walk along the pier, the terrorist agent said,

"I must inform you that your meeting with my superiors will have to take place a lot sooner than you expected. We have lost contact with one of our informants who was placed as an agent inside the Dubai embassy. Unfortunately, we think he has been discovered, and the information that he was relaying to us about the Americans who are trying to capture you has been compromised."

"Are you telling me that this operation is blown?" Assad asked.

"No. The meetings that you're scheduled to have will still go forward, but they will be convening at a different location, outside the city. Our intelligence has told us that this Killian Milson will attempt something that would be detrimental to him and foolish on his part. He may try to covertly cross into Iran. We will have special units from our organization set a trap for him and his group if he carries out this plan. I assure you that if he does, he will not be successful."

"Are you going to use Iranian personnel to assist you, for example, military troops? If not, I think it would be a good idea to use them," Assad said with concern.

"Troops will not be needed. The organization is fully equipped to handle such situations and contingencies. And besides, our Iranian brothers remain unaware of our existence." A devious smirk spread across the individual's face.

"Well, don't be too confident. If this Killian Milson is the type of person, I think he is, he's going to try to do something out of the ordinary. You may need to reconsider asking for help from your so-called Iranian brothers. He's going to use special ops teams. I should know; I was a Navy SEAL years ago, before I joined naval intelligence. I know their tactics and how they work. Trust me, you're going to need all the help you can get. If I were in his shoes, I would be doing the same thing," the former naval officer said.

"Oh, you worry too much, Mr. Assad. We have everything under control. Now if you will follow me, I will see to it that you reach your accommodations on time. This way."

The two men approached a dark-colored automobile parked in a vacant lot. Assad handed the bag over to his companion, who placed it into the trunk of the automobile. Each got into the rear seat of the car, closing their doors simultaneously. Just as the doors closed, the vehicle's engine revved. The car began to move forward in haste, leaving smoke and tire debris in its wake as it accelerated into the darkness of the night.

USS *John Fitzgerald Kennedy*, Persian Gulf, 3:05 a.m.

Both CCM Mk1 boats were ready to get underway. The members of SEAL Team Six were propping up their gear and equipment on the first boat while Milson and his group were preparing the other one. They had to make room for the Delta team, whom they were scheduled to pick up later, and they still had to make arrangements for carrying extra ammo and equipment vital to the mission or to the boat itself. Each group separately had to inspect their own gear because of the time limit. Milson wanted to depart from the *JFK* in fifteen minutes, knowing it would take a considerable amount of time to travel across the gulf, while trying to pick up Troy and his men, and then reach the outskirts of Khorramshahr while they still had the cover of night before the sun rose around six o'clock in the morning. Palmer had the *JFK* driving at 50 knots (equivalent to 57.54 mph), considerable given that her top speed was only 40 to 45 knots. She was able to squeeze some more juice out of her turbines with the aid of her state-of-the-art nuclear reactor.

Milson and Marin were going over the plans in more detail, standing on a platform above the two boats. They each knew that they had only a limited amount of time to make it into Iranian territory without being detected by either aerial or surface radar nets. After concluding their private briefing, Marin called everybody to attention, emphasizing that they should listen to what Milson was about to announce.

"All right, everybody, listen up! We've got a QRF [quick response force] mission to perform! We have exactly ten minutes before we get under way and leave the nest! Chief Milson is about to give us our SOP and sitrep! Pay close attention, because he's only going to say it once!" Marin gave Milson the floor as he cleared his throat to speak.

"You all know what's going on, so I shouldn't have to tell you what's at stake. The only thing we need to worry about is getting in and out of there alive. Everything else is secondary to me besides catching my target package and taking him back to the States. The mission I've been designated to oversee is called Operation Executive Bounty. It consists of the apprehension of a naval intelligence officer by the name of Lieutenant Commander Ad-dam Omar Assad, who went rogue three weeks ago. Assad is responsible for stealing highly classified materials from the Department of Defense and the Pentagon's archives. I and my team have been tracking this guy for weeks. He's been slipping in and out of various countries to hide, but he screwed up in Dubai because he got too comfortable. Now he's on his way to a country that he thinks is safe for him. Big mistake! We're going to extract a Delta Force team from a secluded pickup spot along the Kuwaiti shoreline near to where we need to go. Then we're going to travel up a canal channel that leads to a riverbank.

This river is within Iran's borders. After we penetrate their defenses, we'll set up a temporary perimeter, possibly along a riverbank on the border between Kuwait and Iran. Delta Force is going to set up the perimeter while a third of Commander Marin's squad accompanies me and my team to the city of Khorramshahr. Thanks to a little luck, Agent Weaver, to my right, the CIA liaison of this mission, got a tip a few minutes ago from one of his Kuwaiti-slash-Iraqi SIS contacts, who informed him that the HVT [High-Value Target] identified as Commander Assad was headed toward the designated area to meet with the terrorist group personally! But the meeting is going to take place somewhere outside the city, although the location is still unknown. But they'll have the intel for us when we get there. Weaver's contact knows that he is an HVT wanted by the United States, but he doesn't know the intricacies of his crimes. The big bosses in Washington and Langley want to keep it that way! We're going to meet up with this individual so he can show us where it will transpire. Commander Marin, I, and Ms. Asherah, the young lady you see before you"—Milson pointed directly at her— "who is also familiar with the target, will be going in under cover. We all know the area, and we all can speak Arabic. Everybody else will be both our backup and our eyes and ears out there. Once I identify the target as Commander Assad, I will apprehend him without hesitation. We have two backup plans for escape. The first way is to use the tunnels the Kuwaitis built years ago connecting the two borders, and the second is helicopter pickup, where we will be traveling in four Seahawks with stealth capability. You all know we may encounter resistance from either the Iranians or the terrorists, so there's going to be some CQC [Close-Quarter Combat or Close-Quarter Contingencies] involved! But this will not be a problem; I know all of you will do your jobs to defend yourselves and your shipmates. The problem will be if one of us gets captured by the Iranians or the terrorists. Each of us has been trained to handle scenarios like this, and we're quite aware of the circumstances and the risks that go along with what we're doing. It's not an easy thing to think about and not a pretty possibility to comprehend. But we are no strangers to such dangerous situations and last-minute missions. That is the reason we do the jobs that no one else can do or wants to do! Because we are the ones who have the guts to do it without question! I'm not going to go into a long, tired-ass speech about duty, honor, God, and country, because it's pointless to do so and we just don't have time for it! But what I am going to say to all of you is this: let's go in, get this guy, and get the hell out of there! That's all, people. Let's go to work!"

When Marin saw that Milson was done, he stepped in to give his final say.

"All right, you heard the man! You've got your sitrep, and you know what to do! We've got five minutes left! Get your shit squared away and prepare to get in gear! Let's move!"

Everybody scrambled like a horde of ants around a dirt mound to get to their positions. The ones who had been assigned to their own boats got on board immediately and made last-minute preparations for their departure, including tying down their essential equipment. The ship's remaining crew, who were helping with the outfitting and readiness of the two stealth boats, mechanically aligned the craft on the top of a unique catapult launcher specially designed for deploying small high-speed boats like the ones they were on, the boats obviously located beneath the hangar deck in the rear. The *JFK* was outfitted with this unique style of hangar deck designed specifically to carry, take in, and deploy small boats from the rear. The naval engineers at Norfolk and the admiralty at the Pentagon thought that this design would be beneficial for strategic operations such as the one that is currently being carried out as of now, as well as for emergency procedures if the case were to be made to abandon ship, or in the event of some other catastrophic circumstance, such as the sinking or scuttling of the ship.

The Mk1's were lined up, facing a huge retractable hangar door, and being lowered down into the waters made choppy by the *JFK*'s turbine propellers. Both the SEALs and Milson's team were strapped in and ready to go. The pilots of the two boats were both E-6 petty officers with the necessary qualifications to operate the classified machines. There were also two full-grade lieutenants acting as their skippers (captains of the boats), providing supervisory control. With the water rushing in halfway to allow for buoyancy and support between the two vessels once the steel door had made its touchdown, both lieutenants ordered their NCOs to start up the engines. At first, the roar from the combustible machinery was deafening, but later it smoothed out to a quiet humming or hissing sound, equivalent to a loud whisper if you were up close. The Mark 1's engines were very sophisticated and built magnificently. Each was a high-powered 2 × 2285 MTU-12V396, TE94 turbine, which of course was developed by Norfolk, but later it was redesigned and reintroduced at Maine Marine Manufactures LLC, located at the University of Maine's Advanced Engineering Composite Center. These engines were state-of-the-art and highly advanced, not to mention their stealth capabilities for radar detection.

Once the boats were ready to launch, Captain Cartwright, standing on top of the observation platform, looked down at one of the senior chiefs who oversaw the deck and signaled him to prepare the boats for deployment.

The chief acknowledged by getting on the microphone to contact both vessels.

"SOC-1 and SOC-2, this is Dockmaster Control. Are you ready for departure? Over."

Both lieutenants got on their receivers to answer the chief, one at a time.

"Roger that, Dockmaster. This is SOC-1. We are ready to depart."

"Same here, Control. This is SOC-2. We are also ready to get under way."

The chief looked up at Cartwright to give him the thumbs-up. The XO acknowledged with a quick nod of approval as he stared down at both vessels to watch them leave. The chief got back on the mic to give them the signal to get under way.

"SOC-1 and SOC-2, you are cleared to launch."

"Roger that, Chief. We are go!" both officers said simultaneously.

The first Mark 1, which had the SEALs, revved up her engines and took off at high speed with the help of the catapult underneath her keel. The second one, with Milson and his party, did the same as it jetted out of the boat hangar, leaving a wake. Both boats sped off into the darkness of the night without a single running light on. Each was traveling at a speed of sixty-five knots or better to make time to pick up the Deltas and reach the Iranian coastline. They left the *JFK* so fast that it looked as if the carrier had just spit them out like two torpedoes from a submarine. As the hangar door began to retract, Cartwright called up to the bridge to inform Palmer that Milson and the SEALs were under way. "Bridge, XO!" Cartwright shouted.

"XO, this is bridge. Palmer here. Are the sharks away, Captain?"

"Aye, aye, Skipper. They just left a second ago."

"Very well. I'll have the CIC monitor them and track their movements. But once they move beyond our range and activate their stealth, they're on their own."

"Acknowledged, sir. I just hope they get in and get out without any problems, Admiral."

"Same here, Ron. Same here. Come on back upstairs."

"Aye, aye, sir! On my way!"

Cartwright handed the radio receiver to a sailor standing next to him and stepped off the platform hastily. He walked up to a ramp that led to a nearby hatch on the left side, through which he made his exit. As the *John F. Kennedy* traveled forward to its destination at full speed, the two stealth boats, colored in such a way to make them invisible, continued cutting through the choppy waters of the Persian Gulf at high speeds, the night sky helping to mask their identity.

CHAPTER 10

ENDGAME OF THE HUNT

Karun River, Iranian Coastal Waters, 5:10 a.m.

Milson's boat picked up Troy and his men around four thirty that night at the designated area. Though it was almost morning, the two crafts were still fortunate to have the night atmosphere cloaking them as they quietly entered Iranian territory waters. They had had several close calls with two IRIS Sabalan Alvand-class frigates and three Parvin-class patrol boats, part of the Iranian Islamic Republican Naval Fleet, but were extremely lucky to have had the stealth technology at their disposal as they deepened their trek into hostile waters, escaping detection by the Iranian surface fleet. They came upon several river canals along the gulf's shoreline that split into different fork channels, but only one of these led to the main riverbank, where the water flowed to the Karun River. These channels were obviously waterways leading to both the Tigris and Euphrates. Milson knew he had to take the right one if he were to guide them straight to the city of Khorramshahr and get in touch with Weaver's SIS contact, at which time they could get a head start on Assad by finding the exact location where he was to meet the terrorists. Milson had instructed the boat's skipper to follow the course that had been laid out by the GPS mapping system given to him by Marin and one of his men, both of whom had determined the precise routes they were going to take when they were aboard the *John F. Kennedy*. Marin advised Milson that it would be easier for both groups to go through the narrowest channel along the bank in order not to be seen or detected. They followed the nautical route for thirty to forty-five minutes, and successfully penetrated the Iranian riverbank as planned. Both crafts slowed to a crawl as they drifted into the harbor. Even though it was still dark out, and though the operations of the boats made them damn near invisible, there was still a lot of traffic flowing up and down the river, mostly commercial shipping vessels, but also a portion of military crafts, small coast guard boats, and frigates. There was nothing too large because the river was not broad and could not accommodate full-size ships. Marin's boat and Milson's boat both had to travel very close to one of the shores to prevent them from being spotted by the merchant and naval ships sailing on the river.

As their crafts tiptoed along the side of the channel, they came upon a unique bank that was empty of shipping traffic. It was secluded. To Milson and many others, this was the perfect spot to disembark and set up their operation. The skippers of both boats managed to turn their vessels to the side and close the distance between the boat and the shore, stopping several yards away from shore for the teams to disembark safely and secretly. Each member of the two teams grabbed gear and equipment and rushed off the boat to secure a position on the grassy beach. One of the lieutenants, the captain of Milson's boat, informed Milson that they had to leave immediately before being discovered by the Iranian navy.

"Chief, you have to move fast. The sun will be rising in about thirty minutes from now, meaning we don't have much night cover left to make our escape from Iranian waters. We will make it out of the channel and the canal, but we're going to be visible along the coast."

"Will you still be able to jam their radar?" Milson said in a whisper.

"Yes, most definitely. The boat's outer skin is designed for that. It's coated with a magnetic material that prevents radar detection, but the real problem is them seeing us physically. You saw how many ships we had to duck in order to get in here. We've got to go now, Chief," said the young lieutenant, who was in much of a hurry.

"Yes, go. Get out of here. After the SEALs and Deltas set up the perimeter, we'll make radio contact with the *JFK* on a low-frequency, secure channel. Thanks for the trip, Lieutenant, and good luck getting back safe."

"Same to you, Chief. And get that bastard," the young officer said with an encouraging tone.

"Roger that, Lieutenant." Milson gave the officer a swift handshake and jumped off the boat. He and Troy were the last ones to leave. They made it to the beach and rejoined their teams. All three leaders and their squads watched the two stealth boats leaving the area quietly and quickly to escape detection. All the supervisors got together to discuss their mission, hoping to draw up a plan of attack for contacting their source and entering into the city limits. Milson and Weaver were the first ones to bring up hypothetical scenarios illustrating how they were going to proceed.

"Okay, guys, judging from the GPS, we're twenty to twenty-five miles outside the city limits. We can see the lights from here, so that means we're not that far."

"But we're going to need some transportation to get in there. We obviously can't do this on foot. We're sitting ducks when we're out in the open like this," Troy said.

"That won't be a problem, Major—"

Weaver interrupted, saying, "I got ahold of my SIS contact, who is in Khorramshahr right now. I told him where we're at and how many of us are here. He's going to arrive with several vehicles and some of his own men. He knows exactly where we are and knows of a possible location where Assad and the terrorists are going to meet."

"This SIS agent you know, Agent Weaver, do you have confidence and trust in him?" Marin asked with concern.

Fuller put his opinion in,

"Aye, mate. Remember my guy at the embassy who was my right-hand man? Look what happened in that situation. Are you sure this one is on the level, Jimmy boy?"

Weaver answered both their questions with,

"I hope so, gentlemen. I personally trained this guy when he and a lot of his peers were exchange officers from the Kuwaiti military working in intelligence. Both Iraq and Kuwait sent several of their personnel over to the Farm and to Langley so they could learn from us how to be proficient spies and watch dogs to their next-door neighbors—Iran, Syria, and Turkey."

"Well, that answers my first question, Agent Weaver. Now my second one is, how long will it take for him to get here? The time is five twenty-five in the morning, and that sun is creeping up over the horizon very fast. We're going to be ass-out visible in a matter of minutes if we don't get some cover soon," said Marin.

Everyone in the huddle agreed with Marin. Although the brushy vegetation of the grassy field gave them temporary cover in the little amount of darkness they had left, they desperately needed to get out of view while they still had the element of surprise in their favor. As they continued to discuss their predicament, one of Marin's men came to alert them to something peculiar. "Skipper! Jackson spotted several cars coming our way from the east, three clicks out. Their range is about three thousand meters from us, and they're closing in fast."

"Three thousand meters? That's about a mile and a half from where we are," Milson replied with concern.

At that moment, they all looked up simultaneously to take a peek from the bushes, hoping to see for themselves. Marin, who was overly concerned about the oncoming guest, pulled a set of compact digital binoculars from his cargo pants pocket and pressed them against his face, hoping to get a closer look at the vehicles coming their way.

"Yeah, it's confirmed. We've got company, people. There are six of them coming up on us. Three dark-colored sedans and three SUVs. These guys are traveling in style," Marin said in a whisper.

"That's him!" said Weaver with excitement.

"That's my guy! He's here, fellas!"

"Not so fast!" replied Marin, who instantaneously became cautious.

"We just can't pop up and give away our position. We have to know for sure if it's really your man."

"He's right, James," Milson said.

"We can't take the risk even though we're naked out here. Call him on your phone to see if that's him coming this way."

Weaver quickly acknowledged both men by taking out his satellite phone and dialing the encrypted number from his memory file. He waited for a few seconds, holding the phone up to his ear with his left hand while grappling with a Beretta ARX-160 assault rifle in his right. This was the weapon that had been issued to him from Fuller's armory back at the embassy. Weaver waited for a few seconds, which felt like minutes to the rest of the group, who were looking on. "Enif? Is this you?" Weaver asked cautiously.

"Yes, it's me. Where are you?" asked the voice over the phone.

"Several clicks down to your right. You're coming our way now. We see you. Flick your lights if that's you." Surprisingly, the lights of the oncoming vehicles flashed on and off as if signaling in code. "It's him!" Weaver shouted, jumping up from his squatting position and taking flight toward the incoming vehicles.

Everyone else stayed in their positions, including Milson, Marin, Troy, and Fuller, who were still wary and suspicious. As all six cars gradually slowed and came to a complete stop only a few yards away from the group, who all had their guns drawn and pointed toward the vehicles as they stayed hidden within the brush, Weaver cautiously walked up to the lead vehicle with his own weapon drawn just in case. As they all looked on in anticipation at Weaver and the six vehicles that stood in their crosshairs, the front passenger door of the first car opened, and an individual emerged. Milson and everyone else looking on saw Weaver give a friendly embrace to the individual, who reciprocated with the identical gesture. Then Weaver turned around and walked back, the new person following right behind him.

"Gentlemen, we're good," Weaver said. He sounded exhausted from his short trip, proving that he was out of shape.

"Killian, Commander, Major, this is Enif Saiph of the Kuwaiti/Iraqi Security Intelligence Service. He's our guide to the city, and he knows the whereabouts of our target."

They all shook Saiph's hand and introduced themselves one at a time. After the greetings had been exchanged, Saiph informed them that he had made arrangements for them in a secluded location and that they had to leave immediately.

"It is a pleasure to meet all you gentlemen, but we have to move quickly before the sun rises. The Islamic Republic of Iran Army, with the assistance of the IMMP [Islamic Military Militia Police, otherwise known as the Islamic Republic of Iran Police Agency], does routine patrols in this vicinity quite often. They're scheduled to patrol this area within the next twenty minutes. I strongly advise you and your men to gather your things and head toward the vehicles that await you."

Without argument or hesitation, the SF leaders of both groups ordered their men to head for the six vehicles. Each group swiftly and silently sprinted from the brushy, grassy field and dashed quickly to the confines of the Kuwaitis' automobiles. It was uniquely fortunate and profoundly coincidental that Saiph had brought the correct number of vehicles to transport the Special Forces group. If he had brought fewer vehicles, then things would have been problematic, to say the least, because of the large number of special op troops and the added personnel of Milson's team. It took them only seconds to throw their equipment into the trunks of the vehicles and then get in. When Saiph saw that everyone was in the vehicles, he quickly signaled to the lead car to move out. All six headed out quickly, leaving dust and dirt behind them. The darkness started to fade rapidly as the sun began to rise. After ten minutes had elapsed, four military vehicles with Iranian markings came over the hilly horizon and started their routine patrol of the area. These were obviously the Iranian military whom Saiph was talking about. Two of them were ground force units, identified as soldiers of the IRGC (Islamic Revolutionary Guard Corps), and the second two were definitely the IMMPs. One of them stopped to notice the tracks that the tires of Saiph's cars had left behind, but he did not put much thought into their meaning. At the time, such information was irrelevant and insignificant to Saiph because many vehicles, both military and civilian, travel in and out of this area with great frequency. Both the IRGC and IMMP nonchalantly continued their patrol, ignorant of the fact that American clandestine forces had landed on their soil.

Kuwaiti/Iraqi SIS Safe House outside Khorramshahr, Iran, 7:31 a.m.

The teams had coordinated their efforts with the SIS personnel the moment they arrived. Saiph had established a temporary secluded safe house on the outskirts of the city, about ten miles away from the prying eyes of the natives. As each member of the SEAL and Delta Force team was preparing their equipment and weapons for combat readiness, Milson and the others were discussing their plan for finding and capturing Assad. The discussion between the six of them got a little intense.

Saiph was the first to state his opinion as he announced,

"No, no, no, Agent Milson! That'll be suicidal! The best way for us to go in and get your man is for several of my agents to infiltrate the terrorists and bring Assad out into the open without blowing our cover. If you and your spec-op teams go in with your guns blazing, you'll be identified instantly, and your whole team, including you, will be slaughtered on the spot. We know the area and the background of this city, and we're very familiar with its occupants from previous dealings with the Iranian government and their military forces. We know how they work and how they operate. I and my men have been operating deep under cover within Iranian borders for years. Kuwaiti's SIS forces, in a joint effort with the Iraqi Intelligence Service and Israel's Mossad [Israeli Intelligence and Special Operation Forces], have been watching over the Iranians for years, ever since Iran announced that it had the means to develop its own nuclear arsenal. And if there is an alliance between Iran and this terrorist organization, we should be the first to know about it, and we should discover how to dismantle the organization if the intelligence is accurate."

"Saiph, I'm not disagreeing with you," Milson said.

"On the contrary, I think your expertise in Iranian intelligence is extremely helpful. All I'm saying is that both Marin's and Troy's team will be our safeguard in and outside the city and will be useful in the long run when the proverbial shit really hits the fan out there. You mustn't assume that these terrorists don't have some muscle backing them up, either their own guys or some borrowed from the Iranians. We are clueless about who they really are, what their agenda is, and what type of strategy they'll use in a combat situation. The SEALs and the Deltas are our best weapons for reinforcement and engagement. You can't deny the validity of this statement, and you can't say that this plan to go in and take a terrorist collaborator such as Assad by force would be a solid one without reliable backup. Furthermore, I have my own secret weapon stashed away." Milson pointed in the direction of Asherah, who was in the next room, in the company of Sheppard and several other members of the SEAL and Delta troops, who obviously found her quite appealing given her attractiveness.

"What? You're relying on a woman for the success of this entire mission? What type of intelligence does she have other than knowing the perpetrator personally?" Saiph said with conviction.

"Agent Saiph, that woman is the key to getting Assad. Not only can she ID him, but also, she has the info we need to smoke out this terrorist cell that nobody knows anything about. She also has certain intel that is valuable to us. By using this leverage to our advantage, we, along with you and your government, can solve the mystery shrouding this terrorist organization that has eluded us for who knows how long. I presume that you would welcome this opportunity to be of benefit to your own SIS and to the Kuwaiti and Iraqi governments."

Milson, who was playing to Saiph's psyche and ego, hoped that this comment would sway the proud Iraqi agent who was working for both governments.

"Okay, Agent Milson, you have brought up a compelling argument, and what you say is reasonable. But I must insist that several of my men accompany each of your teams as a precautionary measure, in case something goes wrong."

Milson looked over at both Marin and Troy to get their opinion. Both officers stared at each other, then looked back at Milson. They gave their approval with a nod of the head, each agreeing to the conditions and terms of the partnership.

As they continued their briefing, Troy brought up an issue of great importance.

"Well, since we've gotten that out of the way, what about those tunnels we talked about earlier? Me and my guys brought some equipment with us to determine how deep they are and how far they go."

"That won't be necessary, Major Troy. I have all the information you need about them." Saiph called one of his men to attention by snapping his fingers. The man brought a map that showed the precise coordinates of the underground tunnels.

"There are six or seven tunnels stretching along Iran's borders, coming from the north and going all the way down to the southern tip. Five of these are along Iraq's eastern border. Two are in the north, one is in the middle, and the other two are in the south. The two up north are in the small remote towns of Rayat and Khurmal. The one at the eastern border is in Badrah, and the two down south are close to Jasib al-Muftan and Shaykh Faris. Now the two that stretch along the Iraqi border and into the northern territory of Kuwait are located right here at Abu al-Khasib and at-Tannumah, Iraq. The first five tunnels to have been constructed were used for covert purposes under Saddam Hussein when he went to war with Iran fifty years ago. The last two were built for the same purpose, but after Saddam invaded Kuwait in the early 1990s, the Kuwaiti rebels took control of the tunnels and used them for their own purposes, especially when the Americans came over to help liberate the Kuwaiti people."

"Are they still in use today?" asked Marin, who was intrigued. He had been adamant about the tunnels when he first brought the subject up during the briefing aboard the *JFK*.

"I don't think so, Commander," Saiph said.

"At least the ones I know of in Iraq are not. Three out of the five were dismantled by the Iraqi government during the old regime. The other two, in the south, still exist but are unusable. But I know for sure that the two we have right next door to us are open and usable. In fact, Abu al-Khasib is right across the river from us. It's a little more than twenty-two kilometers from Khorramshahr."

"That's almost fourteen miles away from us. Do you think we can we make it over there after grabbing Assad?" Weaver asked with a little uneasiness in his voice.

"Not on foot. Of course not," said Milson.

"But if we use the transport that brought us here from the riverbank"—Milson looked over at Saiph, hinting that he should recommend they use the same vehicles that picked them up, giving him a small nod of gratitude and appreciation to go with it— "we will have a chance of getting over there in one piece."

"Say no more, Agent Milson. I've already made arrangements for my cars to take you there. The real problem is going to be getting out of there in one piece, as you say," said Saiph.

"Even if you successfully snatch up your target, you very well know, as does everyone else in this room, that the terrorists will have backup of their own. And if they're smart, which we hope they're not, they're going to be prepared and waiting for you."

"That's why we're here, Agent Saiph," said Marin as he continued.

"So, if there are any surprises from our terrorist friends or the Iranian army, my SEALs will be the first ones to burst their bubble."

"Along with my Deltas, who will pull QRF immediately with a full cover strike to finish the job, then pick up the pieces," Troy said, following Marin's analogy with one of his own.

Saiph shook his head repeatedly.

"Wow, so the stories are true about you guys. You Americans are such cowboys. Shoot 'them up, take no prisoners, and all that, huh?" said the sniffling Kuwaiti agent, who was being haughty in his own right.

The proud squad leaders just looked across at each other and answered simultaneously, "Yippee ki yay!" This time everybody shook their heads and laughed hysterically. But soon things became serious again as Milson reiterated the importance of getting out of Iran alive.

"Well, guys, even if getting across the river and to the tunnels is feasible, I still don't want to rule out our other escape plan. The birds will be our best and last alternative if those tunnels fail. Agreed?" Everyone nodded yes to agree with Milson, including Saiph and Marin.

Later from that moment, one of Troy's men interrupted.

"Major, Commander! We have comms up. We've got the *JFK* on a VLF [very low-frequency] channel. They're asking about our sitrep, sir."

Troy and Marin dismissed themselves from the briefing to answer the radio call. The ones left standing around the table were Milson, Saiph, Fuller, and Weaver, who continued their discussion about strategically measuring the mission.

Saiph was a bit skeptical, thinking that too many resources had been made available to capture a man wanted only for a felony, according to what Weaver and the CIA had told him. He brought his misgiving to Milson's attention, saying,

"Mr. Milson, I'm curious. For an individual such as this Commander Assad who is wanted for murder, you sure do have a lot of manpower at your disposal. It's hard for me to believe that an operation of this size and importance is necessary to capture only one man who has committed but one felony in your country. Surely this individual must be of much greater importance than what you and Weaver have told me."

Fuller and Weaver were perplexed at the insinuation. They glanced over in Milson's direction, knowing very well where this conversation was going. Milson, also knowing this, looked up from the table and stared across at Saiph.

"Be honest with me, Mr. Milson. The United States government would not draw on all its resources to build two of the most highly trained and highly classified elite spec-op groups, including four field agents; one of whom is an MI6 agent, to go along and sneak into a country that is considered hostile territory to the Americans and their allies just to catch one man who has killed several people. This man must have done something far worse than what you've been telling me. I believe that I have a right to know what you know, despite my title and my security clearance. I've been with the Kuwaiti and Iraqi Security Intelligence Service long enough to know when someone is, how do you Americans say it, snowballing me. Don't forget, I know how the CIA works and what they're capable of. James was my teacher for two years when I was over there, so I know the tricks of the trade. What did Assad really do apart from taking a few innocent lives?"

The silence in the little room was almost scary when compared to the continuous chatter in the occupied space next door. One could have literally heard a pin drop. Weaver and Fuller remained immovable and mute after the surprising comments made by Saiph. They continued to stare across at Milson, who remained steadfast and relaxed. They knew Milson could not divulge the truth of Assad's crimes to Saiph, which was the reason they were there in the first place, besides his knowing the identity of the terrorist organization that Assad was about to meet. Everyone there, including Fuller, had orders not to reveal the details. Each of them waited for Milson's reaction, anticipating a strong and boastful response from the gritty bounty hunter. But even though the situation was tense from Weaver and Fuller's perspective, Milson did not seem stressed or flustered. He looked calmly across at Saiph and answered only him in Arabic, which was both satisfying and refreshing to the Iraqi agent. Of course, Weaver could not comprehend the Arabic language, but Fuller could, thanks to his years of work with the UAE government and the British Embassy in Abu Dhabi.

The conversation between the two started with Milson saying,

"Agent Saiph, I'm not here to BS you. The service you have provided in assisting us has been most beneficial, and we are very appreciative. It would be stupid on my part to deceive you in such a way that would cause our relationship to turn sour. You are our partner and ally in this war against terrorism. But the circumstances of my mission and the bounty I'm responsible for are of top priority and outweigh any meaningless concerns of foreign relations or any other international coalition or affiliation to certain dignitaries and their employees (speaking mostly on the political and diplomatic side). This man, Commander Assad, is both dangerous and important. His job was counterintelligence for the navy until he became a fugitive. So, you know why he is important to the United States and why they want him back. He is a cold, calculating SOB who is wanted for four counts of murder, three of which are murder in the first degree. The other case involves evidence that is circumstantial at best. Those lives he took are of special concern to certain parties at the top, whom I am not permitted to name at this time. But I can tell you that one of them is a relative of an ONI officer. I say with all due respect that all you need to know is that I am under orders from the president of the United States, the secretary of defense, the secretary of the navy, the director of the CIA, and the director of ONI. That right there should tell you how important this man is and how vital my mission to catch him is. Now, if you want to speculate and offer conspiracy theories or anything else to satisfy your curious mind, then you go right ahead. But the mission that I and my colleagues have been entrusted with, to apprehend this guy, is of the utmost importance. I will not let anyone who feels differently about it stand in the way. Now, if you don't agree with what I said, Agent Saiph, then I am truly sorry. But I hope it doesn't persuade you against helping me and the others, because truthfully, I need you and your people to help us catch this son of a bitch and hopefully bring him to justice."

The room fell quiet again after Milson had spoken his piece. Saiph stood motionless at the other end of the table, staring hard at Milson. Fuller and Weaver, on the other hand, were standing in shock like a captive audience watching an outstanding performance. They did not know how to react to this uncomfortable situation. One could feel the tension in the air as the two combatants hurled verbal assaults at each other. But it was not as confrontational as it seemed. In fact, the verbal sparring resulted in a mutual sense of respect. This was especially true for Saiph, who found Milson's honesty refreshing. He stood upright from his slouched position and said,

"I appreciate your candor and honesty, Mr. Milson. I also appreciate that you addressed me in my native tongue. In my past dealings with American agents such as those from the aforementioned CIA, no one has ever communicated to me like you have with such detail and proficiency. I applaud you on your knowledge of my language and your fluency in speaking it. How did you come to speak Arabic so well?"

"My tours as a young soldier in Iraq. I also studied foreign languages in college and took several mind-blowing trips to Saudi Arabia, Egypt, Libya, and other places in North Africa while a student, all funded by the Central Intelligence Agency," Milson replied facetiously. Saiph laughed at the sarcastic statement.

"Mr. Milson, I have to say that I do like you. Your honesty is very refreshing. You are the first American other than James who has shown true integrity toward me, and for that I give you my sincere appreciation. Even though you work for an agency that tells lies for a living, no offense, I do appreciate your candor in this matter," Saiph said with a tone of solace.

"No offense taken. And just so you know, Agent Saiph, I don't work for the company anymore. I'm strictly freelance. My contract is through naval intelligence, but all I am is a local bail enforcement officer who works for a criminal retrieval agency located in the state of Maryland with special skills that I've acquired from being in the army and the agency—you know, tricks of the trade as you said earlier," Milson replies.

Again, Saiph snickered at the remark. Everyone around the table, including Fuller, laughed, except for Weaver, who couldn't understand Arabic. Weaver, like Milson, is also fluent in several languages, but Arabic was not one of them. For a moment, he felt left out as the group. Feeling irritated, he said,

"All right, guys, the joke's over. Can we all please speak in a language that everyone in this room, including me, is familiar with and can understand?"

"Oh, pipe down, Jimmy boy. You're being ridiculous. I remember four years ago when you and I were stationed in China. You spoke Chinese nonstop in front of those Hong Kong delegates for an entire week, and you bloody well knew I couldn't understand a word of it," Fuller replied, still laughing.

"First of all, it was Mandarin. Second, it was in front of the president and prime minister of China, during the peace talks hosted by the UN and UEA. And third, I was a translator. So, in my opinion, it is very rude to speak in a language that other people don't fully understand," Weaver replied with emotion.

"Oh, quit your whining, you bloody git, and grow a pair," Fuller said. Everyone laughed.

While each of them was taking potshots at Weaver, Marin came over to give them some important news.

"Gentlemen, we've got the *John F. Kennedy* online. Admiral Palmer wants to speak to all of us ASAP."

Without any hesitation, they each dashed out of the room and into the next one. Saiph's people and Troy's Deltas had calibrated a sophisticated communications setup with banks of laptops, radio communicators, and GPS locators that made the underground facility of MICROSCOPE in Langley look like a two-bit electronics store. They had an image of Palmer on a twenty-inch flat-screen monitor that was hooked up to a communications scrambler in case someone was listening in on their conversation and tied in on their frequency. As all of them surrounded the screen, looking at the high-definition image of the admiral's face, Palmer said,

"Chief Milson, are you there?!"

"Yes, Admiral, I'm here, along with Commander Marin, Major Troy, and the rest of us."

"Good! I'm glad to see that all of you made it! Any trouble getting in?"

"No, sir. We sneaked passed their patrol boats and made it to the shore unscathed. We were picked up instantly by Agent Saiph and his men of the Iraqi Intelligence Service. We're now at a safe house near the city of Khorramshahr. We're coordinating our plans to get Assad as we speak. Did the stealth boats make it back?"

"They made it out of Iranian waters but didn't get to us in time. But they were lucky to have made it to neutral waters, to a safe haven port that's part of Kuwaiti territory."

"That's good to hear, Admiral. We're about thirty minutes away from executing Operation Executive Bounty. The intelligence that we've gathered from Agent Saiph puts us in a good position to get Commander Assad, sir."

"I'm glad to hear that, Chief, because I've got some important people on the other line who want to talk to you and your posse! Commander Sloan, tie them into this communication!"

"Aye, aye, sir!" said the voice of Sloan in the background as he patched in another transmission linkup. The screen that held Palmer's image split into two as another face came into view. But in fact, it was several faces being projected on the small monitor.

"Milson, we have you connected to the Pentagon. I hope you're scrambling this transmission on your end, son."

"Yes, sir, we are. The Deltas and the SEALs have rigged up a communications depot on our end that is allowing you to piggyback on an Iranian frequency that they're not aware of. We're scrambling the call so they can't listen in," said Milson.

"Good to hear, son! You already know Admiral Cooper, and Director Richards of the CIA. Meet the secretary of defense, Todd Miller, and the president's national security adviser, Mr. Shawn Atkinson."

Milson addressed them properly, giving each of them their due respect. Then he introduced Marin and Troy, along with Fuller, Weaver, and Sheppard, who were standing right beside him. After the pleasantries from both sides were done, Palmer got right down to business, mentioning why the president's cabinet wanted to communicate with Milson and his party.

"Chief, the secretary and Mr. Atkinson want a sitrep about your mission."

Milson cleared his throat and said, "Admiral, Director, Mr. Secretary, and Mr. Atkinson, at this moment we're about to implement the operation. We have reliable intel that tells us the whereabouts of Commander Assad and the precise location of where he's going next. It's just a matter of time before we capture him and bring him back to the States."

Secretary Miller was the first to step in front of the screen to make his comments to Milson and his group.

"Mr. Milson, I don't have to tell you the importance of your mission, and I don't need to remind you that it must be successful. The president, his cabinet, and his military advisers have a meeting scheduled for early tomorrow morning with both the United Nations and the United Earth Administration's Council on International Affairs regarding foreign countries and their policies. The UN is finishing up its peace talks with the UAE and other middle eastern governments. Soon they'll be coming over here to talk about this selfsame subject. We're going to discuss nonintervention treaties and domestic and international policies related to dealings on foreign soil. Part of this involves noninterference with countries experiencing domestic disputes. No aid will be provided, whether military or humanitarian, unless authorization is given by the governing body of the respective country, and the UN and UEA will refrain from involving themselves diplomatically unless permitted. There are also other stipulations to be considered with this new agreement made by our allies. No other country or government will be allowed to deploy soldiers or military equipment to defuse or investigate foreign disputes or controversies unless permitted by said country or government. This means that military involvement, aid, or action of any kind, either publicly advertised or done in secret, will not be initiated in any foreign country under any circumstances without permission from the country itself or by way of international governing concession. I know this sounds like a lot of political bureaucratic nonsense and diplomatic bullshit, and you're probably wondering what this has got to do with you. But your mission of tracking down a fugitive wanted by the US government, who is in fact an officer of the United States Navy who has entered an Islamic country for reasons that are unknown, falls into the category I just described. The actions that you and your team are about to undertake will be described as unlawful, and it will be said that you entered Iran illegally according to this new policy, given the sanctions imposed by the UN and UEA. And your use of special operations forces (that is, US military personnel) to seize this individual in a foreign country will violate the terms of the agreement, which violation will carry special sanctions and other punishments for the United States and anyone who is partnered or involved with us, such as our English cousins across the Atlantic, who will suffer the same consequences as we. Any action undertaken without the permission of a higher authoritative body will not be tolerated, and violators will suffer immediate repercussions and punishments."

At that moment, Milson and everyone else standing around him in the communications area started to get agitated. All of them, including Fuller and Saiph, who were not subject to the US foreign policy rule, were frustrated as they heard this disappointing but policy making news.

Miller continued with his briefing to Milson, saying,

"That's why you have to catch this son of a bitch before this meeting takes place tomorrow. The president, I, and the chairman of the Joint Chiefs know about your operation, but the UN and the UEA do not. That's why you must apprehend Commander Assad before the deadline. This mission must be signed off on as being finished before any of this happens so we may be in the clear. And if we are asked about it later by anyone from either the UN or UEA, we will of course deny all involvement and feign ignorance. We will deny that we have any knowledge of the involvement of either US forces or independent individuals conducting military operations inside foreign countries without the consent of the UN and the UEA. The meeting will start at either eight or nine o'clock in the morning our time, and it will be held here at the White House. I understand that it's seven or eight o'clock in the morning over there?"

Milson responded,

"Yes, sir, it is. Quarter to eight in the morning to be exact, Mr. Secretary."

"Well, it's fourteen minutes to three in the afternoon over here. So, you've got plenty of time to get that bastard before the meeting takes place tomorrow morning. It's all about timing, gentlemen. And plausible deniability is our key for cleaning up this mess that Assad has put us in, Chief. Being a former CIA agent, you should know that phrase very well. You should also know of the responsibilities that accompany such denial, along with the consequences of invoking it."

With a smile that almost looked to be a reluctant smirk, Milson replied with an ineluctable,

"Yes sir, I most certainly do. It will be done."

Once Miller was finished, Shawn Atkinson brought himself into the proverbial spotlight.

"Chief Milson, I've been talking with Admiral Cooper and Director Richards about this thing with Lieutenant Commander Assad and your involvement in pursuing him. Both of them have told me that you are the right man for the job. They have the utmost confidence in you." Atkinson paused for only a second while the image of his face moved closer toward the screen, staring directly at it as if he were looking at Milson face-to-face.

"It's all on you, son. I know that this is a lot of pressure on you, and it's not going to be easy. But we have a lot riding on you. We need you to grab this guy without the Iranians or anybody else knowing about it. Don't screw it up, Mr. Milson. Get Assad, then get the hell out of that country before he starts World War III."

After that remark, Milson turned his head to look over at Weaver, Fuller, Sheppard, and everyone else who was standing around them. For a moment, it looked as if Milson was annoyed by Atkinson's comments, but surprisingly, he regained his composure and went back to the monitor. "Don't you worry, sir," he said.

"If anyone should know about screwups, it is our own intelligence department. Isn't that right, Director Richards?"

Given the oddity of the statement, Atkinson and Miller turned their heads simultaneously to look over in Richards's direction, hoping to find out what Milson was talking about. But the only reaction that they got from the presiding DCI was a look of confusion, frustration, and embarrassment. Richards was outraged by the remark made by the ex-CIA agent, but he dared not show his ire because he was presently in the company of the president's cabinet. Cooper, on the other hand, found it amusing and quite hilarious. Though it showed disrespect on Milson's part to oust a high-ranking official in front of others, no one on either side seemed to mind it at all, including the presiding secretary and the national security adviser.

Palmer intervened to give notice that the transmission linkup between the two parties would have to be terminated so that no foreign concern could trace or track the call. "Gentlemen, my communications officer is telling me that we have to discontinue this transmission on account of probable Iranian eavesdropping, even though the chief's team is scrambling the frequency. I will personally give you a sitrep on Chief Milson's progress and the mission."

"Very well, Admiral. We'll keep the channels open on our end. Mr. Milson, good luck and good hunting. And to all you men over there, God be with you. Come back safe." The image of Miller's face split and morphed into an image of the faces of the five men, which became one with Palmer's face, which ended up being the only face displayed on the screen.

"Jesus, Chief! Do you have a death wish or something? I can't believe you got away with talking to Richards like that in front of the SECDEF and the president's security adviser. Do you two have some sort of history with each other?" Palmer asked.

Milson drew a breath and sighed.

"In a manner of speaking, yes, sir, we do. The DCI was my boss five years ago when I was with the company. Back then, he was deputy director of my division and was responsible for my termination. So yes, Admiral, we do have a history together."

"Well, I feel your pain, son. Some individuals back in my day used to piss me off too. But sometimes you must swallow your pride, grit your teeth, and get past it in order to achieve your goal. Don't let one asshole shit on your parade. You know what to do and how to do it. Keep that in your head, and to hell with everybody else. If you stick with that, son, you'll have no problems down the road."

Milson chuckled and said, "Aye, aye, Admiral. I'll keep that in mind."

Palmer gave a salute and signed off immediately. After that, Milson told everyone, including the squad leaders of the SF teams, to get their gear ready for the mission. As he was speaking, he happened to glance over into the next room, where he spotted Asherah. Surprisingly, she was interacting with one of the SEALs, who was teaching her combat prep and combat skills on a one-to-one basis. It was not awkward or strange in the sense of being viewable by the public, but it did come off to Milson as a little peculiar. He went over to them and politely said,

"Excuse me, Petty Officer, I need to speak with Ms. Asherah alone. Give us a minute."

Without hesitation or question, the young SEAL gave a

"Yes, sir," followed by a gesturing nod. He walked out by closing the doors behind him to give them privacy.

Both the atmosphere and the conversation within the room was about to become intense. It was Milson who initiated the discussion, after second-guessing his decision, made hours ago, to let her come on this mission. Asherah replied to his concerns about her and the sailor,

"Killian, it's not how it looks. I am clueless about guns. The soldier was showing me some basic steps for handling and using these weapons. I've never had to use a gun before, so I asked him how one operates. It may have looked strange and suspicious, but I assure you, it was neither. It was purely innocent—well, on his part anyway." She chuckled a little, but Milson was not amused. He dismissed what she'd said and got down to the business at hand.

"Listen, Desiree, I'm not here for that. That sailor knows his place if he's done something inappropriate or wrong. And if his head is not on the mission because he is distracted by a pretty face, then his CO and NCO will have his ass in a sling and tear him a new one. I'm here because I think I may have made a mistake. I don't think it was a good idea to bring you with us. I think it would be safer for both of us if you were to stay here at the safe house with Saiph's men until we capture Ad-dam."

In an instant, Asherah got angry. The expression on her face said it all as it switched from pleasantry to outrage. She responded quickly, with furious intensity,

"What?! Are you freaking kidding me?! No, I'm coming with you! I didn't come all this way to stand on the sidelines to be babysit! I'm here to confront Ad-dam and ask him why he did those things then lied about it to my face! No, Killian, I'm going!"

Her rage did not cause Milson to back down or back away from his decision. He was resolute about what he said and was determined to explain the reasons why he had changed his mind. "This is not a game we're playing, Desiree. This is some serious shit that we're about to get into! And I'm not about to jeopardize your life just because you have some emotional concerns to convey to your boyfriend about honesty, trust, and commitment. This is bigger than you and your trust issues with Assad! This is about saving billions of lives and not starting a fucking war! Listen to me, Desiree, this is way too dangerous for you. The conflict of interest alone will cause this mission to become volatile. Never mind that you have no military skills, no military background, and not enough intelligence to handle yourself in a situation like this. I know I agreed to take you along, but now that I think about it, I believe I made a mistake. We're about to go up against a terrorist organization, and probably an entire nation, to apprehend a man who could possibly start World War III because of what he knows and who he is, not to mention the information he is willing to give to these people. The group he's selling to hates the Western world and anyone who is aligned or associated with it. I'm not about to risk the life of an innocent woman who really doesn't have a clue about what's going on and, quite frankly, does not belong here. You could get killed out there, lady. Again, I'm not about to take that chance. I've seen my share of death, and I'm not about to see it happen to someone who does not need to be put in such a position. I'm sorry, but you're staying here until we grab Assad and get him across the border. After that, the SIS can escort you to Kuwait and get you back to Holland, where you belong. You will not be tried criminally for your association with Assad—I will see to that personally—but you are not coming with us."

Asherah grew angrier by the minute. Very adamant and stubborn about going, she completely ignored Milson's explanations and excuses, even though he had attempted to display empathy and concern for her well-being. Asherah was so incensed that she lashed out at Milson, cutting him off.

"You've got some fucking nerve, Milson! I told you how I felt in confidence, and now you're throwing it back in my face?! You are such a self-righteous, hypocritical bastard! You think that this whole thing is about you and your goddamn mission to catch Ad-dam? Well, it's not! It's about a man who manipulated the system to get what he wanted, and he did it perfectly! And now you and your government are pissed off because he made fools out of all of you! Well, you should be pissed! Do you want to know why? Because you trusted a man who knew all your secrets and, at the same time, screwed y'all! Yes, a bitter pill to swallow, isn't it?! Now you know how I feel! I trusted a man who told me that he loved me and would never lie to me, but he did! And on top of that, he used me to get this far, then left me in the middle of a crowded shopping mall in Dubai to save his own ass! How in the hell am I supposed to feel about that? How in the hell should I take that, Milson? I have every right to be here, as much right as you and everyone else out there! I know what's at stake! I know the ramifications if Ad-dam successfully hands over the data and weapons! In a way, it's my fault because of my naivete. I knew what he was doing from the start. That's why I insisted on coming, not only so I can redeem myself, but also so I can find out the truth and determine the kind of man he really is." Asherah's voice began to calm. She moved closer toward Milson.

"Look, Killian, I have a lot invested in this, just as much as you, Weaver, Fuller, Sheppard, and the rest of those guys out there. You cannot shut me out now. Not now, not when we're so close. I need this. Please, don't take this away from me."

Though it seemed that she had concluded after stating her case before Milson, she had much different intentions. She looked at him in a peculiar way, then, without warning, lunged at him and gave him a long passionate kiss. At first, Milson was caught off guard by this. His instinct was to step back and extract himself from the fervent embrace, but soon, feeling the softness of her lips, he ceased all resistance. The embrace lasted for only a couple of seconds, but it seemed like minutes to both of them. In the fraction of time, it took for their sultry interaction, common sense and rationality started to take hold once more, and Milson automatically came to his senses. He discontinued the kiss by forcefully backing off and questioning the action that she exhibited.

"Wait a minute, Desiree. What is this? What are you doing? We can't do this."

At first, Asherah looked at Milson with confusion in her eyes, but she quickly realized the mistake she made. She felt both embarrassed and helpless. She was indeed attracted to Milson, but she had to come to terms with the fact that she still loved Assad despite what he had done and had put her through. Realizing what she was doing, she stepped back from Milson and paused for a moment. Apologizing quickly, she tried to explain her actions. But sympathetic as Milson was, especially now that he was feeling vulnerable and confused in the presence of such a beautiful woman, he dismissed her advances and accepted her apology, forgetting the whole thing. He was attracted to Asherah, but he could not afford to show it. To indulge in such appetites would bring disastrous consequences. So instead of consummating his feelings for her, he took hold of both her shoulders and caressed them softly, consoling her in a more professional, rational sort of way.

A quick knock came at the door. Without an invitation, Sheppard, opened the door wildly as he barged in. He could see that he was interrupting something. Although his curiosity was piqued, he dared not ask any questions.

"Excuse me, Chief. Sorry to bother you, but we've got verified intel on Commander Assad's location. Agent Saiph's men have located him and know where the meeting is going to take place."

"Thanks, Sheppard. I'll be right there." Sheppard was a little reluctant to leave because of his adolescent curiosity, but Milson gave him an eyeful that changed his mind very quickly.

Once Milson and Asherah were alone again, he told her to stay put while he went to check things out. But stubborn and impatient as Asherah was, she dismissed his request and followed right behind him.

Milson and Asherah made their way to the next room, where everybody was gathered. Once again, they were standing in a circle around the comms station, listening to a voice over the speakers that came through staticky and garbled. It was one of Saiph's men, reporting in by way of secure cell phone. After giving a detailed description of Assad, he named the location where he and the terrorists were going to meet. To everyone's surprise, especially Saiph's, the meeting was going to take place right near the border crossing between Iraq and Iran in Abadan, a small city located 10 kilometers (6.2 miles) south of Khorramshahr. Abadan was one of several county capital cities in the Khuzestan province of Iran and was home to one of the largest oil refinery facilities in the Islamic world. When Saiph heard this news, he was ecstatic. This was the perfect opportunity and the perfect location to seize Assad without causing too much collateral damage or bringing attention to themselves.

The Iraqi agent, who had been well briefed about the operation, wanted to know the identity of this mysterious terrorist group operating inside a Muslim country. In the process of digesting the new intel, Saiph instructed his men to stay hidden and to continue gathering as much information as they could. He then turned to the rest of his men and ordered them to get ready.

After observing his Kuwaiti counterpart's actions, Milson reacted in the same way, turning his attention to Marin and Troy, telling them to prepare their men for immediate action. Both men, acknowledging the request without hesitation, ordered their squads to get ready for the mission. Then Milson turned to Weaver, Fuller, and Sheppard to share with them the last-minute details and what would be expected of them.

With everyone scattered about and making preparations for the critical turning point, Asherah, who was standing at Milson's side, seemed bewildered and concerned. Watching in both anticipation and excitement as everyone took off in a frenzy, preparing themselves physically and mentally for the operation, Asherah felt a little antsy. She desperately wanted to be involved but had no way of including herself. But soon an idea popped into her head. She looked over at Milson, who was engaged in a conversation with Fuller, Weaver, and Sheppard about the operation. Without thinking twice, Asherah walked toward Milson and started tugging on his sleeve like a schoolgirl wanting attention from her parents. Still attending to his briefing with his coworkers, he gave Asherah a hand gesture signifying that he did not want to be bothered. Getting the message that he was regarding her as a nuisance, she continued trying to get his attention. Half attentively, he slapped her hand away several times as though she were a bothersome gadfly. Asherah did not give up. Although trying to ignore her, Milson found he could not. Giving in to her persistence, he turned around abruptly and said in a sharp tone,

"Jesus Christ, Desiree, can't you see that I'm busy here? What do you want?"

She responded, "I need to talk to you, Killian, now! It is important."

The aggravated bounty hunter looked at her with frustration, sighing in exhaustion. He then turned to his teammates and instructed them to stand by. As Fuller, Sheppard, and Weaver returned to their preparations, they watched Milson and Asherah walk outside to a secluded area free of onlookers and eavesdroppers. Asherah took the initiative to bring up something important that could help Milson and his group.

"Look, I know what you said back there, and I understand. But you must understand something as well. I have what Ad-dam wants, which is this flash drive." She pulled it out of her pocket and held it in front of him.

"The terrorists need this particular drive because of the info it holds about the undercover operatives. They cannot do anything until they have this drive. Even if Assad gives up the weapons, they still need the two drives as both devices have the original code settings and are digitally encrypted, and both are needed to establish a connection to download the information to their own system. He can't look up the information on a website because intel like this is heavily secured behind firewalls. The two drives together contain all the encryption codes the terrorists will need to access the info once Assad successfully hands them over. If they have one drive without the other, it'll be totally useless to them. And if it is useless to them, then they will definitely kill Assad on the spot. If he sees me, he will know that I have the other drive, which would slightly improve his chances. Please, Killian, let me come with you. You'll have a better chance of catching Assad and discovering who these people are if I'm there."

Again, Milson was reluctant. He kept shaking his head back and forth, a response of *no*. But in his mind, he could not dismiss the fact that what Asherah was saying made sense. Her going along was a terrible risk and was extremely dangerous, but it was an opportunity he could not afford to lose. Apprehending a naval intelligence officer who had gone rogue by threatening international war, and finding out the identity of this new global terrorist group that was a threat to global peace, was worth the risk of taking Asherah along, and Milson knew it. He looked at her one last time. She stared back at him. He said,

"Okay, Desiree, you win. You can come with us. But let me make something perfectly clear to you: you will do as I say at all times. No arguments, no suggestions. Whatever I say goes, understand?" Asherah nodded her head in agreement without a single objection.

"You stick with me like pollen to a bee. You don't wander off, and you don't take the initiative to do anything on your own. If you spot Assad, let me or the others know, and we'll take it from there. Understand?" She indicated her agreement with another nod of her head gesture, which satisfied Milson. When he was through stating his demands, he paused for a moment to consider the intricacies of the mission.

"Desiree, I'm asking you again, are you sure you want to do this? If we get Assad, you know you will not see him again for a very long time. I want you to be clear about the ramifications here. Assad will be incarcerated for life for conspiracy and espionage, and he will probably suffer the death penalty if found guilty of committing murder in the first degree. I understand your feelings for this man, but are you absolutely sure that you want to be present when we take him down? There's still time for you to back out if you want."

Milson gestured with his hands, inviting her to change her mind. In response, Asherah shook her head as she whispered,

"No. No, I want to do this, Killian. I need to do this. I need to see Ad-dam and ask him if everything we've been together was a lie. I'm going, and yes, I know what's at stake."

Milson shook his head and responded,

"All right. I'll talk to the others about this, but right now, I want you to go over there with Ensign Sheppard and have him prep you. Also, tell him that I want him to get with Commander Marin and his radio officer so they can hook you up with a special item I think you'll need." Asherah looked at Milson in a peculiar way, trying to figure what he meant by the term *special item*. He quickly satisfied her curiosity, saying,

"Look, don't worry. I see the confusion on your face. It's nothing to be concerned about. In fact, it's for your own safety. Trust me.

Besides, it will help us in the long run. Just tell Sheppard. He'll know what I'm talking about."

Asherah smiled enthusiastically at Milson and kissed him softly on his left cheek. When she rushed off in Sheppard's direction and began telling him what Milson wanted him to do, Milson just stood there staring at the beautiful, misguided, innocent young woman who had no clue of what was about to happen. He thought to himself, *she really doesn't know what she's getting herself into,* still having second thoughts about involving her. He was dazed, concerned about Asherah and the circumstances that lay ahead of them.

Fuller and Weaver broke Milson's concentration by walking up to him and asking to go over the last-minute details of the operation. Milson talked with them about his decision to include Asherah in the plan. Even though in the back of his mind he knew that this was a bad idea, he also knew that it was their only chance to capture Assad. But still, Milson could not shake the eerie feeling that something bad was going to happen out there. It was eating away at his conscience.

CHAPTER 11

SETUP OF THE HUNT

Abadan, Iran, 10:49 a.m.

The morning was turning to afternoon; Operation Executive Bounty was about to commence. Milson and the others had gotten to the city fifty minutes after the initial sighting of Assad had been verified by Saiph's undercover operatives. The community of Abadan was like any other town in the south of the Islamic Republic of Iran. Rich in history, with a culture influenced by Islam and also with a stunning landscape, Iran, victim of its past indiscretions, had become destitute after decades of conflict and war between Sunnis and Shiites, and war with Iraq in the 1980s, which lasted nine years. All this and more are what led Iran to become poverty-stricken.

Overflowing with natives whose families had resided here since the town's creation, Abadan was a busy place with many merchants occupying the overcrowded streets, selling and buying goods and services in order to make a living. The crowds of people gave Milson and his team the perfect cover, allowing them to blend in. The men and Asherah were positioned within a block's radius of where Saiph's men had first located Assad and the group of individuals who were obviously his contacts.

The stage was set for the operation to go forward. Milson, with Asherah at his side, was stationed in a corner store near the place where Assad had initially been sighted. Milson, dressed like a local, and even though his skin was darker than that of most of the natives, blended in as an Iranian. Asherah, dressed in a traditional burka, which covered her head and face, and a long niqab to hide her body from neck to ankle, found it easier to blend in with the crowd. Even though she was Islamic by heritage, she was a Westerner who normally dressed in casual clothing and lived a more carefree lifestyle. So, she was unhappy with the clothing that she was forced to wear to hide her identity. But she knew she had no choice but to go along with the subterfuge and side with Milson and the others in order to get Assad. Pretending to be Milson's wife, she walked behind him as they made their way through the outskirts of the markets with Fuller, Sheppard, and Weaver yards away.

Marin, along with a small portion of his crew, who were dressed like Milson, was positioned several kilometers away. Troy and his men were there for backup. All of them were positioned perfectly, giving no hint of who they really were or what they were doing. Saiph's men were with them, looking and behaving like ordinary Iranian citizens as they also walked through the crowd. The remainder of Marin's men and Troy's men were stationed a few kilometers outside the city. They were sitting in the same SUVs that had transported them that morning from the riverbank to the safe house in Khorramshahr. Dressed in their tactical gear, with no identifiable markings or rank insignias to give away their identity as US soldiers, they all sat anxiously with their weapons drawn, ready for battle if called upon. Some of Saiph's men were there too, their weapons also drawn, but they also had their ears on as they listened in on a short-range radio frequency tied in to a surveillance channel. Each of them had a small unnoticeable earpiece in one ear. This enabled a connection to every member of each of the different teams—a collective means of communication that kept everyone well-informed and, in the loop, particularly the supervisors of the operation. Everyone was in place and knew their roles.

Asherah, following close behind Milson, pretending to be his wife, soon began to lag behind, her outfit causing her a great deal of discomfort as she fidgeted within it. Milson, turning around and seeing her distress, quickly went to her aid. Asherah did not realize that she was drawing attention to herself, but the people around her did in fact notice her unusual behavior, especially the women, who were dressed in the same fashion as she was. Milson took hold of Asherah and said in a whisper,

"Desiree, what the hell are you doing? You're making a scene."

Without hesitation, she replied,

"This damn thing I'm wearing is very uncomfortable, as is the wire you guys planted on me. It's irritating the hell out of my skin, especially between my breasts and my midsection. This thing is driving me crazy."

Milson quickly took Asherah to the side, getting her away from the people who had noticed her strange behavior, to explain to her the reason the wire was taped to her body.

"Listen to me. You knew the risk in coming with us, along with the consequences and responsibilities. I told you that I didn't want you to come, but you insisted, so deal with the situation. We don't have time to worry about your comfort level or if your dress fits or not. Time is running out for us. We need to catch your boyfriend, like, right now. That wire you're wearing will serve as your safety net if things get really deep and serious out here. It will record everything we need to prove that Assad did act alone and that you are innocent of what he is being accused of. Now, go with the flow, play the part, and act like a good old-fashioned Iranian woman, okay?"

Asherah, who pouted and sneered at Milson's chastising, knew that he was right. Her discomfort in the outfit with the hidden wire was of little consequence compared to what was really at stake. After coming to realize the situation she was in, she quickly composed herself, straightened her posture, and rejoined Milson out among the crowd. When she reappeared, the members of each team immediately thought that something was wrong. But Milson, who was no stranger to undercover work and its procedures, nonchalantly signaled each team that everything was all right. Relieved to see Milson's signal, the men on the teams continued their surveillance, with Fuller, Sheppard, Weaver, and Saiph's men still shadowing every move that Milson and Asherah made.

The couple continued to stroll along the dirt-covered walkway through the outdoor markets, blending in with the pedestrians all around them. Once they made it to the downtown area, Asherah saw a familiar figure from the corner of her eye. She gestured to Milson, frantically tugging at his sleeve to get his attention. He turned to see what the trouble was. She pointed, while whispering in his ear,

"Killian, look! It's him! It's Ad-dam!" Right away, the bounty hunter looked up to see for himself what Asherah was talking about. To his surprise, it was Assad. The bounty Milson had been sent to retrieve was standing right in front of him. It was unquestionably Assad, no doubt about it. He recognized him instantly as he was not in disguise. Standing forty to fifty yards away from them, Assad was dressed in plain casual attire suited for the current atmosphere and was carrying the two duffel bags of stolen weapons. Milson also noticed that he was not alone. He was escorted by three gentlemen, who were probably his contacts or handlers. All four came out of a building to the right and walked along the sidewalk very slowly as though waiting for someone to arrive. Milson nonchalantly signaled the team, confirming Assad's identity. Each team member sprang into action, attentive and alert as the news came over their earpieces. Fuller, Sheppard, and Weaver, who were several feet away from the team, quickly went off in different directions to get a closer look at the renegade officer while still keeping their surveillance intact. Saiph and his operatives performed the same maneuver. Marin and his SEALs followed suit. Each group got a good look at Assad and reported their findings to each other. Marin, along with Saiph, who was perched atop the roof of an abandoned building, saw Assad and his companions.

Marin, the SEAL leader had his scoped AR-15 rifle aimed right at the spot where Assad was now standing. Giddy and anxious to have discovered Assad's location, he said through his microphone,

"I have a visual on the target. Is it confirmed? Repeat, is the target confirmed as Commander Assad?"

Each person, including Milson, gave a nod and a furtive hand signal to confirm the identity of the renegade.

"It's him all right. It's definitely Assad," Milson said with both excitement and calmness in his voice.

"He's several yards away from me with three other guys at his side. They look like they're waiting for something, but I'm not sure."

Everyone was anxious and, on their toes, waiting for the opportunity to apprehend the fugitive. Marin and Saiph were screaming into their microphones.

"If it's a positive confirmation, what are we waiting for? Let's grab him right now before we lose this opportunity," Marin said, clenching his SIG 5.56 mm rifle, which was aimed directly at Assad.

"Agreed. We will never get another chance like this again, gentlemen," Saiph announced.

"Negative! He might lead us to his contacts. This gives us an opportunity to find out who he is working for," Sheppard said.

"The kid's right. We can't afford to snatch him prematurely and blow our cover while we're still in enemy territory. Let him lead us to those goddamn blokes, then we can take them all at once," Fuller added.

Everyone was on pins and needles about capturing Assad, especially Milson, who was agitated and feeling the adrenaline as it ran through his body. Listening to his colleagues spout their opinions about when take to Assad into custody was, to him, nerve-racking and irritating. Listening to the childishness bickering about capturing the traitor, Milson was growing more irritated by the second. Just as he was about to unload over the radio, Weaver came in and refereed the situation.

"All right, guys, enough of the bullshit! All of you are arguing like a couple of teenage girls, and it's getting us nowhere! This is not about who's picking up the tab at a fucking restaurant or who wants to fuck the prettiest girl in school! It's about grabbing a dangerous man who has killed people for his own pleasure and who used the US government to do it!" Weaver, knowing that he was on an open frequency, did not mention the real reason for Assad's treachery. He, along with Milson and the others, knew that he had to keep Assad's real crime a secret from Saiph and his men, being under explicit orders from their superiors to do so.

"This is not your call to make, Enif, nor yours, Commander. It's Milson's. He's the primary on this, and it's his decision whether we execute the plan or not." Everyone went silent in the face of Weaver's moment of clarity. Even Milson was surprised by this outburst from the CIA agent who had previously criticized him.

"Killian, the ball is in your court. What's your play? Do we grab the bastard or not?"

The former army/CIA officer smirked and made a gesture with his head to acknowledge his appreciation of Weaver's insight.

"No, not yet. We follow him and see where he goes. Marin, Saiph, have your guys ready to follow him if he gets into a vehicle with those men. Have a car ready for us when the time comes. Fuller, Sheppard, Weaver, stay close on my six, but keep your distance. We don't want to spook him in any way. He already knows what we look like, especially me, so let's not give him another chance to run or to alert his friends to our presence here. Everybody, keep your surveillance tight and quiet. If we play our cards right, he will lead us to his contacts, and then we'll all be happy campers when we catch him and his asshole friends at the same time. But remember, we don't want to give him a reason to run. Let's see where he's going for now, and then when the time is right, we'll grab him."

Everyone agreed with Milson's decision. They all followed the game plan by staying put in their concealed spots amid the hustle and bustle of the local pedestrians. Milson did not want anyone drawing attention to themselves until the time was right for them to make their move against Assad and party.

Everyone was in sync and in position. Nobody made any unexpected moves or surprises, except one. To Milson's surprise, and to the surprise of everyone else, who stood in shock as they witnessed it, Asherah, who was the first one to spot Assad, ran from Milson's side and sprinted in the direction of her estranged boyfriend. No one could believe what was happening, not even Milson, who stood amazed and silent for a second, only to say her name under his breath as he contended with the questioning thoughts running through his mind. Once again, chatter in the earpieces broke the silence. Then came eardrum-bursting screams of excitement and confusion. "Killian, what's going on? What the hell is she doing?" Marin screamed as he and Saiph witnessed Asherah running toward Assad.

"She's heading toward Assad! Is she crazy? She's going to blow the whole bloody mission!" Fuller was angry, but he had spoken in a low tone so as not to give himself away to the locals.

Even though Milson was angry and outraged by Asherah's actions, he could not give chase right away because he had to maintain his cover. The only thing he could do in this unfortunate predicament was to stand his ground and tell everyone else to do the same.

"Shut the fuck up, for Christ's sake, and stand down! Everybody, stay at your post and relax! For now, let's see what she does. Let's wait it out, people. Remember, she's wired, so we can hear everything she says." Milson's words put everyone at ease, but only for the moment.

Marin, Saiph, and Fuller were already jumping out of their skins at the sight of Asherah's deception, but Sheppard and Weaver kept their cool throughout the entire show. They all watched in disbelief as Asherah continued her trek toward Assad and his cohorts. Milson thought to himself that it had been a good idea to plant a bug on her for this very reason. But in the back of his mind, he blamed himself for having let her come along in the first place. He alone felt responsible for her well-being and was obligated to keep her out of danger. But now he could see that no matter how hard he had tried to change her mind, the beautiful native from Holland had been too stubborn to listen. She was going to see this thing through to the end, even if it meant that she would experience deep hurt upon finding out the truth about her lover's intentions and his diabolical scheme.

The team continued to look at Asherah in disdain and disbelief as she sprinted toward Assad and party. They were each mentally and physically ready for the worst-case scenario, especially Milson, who stood in awe as he watched the beautiful, emotional Asherah rushing off toward the man he had been sent to capture and take back dead or alive. When Asherah finally had closed the distance between her and Assad, she tried to make physical contact with him, only to be stopped by the men he was with, who quickly formed a barricade around him.

At first, Assad did not know who Asherah was because of the burka she was wearing, which hid her identity. But as soon as she pulled the veil from her face, he knew exactly who she was.

"My God, Desiree! What are you doing here? How did you get here?" he exclaimed with excitement, astonished to see her.

Tired from her run, she explained in a general way how she had gotten to Abadan.

"I found you by following what you told me over the phone. I took a plane out of Dubai to Kuwait and traveled the rest of the way by bus to get here."

"Yes, but I told you to meet me in Kuwait and to stay there until I arrived. I did not say that you should come here," Assad said forcefully, scanning the area around him as if he was looking for something or someone.

"I know, but I couldn't be away from you any longer. I missed you very much. And if I would have stayed in Kuwait, you would never have gotten what you need." Asherah showed Assad the flash drive that she had in her possession.

"God!" he said with surprise and amazement.

"You brought the thumb drive with you." Assad anxiously took the drive from her hand, clenching it within his own, then embraced her.

"The Americans didn't suspect that you had this?"

Asherah answered quickly,

"No. I kept it well hidden from them when I was in their custody. They had no idea that I had it on me."

"They didn't search you at all?" Assad asked, confused and uncertain, knowing that as a captive of the United States government, she would have been subjected to a thorough search of her person. Little did he know that indeed the Americans did know about the flash drive, or that Asherah was playing along with them to deceive him.

"Yes, they did, but I kept it in a well-hidden place where no one would think to look."

Assad automatically caught on to what Asherah was saying, mentally picturing the small device concealed in her genitals. Aroused by the notion, he felt the corners of his mouth turn up as a naughty smile spread across his face. With no regard for the situation, they were in, Assad and Asherah began to express their passion and desire for one another. One of the three men who was Assad purposely interrupted by tapping on his shoulder. Speaking in Arabic, the man informed Assad that the transport they had been waiting for had finally arrived.

Snapping his neck to the right, but not wanting to take his gaze off from Asherah, Assad noticed a small, dark-colored BMW; a common automobile that is owned by everyone in the middle east region. It made its way alongside them with two other vehicles of the same make and model right behind it but of two different colors.

After the lead vehicle had come to a stop next to them, one of Assad's men opened the rear door for the four of them to get in. Assad immediately clutched Asherah's right hand and started to make his way to the car, but one of the guards stepped between the couple and invited only Assad to enter the automobile, making it obvious to Asherah, who desperately wanted to accompany him, that she was not welcome. Extremely displeased and irritated, Assad argued his case for allowing Asherah to come too. Frustrated, he would not back down. Surprisingly, his argument changed the guard's mind. Asherah was permitted to join them in the vehicle.

Several yards away, Milson and company watched the pair get into the BMW, about to make their departure. The bounty hunter signaled his colleagues that Assad and Asherah were going to be in the lead vehicle, with the other two behind them, pulling up the rear. As the cars drove off in the same direction, Milson frantically signaled to his team while shouting to Saiph and the others to bring the SUVs around to follow them. The scene was frantic and intense. Milson grew impatient with the enormous crowd of people blocking his view of Assad's convoy as it disappeared into traffic. Gritting his teeth, he said,

"Son of a bitch, the bastard is getting away!" not realizing that Saiph had dispatched the transport seconds ago. But from Milson's perspective, this was not good enough. He could not wait for the vehicles to arrive. In desperation, and thinking only of what was vital at the moment, Milson rushed out from the crowd and into the middle of the street, where he hijacked a car from a local motorist. Speaking in Arabic, he told the individual why he was taking his car while, at the same time, grabbing the man and forcibly removing him from the driver's seat. Milson showed no empathy as he threw the gentleman onto the dirt road and drove away in haste.

Hearing the screams of the old man whom Milson had forced from the automobile, Saiph, Marin, Sheppard, Weaver, and Fuller thought to follow Milson as they rushed toward the dark-colored trucks the Iraqi agent had acquired for them. But they were too late.

The faded sedan that Milson had taken sped off, leaving behind a crowd of confused onlookers and spectators, along with an infuriated gentleman in the middle of a heavily occupied Iranian street. Saiph and Marin, in the lead vehicle, screamed at the pedestrians to get out of the way and let them through. They hoped to catch up to Milson, who was already in pursuit. As the crowd began to disburse in the face of the oncoming black SUVs and their blaring horns, Weaver, Fuller, and Sheppard tried to begin a dialogue with Milson, who was still chasing Assad. But the confusion and frustration they felt upon seeing how Asherah and Milson were behaving had started to undermine their confidence. Saiph especially considered this change in plan to be chaotic and reckless.

Roaring into the microphone, his voice overpowering those of the rest of the team, Saiph said, "Milson, what the hell are you doing?! This wasn't part of the plan!"

Hearing Saiph's voice, but trying hard to ignore it, Milson concentrated on his driving, sticking close to Assad and Asherah while trying not to give his position away. As the line of cars made its way out of the city and onto a congested highway, Milson picked up speed, hoping to catch up with Assad's small convoy. The SUVs behind him began to drive faster too, but the congestion prevented them from going as fast as they would have liked. Milson, determined to follow them, stayed back several yards so as not to draw attention to himself, but he remained close enough to keep them with his sight. Each car was traveling at a speed between fifty and sixty miles per hour, including Milson's, who was sixty or sixty-five yards away from Assad, traveling at the same speed as they were. Saiph and the others were too far behind to catch up, but they were still in hot pursuit.

Saiph was still enraged. He barked,

"Mr. Milson! I demand you answer me at once and tell me what is your position!"

Despite Milson's lack of respect for authority, he decided to answer the Iraqi agent the best way he could.

"Agent Saiph, I demand that you shut the fuck up and let me do what I need to do!"

Hearing his response over the band, Saiph was appalled by the vulgarness of Milson's choice of words and was very adamant about it. But due to the circumstances, he had little choice but to hold his tongue in spite of the situation that just occurred.

Meanwhile, Milson who was in pursuit, gave a play-by-play of what he was doing over the mic to satisfy Saiph's indignant attitude,

"I'm about seventy yards away from them, traveling at speeds between fifty-five and sixty miles per hour! From what I can tell, they have no clue that I'm following them! How far are you guys?"

Weaver got on the mic without letting Saiph answer.

"We're miles away from you, Milson. We'll never catch up in time."

Hearing that, Milson took a moment to rethink the situation.

"Are you guys tracking my position?"

Saiph answered, not giving Weaver or anyone else the chance to do so,

"Yes. We have your position. You are miles ahead, but we're picking up your signal well!"

"Good. Tell Marin and Troy to keep their GPS on me! You should have a lock on the coordinates that I'm traveling. From what I can tell, it looks like they're traveling west, probably to some deserted location. I think he's on his way to meet up with his contacts or that smug bastard I ran into in Dubai!"

"We gotcha, Chief!" shouted Sheppard, who was in the second SUV.

"From your position on the GPS, you're about 50 kilometers ahead of us!"

"That's 31.06 miles! He's not too far!" said Fuller.

"But far enough for us to gain more ground! We need to gain a little more speed if we're going to catch up with him! Milson, don't lose that son of a bitch!" Weaver said.

"I won't! Just be ready to back me up when we get to wherever the hell it is we're going. I have a bad feeling that I'm going to run into a whole bunch of company real soon when this trip is over."

"Don't worry, Milson. That's why we're here, so we can have your six when the proverbial shit hits the fan," Marin said with confidence. Milson smirked, which caused him to feel a little easier than he felt moments ago.

"Thanks, Commander. Just knowing that you navy boys having my back is persuading me more and more to put my faith in the Deltas."

Hearing that, Marin's counterpart, Troy, snickered lightheartedly while the SEAL commander remained silent over the comms. Even though they knew that Milson was joking, they were all aware that this was a serious situation that could go either way. Despite the cards stacked against them, namely, their being in a foreign land with hostile intent, they knew they had to get this guy no matter what.

"Milson, what's your plan when they reach their destination?!" Saiph asked.

The bounty hunter paused for a second to think about how to answer. Then he replied with the most logical statement that came to mind,

"I'm going to do whatever it takes to get this guy, then wait for the cavalry to save my ass!"

After that, the comms went silent. Taking advantage of the situation, Sheppard said to Milson, "Don't worry, Chief! We'll be there to back you up. That's a promise!"

Milson smirked to complement the energetic tone in the young ensign's voice. He said a couple of words under his breath that were meant for his ears only, not to be announced over an open mic.

"I hope so, kid. For God's sake, I hope so," he said, continuing his pursuit of Assad and his accomplices, following the small band of vehicles that were leading him to some unknown destination.

CHAPTER 12

THE SHOWDOWN OF THE HUNT

To Milson, the drive seemed to have lasted for hours, but in reality, it only took fifteen minutes. The group of cars that he followed during that time finally arrived at their destination. As he watched carefully from the rear, he saw them drive down a long desolate road. Their tires throwing up thick clouds of dust, dirt, and debris into the air that made it impossible to see. But on the other hand, the dust served as a concealment for Milson so that the vehicles in front could not see him from behind. But at the same time, it shortened his line of sight, making it hard for him to identify things and see where they were going. Later, as the dust settled and the atmosphere was visibly clear, he was able to see an area that looked deserted and uninhabitable. Milson saw the vehicles continued their long trek along the graveled road. Staying a good distance away he was able to identify the lead car that had Assad and Asherah, as well as the other two cars that were their escort.

The vehicles stopped at a gated entrance that could only be described as decrepit, old and rusty. There were only two figures standing out in front of it, obviously armed sentries who were keeping watch of the entrance. As he looked closer, he noticed that they were wearing headgear with scarfs covering their faces. They were dressed casually, but were wearing bits of tactical gear that made them look like military or militia, and holding what appeared to be Russian-made AK-47's (a Kalashnikov automatic rifle) at their sides. Milson took heed of this and quickly swerved the car in the opposite direction, hoping to stay out of sight so that the small convoy he was following, along with the armed guards, would not see him. While trying to hide himself, he stumbled upon a dirt-covered embankment surrounded by thick vegetation on the opposite side of the road. Without hesitation, he drove slowly toward it without giving his position away. He parked alongside it, thinking that this would give him the perfect cover.

Because of Milson's impetuous decision to chase after Assad solo, the vehicle he'd acquired was no match for the first three automobiles in terms of features and sophistication. As Milson took cover behind the bushes and trees, he surveyed the area around him. He did not have the equipment to perform a full reconnaissance of the surroundings, which otherwise would have made it easier for him to survey. So instead, he relied on his knowledge, skill and foresight as an ex-agent and current bounty hunter. While surveying the area closely to get a good idea of where he was and what he was going to do next, his earpiece, which he'd temporarily forgotten about, abruptly rang out in his left ear. He was nearly deafened by the sound of Saiph's voice shouting from the other end.

"Milson, are you there?! What's your status?!"

Agitated by the device and from Saiph's screeching and annoying voice, which almost led Milson to snatch the small device out of his ear, Milson responded by purposely snapping at his Iraqi counterpart.

"Stop yelling in my ear, you controlling bastard! Wait a second and I'll give you a sitrep!"

Again, Saiph did not appreciate the strong, ill-tempered, rough tone of Milson's retort. But he saw no other choice again than to back down and give the bounty hunter a chance to answer the questions he'd asked.

"I don't know exactly where I am, but I can describe the area in precise detail. This place is isolated with a huge compound in the middle of it. Might be a warehouse or an abandoned building, but whatever it is, it's well fortified and heavily secured. It's surrounded by concrete walls that measure seven to eight feet in height, with two guards posted at a main gate in front. There may be other sentries posted around the area. I'll have to take a closer look to know for sure."

Just as Milson was about to provide additional description of the area, Sheppard interrupted. "Chief, we've got your signal! You're about 20 ½ away from us, which gives us between 20 and 24 minutes to get to you!"

"Perfect. That will give me plenty of time to figure out how to get in and grab Assad without getting myself killed in the process," Milson said sarcastically. He started to realize how big of a mistake he had made when leaving his team behind to follow Assad solo without any backup he might need to capture him and neutralize the drama in front of him. Taking several more glances around the area, something out of the ordinary caught his eye.

"Guys, I think I may have found a way in. I'll let you know when I have Assad in my sights, but for now, stay off the mics. I'll keep you posted if anything else pops up."

Weaver's voice came through the earpiece next, saying,

"Gotcha, Milson! We'll keep the channel open on our end! We're closing in on your position as we speak. We'll be there in 20 minutes or less. Be careful and watch your six!"

"Roger that. If you hear gunplay, please don't hesitate to come in and join the party. Just don't let it be a repeat of Dubai, okay?"

Understanding what Milson was talking about, Weaver and the others responded with their own anecdotes.

Now that the conversation through the comms was over, Milson wasted no time in embarking on his plan. Running the scenario through his mind, he noticed something as he entered the compound: a midsized opening at the bottom of the concrete wall that separated him from the facility. The opening was several feet wide, both deep and wide enough for him to fit through. Remembering his younger days in the army as a sprier soldier, he got down in a prone position and low-crawled through the opening—the perfect opportunity to breach the interior from the outside. While making his attempt, he looked to his left and right to make sure he hadn't been discovered. Once he cleared the hole and the wall, he ran toward one side of the compound to get a better idea of where he was and pinpoint the exact location of Assad and his cohorts. With dozens of ideas racing through his mind as adrenaline pumps through his body from excitement, he looks up at the sky to figure out something. From the position of the sun, Milson realized that he was on the east side of the building, whereas Assad and his party had entered the northwest side. Realizing that it was only a couple of yards away, literally around the corner, Milson started to make his way around the area. He ran quietly against the exterior wall, covering his tracks as he did so. While making his way to the place where he thought Assad might be, he unexpectedly runs into a guard and stops several yards away from him. Oblivious, the guard, careless and indifferent about his actions, did not notice Milson's presence. This gave him the opportunity he was looking for.

While the guard stood against the wall smoking a cigarette, his demeanor carefree and airy, Milson knew what he had to do. The individual needed to be taken out quietly and quickly. Milson was armed with only two of his personal handguns: a forty-caliber SIG Sauer and a forty-caliber Glock, with the SIG in his right hand and the Glock concealed in his waistband at his back. The guard, on the other hand, was formidably armed to the teeth. He too had a midsize AK-47, its belted sling draped around his shoulder and neck and also strapped across his midsection, and a 9 mm Beretta, which he had holstered against his left thigh. He was also equipped with three fully loaded AK-47 magazines, which were strapped to his chest, and a seven-inch tactical knife positioned on the side of his belt. Milson knew he couldn't afford to miss this moment. It was his only chance to infiltrate the facility and nab Assad while having the element of surprise in his favor.

Without hesitating, and relying on both his civilian skills and military skills, he snuck up on the guard from behind and grabbed ahold of the small automatic rifle that was still harnessed to his body. Having made a split-second decision, Milson wrapped the sling around the guard's neck and began to choke him aggressively. At the same time, Milson forcefully puts his hand over the guard's mouth so he would not scream, yell, or shout while being subdued. Still resisting and putting up a valiant fight against Milson, the guard resistance was impeccable, but he was no match to the bounty hunters skill of hand-to-hand combat as well as his determination. Again, without hesitation, and thinking that there was only one outcome to this situation, Milson resigned himself by implementing the only logical solution to his present conundrum. Still holding the guard's mouth and lower jaw, Milson pulled his head to the right with great force, snapping the man's neck in urgency. The guard's body jerked for a moment but soon went limp as he slumped down into Milson's arms. Milson carefully laid him out on the ground and relieved him of his weapon. He also confiscating the extra magazine cartridges and serrated knife that he noticed earlier. He decided to forgo the nine-millimeter Beretta because he had his SIG and Glock, tossing it into the distance. Then, knowing that he needed to get rid of the body quickly before it was discovered by the guard's compadres, Milson dragged the body to a nearby area with a short-sided wall that was divided into several sections. He dumped the body over the wall and then buried the remains beneath a pile of stone, concrete, and rubble. Regaining his composure, he turned his concentration back to his primary objective, getting inside the compound unnoticed. Later, he assumed the identity of the fallen individual he killed in order to infiltrate their facility. When Milson walked around the area, he spotted two other guards standing to his right. These two were not like the other one he subdued. They were neither careless nor nonchalant as the first. Both were alert and immovable, standing on opposite ends of what appeared to be the main entrance to the derelict structure.

CHAPTER 13

THE CONFRONTATION OF THE HUNT

Milson was running out of options. The thoughts in his head were spinning at a rate of one hundred miles an hour as he tried to figure out what to do next. He thought to himself that if he could take down both guards simultaneously, he would gain the advantage. But he also thought it would be too risky. And he'd have to give up the element of surprise because surely there were others in the building who would be alerted at a moment's notice. He thought about trying to wait patiently for his team to arrive as he originally planned, but he knew he was running out of time and could not afford to wait too long. He had to figure something out quickly before his window of opportunity closed. After going over the situation in his mind several times, he was down to the only possible solution for gaining access into the building. He thought about the first guard he'd taken out, who'd been standing around the corner on the other side. Assessing the situation, he quickly returned to the area where he had dumped the body, thinking that if he could disguise himself perfectly as one of the guards, he could easily get in. But he knew he would have to cover his face to guard against being identified by the other two. And if this plan did not work, he would have no other choice but to kill those two guards as well.

Coming upon the corpse of the terrorist soldier, Milson wasted no time in relieving the guard of his headgear and scarf and taking these items for his own. The terrorist also had in his possession an old military-style camouflage jacket: the type worn only by soldiers who were in the army or marine corps, which Milson also took—not because it was the perfect disguise, but because he thought it would look good on him. With no time to waste, he dressed himself in the new clothes, put on the headgear, and draped the scarf across his face. After securing the rifle and the knife he had confiscated earlier, he made his final adjustments. Taking a moment to practice mimicking the guard's demeanor and mannerisms, he casually walked up to the unsuspecting sentries, who noticed him right away. The one to Milson's right, directly facing him, turned and began to walk toward him. Looking at Milson, the guard thought him to be behaving erratically, as if intoxicated. Agitated and disgusted by the behavior, the guard yelled at Milson in an abrasive tone. Milson who spoke and understood fluent Farsi Arabic got a grasp of what the guard was saying to him.

"What the hell are you doing here?! Why aren't you at your post?! Have you been drinking again while on duty?!"

Milson, speaking in Arabic as well, replied in such a way as to confirm the guard's suspicions that he was drunk in order to persuade the illusion. The guard, growing more angrier by the minute as Milson continued his charade of intoxication, pushed Milson several times with great vexation and rage. Knowing that his former plan to approach casually and walk past the guards would never work now, Milson gauged that his only course of action was to take both guards out of the equation, his plan B. The lead guard obviously was unaware of what was about to happen. Milson drew the military-style knife from its hiding place beneath his jacket and held it behind his back. With the guard's hurling more verbal abuse, Milson felt that this was the perfect opportunity to strike. As the guard continued his rant, Milson, catching him off guard, lunged at him, using his left hand to grab the back of the man's neck for leverage and balance, and using his right to force the deadly weapon into his chest cavity. The guard had no time to react to his attack, which was instantaneous and quick. The guard died seconds after being stabbed by the blade. His body dropped heavily to the ground. Milson, wasting no time, went for the second individual to his left.

Unaware of what had transpired, the second guard found himself amid the same circumstances as his comrade. Without warning, Milson sprang into action, sprinting toward him as he remained to look forward. Then from the corner of his eye he saw someone running at him at full speed. Seeing his dead compadre off to the side, he began to raise his weapon and defend himself, but it was too late. Milson grabbed him from behind by the jaw and slashed his throat with the same knife he'd used on the first guard. The gash left by the blade was so deep and long that the guard was nearly decapitated. There was an enormous amount of blood pouring from his neck, which caused the guard to lose his ability to speak or even breathe. Death was instantaneous.

Milson knew he had to act quickly so as not to be discovered. He had no time to dispose of the two bodies properly, so he left them where they lay. Now that the two guards were dead, Milson gathered up the remaining magazines for his small AK-47. After looking once more to ensure no one had discovered him, Milson cautiously entered the building, gently opening the two metal doors in front of him. He soon found himself in a very dark and dusty place. The atmosphere was dry and warm, a result of both the weather and an absent ventilation system. Continuing along, Milson came to a low-lit hallway that stretched for a few yards and then divided into three sections, two on the left and one on the right. Walking silently down the dark corridor, he heard several noises in the distance. They were very faint but were easily recognizable as human voices. The closer he got, the clearer and more understandable the voices became. Whoever it was, was directly ahead and around the corner to the left.

As Milson was making his way toward the voices, little did he know there was another sentry standing guard at the door to the room where the sounds were coming from.

"Shit!" he whispered.

"*They really have this place fortified!*" he thought, at the same time conjuring up another plan. After going through the different scenarios for incapacitating the guard, he made his final choice, which included portraying one of the terrorists again.

Milson walked up to the unsuspecting soldier and began engaging in small talk with him to put him at ease and give him a false sense of security. Then he made his move. Without warning, he grabbed the guard by the lower jaw, covered his mouth with his hand, and forced the knife in, thrusting it under his mandible jaw and up into his throat and tongue. The sound the instrument made when penetrating the guard's flesh was almost unbearable to Milson, but he did it, figuring it was necessary. The guard began convulsing, twitching and jerking violently as if being electrocuted. Milson manages to hold him in tight and restrict his movements. After several seconds, the soldier's body finally collapsed. With a firm hold on the guard's body and mouth, Milson moved him to the other side of the hallway and quietly placed him down on the floor.

Milson had developed the skills required to be a professional killer, something he kept to himself, in the CIA and the army. Of course, he went through boot camp for the army, but when he was hired for intelligence work, he was trained by Special Forces personnel, including Green Berets and Rangers, in close-quarter combat training and fighting techniques. When he was later recruited by the CIA, they taught him about tactical awareness and threat recognition, along with the skills needed to disable and neutralize aggressors/opponents. Milson had thought that he wouldn't ever have to use these dark skills again, but it was necessary in this case.

Seeing a vacant room set apart from the others, Milson dragged his fourth victim into it. Then he went and took up the guard's place, standing in the same spot where he'd found him. As he stood there silently, Milson concluded that Assad, Asherah, and the rest of the terrorists were in that room. He could hear them talking very clearly, as if he were in the room with them. The conversation was conducted mostly in Arabic, but occasionally he heard some English being used. He heard what appeared to be Assad's voice speaking in a contemptuous tone.

"You have no idea what I had to go through to get this for you. I thought your organization was discreet, but from what I've seen, I know now that it is not. I didn't expect the Americans to find out so soon. I'd figured they wouldn't find out until after I'd been compensated for my services."

"Calm down, Assad. The hard tasks are over. Your job is done. You have delivered what we asked for, and we are eternally grateful to you for doing so. With this final transaction of ours complete, we will soon be the most powerful organization in the world. We will all benefit from this glorious stash of firepower you have brought us. You have delivered the weapons we want to cross-engineer for our soldiers to use, and the flash drives we need to crush the Americans and their partners for good. You will be rich beyond your wildest dreams. In addition, you have your lovely companion at your side once again. What more could you want? What more could anyone ask for?"

Milson recognized the voice. It was the same one he'd heard when he and the others were in the basement level of the galleria mall in Dubai: cold, calculating, egotistical, and maniacal. It was a distinctive voice that was intelligent in nature but also malevolent in deception. As he continued to listen, he heard Assad becoming more agitated and irritated than before.

"That may be what you believe, but I don't see it that way. Given everything I've gone through, and since Desiree was captured by the Americans, I think I should be compensated more than we originally agreed. Another two hundred million dollars should be more than sufficient for what I've gone through."

After he said that, there was a long silent pause. One could have heard a pin drop in that room. The silence was so deep and still that Milson could hear sounds from outside the building. He began to get anxious, not knowing whether to continue listening or to burst in, which would compromise his surveillance effort. As he pondered the choice in his mind, he heard a gut-busting laugh suddenly erupt from the room, effectively removing one of his two choices. The laugh had come from the man with the malevolent voice, not Assad.

"Is that a joke, Assad? If it is, it is very amusing. Are you trying to tell me that the three hundred million we originally agreed on is not enough? You want to be compensated more, for a total of five hundred million dollars?"

Again, the room went silent, but only for a second. Assad, his voice breaking the tension, responded,

"That's right. And it is not a joke. I think I deserve a bonus for what I've done for you. I literally put both my ass and my career on the line for you and your organization. And for what? A dishonest employee of yours who tried to kill me and take the plans and the merchandise for himself. You are the one who orchestrated that meeting in the mall garage, assuring me it was safe and secure, but instead we were compromised by the Americans. I barely made my escape. This isn't even counting the fact that I traveled to a country where I knew I could easily be killed simply for who I am, who I once worked for, and where I come from. No, sir. The three hundred million is not good enough, not with the risks I've taken. I want more."

Milson could not believe Assad's audacity. He figured the terrorist leader probably thought the same thing. Also, though, Assad's outrageous demand gave Milson a whole new perspective on his situation. For the first time, he thought to himself that he was being short-changed in his deal with Admiral Cooper and the Justice Department. Cooper had offered him a million dollars to capture Assad and bring him back, but the terrorists, who were calling the shots, had agreed to give Assad three hundred million for the plans and the weapons. Milson thought,

"I'll be damned! This greedy motherfucker is getting three hundred mil and wants more, but I'm only getting one mil for his sorry ass! Cooper and I need to have a chat when I get back!"

The terrorist leader, responding to Assad, said,

"So, you want more, is that correct? You want us to give you—no, you *demand* that we give you—an extra two hundred million because you think you're entitled to it? Is that what I'm being led to understand, Assad?"

Milson did not have to see what was going on inside that room to know that the outcome was not going to be good. He could feel more tension added to the already significant sense of uneasiness in the room, which led him to believe that the circumstances were about to change drastically. His instincts were telling him that he should do something, but his common sense prevailed over his impulses in this case. He knew he was outnumbered and outgunned with no backup to relieve him. If he were to barge in with guns blazing and go toe to toe with them, he knew he would not survive. Milson's only hope was to hold out and wait for the SEALs and Deltas to arrive by saving the day.

As he continued to ponder the situation, things inside the room were getting more intense.

"Well, since we're on the subject of more money, what about the money we asked you to retrieve from Ahmed Shaula when you were in Australia?"

Again, silence took over the room, but only for a few seconds. Assad's voice, more defiant than before, said,

"What?! I told you that I couldn't find it. There was no briefcase when I confronted him. We already went through this! Why are you bringing this up again?!"

The tension became even thicker. Milson could hear the agitation in Assad's voice as he became more and more combative and defiant. This was not good.

"The reason I am confronting you with this issue again, Assad, is that the story you told was a fabrication."

Milson heard the familiar clicking sound of automatic rifles in the background. This meant that the guards had drawn their weapons on Assad after having heard the accusations put forth by their leader.

"When we were in Dubai, I specifically asked you if you had seen the briefcase that Shaula stole from us, and you looked me in my eyes and said no. But the security cameras from the lobby of the hotel in Sydney tell otherwise. We have the surveillance footage from that day. It shows someone who looks exactly like you, disguised as Shaula, leaving the hotel with a small brown briefcase in their possession."

All at once, Assad's demeanor and defiant attitude changed dramatically. The tone in the room had changed also. This was no longer a meeting to carry out an exchange, but rather a venue for making accusations against Assad and his honesty. Milson was very eager to step in. The tension from trying to contain himself and thereby not put his life in jeopardy was causing him great inner conflict. He stood ready, the AK-47 clutched tight in his hands and his right index finger firmly positioned on the trigger guard. He had made up his mind about what to do. But just as Milson was about to storm in through the door, the terrorist leader began speaking again, directing more allegations at the traitorous naval officer.

"Did you explain to Ms. Asherah how you were able to keep that case from your kill? And did you tell her that you lied to us by saying that you never saw it?"

Milson, who had nearly forgotten that Asherah was in the room, heard a sound that only she could have made. It was the sound of a gasp as the air left her throat.

"Kill! What is he talking about, Ad-dam?! What does he mean by *kill*?" Desiree asked, confusion and puzzlement in her voice.

"Oh! He did not tell you about what happened during his stay in Sydney." Milson could hear the individual clearing his throat. Continuing in a devious, conceited tone, the leader replied,

"Well, Ms. Asherah, we instructed your boyfriend to retrieve some money that had been stolen from us—twenty-five million dollars. His orders, which he executed perfectly (no pun intended), were to eliminate Mr. Shaula for his treachery—you see, he embezzled the money from our organization—and return to us the twenty-five million Shaula stole."

Asherah was surprised to hear this as Milson heard her astonishing exhale upon hearing Assad's previous misdeeds.

"What?! You told me that you didn't hurt anyone to get that money! You said that the organization gave you that as a down payment and that you would get the rest of it once you handed over the drives and the weapons! You lied to me, Ad-dam!"

"Oh, that's not the half of it, Ms. Asherah. Your boyfriend had to terminate another individual with whom he was *involved*, and *she* was quite lovely, a woman by the name of Charlene Gardner, I believe."

"Goddamn you! Shut up!" Assad shouted angrily at the terrorist leader, who was obviously enjoying himself. Again, Milson could hear the desperation and distress in Asherah's voice. She could not believe what she was hearing. Assad tried to console her, but Asherah, who was too anguished and too grief-stricken to listen, pulled away from him in haste. He tried to explain himself to her, but the terrorist leader, who was determined to make an example out of him, continued with his revelation of the commander's exploits.

"You see, Ms. Asherah, during his travels between the States and Australia, Ad-dam met up with this beautiful young woman; a former real estate agent who went on to work for a prestigious construction company that we are familiar with. Well, not to get into specifics about your boyfriend's secret liaison. He and Ms. Gardner had a temporary sexual encounter when they were in Sydney. But unfortunately, he had to take her life when she found out the truth about him and what he was doing."

Hearing this startling account for the first time, Desiree was beside herself. Once distressed and tormented, she immediately transformed into a rage-filled individual right in front of everyone. "You lying bastard!" She slapped Assad across the face in outrage and disgust.

"Killian was right! How could you do this to me?!" Screaming abrasively, she continued,

"I asked you to tell me the truth about everything, and you lied right to my face! On top of that, you betrayed me by sleeping with another woman and then killing her?! What kind of person are you, Ad-dam? I thought I knew you! I loved you!"

Embarrassed, Assad tried to console Asherah and explain himself, but she rejected his advances. "Don't you touch me! I don't know who you are anymore. Killian told me about that other woman, but I didn't believe him! He was right about you! He was right about everything!"

Assad took a step back.

"What do you mean, Killian was right about me?" Taking another step back, he pondered what Desiree had just said. Even though they were both currently in danger, Assad took a moment to think of what had happened between the time she was apprehended in Dubai and this moment here in Iran. The expression on his face underwent a dramatic change as something dawned on him.

"Jesus, they got to you, didn't they?" he asked in a speculative tone. Still very upset, Desiree could not answer him. She could only glare at him in resentment and mortification. Still shocked, he continued,

"They didn't let you go right away, did they?! They interrogated you until you cracked! That Killian guy got into your head and told you all sorts of things about me, didn't he?! *Didn't he?!*" His voice was an octave higher than usual.

"You simple little bitch! You believed him and told him everything that we were planning to do, didn't you?!"

Desiree just stood motionless. She was incensed. Her defiance, along with her silence, gave Assad his answer. Seeing her reaction, he grew angrier.

"They didn't let you go; you willingly came here with them! How convenient that you just happened to be here in Iran and spotted me in among a huge crowd of people! You are working with the Americans and that bounty hunter, *aren't you*?! You betrayed me, Desi. How could you do this to me? *How?!*"

When she would not answer, he became even more agitated. He found her silence so irritating that he lost control and lunged at her violently. Grabbing her shoulders so tightly that he caused her to cry out in agony and distress,

"Let me go, Ad-dam! You're hurting me!"

Assad, indifferent to her suffering, replied,

"Oh, I'm going to do much more than hurt you, Desi! I'm going to show you what type of person I really am!"

When Milson, still on the other side of the door, heard this, his instincts took over. No longer playing the role of hidden spectator, he was now protector and savior. Counting back from three to one in his head, he decided to react. With a firm grip on the weapon, he rushed forcibly through the door, breaking it off its hinges as it collapsed to the floor. Milson's sudden appearance in the room was a surprise to everyone, including Assad and Asherah.

"All right, asshole! Why don't you show me what type of person you really are!" Milson said to Assad, pointing his Kalashnikov.

Caught off guard by the sudden entrance of the bounty hunter, the five terrorists present immediately turned their attention from Assad and Asherah to Milson, pointing their weapons directly at him. Milson, full of adrenaline, had his sights on Assad alone, but he knew the other five were focused on him.

Assad drew his pistol from the back of his waistband and pointed it at Milson, still with Asherah in his clutches. Still in a rage because he had just discovered that his longtime girlfriend betrayed him, he directed his anger solely at her.

"So, this is him?! This is the one who got into your fucking head?!" Assad then turned his attention to Milson.

"So, you're the one?! You're the one they sent to find me?! You're the one who turned her against me?!"

Milson, not taking his eyes off Assad, replied,

"Yeah, I'm the one they sent to get you, and I'm the one who's going to bring you in! And to answer your last question, I didn't turn Desiree against you; you did that yourself. I only told her the truth about what you were doing and the consequences that would follow if you continued to do it. I didn't tell her the number of people you killed to do this."

"You are correct, Mr. Milson. I was the one who told Ms. Asherah about Assad's little killing spree."

The sudden interruption from the terrorist leader surprised both men, who turned their attentions away from one another to get a look at the man with the condescending tone. But Milson was shocked to discover that instead of finally getting to lay eyes on this mysterious individual in the flesh, he was looking at a laptop computer sitting in the center of a table in the middle of the room, its screen showing only the silhouette of the man, not his face or any other identifying features. Though disappointed that he wasn't going to get to meet the mastermind in person, Milson kept his attention on Assad and the others. He said to the screen,

"So, here we are again, Mr. Mystery Man. Another secret area, another secluded place, and another Mexican standoff. I'm surprised that you are not here yourself to complete this transaction. I really wanted the chance to meet you in person. Come on, why don't you tell me who, what and where you are, so we can make this date of ours official?"

The leader snickered as he replied,

"Well, Mr. Milson, after our last meeting in Dubai, I and my constituents thought it would be safer if I were to conduct the transaction with Commander Assad by way of satellite feed instead of in person. You know, security reasons and safety precautions. As for your second question, there will be plenty of time for you to know my identity and where I reside. I can assure you of that."

Milson shook his head and chuckled.

"Okay, fair enough. So, let me see if I've got this straight. You decided not to show up in person because you wanted to play it safe. That way, you won't get caught with your pants down around your ankles like the last time. I understand. Typical backstabbing coward who can't do the job himself but wants others to do it for him. I get it."

Because of his silence, it seemed that the terrorist leader was perturbed by Milson's remarks.

"So, once again you're hiding in the shadows like the typical villain we see in movies, cowering in dark corners, shrouded in mystery, afraid to show your face in public, and always trying to manipulate or intimidate your victims into doing whatever it is you want them to do. Wait a minute, I've got it! Now I see what you're doing! You're patterning your behavior after the typical Bond villain who doesn't want his identity revealed until the end! Well, I hate to break it to you, pal, but you've been watching too many James Bond flicks. This isn't a movie or TV; it's reality. Another bit of news I hate to break to you is that the bad guys always get caught in the end. You really should get out more and move out of your mama's basement. It's not good for your self-esteem, Mr. Bad Guy."

The leader laughed.

"Ah, Mr. Killian Milson. You and your vocabulary are very humorous and entertaining. Since we're talking about American pop culture, allow me to suggest that you have patterned yourself after the typical western cowboy we see in those action films… Ah, I got it! You remind me of that Bruce Willis character from the *Die-Hard* films, which I find very enjoyable to watch… But seriously, Mr. Milson, you are indeed a man of many gifts. Still, I applaud you for getting this far. I underestimated you. At first, I was under the impression that you were an underrated, small-time, low-level bail enforcement officer who chases cretins, Neanderthals, and troglodytes who no longer have the good sense that Allah gave them. But now I stand corrected. You are a man of many gifts and much promise who has exceeded my expectations. Your talents as an ex-spy and a tracker could go very far in our organization. Your knowledge, experience, and expertise could be of great use to us. What would you say if I were to offer you a position in our organization?"

Milson, going along with the charade, replied sarcastically,

"Very interesting. I think I may take you up on that offer. I've got an idea. Why don't you give me your phone number, your address, and the name of the company you work for? I would love to know who this organization is and where I can find them, so I can send you an email with my résumé attached and also have my current employer contact you directly, so we can touch base with one another. You know, recommendations, qualifications, and so on. Oh, by the way, thank you for saying I remind you of John McClane from *Die Hard*. Sometimes I think of myself as that character when he kills all those terrorist assholes at the end of the movie, just as I'm about to do to your boys right now if they don't lay down their guns."

Again, the leader laughed, but this time it was more of a mordacious chuckle.

"At first, I thought your sense of humor was amusing, but now I find it taxing and annoying. You have no idea who you are dealing with, Mr. Milson."

"You have no idea who you're dealing with either, Mr. Mystery Man. You think I came alone? Right behind me are several spec-op forces waiting on my signal to rush in. If they don't hear from me within the next few seconds, this place is going to be surrounded by SEALs, Delta Force, and Iraqi SIS forces."

The leader fell silent for a moment. Then he said,

"You're bluffing, Mr. Milson. You and your government would not take so great a chance as to order US troops to operate illegally within Iranian territory. To do so is a violation of the UEA and

UN regulations concerning the covert operation of foreign military troops."

"I don't bluff. But if you think I am bluffing, go ahead and try me. Two teams of Special Forces, along with Iraqi forces, are going to storm in here with guns blazing if you and Assad don't surrender now."

Assad, who was already high-strung, his gun still pointing at Milson, looked over at the image of the leader on the screen.

"Bullshit! He's lying! The Americans wouldn't take the chance to intervene militarily if it would cause them diplomatic problems in the future! They wouldn't dare risk it!"

Milson replied,

"No. At one time they wouldn't, but you changed that when you decided to turn traitor and sell out your country to these assholes! You've put millions of American lives at risk, and for what? To be an expendable stooge for this wanna-be clown?! This is why I'm here, Commander, to take your ass back to the States dead or alive! Personally, I prefer alive, because then I won't have to haul your sorry carcass all the way back to Washington!" Still pointing his weapon at Assad, Milson turned his gaze back toward the computer.

"I may not get a chance today to find out who you are or what group you represent, but I guarantee you that I will find out soon. And when I do, you will have nowhere to hide."

The leader, laughing maniacally, said,

"Mr. Milson, haven't you ever heard of hiding in plain sight? Well, I don't need to hide when I've been standing right in front of you all this time."

Milson and Assad both drew back, each wondering what the terrorist was implying. Milson suddenly heard a faint staticky voice coming through his earpiece.

"Milson, do you read me?" The voice came in fits and starts because of the poor connection. "Weaver here. Several yards outside the compound. Engaging on your location." This was like music to Milson's ears. He was now in a better position to turn the tide in his favor. He looked over at Assad and saw that his demeanor and attitude had changed. He was not as confident or abrasive as he'd been only minutes ago. Quite the opposite, in fact. He was nervous, confused, and very apprehensive about what was happening.

Milson, seeing this and wanting to use it to his advantage, turned away from the computer screen and concentrated all his attention on Assad.

"Ad-dam, listen to me. I know we're in a tight spot right now, but it's not too late for you. You can still change your mind and walk away from this in one piece if you surrender now and hand the drive and the weapons to me. If you give this up right now, I promise you that the Justice Department and the navy will show leniency toward you. I'll personally put in a good word for you with Admiral Cooper and the DOJ if you stop this right now. I wasn't kidding about the spec-op forces I mentioned earlier. Both Iraqi ground forces and some of our own troops are already here, right outside the compound, waiting for me to give the word. Remember your friend Commander Dixon?" Assad's eyes widened when he heard his best friend's name.

"Well, he asked me to ask you if this has all been worth it, and if the money was so high that you had to stab your country in the back to do it? Well, Commander? Was it worth it?" Milson told Assad what Dixon had said to him in confidence when briefing him on Assad at ONI. Hearing this, Assad went from anxious to melancholic within a matter of seconds. Milson hoped to use this to his advantage to get through to Assad. From Milson's point of view, it seemed that Assad was realizing what he had done, the consequences of his actions being irrefutable, but his circumstances had not changed, meaning that the situation in the room remained the same as ever.

Milson announced that his backup had arrived. The terrorist leader ordered one of his five men to go see for himself.

The guard rushed to a window that was covered in soot and dust. Quickly wiping off the dirt to get a clearer view, he looked out and saw several vehicles quickly approaching. He ran back to the computer to report on what he'd seen. Speaking in Farsi Arabic, he said,

"The American is correct, sir! Six or seven vehicles are approaching!"

Milson sneered as he addressed the terrorist leader.

"Did you think I was kidding about what I said? It's over, Blofeld," he said sarcastically as to, refer to a main villain from the James Bond series.

"Tell your men to stand down and surrender."

In spite of all that was going on, a soft, rational voice interceded.

"Ad-dam, please don't do this. Listen to what Killian is saying. Listen to me. It's not worth your life. We can still have a future together if you give this up. I forgive you. I forgive you for everything you've done. Please. I still love you." Asherah said with compassion.

Assad, still anxious and uncertain, looked over at her and saw tears in her eyes. Even with all the tension, he found it impossible to turn away from her. Thinking about the situation he had gotten himself into, he began to have second thoughts, knowing very well the danger of his current predicament.

Asherah slowly reached her hand out toward Assad's pistol, which was still gripped tightly in his hand and still pointing at Milson. Meeting no resistance, she gently pushed down on the gun to lower it, implicitly persuading Assad to do the right thing. The terrorist leader, obviously displeased by this sudden change in behavior, ordered his soldiers to aim their weapons at the couple and fire. Milson, standing opposite the leader, transferring his aggression from Assad to the guards, drew his compact Kalashnikov and pointed it at them. The leader said,

"Oh, Assad, you really disappoint me. You could've been rich beyond your wildest dreams and had the full protection of the organization behind you. But instead, you chose sentiment and the guiles of a charming woman. Pathetic!"

Assad turned his head toward the screen and said,

"You're right, I am pathetic. Pathetic for letting you and your organization talk me into betraying my country, my friends, my family, and others who cared about me. I can't bring back the lives I took, but I can tell the American government all about you and the people you work for."

"What makes you think that you, Ms. Asherah, and Mr. Milson will get out of this building alive and be able to tell your government about us?"

Once again, the guards cocked their weapons, ready to discharge a cache of bullets. Milson performed the same action, telegraphing his intentions as well. Reviewing the entire situation as it unfolded in front of his eyes, Assad finally came to the realization that he had been deceit was about to happen. He looked over at the screen with disdain and said to the leader,

"This was a double-cross from the start! You were never going to pay me for the merchandise, were you?! Your plan was to take the information on the drives, take the modified weapons, and kill both of us afterward, wasn't it?!"

The leader's head, shown in shadow, nodded as he answered,

"On the contrary, Commander. We are an organization of people who are true to our word. We were going to pay you the agreed upon sum in its entirety, but when we found out that you lied about the twenty-five million, my associates and I decided that you were an unreliable person, someone who could not be trusted. We thought long and hard about our decision to recruit you based on the expertise and knowledge you bring to the table, but that single untrustworthy act of yours turned you into a liability. So, yes, we were going to"—he paused meaningfully— "terminate your contract as soon as you handed over the drives and weapons. Though you may think of us as an evil, diabolical, villainous group, as Mr. Milson described us to be. We also believe in loyalty, honesty, and most importantly, trust. But in this circumstance, it seems that you have none of the three qualities we're looking for. You are indeed a flawed character, Commander."

Assad shook his head, but more from disbelief than anything else. He finally realized what he had done, his moral compass pointing in such a way as to cause him regret for the decisions he'd made. He also felt disillusioned by the dishonest terrorist organization that had seduced him. Beginning to have a change of heart, he regrets the crimes he committed and loathed the blanket authority that the corrupt terrorist leader had over him. This was what occupied his mind as he continued to stare at the image on the screen with anger and contempt.

Two of the five guards alerted their leader to a surprising development.

"Zaiem," one of them said, using the Arabic word for leader,

"Seven vehicles have breached the front entrance! Our men are under attack!"

Milson was given the same report through his earpiece by Weaver.

"Killian, we've broken through! Engaging hostiles! Taking heavy fire! SEALs, Deltas, and Iraqi forces are outflanking them! What is your status? Over."

Milson grabbed his mic and told Weaver to stand by. He looked at Assad one last time and said, "This is it, Commander! We're running out of time! Decide! It's either them or us!"

Assad, slumped over the table in grief, slowly raised himself up in a way that can only be described as nonchalant. Turning to Milson, he said softly,

"Okay, Chief. You win. I surrender."

Milson, who was already anxious, was gratified upon learning of this last-minute decision made by the former naval officer. All that aside, his life was still in danger.

"Well, it looks like you lost today, Mystery Man," Milson said, sneering.

"Now tell your men to stand down and surrender. The entire compound is surrounded."

The terrorist leader fell silent, but only for a moment. His silhouetted image turned slightly to the left as if he were talking to someone in the background, then he turned his attention back to the screen. He gave a soft mocking laugh at Milson, then said tauntingly,

"This day is yours, Mr. Milson. You have won this battle, but the war is far from over. As you said before, we will meet again. And I assure you, it will be sooner than you think!" Milson took the threat seriously. The leader shouted a command to his soldiers, who were already in position: "Akotlhm," Arabic for "Kill them!"

CHAPTER 14

THE GUNFIGHT OF THE HUNT

Hearing this, Milson and Assad reacted quickly. The guards opened fire, spraying bullets in their direction. Milson dashed to the left and crouched behind an old rusted metal table that provided adequate cover and protection. Proceeding in the same fashion, Assad and Asherah turned the table in front of them on its end, knocking the laptop off of it. Everyone in the room began exchanging fire. Milson was able to take out one of the five guards while he himself was pinned down in place because of the large number of rounds being fired towards him. Assad, armed only with his Walther, managed to wound one of the guards but was still outgunned with too much firepower coming from the terrorist's weapons.

Seeing that Milson and Assad were in dire straits of defending themselves against an onslaught of heavy gunfire, Asherah wanted to help out in some way. She suggested to Assad that she recover the weapon from the terrorist Milson had killed. Objecting to her idea, he told her to stay down and take cover. Milson was able to intuit what Asherah was contemplating. He told her and Assad that he would direct ample suppressive fire in the terrorists' direction to cover Asherah as she went to retrieve the weapons. Assad would not permit it. But Asherah, stubborn and headstrong, wanted to do it anyway, no matter how dangerous and risky it was.

Milson removing the spent magazine cartridge from his AK and replacing it with a fresh one, yelled at them to make their decision fast. Assad looked at Asherah with concern, fearing the worst if she were to carry out such a perilous stunt. But Asherah was determined to carry it out no matter the consequences or the ultimate outcome. Apprehensive as he was about the idea, but knowing it could potentially benefit them, Assad gave her his blessing to go forward with her plan. He told her to stay low to the ground so as not to get hit by any bullets, also advising her to run as fast as her legs could carry her to retrieve the gun and then return to him. She nodded in acknowledgment, holding her hands against her ears to protect them from the sound of gunfire and the bullets ricocheting off the walls.

As the three continued to be pelted with the deadly projectiles, Assad made a desperate gesture to Milson, indicating that it was time for him to cover Asherah. Milson, seeing his opening, stood from his crouched position behind the table. Aiming at his target, he fired a barrage of bullets, aiming to kill or at least maim. But his main purpose was to provide cover for Asherah, so she could obtain one of the AK rifles. As Milson was doing his part, with Assad assisting, Asherah did exactly what Assad had told her to do. Fixing her eyes on the AK lying beside the dead terrorist, she ran straight for it. Keeping her body close to the ground, she managed to grab the weapon and ran back seeking cover. The exchange of gunfire between the two opposing sides was so heavy, that she could not make it back to where Assad was waiting for her. Noticing an overturned table, she ran toward it, bullets flying over her head as she did so, and crouched down behind it. Assad was worried about her. Seeing that she was in need, he tried to run to her, but the barrage of bullets was too great, so he stayed put.

Milson, on the opposite side of the room, wanted to assist Asherah, but the four men firing, making it impossible for him to move. Asherah, trapped in the center of the room, tried to operate the weapon but had trouble loading the cartridge. Assad, seeing what she was trying to do, gave her some quick instructions on how to use the weapon. She took heed of what he said and successfully loaded the magazine into the feed well, then pulled back the firing pin. Her AK was ready. She looked over at Assad and gestured to him that she was all right. Milson, who was still in combat mode, tried again to reach Asherah so he could help her, but the same terrorist kept his weapon trained on him, continuing his lethal assault. Asherah knew that she could not get to either Milson or Assad. Her mind was set on getting back to Assad and giving him the weapon to use, but the scenario did not play out as she had planned. So, she decided to use the gun herself. Assad looked over at her and realized what she was about to do. Frightened, he yelled at her to stay down, but she did not hear him. She got herself into a good stance, took a deep breath, and counted backward. Doing the unthinkable, she stood up from behind the table, the only thing protecting her, and squeezed the trigger, unleashing a barrage of gunfire so intense that the rival combatants immediately ducked for cover. Milson and Assad were both stunned by her action. She herself could not believe what she had done, realized that at a pivotal moment, she had chosen to protect the man she loved, which was something that she was proud to do.

Caught up in her own amazement, and satisfied for her actions, Asherah was unaware that one of the terrorists who had been incapacitated in the fight previously had his sights set on her with the intent of shooting her. Seeing the injured gunman pointing his weapon at her, Assad screamed at her to get down and take cover. Milson, who also witnessed the intention, started maneuvering toward Asherah as well. Showing disregard for his own safety, Milson was only able to reach several meters towards her location, but was not able to get to her on time because of the heavy gunfire. Assad was horrified to learn that the prediction he'd made previously was about to come true.

The terrorist opened fire, shooting Asherah three times, twice in the abdomen and once in the chest. She fell to the ground instantly.

Assad saw this. Traumatized, he screamed

"*No!*" In agony and anguish, frozen in shock and disbelief, he could not fathom to what his eyes were witnessing. Asherah lay motionless with her arms stretched out as if she was reaching for him. He felt paralyzed: physically, emotionally and mentally. Despair consumed him as he stood looking at her with grief and pain in his eyes. Showing no regard for his own safety or well-being, Assad attempted to make his way to Asherah, desperately wanting to find some way to help and secure her. Milson, who was also deeply affected by this terrible scene, began firing round after round at the man who had shot her. With everyone else engaged in the gun battle, Assad was able to make it over to where Asherah lay. He pulled her back behind the table for cover, bullets whizzing past his head. At that moment he cared about nothing and no one but her. All he wanted to do was to be by her side and hold her.

Taking her body in his arms, Assad comforted Asherah as she tried to maintain consciousness. Blood from the bullet wounds trickled from her body as he tried to apply pressure to them. Tears poured from Assad's eyes as he comforts her with gentle words of hope saying,

"Desi, baby, you're okay. It's not bad. We're going to get you out of here, I promise."

Hearing Assad's voice, which gave her comfort and relief, Asherah slowly opened her eyes. She gathered the strength to put her hand on his cheek while saying,

"Ad-dam, I know it's bad. I'm not going to make it. But I want you to know this: I love you. I've always loved you. From the time we were kids to now. You mean everything to me, and I'm glad you changed your mind about what you were going to do."

Assad, unable to accept what was happening, said,

"Baby, stop talking. Conserve your energy. We're going to get you some medical attention right now."

Asherah shook her head, knowing the truth of her condition. Again, she put her hand to his face, with her thumb pressed softly against his lips to stop him from speaking.

"No. All I want you to do is to get Killian and yourself out of here alive and clear your name. You're a good man, Ad-dam. I know this. You only did what you thought was right at the time. Be the man I know you are. Do the right thing, my love."

Assad, enraged and stricken with anguish, cried,

"Why?! Why did you take it upon yourself to shoot back?! I told you to grab the gun and come back to me! I didn't want you to put yourself in danger like that! Why?! *Why?!*"

Asherah smiled as she wiped the tears from Assad's eyes.

"Because your life is more important to me than my own. You are more important to me than anything else. That's why I did it, because I love you. And I forgive you."

Knowing she was close to the end, Asherah was serene and calm. Assad could no longer hold back his emotions. He felt her slipping away as he held her tighter. She looked upon his face one last time as she smiled gently, staring into his eyes with the love and tenderness she felt for him. At that moment, Assad saw her pupils dilate as she fell unconscious, then peacefully passed away. The hand that was pressed against his face earlier had slowly fallen to her side, where it now lay lifeless and still. He had felt her life force leaving her body just as he heard the final whisper of breath escape from her mouth. Heartbroken and devastated, Assad was now a shell of a man. He cried out so loud that the sound echoed throughout the room, audible over the gunfire. Both Milson and the terrorists heard Assad cry out, but they did not let it tear them away from the gun battle.

Milson, who was running out of ammo, tried to get Assad's attention, but Assad, in a pit of grief and loss, was not fully attentive to what was going on around him. Milson saw Assad cradling Asherah in his arms as if she were a newborn baby he would not let go of. Milson tried to reason with him, saying they now had to focus on their own survival, but Assad was too far gone to listen.

At that moment, the bounty hunter knew that he was truly alone. Almost out of ammo, he had only one magazine left in his pouch, with the one currently in the AK nearly empty. Milson couldn't get in contact with Weaver and the rest of the group; he heard nothing but static from his earpiece when trying to call them for help. Not that it would have been any better if the connection had been clear; Weaver and the others were too busy dealing with their own touchy situation outside to be able to come and help him.

The situation was not looking good for Milson. He was down to his last cartridge, with only his SIG and his Glock as backup. He was literally on his own against the four terrorists, who were armed to the max, continuing to discharge their weapons at him. Milson, knowing that Assad was in no position to help, decided to put all his knowledge and skills to the test and confront the no-win scenario he was in. He was about to raise up and start shooting, knowing that it might cost him his own life, but then he noticed Assad. Greatly affected by the death of Asherah, so much so that his sorrow had transformed into a well of rage. Assad stared at the terrorists with hatred and malice in his eyes, knowing that they were the ones who had killed the woman he loved. His eyes went from watery tears to crimson red in a matter of seconds. Though he was still taking fire from the opposite side, he would not be swayed from the horror that he witnessed. Every moral or ethical notion that Assad may have had was now gone. His imperative goal was to murder and kill everyone who had had a hand in the death of his child hood girlfriend.

Picking up the gun Asherah had taken from the dead terrorist, Assad began firing at his adversaries with hatred and extreme prejudice. Milson, who was keeping himself pinned down in a corner of the room, was surprised to see him behaving so aggressively. Looking as though he was possessed by the devil himself. Standing upright with neither fear nor compassion in his eyes, fueled by raw aggression, fury, and rage, which stimulated his soul. Assad was bent on pure homicidal intent. He was a man with one thing on his mind: to eliminate anyone who was responsible for the death of the woman he loved; mercilessly and without leniency. Not once did he cringe or flinch when projectiles of bullets streaked through the air as they came inches across his body. Not even a single one made contact with him as he walked toward the adversarial group. Determined to kill each and every one of them as if he were the Terminator himself, showing neither mercy nor remorse. Keeping his finger on the trigger guard as he sprayed a number of rounds continuously without a single pause in his stride. Assad was truly possessed and did not stop until all of these men were dead.

Still consumed with the rage that fueled his actions, Assad was gratified to learn that he had taken out three of the four terrorists, including the one who'd been injured that laid helpless on the ground—the one who was responsible for Asherah. Assad was satisfied with this outcome. Milson, however, was not. He took out the last man remaining with several shots to the body. The gunfight, which had lasted somewhere between five and ten minutes, was finally over. Milson and Assad were considered the victors as they neutralized the threat that almost cost them their lives. Both men stood over the bodies; the carnage they created which laid riddles of bullets, shrapnel, debris, and blood. While Milson went and check the corpses for a pulse, wanting to ensure that they were truly dead, Assad, still in torment, dropped his weapon on the ground and plodded back to Asherah's remains. He sat down beside her and took her gently in his arms again, cradling her as if she were a newborn baby.

Milson, seeing that Assad was devastated, went to comfort him.

"Ad-dam, I'm so sorry about Desiree… But we have to go. We'll take her with us and take care of her properly, but we must get out of here now. Judging by the way this whole thing went down, the Iranians are going to be coming in here any minute with an army and police force. We definitely don't want to be here when they show up."

Still grieving over Asherah, Assad ignored Milson's warning. Clutching her body to his, he was not about to let go for any reason, and Milson knew this to be so. Wishing he could give him ample time to grieve, but knowing that doing so would leave them vulnerable, Milson made the best decision he could give due to their current situation. Grabbing onto Asherah's arm, he attempted to assist Assad, who still had her body in his possession. Assad lashed out, pushing Milson away and shouting at him in a fit of rage,

"Get away from her, you bastard! This is your fault! You're the one who brought her here! You're the one who did this!"

Knowing how distraught he was, Milson took no offense to this. He understood what Assad was going through. And while he wanted to help, he also knew that they were running out of time. They needed to leave before the Iranians showed up.

Once again, Weaver's voice came over Milson's earpiece, saying,

"Killian, it's Weaver! Do you read me? Over."

Milson replied,

"I read you. What's going on? Send it."

"Do you have the target package?"

"Roger that. I have Assad. What's your sitrep?"

"We have neutralized all enemy combatants out here! There are some stragglers who are resisting, but the compound is nearly secured!"

"Roger that. Enemy combatants inside are neutralized as well. Data drives and weapons have been secured and are currently in my possession."

"Good! Because we need to get out of here, like, right now! One of Major Troy's men on comms just picked up an Iranian transmission indicating that they saw our little skirmish out here and are about to deploy their militia. He says that they're about twenty-five klicks [twenty-five kilometers measured by fifteen miles] away from our location and headed this way. We need to evac now!"

"Roger that. We are on our way now." Milson, wanting to be sympathetic but having no time to accommodate Assad's emotional distress of remaining with Asherah and mourn for her, leaned over and said,

"Assad, listen to me. We don't have time for this! The Iranians are on their way as we speak. If they catch us, we're as good as dead. I am very sorry about Desiree, I truly am, but we don't have time to sit here and shed tears over her. We'll take her with us, then both you and I will see to it that she is properly taken care of. In the meantime, we need to get the hell out of here!"

Assad, still overcome with grief, again burst out in an angry rage, and physically shoved Milson across the room. Milson did not retaliate, understanding the emotional turmoil he was experiencing.

"Commander, you do not want to do this. I know that you're angry and upset, but in twenty minutes, we are going to be surrounded by Iranian forces with no chance of escape. We must get out of here now. Desiree would not want you to do this."

Hearing Asherah's name come out of Milson's mouth caused him to become even more enraged. "How do you know what Desi would have wanted?! You're the one who brought her here in the first place! I didn't want her here! I wanted her to stay in Kuwait as we originally planned! But somehow you convinced her to come here, and now she's dead! She's dead because of you!"

Taking offense to what he said, Milson finally had enough of his recriminations and blame. "She's dead because of me? No, Commander, she's dead because of you! You are to blame for all of this! You are the one who committed espionage! You are the one who committed treason! And you are the one who involved her in the first place! Desiree wanted to come because she wanted to know the truth about you and what you did! She didn't want to believe it at first, but with everything that happened, she couldn't dismiss the reality of who you are or the type of man you've become! So, if you want to blame somebody for her death, you should look in the mirror and blame your goddamn self for it. If it weren't for your greed, lies, and manipulation, she would be alive right now! You did this! You put her life in danger, and you put her in this situation! All of this is your doing, not mine! You killed her, you sanctimonious, selfish son of a bitch! You, not me! This is all on you!"

Stunned by Milson's brutal honesty, Assad was taken aback. He had no verbal response to the accusations leveled against him because, deep down, he knew those allegations were true. Egotistical and arrogant as he was, he could not openly admit his faults, his inadequacy, or his wrongdoings, let alone the crimes he had committed that led to this current state of affairs. Brilliant as Assad was, he was also a narcissist and very pretentious. His strongest characteristics were his intellect and adaptability, whereas his greatest weakness was his pride and ego. His self-admiration would not permit him take the blame for anything, not even things in which he was directly involved. He would never do anything to damage his reputation, even though he considered himself to be beyond reproach. But in this situation, his self-centeredness had cost him the love of his life, which was something he was finding very difficult to bear. Because of the pain it caused him, he would not accept that in fact his actions had led to Asherah's death. Rejecting Milson's frank suggestion that he was indeed the guilty party here, Assad's anger reignited which made it turn physical. Assad made a fist and struck Milson across the face. Then he lunged at him as if he were a raging bull trying to gore a matador. Both men fell to the ground, where they began grappling with one another. Assad mounted Milson and was striking him hard to the face and body. Milson, who was no stranger to this fighting technique, was able to defend himself against the blows by using Assad's own body weight against him, turning him on his side and then overpowering him as he was now in the mounted position. Though they were evenly matched in terms of size, strength, and weight, not to mention their skill set in hand-to-hand combat, owing to their past military training and previous encounters, Assad seemed to have the upper hand. Driven with intense, uncontrollable rage, he delivered several brutal blows and strikes to Milson's body. Milson found it difficult to answer back. To a spectator, it would have seemed that Assad was winning because he had the upper hand, conducting himself as an MMA (mixed martial arts) fighter. He fought with a ferociousness and savagery that made him seem to be a barbarian fighting against an unworthy opponent who was struggling to survive. But Milson was far from being an unworthy opponent, and he was not about to be counted out from this brawl.

Determined to overpower his combatant, Milson punched Assad in his midsection, rendering him momentarily defenseless. Taking advantage of the situation, he landed several hard-hitting punches, also delivering heavy elbow strikes to Assad's head, upper body, and torso, adding a few knee strikes and kicks to his repertoire. Assad tried several times to answer with countermeasures but was too exhausted to do so. Soon, Assad's legs gave out and he fell to the floor. With that exchange, the fight was over, and Milson was the victor.

Milson stood over the beaten, bloodied, broken body of Assad. Concluding that he had no chance of recovering or responding. Milson, also tired from the fight, struggled to remain upright, determined to show his defeated competitor that he was the winner and was not going to tolerate any more retaliation. He forced Assad to turn over and lie on his stomach, then ordered him to place his arms behind his back so he could bind his hands together with zip ties. Exhausted from the fight, Milson plopped down onto the floor without even considering what was going on outside. He knew the Iranians were coming and knew he had to get his bounty and his team out of there before they arrive.

Scrambling to operate his earpiece, Milson was hoping to get in contact with Weaver or anyone who could hear his voice. Just when he was about to make the call, he heard several familiar voices echoing through the corridors of the building. It was Fuller, Sheppard, and Weaver shouting his name. "Milson! Where are you?!" Weaver shouted first. Recognizing their voices, Milson answered by telling them where to locate him.

"I'm here! Follow my voice! You'll see a door with bullet holes to your left! You can't miss it!"

Within seconds, all three men rushed in, with several of Marin's and Troy's men right behind them. Milson, who was very glad to see them, smiled and laughed whole heartedly.

"What the bloody hell?!" Fuller said, looking around at the carnage.

"Looks like Jack the Ripper paid you blokes a visit in here. You okay, mate?" Fuller asked Milson, who was still on the ground.

Milson replied by giving a slow thumbs-up and a nod to assure Fuller that he was all right. As the rest of them looked around at the bodies of the terrorists scattered about, they also saw Assad lying on the ground, unconscious and shackled. Then they saw something that shocked them all: Asherah's remains lying at the end of the room opposite Assad. All three were stunned as they looked at her dead body.

Weaver looked over at Milson and ask him what had happened, but all Milson could do was to shake his head in sorrow, unable to utter a single word. Weaver, understandably, nodded back in a gesture of sympathy and solace. Milson appreciated the sentiment. He asked for help with his injuries.

"Thank God you guys showed up," he said.

"I was getting my ass handed to me on a silver platter."

Weaver and Sheppard laughed at Milson's statement while rendering him aid. Once they had him cleaned and bandaged up, they were ready to go. Weaver said,

"Come on, let's get out of here. The Iranians are on their way. If they catch us, we'll all be up shit's creek without a paddle."

As Weaver and Sheppard helped Milson to his feet, Fuller saw the two black bags at the other end of the room.

"Killian?" he shouted with interest.

"Are those the guns?"

Milson looked over and gave him two quick nods in response. His curiosity satisfied, Fuller asked,

"What about the thumb drives? Did you get them too?"

Groggy and still feeling the effects of the fight, Milson managed to pull both devices from his pocket, hoping to set the mind of the MI6 agent at ease.

"Now if you're through with the questions, Sherlock Holmes, can we please get the hell out of here?!" Milson said mockingly and with sarcasm.

Fuller, who did not appreciate Milson's tone, sneered a bit but knew Milson was right about leaving immediately. Seeing that Weaver and Sheppard were busy attending to Milson, Fuller ordered one of the spec-op soldiers to seize the two bags and give them to his CO. Later, he gave a sitrep to Marin, Troy, and Saiph through his mic, saying that the area inside was secure and that they had recovered both the renegade officer and the stolen items. He also took it upon himself, enlisting the help of another soldier, to take Assad into custody. Just as they made their move to escort Assad outside to be transported, Milson, looking over his right shoulder and seeing Asherah's body, far away from everyone else, stopped them by suggesting,

"Guys, we're not leaving Desiree here. We're taking her with us. She deserves better than this. She sacrificed her life to save us. I owe her for that."

All three stood in agreement with him. Sheppard, who was closest to Asherah, carefully picked her off the floor and gently positioned her in his arms, treating her as a delicate vessel. Acknowledging that she was deserving the respect and dignity that she was due because of her sacrifice and her selflessness in helping to save Milson and the man she thought she loved, they all treated her as if she was a fallen soldier in battle. They quickened their pace and left through the door, hurrying because the Iranians were on their way. Leaving behind the bodies of the terrorists and the remains of a demolished compound. All four men, including Assad, who was physically dragged from the building by his captors, exited the main entrance and escorted to one of the SUVs. Saiph, Marin, Troy, and their subordinates all stood watch as the four emerged from the compound with both satisfaction and disappointment written on their faces: satisfaction because they'd captured the fugitive and retrieved the items, and disappointment because the conflict had caused an innocent civilian to lose her life.

The men made their way to their respective SUVs, with Marin and Troy providing cover. Both the SEALs and the Deltas gathered up their equipment and made their way to the vehicles. Saiph informed them that there were four heavily armed US Navy Seahawk helicopters waiting for them back at the safe house. Each man was relieved to hear this news, even though knowing that they were still inside enemy territory. The vehicles rushed out of the compound area, their tires leaving behind a cloud of dust, dirt, and debris. All seven SUVs made it out onto an open pavement road without incident. Several minutes after their escape, they saw a convoy of heavily armored Iranian military trucks and vehicles passing them on the opposite side of the road. Milson, who was in the second truck with Weaver, Fuller, along with Assad, who was still unconscious after his ordeal with the bounty hunter, sighed in relief as the Iranian military passed them by without suspicion. They all were relieved once they finally made it outside the city limits of Abadan and into the suburbs of Khorramshahr. All of them hoping to make it to the safe house in one piece with no delays or surprises.

CHAPTER 15

END OF THE HUNT

Kuwaiti/Iraqi SIS Safe House outside Khorramshahr, Iran

Dusk was falling rapidly as the seven SUVs departed from Abadan to arrive safely at the Iraqi SIS safe house. While making their approach, they saw the four navy Seahawk helicopters that Saiph had mentioned earlier. Each one gray in color with no recognizable markings or insignias that would identify them as US owned aircraft. As the vehicles moved closer, the occupants could feel the wind kicking up from the Seahawks' powerful rotors, which were spinning ferociously in the air, seemingly able to lift the vehicles from the ground. Each Seahawk was heavily armed, with dual six-barrel M134 rotary machine miniguns attached on each side, manned by either marine or navy personnel. Milson and his party felt relieved when they saw how heavily armored the helicopters were. They were also satisfied that they did not have to resort to their second contingency plan of escape by using the underground tunnels as their final option.

Milson, his crew, and the Special Forces detail, not waiting for the SUVs to stop, jumped out raucously while the vehicles were still in motion. Then, once the SUVs had come to a complete stop, they gathered up their gear and ran toward the Seahawks. Milson and Weaver pulled Assad from the rear of the truck and ordered two spec-op soldiers to get him aboard one of the helicopters. Still a little dazed and weary, Assad slowly regained his senses. He began to realize that he had been apprehended and was in restraints. Feeling anguish and sadden in the wake of Asherah's death, he also felt disdain and disgust as he turned to look at Milson one last time before entering the aircraft. Milson noticed the expression of hatred on his face, but he dismissed it without giving a second thought to it.

Watching Assad being put into the helicopter, Milson turned his attention to the Iraqi agent. "Enif, I would like to thank you." Milson stretched out his hand in gratitude.

"If it hadn't been for your resources, we wouldn't have gotten this far to grab him." Saiph gratefully reciprocated the gesture.

"Even though you were a pain in the ass and a controlling prick," Milson continued.

"I'm glad I got to know you. And I'm grateful for your help."

The Iraqi agent, knowing that Milson was joking, took no offense as he to snickered to his sense of humor. He retorted by saying,

"You know, I was wrong about you Americans. You're not as conceited or narcissistic as I've been led to believe." They both laughed boastfully at one another's expense.

Interrupting Saiph and Milson's conversation, one of the spec-op soldiers asked Milson what was to be done with Asherah's body. Milson told the soldier to put her in a bag and place it on one of the four helicopters. The soldier complying to Milson's order, asked two of his peers to assist with the detail. As the soldiers carried Asherah's body from the truck to the helicopter, Milson and party looked on with grief and sorrow. Saiph's eyes fixed on the body of what was once been a beautiful young woman, said to Milson in a somber but gracious tone,

"You have my sympathy, Killian. I'm sorry that this had to end so tragically with the loss of that young girl's life. I will pray to Allah for her and her family. Offer them condolences on my behalf and on behalf of my government."

Milson accepted Saiph's gesture and compliments with a grin that could only be described as blasé. But he did appreciate the empathy so much so that he gave the Iraqi agent a full-hearted handshake of gratitude. "Thank you, Enif. I will make sure her family receives your condolences."

Weaver came up to them. "Fellas, I hate to get between this lovely relationship you guys have, but we need to get on those birds and evac now. The Iranian air force does routine air patrols all across this region, and the Seahawk pilots say that we need to go now so we can get an open window and not under their radar."

As everyone understood the seriousness of the situation, they bid their final farewells, shaking each other's hands and waving. Milson and party were the last to get on the helicopters; Marin, Troy, and their men were already on board the other three. After Milson had stepped inside one of the Seahawks, all four lifted off the ground, their rotors leaving a spray of dust and dirt in the air. In a single line formation, the helicopters climbed high into the atmosphere. Milson was unable to see Saiph and his men as they climbed higher from the ground. He sat back in his seat and secured himself with the safety harness because of the heavy turbulence. As he thought of finally having captured his executive bounty and delivering him to the authorities, he turned towards Weaver asking him a question of importance.

"James, did you contact Cooper and Richards about Assad?!" Milson yelled, making his voice heard over the noise of the engines.

Weaver replied,

"Affirmative! I got on the horn and used a relay through the *JFK* to give them the sitrep. They're ecstatic that we captured Assad before the signing of the treaty between the UEA and the UAE!"

"Speaking of the *JFK*, what's our ETA to reach her?!" Milson asked.

"An hour-in-a-half if we stay on this route. She's parked eighty-five miles off the coast of Kuwait. The Iranians can't say shit about her because she's in Kuwaiti waters and far from their borders. We've got a clear road ahead, Killian. You did it!"

Milson gave a thumbs-up and relaxed in his seat. Pondering the whole situation in his head, he still wondered if the circumstances would have been different if Asherah had not come along and stayed where she was. He had asked himself that question a hundred times, and he came up with the same one every time: *yes, because she would still be alive and Assad would still be on the run*. Milson realized that he would have to live with that decision for the rest of his life, but still he knew that life-or-death situations were always fraught with risk. On that note, he laid his head against the cushioned headrest and closed his eyes in tranquility. The four helicopters flew towards the sunset horizon within the Iranian airspace in order to reach their final destination to a safe haven of a US aircraft carrier.

ONI Headquarters, Suitland, Silver Hill, Maryland

One year had passed since the capture and apprehension of Ad-dam Omar Assad. The former naval officer was now serving a life sentence at USDB (United State Disciplinary Barracks) Military Facility Prison located at Fort Leavenworth, Kansas. He had been stripped of his title and rank and had received a dishonorable discharge due to his actions. He was tried by a military tribunal and received a court-martialed for his treasonous acts of espionage, desertion, and illegal distribution of US military materials and governmental intelligence, and for three counts of murder. Assad was now serving his life sentence plus fifty years without the possibility of parole for the murder of Muhammad Kareem, Ahmed Shaula, and Charlene Gardner. Though the first two were foreign nationals, making the crimes fall outside US jurisdiction, Gardner was a US citizen, so her homicide fell within the boundaries of the American criminal justice system and its laws. The judge found that a commissioned officer of the United States military—Ad-dam Assad—was guilty of her murder and was to receive the highest punishment to fit such a crime. Assad was held temporarily at the Naval Brig CCU (Consolidated Confinement Unit), Norfolk Naval Station, Norfolk, Virginia. After Milson had brought him back to the States, where he was kept until his court-martial proceedings began, he was later shipped off to Leavenworth to begin his sentencing. Assad was now being held in solitary confinement for security and safety reasons, to protect him from both himself and other inmates who might wish to do him harm because of his actions. Admiral Cooper was the first to see Assad in custody and was also one of the many to sign off on his court-martial and detention. He along with the POTUS (President Of The United States), SECDEF (Secretary of Defense), SECNAV (Secretary of the Navy), the CJCS (Chairman of the Joint Chiefs of Staff), the chief of naval operations, and the US attorney general.

Assad's paperwork was voluminous, scattered across the admiral's desk in his office as if there was no end in sight. The paperwork was months old, but the information it reported was very important, needing to be stored in the ONI database to show that Assad, a person from within their ranks, had attempted espionage within the United States and its military. As Admiral Cooper hurriedly gathered up the many pages and forms of Assad's paper work, he suddenly pushed them all aside when he saw a document that he viewed as being much more important. It had been given to him directly by the directors of the CIA and NSA. As he read it, Cooper became intrigued, taking off his glasses to rub his eyes several times before taking another look. As he read over the document for the second time, his secretary buzzed in on the intercom to tell him that he had a visitor.

"Admiral, your appointment is here to see you, sir."

Cooper gently pushed the button on the intercom to relay his answer.

"Send him through, Lieutenant." Just as he finished speaking, the door flew open. Cooper was not surprised to see that it was Milson himself.

"Welcome, Chief, welcome. Good to see you again after all these months."

"Likewise, sir. It has been almost a year since the last time we got together," Milson responded.

Cooper shook Milson's hand, immensely grateful.

"How have you been, Chief? I hope you haven't spent all that money we paid you."

Milson laughed softly as he replied sincerely,

"No, not at all, Admiral. I paid off some bills and debts, and invested the rest." The director smiled with enthusiasm.

"I see some changes have been made around here since I saw you last, sir."

"Oh, like what, Chief?" Cooper asked, curious.

"Like another star on your collar, sir. I see that congratulations are in order."

Cooper nodded his head as he acknowledged Milson's recognition of his new status. "Yes, I suppose so. Thank you, Chief. But if you look at it in another way, I should be thanking you for this second star. After all, you're the one who apprehended Assad and brought him back in one piece. The work you did saved a lot of lives and also kept our intel out of the hands of the terrorists. I sent my recommendation to reward you for having captured Assad straight to the president. With the president's approval, and with the approval of the CJCS, the navy decided to promote me to rear upper status [two-star rear admiral] all because of what you did, son. Thank you again."

Milson, humble in the face of Cooper's gratitude, politely shook his head.

"I was just doing the job you hired me to do, Admiral. I appreciate that you had confidence in me, sir. But I must admit, the task of retrieving Assad was not an easy one."

Again, Cooper smiled.

"I bet it wasn't. After reading your report, Chief, I see you had a lot of close calls toward the middle and at the end. You had to go to three different countries to find out where he was, sneak into Iran's backyard, and chase Assad into a fortified compound full of armed foreign nationals. I don't think that I would've gone to such lengths in pursuit of an objective like that, and I was once a SEAL doing the same dangerous stuff that you did. You went above and beyond your means, son, and I sincerely appreciate it. You, Mr. Milson, have my respect from now until the day I die. I knew I picked the right man for this assignment; I knew that you were the one. You are one hell of a bounty hunter and one hell of a soldier, Chief."

Milson was overwhelmed by Cooper's admiration and appreciation, but he still welcomed it. It had been long time since he'd been shown this much gratitude and recognition. He showed that he was moved by thanking the admiral with another firm handshake.

"I'm glad you feel that way, Admiral, and again, I appreciate that you had confidence in me, but I wish I had gotten more info on that terrorist organization. I also wish I had discovered the identity of their leader. From the little intel I was able to gather, they are well connected, very well organized, and have a good deal of financial backing. And the leader is very intuitive and intelligent—cold, calculating, manipulative, and cunning. The son of a bitch knew what we were going to do before we did it. He also knew about our intelligence community and our protocols. To be honest, Admiral, I don't think we're dealing with a group of amateurs here. These people are professionals—organized, sophisticated, and very knowledgeable about many things, sir. I don't think we've seen the last of them or their mysterious leader. I have a feeling that we're going to run into them again sometime very soon," Milson said.

Cooper waved it off with a hand gesture as he sat down in his chair.

"It's possible, Chief. The number of terrorist organizations that have fallen during our twenty-year occupation of Iraq and

Afghanistan is substantial. Since the fall of al-Qaeda, ISIS, and the Taliban, and with the help of coalition forces and the UEA, little fly-by-night terrorist cells and groups have been sprouting up, wanting to fill the shoes left empty by those larger organizations, but intel reports show that these groups in no way present a threat to us or the world. But it looks like this new one you've reported is quite different. It seems to me that, being the new kids on the block, they want to show their muscle. The good thing about all this is that you caught Assad before he could give them the goods on us. If they would have gotten their hands on our intelligence and weaponry, we would be having a very different conversation right now. But I assure you, Chief, we will deal with them when the time comes."

Milson nodded several times.

"Understood, Admiral. But I know you didn't call me to come all this way from Baltimore so we could reminisce about Assad. What can I do for you, sir?"

Cooper's expression changed from jovial to stern in a matter of seconds as he gestured to Milson to take a seat.

"We've had several intelligence reports from the CIA, NSA, and ATF about illegal shipments of arms overseas. Syria, Mexico, and certain countries in Africa and South America, have been receiving aid in the form of illegal weapons from a source they cannot identify. I have my suspicions but that's all they are, just suspicions. Judging from the reports, these shipments are all US-manufactured firearms and other heavy ordnance. The intelligence agencies believe that large numbers of these weapons are being distributed to these areas by individuals who used to have ties in the military."

Milson cleared his throat and raised his left eyebrow. Cooper was about to continue, but Milson edged off a question that was a little disparaging. "Admiral, are you telling me that we may have another Assad dilemma on our hands?"

Cooper leaned over across his desk while crossing his arms together. He shook his head in response.

"No, Chief, this is entirely different," he said. Milson was visibly relieved.

"This is not another breach of security or another episode of intel being taken from our house. This is outside the norms of standard protocol. I believe we are looking at a group of people who used to serve or an independent militia with intentions of their own."

Milson, curious to know what Cooper was talking about, leaned forward, hoping to hear more. Cooper proceeded to ask Milson a question that only he could answer:

"Chief, how good are you at tracking down and capturing *mercenaries*?" Milson looked at Cooper with an expression that only fitted his persona. He made a devilish grin followed by a nonchalant response.

"As good as to be expected, sir."

Stay tuned for the next novel in this series, *Soldiers of Fortune.*

CPSIA information can be obtained
at www.ICGtesting.com
Printed in the USA
LVHW041445071222
734629LV00028B/361

9 781959 182245